# Elric of Melniboné
# and Other Stories

# The Michael Moorcock Collection

The Michael Moorcock Collection is the definitive library of acclaimed author Michael Moorcock's SF & fantasy, including the entirety of his Eternal Champion work. It is prepared and edited by John Davey, the author's long-time bibliographer and editor, and will be published, over the course of two years, in the following print omnibus editions by Gollancz, and as individual eBooks by the SF Gateway (see http://www.sfgateway.com/authors/m/moorcock-michael/ for a complete list of available eBooks).

ELRIC

Elric of Melniboné and Other Stories

Elric: The Fortress of the Pearl

Elric: The Sailor on the Seas of Fate

Elric: The Sleeping Sorceress

Elric: The Revenge of the Rose

Elric: Stormbringer!

Elric: The Moonbeam Roads
comprising –
*Daughter of Dreams*
*Destiny's Brother*
*Son of the Wolf*

CORUM

Corum: The Prince in the Scarlet Robe
comprising –
*The Knight of the Swords*
*The Queen of the Swords*
*The King of the Swords*

Corum: The Prince with the Silver Hand
comprising –
*The Bull and the Spear*
*The Oak and the Ram*
*The Sword and the Stallion*

HAWKMOON

Hawkmoon: The History of the Runestaff
comprising –
*The Jewel in the Skull*
*The Mad God's Amulet*
*The Sword of the Dawn*
*The Runestaff*

Hawkmoon: Count Brass
comprising –
*Count Brass*
*The Champion of Garathorm*
*The Quest for Tanelorn*

JERRY CORNELIUS

The Cornelius Quartet
comprising –
*The Final Programme*
*A Cure for Cancer*
*The English Assassin*
*The Condition of Muzak*

Jerry Cornelius: His Lives and His Times (short-fiction collection)

A Cornelius Calendar
comprising –
*The Adventures of Una Persson
and Catherine Cornelius in
the Twentieth Century*
*The Entropy Tango*
*The Great Rock 'n' Roll Swindle*
*The Alchemist's Question*
*Firing the Cathedral/Modem
Times 2.0*

Von Bek
comprising –
*The War Hound and the World's
Pain*
*The City in the Autumn Stars*

The Eternal Champion
comprising –
*The Eternal Champion*
*Phoenix in Obsidian*
*The Dragon in the Sword*

The Dancers at the
End of Time
comprising –
*An Alien Heat*
*The Hollow Lands*
*The End of all Songs*

Kane of Old Mars
comprising –
*Warriors of Mars*
*Blades of Mars*
*Barbarians of Mars*

Moorcock's Multiverse
comprising –
*The Sundered Worlds*
*The Winds of Limbo*
*The Shores of Death*

The Nomad of Time
comprising –
*The Warlord of the Air*
*The Land Leviathan*
*The Steel Tsar*

Travelling to Utopia
comprising –
*The Wrecks of Time*
*The Ice Schooner*
*The Black Corridor*

The War Amongst the Angels
comprising –
*Blood: A Southern Fantasy*
*Fabulous Harbours*
*The War Amongst the Angels*

Tales From the End of Time
comprising –
*Legends from the End of Time*
*Constant Fire*
*Elric at the End of Time*

Behold the Man

Gloriana; or, The Unfulfill'd Queen

SHORT FICTION
My Experiences in the Third World
War and Other Stories: The Best
Short Fiction of Michael Moorcock
Volume 1

The Brothel in Rosenstrasse and
Other Stories: The Best Short Fiction
of Michael Moorcock Volume 2

Breakfast in the Ruins and Other
Stories: The Best Short Fiction of
Michael Moorcock Volume 3

MICHAEL MOORCOCK (1939–) is one of the most important figures in British SF and Fantasy literature. The author of many literary novels and stories in practically every genre, he has won and been shortlisted for numerous awards including the Hugo, Nebula, World Fantasy, Whitbread and Guardian Fiction Prize. He is also a musician who performed in the seventies with his own band, the Deep Fix; and, as a member of the space-rock band, Hawkwind, won a platinum disc. His tenure as editor of NEW WORLDS magazine in the sixties and seventies is seen as the high watermark of SF editorship in the UK, and was crucial in the development of the SF New Wave. Michael Moorcock's literary creations include Hawkmoon, Corum, Von Bek, Jerry Cornelius and, of course, his most famous character, Elric. He has been compared to, among others, Balzac, Dumas, Dickens, James Joyce, Ian Fleming, J.R.R. Tolkien and Robert E. Howard. Although born in London, he now splits his time between homes in Texas and Paris.

For a more detailed biography, please see Michael Moorcock's entry in *The Encyclopedia of Science Fiction* at: http://www.sf-encyclopedia.com/

For further information about Michael Moorcock and his work, please visit www.multiverse.org, or send S.A.E. to The Nomads Of The Time Streams, Mo Dhachaidh, Loch Awe, Dalmally, Argyll, PA33 1AQ, Scotland, or P.O. Box 385716, Waikoloa, HI 96738, USA.

# Elric of Melniboné and Other Stories

## MICHAEL MOORCOCK

### Edited by John Davey

This edition published in Great Britain in 2013 by
Gollancz
An imprint of the Orion Publishing Group
Orion House, 5 Upper St Martin's Lane,
London WC2H 9EA

An Hachette UK Company

The authorised representative in the EEA is Hachette Ireland,
8 Castlecourt Centre, Dublin 15, D15 XTP3, Ireland (email: info@hbgi.ie)

10

A CIP catalogue record for this book is
available from the British Library

ISBN 978 0 575 11309 1

Typeset by Jouve (UK), Milton Keynes

Printed and bound in Great Britain by Clays Ltd, Elcograf S.p.A.

The Orion Publishing Group's policy is to use papers
that are natural, renewable and recyclable products and
made from wood grown in sustainable forests. The logging
and manufacturing processes are expected to conform to
the environmental regulations of the country of origin.

www.multiverse.org
www.sfgateway.com
www.gollancz.co.uk
www.orionbooks.co.uk

# Introduction to
## *The Michael Moorcock Collection*
### *John Clute*

H E IS NOW over 70, enough time for most careers to start and end in, enough time to fit in an occasional half-decade or so of silence to mark off the big years. Silence happens. I don't think I know an author who doesn't fear silence like the plague; most of us, if we live long enough, can remember a bad blank year or so, or more. Not Michael Moorcock. Except for some worrying surgery on his toes in recent years, he seems not to have taken time off to breathe the air of peace and panic. There has been no time to spare. The nearly 60 years of his active career seems to have been too short to fit everything in: the teenage comics; the editing jobs; the pulp fiction; the reinvented heroic fantasies; the Eternal Champion; the deep Jerry Cornelius riffs; NEW WORLDS; the 1970s/1980s flow of stories and novels, dozens upon dozens of them in every category of modern fantastika; the tales of the dying Earth and the possessing of Jesus; the exercises in postmodernism that turned the world inside out before most of us had begun to guess we were living on the wrong side of things; the invention (more or less) of steampunk; the alternate histories; the *Mitteleuropean* tales of sexual terror; the deep-city London riffs: the turns and changes and returns and reconfigurations to which he has subjected his oeuvre over the years (he expects this new Collected Edition will fix these transformations in place for good); the late tales where he has been remodelling the intersecting worlds he created in the 1960s in terms of twenty-first-century physics: for starters. If you can't take the heat, I guess, stay out of the multiverse.

His life has been full and complicated, a life he has exposed and hidden (like many other prolific authors) throughout his work. In *Mother London* (1988), though, a nonfantastic novel published at what is now something like the midpoint of his career, it may be possible to find the key to all the other selves who made the 100 books. There are three protagonists in the tale, which is set from about 1940 to about 1988 in the suburbs and inner runnels of the vast metropolis of Charles Dickens and Robert Louis Stevenson. The oldest of these protagonists is Joseph Kiss, a flamboyant self-advertising fin-de-siècle figure of substantial girth and a fantasticating relationship to the world: he is Michael Moorcock, seen with genial bite as a kind of G.K. Chesterton without the wearying punch-line paradoxes. The youngest of the three is David Mummery, a haunted introspective half-insane denizen of a secret London of trials and runes and codes and magic: he too is Michael Moorcock, seen through a glass, darkly. And there is Mary Gasalee, a kind of holy-innocent and survivor, blessed with a luminous clarity of insight, so that in all her apparent ignorance of the onrushing secular world she is more deeply wise than other folk: she is also Michael Moorcock, Moorcock when young as viewed from the wry middle years of 1988. When we read the book, we are reading a book of instructions for the assembly of a London writer. The Moorcock we put together from this choice of portraits is amused and bemused at the vision of himself; he is a phenomenon of flamboyance and introspection, a poseur and a solitary, a dreamer and a doer, a multitude and a singleton. But only the three Moorcocks in this book, working together, could have written all the other books.

It all began – as it does for David Mummery in *Mother London* – in South London, in a subtopian stretch of villas called Mitcham, in 1939. In early childhood, he experienced the Blitz, and never forgot the extraordinariness of being a participant – however minute – in the great drama; all around him, as though the world were being dismantled nightly, darkness and blackout would descend, bombs fall, buildings and streets disappear; and in the morning, as though a new universe had taken over from the old one and the world had become portals, the sun would rise on glinting rubble, abandoned tricycles, men and women going about their daily tasks as though nothing had happened, strange shards of ruin poking into altered air. From a very early age, Michael Moorcock's security reposed in a sense that everything might change, in the blinking of an eye, and be *rejourneyed* the next day (or the next book). Though as a writer he has certainly elucidated the fears and alarums of life in Aftermath Britain, it does seem that his very early years were marked by the epiphanies of war, rather than the inflictions of despair and beclouding amnesia most adults necessarily experienced. After the war ended, his parents separated, and the young Moorcock began to attend a pretty wide variety of schools, several of which he seems to have been expelled from, and as soon as he could legally do so he began to work full time, up north in London's heart, which he only left when he moved to Texas (with intervals in Paris) in the early 1990s, from where (to jump briefly up the decades) he continues to cast a Martian eye: as with most exiles, Moorcock's intensest anatomies of his homeland date from after his cunning departure.

But back again to the beginning (just as though we were rimming a multiverse). Starting in the 1950s there was the comics and pulp work for Fleetway Publications; there was the first book (*Caribbean Crisis*, 1962) as by Desmond Reid, co-written with his early friend the artist James Cawthorn (1929–2008); there was marriage, with the writer Hilary Bailey (they divorced in 1978), three children, a heated existence in the Ladbroke Grove/Notting Hill Gate region of London he was later to populate with Jerry Cornelius and his vast family; there was the editing of NEW WORLDS, which began in 1964 and became the heartbeat of the British New Wave two years later as writers like Brian W. Aldiss and J.G. Ballard, reaching their early prime, made it into a tympanum, as young American writers like Thomas M. Disch, John T. Sladek, Norman Spinrad and Pamela Zoline found a home in London for material they could not publish in America, and new British writers like M. John Harrison and Charles Platt began their careers in its pages; but before that there was Elric. With *The Stealer of Souls* (1963) and

*Stormbringer* (1965), the multiverse began to flicker into view, and the Eternal Champion (whom Elric parodied and embodied) began properly to ransack the worlds in his fight against a greater Chaos than the great dance could sustain. There was also the first SF novel, *The Sundered Worlds* (1965), but in the 1960s SF was a difficult nut to demolish for Moorcock: he would bide his time.

We come to the heart of the matter. Jerry Cornelius, who first appears in *The Final Programme* (1968) – which assembles and co-ordinates material first published a few years earlier in NEW WORLDS – is a deliberate solarisation of the albino Elric, who was himself a mocking solarisation of Robert E. Howard's Conan, or rather of the mighty-thew-headed Conan created for profit by Howard epigones: Moorcock rarely mocks the true quill. Cornelius, who reaches his first and most telling apotheosis in the four novels comprising *The Cornelius Quartet*, remains his most distinctive and perhaps most original single creation: a wide boy, an agent, a *flaneur*, a bad musician, a shopper, a shapechanger, a trans, a spy in the house of London: a toxic palimpsest on whom and through whom the *zeitgeist* inscribes surreal conjugations of 'message'. Jerry Cornelius gives head to Elric.

The life continued apace. By 1970, with NEW WORLDS on its last legs, multiverse fantasies and experimental novels poured forth; Moorcock and Hilary Bailey began to live separately, though he moved, in fact, only around the corner, where he set up house with Jill Riches, who would become his second wife; there was a second home in Yorkshire, but London remained his central base. *The Condition of Muzak* (1977), which is the fourth Cornelius novel, and *Gloriana; or, The Unfulfill'd Queen* (1978), which transfigures the first Elizabeth into a kinked Astraea, marked perhaps the high point of his career as a writer of fiction whose font lay in genre or its mutations – marked perhaps the furthest bournes he could transgress while remaining within the perimeters of fantasy (though *within* those bournes vast stretches of territory remained and would, continually, be explored). During these years he sometimes wore a leather jacket constructed out of numerous patches of varicoloured material, and it sometimes seemed perfectly fitting that he bore the semblance, as his jacket flickered and fuzzed from across a room or road, of an illustrated man, a map, a thing of shreds and patches, a student fleshed from dreams. Like the stories he told, he seemed to be more than one thing. To use a term frequently applied (by me at least) to twenty-first-century fiction, he seemed equipoisal: which is to say that, through all his genre-hopping and genre-mixing and genre-transcending and genre-loyal returnings to old pitches, *he was never still*, because 'equipoise' is all about *making stories move*. As with his stories, he cannot be pinned down, because he is not in one place. In person and in his work, it has always been sink or swim: like a shark, or a dancer, or an equilibrist...

The marriage with Jill Riches came to an end. He married Linda Steele in 1983; they remain married. The Colonel Pyat books, *Byzantium Endures* (1981), *The Laughter of Carthage* (1984), *Jerusalem Commands* (1992) and *The Vengeance of Rome* (2006), dominated these years, along with *Mother London*. As these books, which are non-fantastic, are not included in the current *Michael Moorcock Collection*, it might be worth noting here that, in their insistence on the irreducible difficulty of gaining anything like true sight, they represent Moorcock's mature modernist take on what one might call the rag-and-bone shop of the world itself; and that the huge ornate postmodern edifice of his multiverse *loosens* us from that world, gives us room to breathe, to juggle our strategies for living – allows us ultimately to escape from prison (to use a phrase from a writer he does not respect, J.R.R. Tolkien, for whom the twentieth century was a prison train bound for hell). What Moorcock may best be remembered for in the end is the (perhaps unique) interplay between modernism and postmodernism in his work. (But a plethora of discordant understandings makes these terms hard to use; so enough of them.) In the end, one might just say that Moorcock's work as a whole represents an extraordinarily multifarious execution of the fantasist's main task: which is to *get us out of here*.

Recent decades saw a continuation of the multifarious, but with a more intensely applied methodology. The late volumes of the long Elric saga, and the Second Ether sequence of meta-fantasies – *Blood: A Southern Fantasy* (1995), *Fabulous Harbours* (1995) and *The War Amongst the Angels: An Autobiographical Story* (1996) – brood on the real world and the multiverse through the lens of Chaos Theory: the closer you get to the world, the less you describe it. *The Metatemporal Detective* (2007) – a narrative in the Steampunk mode Moorcock had previewed as long ago as *The Warlord of the Air* (1971) and *The Land Leviathan* (1974) – continues the process, sometimes dizzyingly: as though the reader inhabited the eye of a camera increasing its focus on a closely observed reality while its bogey simultaneously wheels it backwards from the desired rapport: an old Kurasawa trick here amplified into a tool of conspectus, fantasy eyed and (once again) rejourneyed, this time through the lens of SF.

We reach the second decade of the twenty-first century, time still to make things new, but also time to sort. There are dozens of titles in *The Michael Moorcock Collection* that have not been listed in this short space, much less trawled for tidbits. The various avatars of the Eternal Champion – Elric, Kane of Old Mars, Hawkmoon, Count Brass, Corum, Von Bek – differ vastly from one another. Hawkmoon is a bit of a berk; Corum is a steely solitary at the End of Time: the joys and doleurs of the interplays amongst them can only be experienced through immersion. And the Dancers at the End of Time books, and the Nomad of the Time Stream books, and the Karl Glogauer books, and all the others. They are here now, a 100 books that make up one book. They have been fixed for reading. It is time to enter the multiverse and see the world.

September 2012

# Introduction to
## *The Michael Moorcock Collection*
### *Michael Moorcock*

B Y 1964, AFTER I had been editing NEW WORLDS for some
months and had published several science fiction and fantasy
novels, including *Stormbringer*, I realised that my run as a writer
was over. About the only new ideas I'd come up with were mini-
ature computers, the multiverse and black holes, all very crudely
realised, in *The Sundered Worlds*. No doubt I would have to return
to journalism, writing features and editing. 'My career,' I told my
friend J.G. Ballard, 'is finished.' He sympathised and told me he
only had a few SF stories left in him, then he, too, wasn't sure
what he'd do.

In January 1965, living in Colville Terrace, Notting Hill, then an
infamous slum, best known for its race riots, I sat down at the
typewriter in our kitchen-cum-bathroom and began a locally
based book, designed to be accompanied by music and graphics.
*The Final Programme* featured a character based on a young man
I'd seen around the area and whom I named after a local green-
grocer, Jerry Cornelius, 'Messiah to the Age of Science'. Jerry was
as much a technique as a character. Not the 'spy' some critics
described him as but an urban adventurer as interested in his
psychic environment as the contemporary physical world. My
influences were English and French absurdists, American noir
novels. My inspiration was William Burroughs with whom I'd
recently begun a correspondence. I also borrowed a few SF ideas,
though I was adamant that I was not writing in any established
genre. I felt I had at last found my own authentic voice.

I had already written a short novel, *The Golden Barge*, set in a
nowhere, no-time world very much influenced by Peake and the

surrealists, which I had not attempted to publish. An earlier auto-biographical novel, *The Hungry Dreamers*, set in Soho, was eaten by rats in a Ladbroke Grove basement. I remained unsatisfied with my style and my technique. *The Final Programme* took nine days to complete (by 20 January, 1965) with my baby daughters sometimes cradled with their bottles while I typed on. This, I should say, is my memory of events; my then wife scoffed at this story when I recounted it. Whatever the truth, the fact is I only believed I might be a serious writer after I had finished that novel, with all its flaws. But Jerry Cornelius, probably my most successful sustained attempt at unconventional fiction, was born then and ever since has remained a useful means of telling complex stories. Associated with the 60s and 70s, he has been equally at home in all the following decades. Through novels and novellas I developed a means of carrying several narratives and viewpoints on what appeared to be a very light (but tight) structure which dispensed with some of the earlier methods of fiction. In the sense that it took for granted the understanding that the novel is among other things an internal dialogue and I did not feel the need to repeat by now commonly understood modernist conventions, this fiction was post-modern.

Not all my fiction looked for new forms for the new century. Like many 'revolutionaries' I looked back as well as forward. As George Meredith looked to the eighteenth century for inspiration for his experiments with narrative, I looked to Meredith, popular Edwardian realists like Pett Ridge and Zangwill and the writers of the *fin de siècle* for methods and inspiration. An almost obsessive interest in the Fabians, several of whom believed in the possibility of benign imperialism, ultimately led to my Bastable books which examined our enduring British notion that an empire could be essentially a force for good. The first was *The Warlord of the Air*.

I also wrote my *Dancers at the End of Time* stories and novels under the influence of Edwardian humourists and absurdists like Jerome or Firbank. Together with more conventional generic books like *The Ice Schooner* or *The Black Corridor*, most of that work was done in the 1960s and 70s when I wrote the Eternal Champion supernatural adventure novels which helped support my own and others' experiments via NEW WORLDS, allowing me also to keep a family while writing books in which action and fantastic invention were paramount. Though I did them quickly, I didn't write them cynically. I have always believed, somewhat puritanically, in giving the audience good value for money. I enjoyed writing them, tried to avoid repetition, and through each new one was able to develop a few more ideas. They also continued to teach me how to express myself through image and metaphor. My Everyman became the Eternal Champion, his dreams and ambitions represented by the multiverse. He could be an ordinary person struggling with familiar problems in a contemporary setting or he could be a swordsman fighting monsters on a far-away world.

Long before I wrote *Gloriana* (in four parts reflecting the seasons) I had learned to think in images and symbols through reading John Bunyan's *Pilgrim's Progress*, Milton and others, understanding early on that the visual could be the most important part of a book and was often in itself a story as, for instance, a famous personality could also, through everything associated with their name, function as narrative. I wanted to find ways of carrying as many stories as possible in one. From the cinema I also learned how to use images as connecting themes. Images, colours, music, and even popular magazine headlines can all add coherence to an apparently random story, underpinning it and giving the reader a sense of internal logic and a satisfactory resolution, dispensing with certain familiar literary conventions.

When the story required it, I also began writing neo-realist fiction exploring the interface of character and environment, especially the city, especially London. In some books I condensed, manipulated and randomised time to achieve what I wanted, but in others the sense of 'real time' as we all generally perceive it was more suitable and could best be achieved by traditional nineteenth-century means. For the Pyat books I first looked back to the great German classic, Grimmelshausen's *Simplicissimus* and other early picaresques. I then examined the roots of a certain kind of moral fiction from Defoe through Thackeray and Meredith then to modern times where the picaresque (or rogue tale) can take the form of a road movie, for instance. While it's probably fair to say that Pyat and *Byzantium Endures* precipitated the end of my second marriage (echoed to a degree in *The Brothel in Rosenstrasse*), the late 70s and the 80s were exhilarating times for me, with *Mother London* being perhaps my own favourite novel of that period. I wanted to write something celebratory.

By the 90s I was again attempting to unite several kinds of fiction in one novel with my Second Ether trilogy. With Mandelbrot, Chaos Theory and String Theory I felt, as I said at the time, as if I were being offered a chart of my own brain. That chart made it easier for me to develop the notion of the multiverse as representing both the internal and the external, as a metaphor and as a means of structuring and rationalising an outrageously inventive and quasi-realistic narrative. The worlds of the multiverse move up and down scales or 'planes' explained in terms of mass, allowing entire universes to exist in the 'same' space. The result of developing this idea was the *War Amongst the Angels* sequence which added absurdist elements also functioning as a kind of mythology and folklore for a world beginning to understand itself in terms of new metaphysics and theoretical physics. As the cosmos becomes denser and almost infinite before our eyes, with black holes and dark matter affecting our own reality, we can explore them and observe them as our ancestors explored our planet and observed the heavens.

At the end of the 90s I'd returned to realism, sometimes with a dash of fantasy, with *King of the City* and the stories collected in *London Bone*. I also wrote a new Elric/Eternal Champion sequence, beginning with *Daughter of Dreams*, which brought the fantasy worlds of Hawkmoon, Bastable and Co. in line with my realistic and autobiographical stories, another attempt to unify all my fiction, and also offer a way in which disparate genres could be reunited, through notions developed from the multiverse and the Eternal Champion, as one giant novel. At the time I was finishing the Pyat sequence which attempted to look at the roots of the Nazi Holocaust in our European, Middle Eastern and American cultures and to ground my strange survival guilt while at the same time examining my own cultural roots in the light of an enduring anti-Semitism.

By the 2000s I was exploring various conventional ways of story-telling in the last parts of *The Metatemporal Detective* and through other homages, comics, parodies and games. I also looked back at my earliest influences. I had reached retirement age and felt like a rest. I wrote a 'prequel' to the Elric series as a graphic novel with Walter Simonson, *The Making of a Sorcerer*, and did a little online editing with FANTASTIC METROPOLIS.

By 2010 I had written a novel featuring Doctor Who, *The Coming of the Terraphiles*, with a nod to P.G. Wodehouse (a boyhood favourite), continued to write short stories and novellas and to work on the beginning of a new sequence combining pure fantasy and straight autobiography called *The Whispering Swarm* while still writing more Cornelius stories trying to unite all the various genres and sub-genres into which contemporary fiction has fallen.

Throughout my career critics have announced that I'm 'abandoning' fantasy and concentrating on literary fiction. The truth is, however, that all my life, since I became a professional writer and editor at the age of 16, I've written in whatever mode suits a story best and where necessary created a new form if an old one didn't work for me. Certain ideas are best carried on a Jerry Cornelius story, others work better as realism and others as fantasy or science fiction. Some work best as a combination. I'm sure I'll write whatever I like and will continue to experiment with all the ways there are of telling stories and carrying as many themes as possible. Whether I write about a widow coping with loneliness in her cottage or a massive, universe-size sentient spaceship searching for her children, I'll no doubt die trying to tell them all. I hope you'll find at least some of them to your taste.

One thing a reader can be sure of about these new editions is that they would not have been possible without the tremendous and indispensable help of my old friend and bibliographer John Davey. John has ensured that these Gollancz editions are definitive. I am indebted to John for many things, including his work at

Moorcock's Miscellany, my website, but his work on this edition has been outstanding. As well as being an accomplished novelist in his own right John is an astonishingly good editor who has worked with Gollancz and myself to point out every error and flaw in all previous editions, some of them not corrected since their first publication, and has enabled me to correct or revise them. I couldn't have completed this project without him. Together, I think, Gollancz, John Davey and myself have produced what will be the best editions possible and I am very grateful to him, to Malcolm Edwards, Darren Nash and Marcus Gipps for all the considerable hard work they have done to make this edition what it is.

Michael Moorcock

# Contents

THE YOUNG KINGDOMS

THE SIGHING DESERT

THE RAGGED PILLARS

TANELORN

• QVARZHASAAT

TO PHUM AND
YESHPOTOOM
KAHLAI
ELWHER

• ILMAR

ILMIORA

KARLAAK

GORTHAN

THE
WEEPING
WASTE

BAKSHAAN

ORG
FOREST
OF TROOS

NADSOKOR

RIGHARIOM

TO
OKARA
CHANG SHAI

VILMIR

TARMAR

OLD
HROLMAR

STRAITS of VILMIR

THE FORTRESS of EVENING

MENII

THE ISLE OF THE
PURPLE
TOWNS

TREPESAZ

STAGASAZ

RASCHIL

SHALAL

STAGASAZ

FILKHAR

ARGHILIAR

RIVER CHA

RIVER SCHLAN

IOSAZ

PIKARAYD

RIVER ZAPROZ TREPECK

DHRIYR

ALORASAZ

J. CAWTHORN · 92

ADAPTED FROM THE MAP BY
JOHN COLLIER & WALTER ROMANSKI

*To the memory of Harry Harrison,*
*Elric's godfather and a fellow spirit*

# The Return of the
# Thin White Duke

*Foreword by Alan Moore*

I REMEMBER MELNIBONÉ. Not the empire, obviously, but its aftermath, its débris: mangled scraps of silver filigree from brooch or breastplate, tatters of checked silk accumulating in the gutters of the Tottenham Court Road. Exquisite and depraved, Melnibonéan culture had been shattered by a grand catastrophe before recorded history began – probably sometime during the mid-1940s – but its shards and relics and survivors were still evident in London's tangled streets as late as 1968. You could still find reasonably priced bronze effigies of Arioch amongst the stalls on Portobello Road, and when I interviewed Dave Brock of Hawkwind for the English music paper SOUNDS in 1981 he showed me the black runesword fragment he'd been using as a plectrum since the band's first album. Though the cruel and glorious civilisation of Melniboné was by then vanished as though it had never been, its flavours and its atmospheres endured, a perfume lingering for decades in the basements and back alleys of the capital. Even the empire's laid-off gods and demons were effectively absorbed into the ordinary British social structure; its Law Lords rapidly became a cornerstone of the judicial system while its Chaos Lords went, for the most part, into industry or government. Former Melnibonéan Lord of Chaos Sir Giles Pyaray, for instance, currently occupies a seat at the Department of Trade and Industry, while his company Pyaray Holdings has been recently awarded major contracts as a part of the ongoing reconstruction of Iraq.

Despite Melniboné's pervasive influence, however, you will find few public figures ready to acknowledge their huge debt to this all-but forgotten world, perhaps because the wilful decadence

1

and tortured romance that Melniboné exemplified has fallen out of favour with the resolutely medieval world view we embrace today throughout the globe's foremost Neoconservative theocracies. Just as with the visitors' centres serving the Grand Canyon that have been instructed to remove all reference to the canyon's geologic age lest they offend creationists, so too has any evidence for the existence of Melniboné apparently been stricken from the record. With its central governmental district renamed Marylebone and its distinctive azure ceremonial tartans sold off in job lots to boutiques in the King's Road, it's entirely possible that those of my own post-war generation might have never heard about Melniboné were it not for allusions found in the supposedly fictitious works of the great London writer, Michael Moorcock.

My own entry to the Moorcock oeuvre came, if I recall correctly, by way of a Pyramid Books 'science fantasy' anthology entitled *The Fantastic Swordsmen*, edited by the ubiquitous L. Sprague de Camp and purchased from the first science fiction, fantasy and comics bookshop, Dark They Were And Golden Eyed, itself a strikingly neo-Melnibonéan establishment. The paperback, touchingly small and underfed to modern eyes, had pages edged a brilliant Naples yellow and came with the uninviting cover image of a blond barbarian engaged in butchering some sort of octopus, clearly an off-day from the usually inspired Jack Gaughan. The contents, likewise, while initially attractive to an undiscriminating fourteen-year-old boy, turned out upon inspection to be widely varied in their quality, a motley armful of fantastic tales swept up under the loose rubric of sword-and-sorcery, ranging from a pedestrian early outing by potboiler king John Jakes, through more accomplished works by the tormented would-be cowboy Robert Howard, or a dreamlike early Lovecraft piece, or one by Lovecraft's early model, Lord Dunsany, to a genuinely stylish and more noticeably modern offering from Fritz Leiber. Every story had a map appended to it, showing the geographies of the distinct imaginary worlds in which the various narratives were set, and all in all it was a decent and commendable collection for its genre, for its time.

And then, clearly standing aloof and apart from the surrounding mighty-thewed pulp and Dunsanian fairy tales, there was the Elric yarn by Michael Moorcock.

Now, at almost forty years remove, I can't even recall which one it was – one of the precious handful from *The Stealer of Souls*, no doubt – but I still remember vividly its impact. Elric, decadent, hallucinatory and feverish, its alabaster hero battled with his howling, parasitic blade against a paranoiac backdrop that made other fantasy environments seem lazy and anaemic in their Chinese-takeaway cod orientalism or their snug Arcadian idylls. Unlike every other sword-wielding protagonist in the anthology, it was apparent that Moorcock's wan, drug-addicted champion would not be stigmatised by a dismaying jacket blurb declaring him to be in the tradition of J.R.R. Tolkien: the Melnibonéan landscape, seething, mutable, warped by the touch of fractal horrors, was an anti-matter antidote to Middle Earth, a toxic and fluorescing elf-repellent. Elric's world churned with a fierce and unselfconscious poetry, churned with the breakneck energies of its own furious pulp-deadline composition. Not content to stand there shuffling uneasily beneath its threadbare sword-and-sorcery banner, Moorcock's prose instead took the whole stagnant genre by its throat and pummelled it into a different shape, transmuted Howard's blustering over-compensation and the relatively tired and bloodless efforts of Howard's competitors into a new form, a delirious romance with different capabilities, delivered in a language that was adequate to all the tumult and upheaval of its times, a voice that we could recognise.

Moorcock was evidently writing from experience, with the extravagance and sheer exhilaration of his stories marking him as from a different stock than the majority of his contemporaries. The breadth and richness of his influences hinted that he was himself some kind of a Melnibonéan ex-pat, nurtured by the cultural traditions of his homeland, drawing from a more exotic pool of reference than that available to those who worked within the often stultifying literary conventions found in post-war England. When Moorcock commenced his long career while in his teens he showed no interest in the leading authors of the day, the former

Angry Young Men who were in truth far more petulant than angry and had never been that young, cleaving instead to sombre, thoughtful voices such as that of Angus Wilson, or to marvellous, baroque outsiders such as Mervyn Peake. After solid apprentice work on his conventional blade-swinging hero Sojan in the weekly TARZAN comic book, or in the Sexton Blake adventures that he penned alongside notables such as the wonderful Jack Trevor Story (and, as rumour has it, even Irish genius Flann O'Brien), Moorcock emerged as a formidable rare beast with an extensive reach, as capable of championing the then-unpublished *Naked Lunch* by Burroughs (W.S.) as he was of appreciating the wild colour and invention that was to be found in Burroughs (E.R.). Whether by virtue of his possibly Melnibonéan heritage or by some other means, Moorcock was consummately hip and brought the sensibilities of a progressive and much wider world of art and literature into a field that was, despite the unrestrained imagination promised by its sales pitch, for the most part both conservative and inward-looking.

Growing out of a mid-1950s correspondence between the young writer and his long-serving artist confederate James Cawthorn, the first Elric stories were an aromatic broth of Abraham Merritt and Jack Kerouac, of Bertholt Brecht, and Anthony Skene's Monsieur Zenith, the albino drug-dependent foe of Sexton Blake who'd turned out to have more charisma than his shrewd detective adversary. With the series finally seeing daylight in Carnell's SCIENCE FANTASY in 1961, it was immediately quite clear that a dangerous mutation had occurred within the narrow gene pool of heroic fantasy, a mutation just as elegant and threatening as Elvis Presley had turned out to be in the popular music of this decade, or that James Dean represented in its cinema. Most noticeably, Elric in no way conformed to the then-current definition of a hero, being instead a pink-eyed necromaniac invalid, a traitor to his kind and slayer of his wife, a sickly and yet terrifying spiritual vampire living without hope at the frayed limits of his own debatable humanity. Bad like Gene Vincent, sick like Lenny Bruce and haunted by addiction like Bill Burroughs, though Elric ostensibly existed in a dawn world of antiquity this was belied by his being so obviously a creature of his Cold War brothel-creeper times, albeit one whose languid decadence placed him slightly ahead of them and presciently made his pallid, well-outfitted figure just as emblematic of the psychedelic '60s yet to come.

By 1963, when first the character appeared in book form, Britain was beginning to show healthy signs of energetic uproar and a glorious peacock-feathered blossoming, against which setting Elric would seem even more appropriate. The Beatles had, significantly, changed the rules of English culture by erupting from a background of the popular and vulgar to make art more vital and transformative than anything produced by the polite society-approved and -vetted artistic establishment. The wrought-iron and forbidding gates had been thrown open so that artists, writers and musicians could storm in to explore subjects that seemed genuinely relevant to the eventful and uncertain world in which they found themselves; could define the acceptable according to their own rules. Within five years, when I first belatedly discovered Elric sometime during 1968, provincial English life had been transmuted into a fantasmagoric territory, at least psychologically, so that the exploits of this fated, chalk-white aesthete somehow struck the perfect resonance, made Moorcock's anti-hero just as much a symbol of the times as demonstrations at the US embassy in Grosvenor Square, or Jimi Hendrix, or the OZ trial.

Naturally, by then Moorcock himself had moved on and was editing NEW WORLDS, the last and the best of traditional science fiction magazines published in England. Under Moorcock's guidance, the magazine became a vehicle for modernist experiment, gleefully re-imagining the SF genre as a field elastic enough to include the pathological and alienated 'condensed novels' of J.G. Ballard, the brilliantly skewed and subverted conventional science fiction tropes of Barrington Bayley, and even the black urban comedies dished up by old Sexton Blake mucker Jack Trevor Story. Moorcock's own main contribution to the magazine, aside from his task as commander of the entire risky, improbable venture, came in the form of his Jerry Cornelius stories.

Cornelius, a multiphasic modern pierrot with his doings catalogued by most of Moorcock's NEW WORLDS writing stable at one time or other, rapidly became an edgy mascot for the magazine and also for the entire movement that the magazine was spearheading, an icon of the fractured moral wasteland England would become after the wild, fluorescent brushfire of the 1960s had burned out. His début, starting in the pages of NEW WORLDS in 1965 and culminating in Avon Books' publication of *The Final Programme* during 1968 was a spectacular affair – 'Michael Moorcock's savagely satirical breakthrough in speculative fiction, *The Final Programme*, a breathtakingly vivid, rapid-fire novel of tomorrow that says things you may not want to hear about today!' – and a mind-bending apparent change of tack for those readers who thought that they knew Moorcock from his Elric or his Dorian Hawkmoon fantasies. Even its dedication, 'To Jimmy Ballard, Bill Burroughs, and the Beatles, who are pointing the way through', seemed dangerously avant-garde within the cosy rocket-robot-raygun comfort zone of early '60s science fiction. As disorienting as *The Final Programme* was, however, its relentless novelty was undercut by a peculiar familiarity: Cornelius's exploits mirrored those of Elric of Melniboné almost exactly, blow for blow. Even a minor character like the Melnibonéan servant, Tanglebones, could turn up anagrammatised as the Cornelius family's retainer John Gnatbeelson. It became clear that far from abandoning his haunted and anaemic prince of ruins, Moorcock had in some way cleverly refracted that persona through a different glass, until it looked and spoke and acted differently, became a different creature fit for different times, while still retaining all the fascinating, cryptic charge of the original.

As Moorcock's work evolved into progressively more radical and startling forms over the coming decades, this process of refracting light and ideas through a prototypical Melnibonéan gemstone would continue. Even in the soaring majesty of *Mother London* or the dark symphony of Moorcock's Pyat quartet, it is still possible to hear the music of Tarkesh, the Boiling Sea, or Old Hrolmar. With these later works and with Moorcock's ascent to literary landmark, it has become fashionable to assert that only in such offerings as the exquisite *Vengeance of Rome* are we seeing the real Moorcock; that the staggering sweep of glittering fantasy trilogies that preceded these admitted masterpieces are in some way minor works, safely excluded from the author's serious canon. This is to misunderstand, I think, the intertextual and organic whole of Moorcock's writings. All the blood and passion that informs his work has the genetic markers of Melniboné, stamped clearly on each paragraph, each line. No matter where the various strands of Moorcock's sprawling opera ended up, or in what lofty climes, the bloodline started out with Elric. All the narratives have his mysterious, apocalyptic eyes.

These tales are among the first rush of that blood, the first pure spurts from what would prove to be a deep and never-ending fountain. Messy, uncontrolled and beautiful, the stories are the raw heart of Michael Moorcock, the spells that first drew me and all the numerous admirers of his work with whom I am acquainted into Moorcock's luminous and captivating web. Read them and remember the frenetic, fiery world and times that gave them birth. Read them and recall the days when all of us were living in Melniboné.

*Alan Moore*
*Northampton*
*31 January, 2007*

# At the Beginning

I'm inclined to forget how many contributions I made to fanzines between, say, 1955 and 1965. I continued to contribute to them while I was editor of TARZAN ADVENTURES and even wrote the odd letter while I was editing NEW WORLDS. One of the finest of these fanzines was AMRA, essentially a serious magazine for that handful of people then interested in fantasy fiction and specifically, thus the title, the work of Robert E. Howard. Run by an enthusiast, George Scithers, who was still involved in enthusiast-publishing (most recently WEIRD TALES) up to his death in 2010. By the evidence of my approach, I must suppose that Fritz Leiber had not yet taken part in the correspondence and had therefore not come up with the terms 'sword and sorcery' or 'heroic fantasy'. Actually, I still prefer my own suggestion. I would not include the Peake books in that list any more and there are a few others I would mention if writing the piece today. It was probably written in the middle of 1960. I reprint it here because, with my 'Aspects of Fantasy' essays, which became *Wizardry and Wild Romance*, it immediately precedes the Elric stories and gives some idea of the atmosphere in which they were first published, at a time when supernatural adventure fantasy (to give it another tag) was thought to have only a very limited readership...

# Putting a Tag on It

## (1960)

I'VE ALWAYS KIDDED myself, and until recently had convinced myself, that names were of no importance and that what really mattered was the Thing Concerned, not the tag which was put on said Thing. Although in principle I still agree with the idea, I am having to admit to myself that names are convenient and save an awful lot of wordage. Thus with 'Science Fiction': a much disputed tag, agreed, but one which at least helps us to visualise roughly what someone who uses the words means.

We have two tags, really – SF and 'Fantasy' – but I feel that we should have another general name to include the sub-genre of books which deal with Middle Earths and lands and worlds based on this planet, worlds which exist only in some author's vivid imagination. In this sub-genre I would classify books like *The Worm Ouroboros, Jurgen, The Lord of the Rings, The Once and Future King*, the Grey Mouser/Fafhrd series, the Conan series, *The Broken Sword, The Well of the Unicorn*, etc.

Now all these stories have several things in common – they are fantasy stories which could hardly be classified as SF, and they are stories of high adventure, generally featuring a central hero very easy to identify oneself with. For the most part they *are* works of escapism, anything else usually being secondary (exceptions, I would agree, are *Jurgen* and *The Once and Future King*). But all of them are tales told for the tale's sake, and the authors have obviously thoroughly enjoyed the telling.

The roots of most of these stories are in legendry, classic romance, mythology, folklore, and dubious ancient works of 'History'.

In a recent letter, Sprague de Camp called this stuff Prehistoric-Adventure-Fantasy and this name, although somewhat unwieldy, could apply to much of the material I have listed. PAF? Then again, you could call it Saga-Fantasy or Fantastic-Romance (in the sense of the Chivalric Romances).

What we want is a name which might not, on analysis, include every book in this category, but which, like 'Science Fiction', would give readers some idea what you're talking about when you're doing articles, reviews, etc., on books in this genre. Or for that matter it would be useful to use just in conversation or when forming clubs, launching magazines, etc.

*Epic Fantasy* is the name which appeals most to me as one

which includes many of these stories – certainly all of the ones I have mentioned.

Most of the tales listed have a basic general formula. They are 'quest' stories. The necessary sense of conflict in a book designed to hold the reader's interest from start to finish is supplied by the simple formula:

A) Hero must get or do something,
B) Villains disapprove,
C) Hero sets out to get what he wants anyway,
D) Villains thwart him one or more times (according to length of story), and finally
E) Hero, in the face of all odds, does what the reader expects of him.

Of course E) often has a twist of some kind to it but in most cases the other four parts are there. This is not so in *Jurgen* nor in White's tetralogy admittedly, but then *Jurgen* is definitely an allegory, while in *The Sword in the Stone* and its sequels it is the characters which are of main importance to the author. *Jurgen* only just manages to squeeze into the category anyway.

Also, it can be argued that this basic plotline can apply to most stories. Agreed, but the point is that here the plotline tends to dominate both theme and hero, and is easily spotted for what it is.

Conan and the Grey Mouser generally have to start at point A), pass wicked points B) and D), and eventually win through to goal – point E. Anything else, in the meantime, is extra – in fact, the extra is that which puts these stories above many others. The Ringbearers in Tolkien's magnificent saga do this also.

Now, the point is that every one of these tales, almost without exception, follows the pattern of the old Heroic Sagas and Epic Romances. Basically, Conan and Beowulf have much in common; Ragnar Lodbrok and Fafhrd also; Gandalf and Merlin; Amadis of Gaul and Airar (of *The Well of the Unicorn*). And I'm sure many of the unhuman characters (elves, orcs, wizards and such) and monsters these heroes encounter can trace their ancestry right back to the Sidhe, Lord Soulis, Urganda the Unknown, Grendel, Siegfried's dragon, Cerberus, and the various hippogriffs, firedrakes, and serpents of legend and mythology.

As de Camp showed in his 'Exegesis of Howard's Hyborian Tales' and as I did in my earlier and not nearly so complete article 'Historical Fact and Fiction in Connection with the Conan Series' [BURROUGHSANIA V. 2 #16, Aug 1957], the names for characters and backgrounds in Howard's wonderful series were nearly all culled from legendry. Most of Howard's sources are easily traced, for he did not even change names. The same goes for *The Broken Sword*; and the Ring tetralogy is obviously based (only *based* mind you) on Anglo-Saxon foundations.

This, of course, does not detract one iota from the stories themselves. In fact all the authors have done much, much more than simply rehash old folk literature – they have taken crudely formed and paradoxical tales as their bases and written new, subtler stories which are often far better than the ones which undoubtedly influenced them. Also, when I compare Conan with Beowulf and so on, I am not saying that these characters were the originals upon which Howard, Leiber, Tolkien and the others based their own heroes and villains – I am simply trying to point out that the *influence* was there.

So, all in all, I would say that *Epic Fantasy* is about the best name for the sub-genre, considering its general form and roots. Obviously, Epic Fantasy includes the Conan, Kull, and Bran Mak Morn stories of R.E. Howard; the Grey Mouser/Fafhrd stories by Fritz Leiber; the Arthurian tetralogy by T.H. White; the Middle Earth stories of J.R.R. Tolkien; *The Worm Ouroboros* by E.R. Eddison; the Zothique stories of Clark Ashton Smith; some of the works of Abraham Merritt (*The Ship of Ishtar*, etc.); some of H. Rider Haggard's stories (*Allan and the Ice Gods*, etc.); *The Broken Sword* by Poul Anderson; the Gormenghast trilogy of Mervyn Peake (it just gets in, I think); the Poictesme stories of James Branch Cabell (including *Jurgen, The Silver Stallion*, and others); and *The Well of the Unicorn* by Fletcher Pratt.

I would appreciate other suggestions for possible inclusions. *Titus Groan* and its sequels by Mervyn Peake actually do not have the form nor roots I have described but they have the general atmosphere and are certainly set outside of our own space-time Earth.

The question might be raised as to whether or not to include Alternate Space-Time Continuum stories such as de Camp's and Pratt's Harold Shea tales, Anderson's *Three Hearts and Three Lions*, Mark Twain's *A Connecticut Yankee at the Court of King Arthur* (obviously the main influence for many subsequent stories), L. Ron Hubbard's *Masters* and *Slaves of Sleep*, etc., in which present-day heroes enter worlds of legend and myth and don't take the idea altogether seriously. The basic difference is in the treatment, I think. In the Epic Fantasy group the author more or less asks you to accept the background and so on as *important* because his characters consider it important, then take the story from there, respecting the laws and logic which are to be taken for what they are, and taken seriously.

In the AS-TC group the treatment is often humorous, the author having the attitude of a teller of tall stories who doesn't expect to be believed but knows that he is entertaining his hearers – which is all that is required of him. Thus, although several of the AS-TC group could just about fall into the Epic Fantasy group, I consider it best to describe them as simply 'Fantasy' (which I usually interpret to mean the kind of stuff which filled the majority of UNKNOWN's pages).

What do you think?

# Master of Chaos

## (Earl Aubec)

FROM THE GLASSLESS window of the stone tower it was possible to see the wide river winding off between loose, brown banks, through the heaped terrain of solid green copses which blended very gradually into the mass of the forest proper. And out of the forest, the cliff rose, grey and light green, up and up, the rock darkening, lichen-covered, to merge with the lower, and even more massive, stones of the castle. It was the castle which dominated the countryside in three directions, drawing the eye from river, rock or forest. Its walls were high and of thick granite, with towers; a dense field of towers, grouped so as to shadow one another.

Aubec of Malador marvelled and wondered how human builders could ever have constructed it, save by sorcery. Brooding and mysterious, the castle seemed to have a defiant air, for it stood on the very edge of the world.

At this moment the lowering sky cast a strange, deep yellow light against the western sides of the towers, intensifying the blackness untouched by it. Huge billows of blue sky rent the general racing greyness above, and mounds of red cloud crept through to blend and produce more and subtler colourings. Yet, though the sky was impressive, it could not take the gaze away from the ponderous series of man-made crags that were Castle Kaneloon.

Earl Aubec of Malador did not turn from the window until it was completely dark outside; forest, cliff and castle but shadowy tones against the overall blackness. He passed a heavy, knotted hand over his almost bald scalp and thoughtfully went towards the heap of straw which was his intended bed.

The straw was piled in a niche created by a buttress and the outer wall and the room was well-lighted by Malador's lantern. But the air was cold as he lay down on the straw with his hand close to the two-handed broadsword of prodigious size. This was his only weapon. It looked as if it had been forged for a giant – Malador was virtually that himself – with its wide crosspiece and heavy, stone-encrusted hilt and five-foot blade, smooth and broad. Beside it was Malador's old, heavy armour, the casque balanced on top with its somewhat tattered black plumes waving slightly in a current of air from the window.

Malador slept.

His dreams, as usual, were turbulent; of mighty armies surging across the blazing landscapes, curling banners bearing the blazons of a hundred nations, forests of shining lance-tips, seas of tossing helmets, the brave, wild blasts of the war-horns, the clatter of hoofs and the songs and cries and shouts of soldiers. These were dreams of earlier times, of his youth when, for Queen Eloarde of Klant, he had conquered all the Southern nations – almost to the edge of the world. Only Kaneloon, on the very edge, had he not conquered, and this because no army would follow him there.

For one of so martial an appearance, these dreams were surprisingly unwelcome, and Malador woke several times that night, shaking his head in an attempt to rid himself of them.

He would rather have dreamed of Eloarde, though she was the cause of his restlessness, but he saw nothing of her in his sleep; nothing of her soft, black hair that billowed around her pale face, nothing of her green eyes and red lips and her proud, disdainful posture. Eloarde had assigned him to this quest and he had not gone willingly, though he had no choice, for as well as his mistress she was also his queen. The Champion was traditionally her lover – and it was unthinkable to Earl Aubec that any other condition should exist. It was his place, as Champion of Klant, to obey and go forth from her palace to seek Castle Kaneloon alone and conquer it and declare it part of her empire, so that it could be said Queen Eloarde's domain stretched from the Dragon Sea to World's Edge.

Nothing lay beyond World's Edge – nothing save the swirling stuff of unformed Chaos which stretched away from the Cliffs of Kaneloon for eternity, roiling and broiling, multicoloured, full of monstrous half-shapes – for Earth alone was Lawful and constituted of ordered matter, drifting in the sea of Chaos-stuff as it had done for aeons.

In the morning, Earl Aubec of Malador extinguished the lantern which he had allowed to remain alight, drew on greaves and hauberk, placed his black plumed helm upon his head, put his broadsword over his shoulder and sallied out of the stone tower which was all that remained whole of some ancient edifice.

His leathern-shod feet stumbled over stones that seemed partially dissolved, as if Chaos had once lapped here instead of against the towering Cliffs of Kaneloon. That, of course, was quite impossible, since Earth's boundaries were known to be constant.

Castle Kaneloon had seemed closer the night before and that, he now realised, was because it was so huge. He followed the river, his feet sinking in the loamy soil, the great branches of the trees shading him from the increasingly hot sun as he made his way towards the cliffs. Kaneloon was now out of sight, high above him. Every so often he used his sword as an axe to clear his way through the places where the foliage was particularly thick.

He rested several times, drinking the cold water of the river and mopping his face and head. He was unhurried, he had no wish to visit Kaneloon, he resented the interruption to his life with Eloarde which he thought he had earned. Also he, too, had a superstitious dread of the mysterious castle, which was said to be inhabited only by one human occupant – the Dark Lady, a sorceress without mercy who commanded a legion of demons and other Chaos creatures.

He arrived at the cliffs by midday and regarded the path leading upwards with a mixture of wariness and relief. He had expected to have to scale the cliffs. He was not one, however, to take a difficult route where an easy one presented itself, so he looped a cord around his sword and slung it over his back, since it was too long and cumbersome to carry at his side. Then, still in bad humour, he began to climb the twisting path.

The lichen-covered rocks were evidently ancient, contrary to the speculations of certain philosophers who asked why Kaneloon had only been heard of a few generations since. Malador believed in the general answer to this question – that explorers had never ventured this far until fairly recently. He glanced back down the path and saw the tops of the trees below him, their foliage moving slightly in the breeze. The tower in which he'd spent the night was just visible in the distance and, beyond that, he knew, there was no civilisation, no outpost of Man for many days' journey north, east, or west – and Chaos lay to the south. He had never been so close to the edge of the world before and wondered how the sight of unformed matter would affect his brain.

At length he clambered to the top of the cliff and stood, arms akimbo, staring up at Castle Kaneloon which soared a mile away, its highest towers hidden in the clouds, its immense walls rooted on the rock and stretching away, limited on both sides of the cliff, Malador watched the churning, leaping Chaos-substance – predominantly grey, blue, brown and yellow at this moment, though its colours changed constantly – spew like sea-spray a few feet from the castle.

He became filled with a feeling of such indescribable profundity that he could only remain in this position for a long while, completely overwhelmed by a sense of his own insignificance. It came to him, eventually, that if anyone did dwell in the Castle Kaneloon, then they must have a robust mind or else must be insane, and then he sighed and strode on towards his goal, noting that the ground was perfectly flat, without blemish, green, obsidian and reflecting imperfectly the dancing Chaos-stuff from which he averted his eyes as much as he could.

Kaneloon had many entrances, all dark and unwelcoming, and had they all not been of regular size and shape they might have been so many cave-mouths.

Malador paused before choosing which to take, and then walked with outward purposefulness towards one. He went into blackness which appeared to stretch away for ever. It was cold; it was empty and he was alone.

He was soon lost. His footsteps made no echo, which was unexpected; then the blackness began to give way to a series of angular outlines, like the walls of a twisting corridor – walls which did not reach the unsensed roof, but ended several yards above his head. It was a labyrinth, a maze. He paused and looked back and saw with horror that the maze wound off in many directions, though he was sure he had followed a straight path from the outside.

For an instant, his mind became diffused and madness threatened to engulf him, but he battened it down, unslung his sword, shivering. Which way? He pressed on, unable to tell, now, whether he went forward or backward.

The madness lurking in the depths of his brain filtered out and became fear and, immediately following the sensation of fear, came the shapes. Swift-moving shapes, darting from several different directions, gibbering, fiendish, utterly horrible.

One of these creatures leapt at him and he struck at it with his blade. It fled, but seemed unwounded. Another came and another and he forgot his panic as he smote around him, driving them back until all had fled. He paused and leaned, panting, on his sword. Then, as he stared around him, the fear began to flood back into him and more creatures appeared – creatures with wide, blazing eyes and clutching talons, creatures with malevolent faces, mocking him, creatures with half-familiar faces, some recognisable as those of old friends and relatives, yet twisted into horrific parodies. He screamed and ran at them, whirling his huge sword, slashing, hacking at them, rushing past one group to turn a bend in the labyrinth and encounter another.

Malicious laughter coursed through the twisting corridors, following him and preceding him as he ran. He stumbled and fell against a wall. At first the wall seemed of solid stone, then, slowly it became soft and he sank through it, his body lying half in one corridor, half in another. He hauled himself through, still on

ELRIC OF MELNIBONÉ AND OTHER STORIES

hands and knees, looked up and saw Eloarde, but an Eloarde whose face grew old as he watched.

*I am mad*, he thought. *Is this reality or fantasy – or both?*

He reached out a hand, *'Eloarde!'*

She vanished but was replaced by a crowding horde of demons. He raised himself to his feet and flailed around him with his blade, but they skipped outside his range and he roared at them as he advanced. Momentarily, while he thus exerted himself, the fear left him again and, with the disappearance of the fear, so the visions vanished until he realised that the fear preceded the manifestations and he tried to control it.

He almost succeeded, forcing himself to relax, but it welled up again and the creatures bubbled out of the walls, their shrill voices full of malicious mirth.

This time he did not attack them with his sword, but stood his ground as calmly as he could and concentrated upon his own mental condition. As he did so, the creatures began to fade away and then the walls of the labyrinth dissolved and it seemed to him that he stood in a peaceful valley, calm and idyllic. Yet, hovering close to his consciousness, he seemed to see the walls of the labyrinth faintly outlined, and disgusting shapes moving here and there along the many passages.

He realised that the vision of the valley was as much an illusion as the labyrinth and, with this conclusion, both valley and labyrinth faded and he stood in the enormous hall of a castle which could only be Kaneloon.

The hall was unoccupied though well-furnished, and he could not see the source of the light, which was bright and even. He strode towards a table, on which were heaped scrolls, and his feet made a satisfying echo. Several great metal-studded doors led off from the hall, but for the moment he did not investigate them, intent on studying the scrolls and seeing if they could help him unravel Kaneloon's mystery.

He propped his sword against the table and took up the first scroll.

It was a beautiful thing of red vellum, but the black letters upon it meant nothing to him and he was astounded for, though dialects varied from place to place, there was only one language in all the lands of the Earth. Another scroll bore different symbols still, and a third he unrolled carried a series of highly stylised pictures which were repeated here and there so that he guessed they formed some kind of alphabet. Disgusted, he flung the scroll down, picked up his sword, drew an immense breath and shouted:

'Who dwells here? Let them know that Aubec, Earl of Malador, Champion of Klant and Conqueror of the South claims this castle in the name of Queen Eloarde, Empress of all the Southlands!'

In shouting these familiar words, he felt somewhat more comfortable, but he received no reply. He lifted his casque a trifle and scratched his neck. Then he picked up his sword, balanced it over his shoulder, and made for the largest door.

Before he reached it, it sprang open and a huge, manlike thing with hands like grappling irons grinned at him.

He took a pace backwards and then another until, seeing that the thing did not advance, he stood his ground observing it.

It was a foot or so taller than he, with oval, multifaceted eyes that, by their nature, seemed blank. Its face was angular and had a grey, metallic sheen. Most of its body was composed of burnished metal, jointed in the manner of armour. Upon its head was a tight-fitting hood, studded with brass. It had about it an air of tremendous and insensate power, though it did not move.

'A golem!' Malador exclaimed for it seemed to him that he remembered such man-made creatures from legends. 'What sorcery created *you*!'

The golem did not reply but its hands – which were in reality composed of four spikes of metal apiece – began slowly to flex themselves; and still the golem grinned.

This thing, Malador knew, did not have the same amorphous quality of his earlier visions. This was solid, this was real and strong, and even Malador's manly strength, however much he exerted it, could not defeat such a creature. Yet neither could he turn away.

With a scream of metal joints, the golem entered the hall and stretched its burnished hands towards the earl.

Malador could attack or flee, and fleeing would be senseless. He attacked.

His great sword clasped in both hands, he swung it sideways at the golem's torso, which seemed to be its weakest point. The golem lowered an arm and the sword shuddered against metal with a mighty clang that set the whole of Malador's body quaking. He stumbled backwards. Remorselessly, the golem followed him.

Malador looked back and searched the hall in the hope of finding a weapon more powerful than his sword, but saw only shields of an ornamental kind upon the wall to his right. He turned and ran to the wall, wrenching one of the shields from its place and slipping it onto his arm. It was an oblong thing, very light and comprising several layers of cross-grained wood. It was inadequate, but it made him feel a trifle better as he whirled again to face the golem.

The golem advanced, and Malador thought he noticed something familiar about it, just as the demons of the labyrinth had seemed familiar, but the impression was only vague. Kaneloon's weird sorcery was affecting his mind, he decided.

The creature raised the spikes on its right arm and aimed a swift blow at Malador's head. He avoided it, putting up his sword as protection. The spikes clashed against the sword and then the left arm pistoned forward, driving at Malador's stomach. The shield stopped his blow, though the spikes pierced it deeply. He yanked the buckler off the spikes; slashing at the golem's leg-joints as he did so.

Still staring into the middle distance, with apparently no real interest in Malador, the golem advanced like a blind man as the earl turned and leapt onto the table, scattering the scrolls. Now he brought his huge sword down upon the golem's skull, and the brass studs sparked and the hood and head beneath it was dented. The golem staggered and then grasped the table, heaving it off the floor so that Malador was forced to leap to the ground. This time he made for the door and tugged at its latch-ring, but the door would not open.

His sword was chipped and blunted. He put his back to the door as the golem reached him and brought its metal hand down on the top edge of the shield. The shield shattered and a dreadful pain shot up Malador's arm. He lunged at the golem, but he was unused to handling the big sword in this manner and the stroke was clumsy.

Malador knew that he was doomed. Force and fighting-skill were not enough against the golem's insensate strength. At the golem's next blow he swung aside, but was caught by one of its spike-fingers which ripped through his armour and drew blood, though at that moment he felt no pain.

He scrambled up, shaking away the grip and fragments of wood which remained of the shield, grasping his sword firmly.

*The soulless demon has no weak spot*, he thought, *and since it has no true intelligence, it cannot be appealed to. What would a golem fear?*

The answer was simple. The golem would only fear something as strong or stronger than itself.

He must use cunning.

He ran for the upturned table with the golem after him, leapt over the table and wheeled as the golem stumbled but did not, as he'd hoped, fall. However, the golem was slowed by its encounter, and Aubec took advantage of this to rush for the door through which the golem had entered. It opened. He was in a twisting corridor, darkly shadowed, not unlike the labyrinth he had first found in Kaneloon. The door closed, but he could find nothing to bar it with. He ran up the corridor as the golem tore the door open and came lumbering swiftly after him.

The corridor writhed about in all directions and, though he could not always see the golem, he could hear it and had the sickening fear that he would turn a corner at some stage and run straight into it. He did not – but he came to a door and, upon opening it and passing through it, found himself again in the hall of Castle Kaneloon.

He almost welcomed this familiar sight as he heard the golem, its metal parts screeching, continue to come after him. He needed another shield, but the part of the hall in which he now found himself had no wall-shields – only a large, round mirror of bright, clear-polished metal. It would be too heavy to be much use, but he seized it, tugging it from its hook. It fell with a clang and he hauled it up, dragging it with him as he stumbled away from the golem which had emerged into the room once more.

Using the chains by which the mirror had hung, he gripped it before him and, as the golem's speed increased and the monster rushed upon him, he raised this makeshift shield.

The golem shrieked.

Malador was astounded. The monster stopped dead and cowered away from the mirror. Malador pushed it towards the golem and the thing turned its back and fled, with a metallic howl, through the door it had entered by.

Relieved and puzzled, Malador sat down on the floor and studied the mirror. There was certainly nothing magical about it, though its quality was good. He grinned and said aloud:

'The creature *is* afraid of something. It is afraid of itself!'

He threw back his head and laughed loudly in his relief. Then he frowned. 'Now to find the sorcerers who created him and take vengeance on them!' He pushed himself to his feet, twisted the chains of the mirror more securely about his arm and went to another door, concerned lest the golem complete its circuit of the maze and return through the door. This door would not budge, so he lifted his sword and hacked at the latch for a few moments until it gave. He strode into a well-lit passage with what appeared to be another room at its far end – the door open.

A musky scent came to his nostrils as he progressed along the passage – the scent that reminded him of Eloarde and the comforts of Klant.

When he reached the circular chamber, he saw that it was a bedroom – a woman's bedroom full of the perfume he had smelled in the passage. He controlled the direction his mind took, thought of loyalty and Klant, and went to another door which led off from the room. He lugged it open and discovered a stone staircase winding upwards. This he mounted, passing windows that seemed glazed with emerald or ruby, beyond which shadow-shapes flickered so that he knew he was on the side of the castle overlooking Chaos.

The staircase seemed to lead up into a tower, and when he finally reached the small door at its top he was feeling out of breath and paused before entering. Then he pushed the door open and went in.

A huge window was set in one wall, a window of clear glass through which he could see the ominous stuff of Chaos leaping. A woman stood by this window as if awaiting him.

'You are indeed a champion, Earl Aubec,' said she with a smile that might have been ironic.

'How do you know my name?'

'No sorcery gave it me, Earl of Malador – you shouted it loudly enough when you first saw the hall in its true shape.'

'Was not *that*, then, sorcery,' he said ungraciously, 'the laby-rinth, the demons – even the valley? Was not the golem made by sorcery? Is not this whole cursed castle of a sorcerous nature?'

She shrugged. 'Call it so if you'd rather not have the truth. Sor-cery, in your mind at least, is a crude thing which only hints at the true powers existing in the multiverse.'

He did not reply, being somewhat impatient of such state-ments. He had learned, by observing the philosophers of Klant, that mysterious words often disguised commonplace things and ideas. Instead, he looked at her sulkily and over-frankly.

She was fair, with green-blue eyes and a light complexion. Her long robe was of a similar colour to her eyes. She was, in a secret sort of way, very beautiful and, like all the denizens of Kaneloon he'd encountered, a trifle familiar.

'You recognise Kaneloon?' she asked.

He dismissed her question. 'Enough of this – take me to the masters of this place!'

'There is none but me, Myshella the Dark Lady – and I am the mistress.'

He was disappointed. 'Was it just to meet you that I came through such perils?'

'It was – and greater perils even than you think, Earl Aubec. Those were but the monsters of your own imagination!'

'Taunt me not, lady.'

She laughed. 'I speak in good faith. The castle creates its defences out of your own mind. It is a rare man who can face and defeat his own imagination. Such a one has not found me here for two hundred years. All since have perished by fear – until now.'

She smiled at him. It was a warm smile.

'And what is the prize for so great a feat?' he said gruffly.

She laughed again and gestured towards the window which looked out upon the edge of the world and Chaos beyond. 'Out there nothing exists as yet. If you venture into it, you will be confronted again by creatures of your hidden fancy, for there is nothing else to behold.'

She gazed at him admiringly and he coughed in his embarrassment. 'Once in a while,' she said, 'there comes a man to Kaneloon who can withstand such an ordeal. Then may the frontiers of the world be extended, for when a man stands against Chaos it must recede and new lands spring into being!'

'So that is the fate you have in mind for me, sorceress!'

She glanced at him almost demurely. Her beauty seemed to increase as he looked at her. He clutched at the hilt of his sword, gripping it tight as she moved gracefully towards him and touched him, as if by accident. 'There is a reward for your courage.' She looked into his eyes and said no more of the reward, for it was clear what she offered. 'And after – do my bidding and go against Chaos.'

'Lady, know you not that ritual demands of Klant's Champion that he be the queen's faithful consort? I would not betray my word and trust!' He gave a hollow laugh. 'I came here to remove a menace to my queen's kingdom – not to be your lover and lackey!'

'There is no menace here.'

'That seems true...'

She stepped back as if appraising him anew. For her this was unprecedented – never before had her offer been refused. She rather liked this solid man who also combined courage and imagination in his character. It was incredible, she thought, how in a few centuries such traditions could grow up – traditions which could bind a man to a woman he probably did not even love. She looked at him as he stood there, his body rigid, his manner nervous.

'Forget Klant,' she said, 'think of the power you might have – the power of true creation!'

'Lady, I claim this castle for Klant. That is what I came to do and that is what I do now. If I leave here alive, I shall be judged the conqueror and you must comply.'

She hardly heard him. She was thinking of various plans to convince him that her cause was superior to his. Perhaps she could still seduce him? Or use some drug to bewitch him? No, he was too strong for either; she must think of some other stratagem.

She felt her breasts heaving involuntarily as she looked at him. She would have preferred to have seduced him. It had always been as much her reward as that of the heroes who had earlier won over the dangers of Kaneloon. And then, she thought, she knew what to say.

'Think, Earl Aubec,' she whispered. 'Think – new lands for your queen's empire!'

He frowned.

'Why not extend the empire's boundaries further?' she continued. 'Why not *make* new territories?'

She watched him anxiously as he took off his helm and scratched his heavy, bald head. 'You have made a point at last,' he said dubiously.

'Think of the honours you would receive in Klant if you succeeded in winning not merely Kaneloon – but that which lies *beyond*!'

Now he rubbed his chin. 'Aye,' he said, 'Aye...' His great brows frowned deeply.

'New plains, new mountains, new seas – new populations,

even – whole cities full of people fresh-sprung and yet with the memory of generations of ancestors behind them! All this can be done by *you*, Earl of Malador – for Queen Eloarde and Klant!'

He smiled faintly, his imagination fired at last. 'Aye! If I can defeat such dangers here – then I can do the same out there! It will be the greatest adventure in history! My name will become a legend – Malador, Master of Chaos!'

She gave him a tender look, though she had half-cheated him.

He swung his sword up onto his shoulder. 'I'll try this, lady.'

She and he stood together at the window, watching the Chaos-stuff whispering and rolling for eternity before them. To her it had never been wholly familiar, for it changed all the time. Now its tossing colours were predominantly red and black. Tendrils of mauve and orange spiralled out of this and writhed away.

Weird shapes flitted about in it, their outlines never clear, never quite recognisable.

He said to her: 'The Lords of Chaos rule this territory. What will they have to say?'

'They can say nothing, do little. Even they have to obey the Law of the Cosmic Balance which ordains that if man can stand against Chaos, then it shall be his to order and make Lawful. Thus the Earth grows, slowly.'

'How do I enter it?'

She took the opportunity to grasp his heavily muscled arm and point through the window. 'See – there – a causeway leads down from this tower to the cliff.' She glanced at him sharply. 'Do you see it?'

'Ah – yes – I had not, but now I do. Yes, a causeway.'

Standing behind him, she smiled a little to herself. 'I will remove the barrier,' she said.

He straightened his helm on his head. 'For Klant and Eloarde and only those do I embark upon this adventure.'

She moved towards the wall and raised the window. He did not look at her as he strode down the causeway into the multicoloured mist.

As she watched him disappear she smiled to herself. How easy it was to beguile the strongest man by pretending to go his way! He might add lands to his empire, but he might find their populations unwilling to accept Eloarde as their empress. In fact, if Aubec did his work well, then he would be creating more of a threat to Klant than ever Kaneloon had been.

Yet she admired him, she was attracted to him, perhaps, because he was not so accessible, a little more than she had been to that earlier hero who had claimed Aubec's own land from Chaos barely two hundred years before. Oh, he had been a man! But he, like most before him, had needed no other persuasion than the promise of her body.

Earl Aubec's weakness had lain in his strength, she thought. By now he had vanished into the heaving mists.

She felt a trifle sad that this time the execution of the task given her by the Lords of Law had not brought her the usual pleasure.

Yet perhaps, she thought, she felt a more subtle pleasure in his steadfastness and the means she had used to convince him.

For centuries had the Lords of Law entrusted her with Kaneloon and its secrets. But the progress was slow, for there were few heroes who could survive Kaneloon's dangers – few who could defeat self-created perils.

Yet, she decided with a slight smile on her lips, the task had its various rewards. She moved into another chamber to prepare for the transition of the castle to the new edge of the world.

Thus were the seeds sown of the Age of the Young Kingdoms, the Age of Men, which was to produce the downfall of Melniboné.

*Elric:*
*The Making of a Sorcerer*

A graphic novel
drawn by Walter Simonson

Book One

*The Dream of One Year:*
*The Dream of Earth*

Bargains in Blades

# Chapter One

## *Friends at Court*

FOR TEN THOUSAND years the Bright Empire of Melniboné ruled the world – drawing her power from terrifying compacts with the supernatural.

Some say she's invulnerable and will rule for another ten thousand...

Some say corruption already comes from within...

Some say her doom will fall from outside...

But, decidedly, doom is written in her future.

In mysterious realms of the multiverse ruled by the Lords of the Higher Worlds omens and portents proliferate.

Even in the corridors of dreaming Imrryr – capital of the empire – forbidden words are whispered.

They say the empire will live or die according to which of two youths becomes the next emperor.

Meanwhile, plots are hatched and abandoned.

Even the Tower of D'a'rputna, home to the emperor's own kin and court, festers and itches with hitherto unthinkable thoughts.

*(Note on style: Make towers very elongated wigwams – cowled rather than roofed. The designs and dominant styles – braided hair or shaven scalp with single lock – are Plains and forest Indian, as if these early Americans had risen to the skills of building a huge city like this and practising advanced metallurgy. No feathers as such, but some have crowns of metal feathers and so on. The colours are native American. Nothing too obvious, but that's the underlying style.)*

*Opening shot of Imrryr, the Dreaming City of ancient towers, rising up upon a volcanic mound like a choir of angels, a chord of music made into subtle, complex architecture. The characteristic architecture of Melniboné is tall towers, with a single large room at each level of each tower. They rise above the warehouses and trading sheds of the ancient harbour – itself surrounded by jagged cliffs, the same cliffs which guard the entrances to the sea-maze which leads to the port.*

*High above all this, in the tallest, perhaps even slenderest, tower, dwells the royal family of Melniboné – Sadric the emperor, Elric his son, a youth, his sister-in-law Ederin, mother to daughter Cymoril (on whom she dotes), son Yyrkoon (whom she mistrusts and dislikes) also certain members of the Tvar family, who are all expert Dragon Masters and are close kin to the emperor. And there is also a human servant woman, Arisand, whose secret ambitions are not inconsiderable...*

*Arisand moves from floor to floor. We identify some of our characters in their various rooms of the Tower of D'a'rputna, The Emperor's Tower... She enters the highest chamber of the tower, flanked by what appear to be great buttresses, where looms the shadow of Sadric, the King Emperor... (Ivan the Terrible but with less charm).*

*But first, a few floors down, we are introduced to Yyrkoon (Olivier as Richard III, Walter? Sans hump?) in his bed of concubines.*

He is dismissing certain officers of his acquaintance.

YYRKOON: 'You may go, but consider carefully what I have said. All our fates depend on this moment!'

*On the steps outside this room some soldierly types confer. A slave closes a door on them as they leave. Three captains pause for a moment on the top stair before it curves out of sight.*

FIRST CAPTAIN: 'Prince Yyrkoon doesn't persuade me. My loyalty's still to Elric.'

SECOND CAPTAIN: 'Elric's weak. He's sick. How many years can he live? Only sorcery sustains him. Ambitious and aggressive, Yyrkoon will claw us back our former power.'

THIRD CAPTAIN: 'He'll defend and expand the old dragon fief-doms. The Young Kingdoms shall be no more. Each captain shall rule a province!'

SECOND CAPTAIN: 'Conquest will revive our blood. Our wives will again bear healthy children. The empire will rule with all her old arrogance... yet it's hard to turn against traditional loyalties...'

FIRST CAPTAIN: 'Treachery doesn't taste too good, eh? Well I hope the rest of you have equally delicate palates. Think long and hard before you betray our rightful lord.' *(He's emphatic, almost mocking them... He indicates a portrait which hangs below them on the curve of the stair, half-seen from above – another Melnibonéan albino...)* 'Six thousand years ago, the silver kings brought our nation greatness and honour. Some "silverskins" attract great fortune to the Ruby Throne. Think on that, my captains. Then dare treason...'

*He throws this behind him as he disappears down the spiral staircase of the tower.*

At this moment, Prince Elric, the only rightful inheritor of the mantle of empire, is oblivious to talk of treason.

He's oblivious to any talk. Or action. He's ignorant of where his own body lies. He is elsewhere...

*The last face we'll see is young Elric, apparently dead, but actually sleeping on his dream couch, soon to be awakened by Doctor Tanglebones.*

*The black raven Sepiriz settles on Doctor Tanglebones's ungainly shoulder.*

DOCTOR TANGLEBONES: 'Wake now, my lord. Gently, my lord.'

*Elric blinks but is fairly blank still. Tanglebones is pleased. He realises Elric is alive and safe from his dream-quest.*

TANGLEBONES: 'Aha! Back with us. Safe and sound from the inner landscapes of your common memory... You've learned much, though you won't remember how you learned it...'

TANGLEBONES: 'Ha! Ha! Good lad! Brave, resourceful lad!'

*Elric begins to rise on the couch. But he is weak. He falls back onto one elbow. Totally wiped out. Tanglebones, old as he is, has to assist him. A woman's hand extends into the picture, she is holding tongs holding a hanging brazier on which a copper dish cooks herbs into a single sticky sap...*

TANGLEBONES: 'There's never been a better dream-scholar –'

*He reaches towards the copper dish... Rapidly scooping the still-viscous sap into an earthenware cup to which he swiftly adds wine, which steams and bubbles. Stirring it, he hands this to Elric to drink.*

TANGLEBONES: '– nor one stranger... Drink this down. All of it, mind! It will help you recover your strength.'

*Elric drinks the potion. He is immediately invigorated, handing the dish back to Tanglebones.*

ELRIC: 'Ugh! I'll suffer no more such fearful dream-quests, Doctor Tanglebones. Surely there are easier ways of earning my people's wisdom?'

*Elric looks out of the picture to where the unseen woman no doubt still stands. He begins to smile.*

TANGLEBONES: 'None more effective. Rest for a few days. Ready yourself for the long dreams.'

TANGLEBONES: 'The first is the Dream of One Year. The Dream of Earth. I'll give you a week to prepare...'

ELRIC: 'You delight to torture me, doctor. It's unseemly in a physician, especially a royal one!'

*Elric is as outraged as any student being given an especially hard schedule. He wants to argue. Then that same female hand falls on his arm. He turns to see his beautiful, slender, dark-haired cousin Cymoril come to welcome him back to the world's reality. Again he smiles, immediately courteous, relaxed and friendly.*

CYMORIL: 'Hush, Elric, you mustn't tease Doctor Tanglebones. I waited with him to be sure you awakened…'

ELRIC: 'Cousin, you're the best friend I have! For your sake and yours alone… I will forgive the old fraud.'

*He is invigorated by the drink but also rather flattered by Cymoril's attention. He has something of a swagger now. He wants to show his individualism.*

ELRIC: 'Besides, in all fairness, his vile decoction begins to improve my outlook.'

*In defiance, with an exaggerated gesture, Elric bows and shows Cymoril the way to the door…*

ELRIC: 'Come, sweet Cymoril. Let's ride to the wilder reaches of our island.'

*Cymoril looks to Doctor Tanglebones, who is grave.*

TANGLEBONES: 'You must prepare yourself mentally and bodily for your coming trials.'

TANGLEBONES: 'My lord, you must rest…'

ELRIC: 'And so I shall, good doctor. so I shall.'

*He's determined to enjoy this sense of release, to get the most out of it. He is a boy overburdened with duty and destiny.*

*Cymoril goes with him when he leaves the chamber. She shares his grin as they head for the stables.*

*Shot of them riding hell for leather from the walls of Imrryr, into the craggy beauty of the island's interior.*

But, of course, in Melniboné royal princes and princesses rarely go unwatched…

*Wearing his crown of iron feathers, Old Sadric, gaunt and haunted, stares from a window at his departing son, then turns his mind to more important matters.*

Sadric, the old Sorcerer Emperor, hated his son, blamed Elric for killing his mother in childbirth.

Sadric had read the portents, heard the omens.

Was there any other interpretation?

Elric must bring shame to his own blood and drag destruction down on all the world...

*Watched by the human woman Arisand, who holds back in a gesture of supplication, Sadric pushes open the doors of the great Hall of Steel. Here are the weapons, banners and armour of his ancestors.*

So Sadric cared little where his son rode or with whom. Sadric had a colder choice to make...

*Sadric has come to stand before the traditional armour of a Melnibonéan Sorcerer Emperor. This is constituted pretty much how Whelan depicts it on the DAW covers. A breastplate decorated with dragon motif, back-plate matching. The dragon helm – crowned by a slender dragon about to take flight, with pieces protecting nose, eyes, ears. Grieves and gauntlets of similar design. A great war-shield, also of similar design. He's reaching to take down the helmet...*

SADRIC: 'My old armour. The armour of all Melniboné's emperors.'

*As he removes it, the helmet falls from his ancient, palsied hands and rolls on the stone slabs at his feet.*

*Proudly, Sadric peers down at the helm.*

SADRIC: 'Not a dent. Not a scratch. Sorcery or science? I once knew what it was. But I forget everything. So addictive, so corrosive, that ancient magic...'

*He runs a still-sensuous hand over the complicated metalwork.*

SADRIC: 'I had a warrior's body once, to match a warrior's heart. Now, my hands can barely hold such power.'

*He replaces the helmet.*

SADRIC: 'Who shall wear it? My strong, cruel nephew. Or my weakling son. To survive we have always been ruthless. It is our duty.'

*He inspects obscene-looking daggers, mysterious cutting weapons, odd armour.*

*Wearing his crown of iron plumes, Sadric is in the upper part of the tower. From this curve four apparent flying buttresses. These also house the great chambers, such as the Hall of Steel, off his main living quarters. Now he looks out across the forest of ancient towers which is Melniboné. Behind him stands the human girl Arisand.*

ARISAND: 'A human is neither as wise nor as well educated as a Melnibonéan, master. But it seems to me your son puts aside his youthful weaknesses and becomes increasingly what you would wish him to be.'

SADRIC (*coolly*): 'Deficient blood, my dear. That's the problem. The test will come on the dream couches. That is where one or the other will prove their fitness. Now...'

*He waves her away and she leaves through a door.*

SADRIC: '... I must return to my grimoires...'

*Next we see her making an entrance, slipping through another curtain. She has removed her over-dress. She is more sensuously clad.*

*Yyrkoon's bed of concubines is not far from where she now seats herself in a great, baroque chair.*

*Yyrkoon has his back to us. He will be seen to be leaning towards the great port of Imrryr, with its cliffs surrounding the harbour not fronted by the city. The sea-maze swirls. Ships are still loading and unloading.*

*Without looking back at her, Yyrkoon speaks to Arisand:*

YYRKOON: 'So, madam.'

YYRKOON: 'A score of our finest merchantmen will sail with the evening tide when they should have been warships!'

*He turns. She smiles.*

YYRKOON: 'Did you discover my uncle's wishes? Will he make *me* his heir over that weakling?'

ARISAND: 'He cannot bring himself to choose. All will be decided on the couches. If Elric survives the four dream-quests, he will rule.'

*Yyrkoon takes this information thoughtfully. Then he grins as if to Arisand, but actually directly addressing us, like a knowing, Jacobean villain...*

YYRKOON: 'That is good news for me, I think. We can challenge destiny!'

*Last panel will be a small one of Elric and Cymoril riding over open, if slightly weird, countryside. We read Yyrkoon's words over this panel...*

YYRKOON: 'In past times, many perished hideously on those dream couches. Soon Elric will be one mummy amongst many – in the burial vaults of our ancestors.'

# Chapter Two

## *The Vaults of our Ancestors*

*O*UT OF SIGHT *of the city, Cymoril and Elric pull their horses up before a great slab of limestone, surrounded by shrubs and small trees, moss, a few small streams making tears in the massive face.*

ELRIC: 'Ha! Here's my chance to show you something I learned during my dream-quests.'

CYMORIL: 'Could we not ride around it, my lord?'

*Elric shuts his eyes and his face contorts almost to Mr Hyde transformation as his fingers stretch to Hogarthian proportions and he utters an unholy word in an alien language – Cymoril covers her ears.*

ELRIC: '←←←←⊐⋇⋶⋌ᘜↃ⇂⇂⇂⇂⊅⌣  →⊐⫞ᘜ५∧⋶←←← ←←←←←←←'

*(check spelling)*

*With an enormous cracking noise, the rockface splits – and keeps on splitting until it is a great fissure, large enough to admit human bodies. The horses are not taking this well. They will go forward no more.*

ELRIC *(dismounts)*: 'There are some practical skills to be learned from those dream-quests. Our horses will find their way home. Come!'

*Cymoril is not a little uncertain about this venture... She holds back but he insists, holding out his hand. Trusting him, but uncertain still, she goes with him. Down into the dank depths of the earth. The horses turn and gallop away home.*

*And when we have seen the last of Elric's and Cymoril's heads, descending into the darkness, the slab closes again with a sense of finality.*

*Elric is not alarmed and comforts Cymoril. Dark and dank as it is, there are fires flaring intermittently below. Enough light to allow them to make their way down a rocky spiral road towards the bottom.*

*Then a huge shape goes past them with a PHUNK, almost knocking them from the ledge, but Elric is laughing up at the shape –*

CYMORIL: 'Elric!'

*– which, as it spirals towards the ground, a tiny rider on its back, proves to be a young Phoorn. A young dragon… The fires themselves come from the combustible venom which drips from the fangs of the mature dragons who sleep or raise drowsy eyes and snort clouds of steam through their nostrils.*

ELRIC: 'Do not worry, my lady. These are the Dragon Caves of Imrryr.'

*As the young couple descend the path, another young Melnibonéan ascends it to greet them. He's the laughing rider of the dragon, and still wears his dragon leathers, holds part of a bridle. In the other hand is his great dragon lance – a long, leaf-shaped blade which is set in a red jewel from the other end of which comes the haft of the lance. This will show a distinct similarity of design with the Black Sword, but where the Black Sword will have a red Actorios, this has a light blue sapphire. The bearer is Dyvim Tvar, Elric's best male friend.*

DYVIM TVAR: 'Dear cousins! How good of you to visit me in my murky lair.'

ELRIC: 'Well met, Dyvim Tvar.'

*Dyvim Tvar bows and displays the rows of dragons who sleep in orderly ranks around the rim of a bay which is almost a perfect oval, an underground sea beneath the stalactites.*

DYVIM TVAR: 'Forgive me for startling you. We watch for intruders these days. More than we used to.'

DYVIM TVAR (*with a hospitable gesture*): 'Come, meet the Phoorn, my family. The few who are presently awake!'

*The Melnibonéans stand looking up at a massive snout from which pour, like drool, rivulets of venom. Some of this venom has scarred the rock on which the dragon sleeps. Some still flickers, for it becomes fire when it meets air... Fiery streams run on both sides of the figures as they regard the huge, sleepy, half-open eye which regards them. Dyvim Tvar speaks to the Phoorn in their own language.*

DYVIM TVAR (*runes*): '!@@###$% )))(*&&^^^', etc.

DRAGON (*answers in the same language*): '++%%$$##@@'

ELRIC: 'I envy your knowledge of the dragon tongue.'

DYVIM TVAR: 'Once, when our folk were the simple Mernii, we and the Phoorn shared a common language. Now it cannot be learned. It has to be remembered...'

*He guides them up some rather more recently built stone stairs towards a door which he opens for them.*

*They look back at the great near-circle of resting and sleeping dragons. Dyvim Tvar puts his hand on Elric's shoulders.*

DYVIM TVAR: 'Prince Yyrkoon will never have help. My loyalty's to you, my dragons and to our traditions.'

*They are out on a long, straight staircase which leads upwards from the Dragon Caves. They are briefly in an underground passage. Then on a spiral staircase. Then they are entering a chamber at the base of the Imperial Tower.*

*But these chambers are spare. A craftsman's rooms. Various heavy, ornate bits of dragon bridle hang on the walls. The furniture is sturdy but not ornate. Dyvim Tvar provides food, which they do not eat, and wine, which they drink. Elric tilts his chair back, enjoying this simple pleasure.*

ELRIC: 'What I would not give, dear friend, to be a simple Dragon Master...'

DYVIM TVAR (*smiles at this*): 'Well, I must say I don't envy you your sorcerous learning... nor the means by which it's gathered. I am content. The dragons sleep. Only a few need tending.'

*He looks almost dreamy as he adds:*

DYVIM TVAR: 'Perhaps one day the Phoorn will again fly in a phalanx blotting out the sun – a final, mighty flight...'

*He claps his hand on Elric's shoulder.*

DYVIM TVAR: 'And you'll be with me. Riding side by side on twin dragons. Flying above our empire.'

*Elric embraces Cymoril.*

ELRIC: 'Where shall we go now?'

CYMORIL: 'To our beds. And tomorrow, my lord, to your studies. I shall not see you until you begin the first of your most important dreams...'

*A montage of Elric studying, being taught by old Tanglebones – to fence, learn an incantation, summoning a small demon, sleep in exhausted slumber. Until Doctor Tanglebones wakes him before dawn and, carrying a lantern, leads the way. Washed by slaves, Elric next ascends the dream couch with its hard, marble head-rest, its decorated stonework and woodwork.*

And so begins the first long dream: the Dream of Earth...

# Chapter Three
## *Talking in Silence*

*O*BSERVED BY THE *raven Sepiriz, which flies from Tanglebones's shoulder into the dream sequence, Elric's astral body leaves the couch and becomes this very good physical body – his own in its best possible condition. His hair is braided. He is stripped to the waist, wearing only a short jacket. He has a quiver of arrows, an unstrung bow, a long knife, leggings, breechclout, deerskin boots. And he is entering what seems to be an amphitheatre – Pueblo-style dwellings, with ladders and cave entrances at every level. Some short, squat, sturdy dwarfish Mayan types (Puk Wa D'Jee, Pukwadji) stare out at Elric. Elric is now White Crow. Throughout this sequence the huge black raven is evident. White Crow greets the Pukwadji cheerfully.*

WHITE CROW/ELRIC: 'Hey, little allies. Have the Pukwadji no welcome for White Crow?'

*Suddenly Elric has more friends than he needs. They are jumping on him, hitting him with clubs, holding him wherever they can. He attempts to fight them and sends several flying, but eventually they overwhelm him.*

ELRIC: 'I gather we're no longer allies. The last I knew, our peoples neared agreement...'

*He is trussed in rawhide.*

PUKWADJI LEADER: 'Your folk betray us. We'll never return their ships now. They have no right to keep the black blade when it threatens our very existence.'

PUKWADJI SHAMAN: 'King Grome will destroy us if we do not return the black blade. But your folk will not trade it back. So Grome keeps your ships. and we feed him the few of your folk we catch – to placate him in his terrible distress.'

ELRIC: 'You attacked us, dragging our ships underground, stranding us, making our journey impossible to finish.'

SHAMAN: 'We used our last great pact with Grome to take those ships. We have little left to fight with. We'll keep the ships until we get the blade.'

SHAMAN: 'Meanwhile – we sacrifice you to King Grome, the earth-lord...'

*Shaman holds up a skull with a crown of metal feathers stuck on it.*

*They carry the tied Elric deep, deep underground, down tunnels, passages, through chambers, through natural caverns, down and down until they come to where Grome awaits them, far below. Grome is gnarled and knotted, made of great tree roots, and clumps of earth and boulders and grass and moulds and fungus.*

KING GROME: 'A morsel to distract me from my pain? You fail to understand the importance of this matter. We are doomed unless you bring me the blade. You must bring me the blade! All are imperilled!'

FIRST PUKWADJI: 'A morsel is all we can offer, great king of the earth. We are too weak to defeat the Mernii intruders. We are sorry we bartered the black blade.'

GROME: 'You will perish. I will punish you. King Grome still has his powers! And his pride.'

*Flashback of the Mernii ships breaking through dimensions onto a river. As the Mernii run for it, Grome buries all the ships, including the river, under huge mounds of earth...*

*But Grome is hungry, too...*

GROME: 'Oh, very well, give me the morsel...'

*Elric is thrown down to Grome who catches him expertly with his strange, earthy, rooty hand.*

GROME: 'What bloodless thing is this?'

ELRIC: 'I can assure you, your majesty, that I am better conversation than I am a canapé.'

*Grome continues to lift Elric towards his gaping maw.*

GROME: 'That blade brings doom upon the world. Unless I can put it back in the rock from which it was taken.'

ELRIC: 'I'll strike a bargain with you. Let me explain this to my people. Surely they purchased the black blade for a special reason.'

GROME (*now hesitates and thinks*): Mmmmmmmmmmmmm mmmmmm.

*Grome returns Elric to the ground, releasing his bonds.*

*Puzzled Pukwadji return Elric's bow and arrows, etc. Set him on his way, scowling and unsure.*

SHAMAN: 'But if you fail to keep your bargain with him, King Grome will find you and eat you wherever you hide. Go!'

ELRIC: 'I doubt my own folk will welcome me much more warmly.'

*Elric now approaches a mountain which those with sharp eyes might notice to resemble the contours of the Isle of Melniboné. On the side of this (where the harbour is now) stands a very elaborate and wealthy camp, protected by a tall, wooden fence. Within the compound are wigwam-style tents, very tall, with slender lodgepoles and cowled tops. They are versions of the towers of Melniboné. A young Mernii guard looks at Elric with a mixture of humour and contempt.*

GUARD: 'Good afternoon, renegade. Have you received an order to return...?'

ELRIC: 'No, kinsman, but I come in some urgency.'

*Within the camp, which has a temporary quality to it, Elric is greeted by a group of aggressive young men.*

LEADER (*of aggressive young men*): 'Renegade! Our king is too lenient.'

ELRIC: 'A pleasant day, Tvarim Kha.'

TVARIM KHA: 'Both you and he deserve to die!'

*But Elric pushes past them. They are glowering, reaching towards their swords.*

*Wearing the iron-feathered crown of kingship, King Varnik is still relatively young and fit. He is clearly White Crow's elder brother. He turns an unwelcoming gaze on Elric as he arrives in the big wigwam. The black blade (sans runes) is laid on a sort of altar, guarded by tall, grim Mernii (Melnibonéans). It appears to be a lance-blade and there is a half-moon fitting at the top, supposedly for a shaft, but actually it is where the throbbing scarlet Actorios stone should sit.*

KING VARNIK: 'You return early from your banishment, sir trickster...'

ELRIC: 'Brother, I am hoping to end a war destroying both sides. How can we get our ships back and let them have the black blade?'

*Varnik is interested.*

ELRIC: 'Grome will destroy the dwarves if they do not return the blade.'

VARNIK: 'Let him destroy them. Without the blade we'll have no means of pursuing our journey. The loss of the ships was terrible, but we can't give them back the blade.'

ELRIC: 'Destroying the dwarves, Grome will then begin killing us. Until he has the blade...'

VARNIK: 'The blade has a special purpose. Our people will not survive without it. We must keep it.'

ELRIC: 'Will you still need it when it has performed this purpose?'

VARNIK: 'Need it or not, it is ours by tradition. We'll never return it.'

ELRIC: 'So we'll never see our ships again, and yet the blade will be useless until we regain the Actorios stone. Would you bargain with Grome if I found you the stone?'

*Varnik leans forward, laughing at Elric.*

VARNIK: 'You would have to bring back the Actorios in just over a year... For that is the time of the next great astral conjunction, when the sword is needed.'

ELRIC: 'Legend has it the Actorios was stolen from us before we owned the sword. The thief was a northern giant, too quick for any to follow, and not one of our warriors who sought him ever returned.'

VARNIK: 'Can you do what our greatest heroes failed to do? If so I give you my word – bring me the Actorios, the Dragon Stone... and Grome shall have his sword returned... after we have used it.'

ELRIC: 'Then clearly, my lord, I must find the Actorios for you... within the year!'

*The leader of the belligerent young men is cheered by what he overhears.*

LEADER (*whispers*): 'They'd trade away our birthright, but one will die on his quest, and the other's easily finished...'

# Chapter Four
## *The Dragon Stone*

A ND SO WHITE Crow journeyed north...

*With the basic kit for a long journey on foot, White Crow sets off away from the tall lodges of his people. This page could be done like Indian pictograms.*

*Basically it will be four panels depicting the seasons, in which White Crow makes a journey across the North American continent from south to north.*

*(Summer)*

... Risking death...

*In this sequence White Crow is attacked by a white mountain lion and defeats it.*

*(Fall)*

... Learning wisdom...

*In this sequence White Crow sits with human people, passing the peace pipe and listening while wise oldsters read from long wampum belts.*

*(Winter)*

... Controlling his powers...

*Winter on prairie, White Crow uses his magic – to stop a charging white buffalo.*

*(Spring)*

... Defending life...

*We see White Crow binding the leg of a bear, helping a deer out of a ravine, setting a white beaver on its way...*

BEAVER: 'I am grateful, White Crow...'

BEAVER: '... But I will not accompany you. We shun the longhouse you seek. It lies due north. It is fairly well defended.'

Beavers are famous for their understatement...

... and had good reason to shun the giants' 'longhouse'.

*Elric arrives at last at the Giants' great longhouse – actually a massive ziggurat-shaped metropolis, with all kinds of city activity taking place in its galleries, between private windows and public walkways. But, save for a narrow, heavily defended causeway, there seems no way into the city, for the great lake around it boils with molten lava. Which does not concern those citizens. At the very top of the ziggurat is the Temple of the Actorios. You can see its red light burning, even in day. Giants have a distinctively Iroquois sort of look. Maybe we should save whole view of the ziggurat until next page...*

ELRIC (*thinks*): A lake of molten lava. With only one way to cross. Yet there's the Actorios they prize – atop their city's proudest point.

*Elric's tiny in this picture, with the vast city dominating everything. Closer to foreground maybe is Sepiriz the raven – young Elric's mentor in these dreams. Sepiriz is, of course, an omen-ous bird.*

ELRIC: 'No mortal can cross that!'

SEPIRIZ: 'With native skill and demon's lore
On supernatural wing's ye'll soar...
With sorcerous cunning and feline stealth...
A prince shall filch a giant's wealth...

*Elric is almost amused by the appearance of his familiar.*

ELRIC: 'There you are, Master Sepiriz. Come to give me advice. As always. I'm glad to see you.'

*We see him beginning to puzzle out the spell – aha! –*

ELRIC: 'The flying demon! A recently learned spell...'

*... and as he does so we fade to him actually doing the conjuring of the grumpy winged demon –*

GRUMPY DEMON: 'I do this because your spell grants you one wish of me.'

*– and forcing it to take him over to the longhouse.*

*Grumbling, yet triumphant, the demon flies off, leaving Elric on the dais up to the brazier which holds the Actorios Stone, the Dragon Stone. This has awakened a huge giant who looks up and sees Elric.*

DEMON: 'I said I'd carry you there. I said nothing of taking you back. My bargain's done!'

*As the giant comes roaring up to defend the Actorios, Elric gets between him and the glaring red crystal. Puts fluence on giant, using the crystal as a sort of amplifier of his powers.*

ELRIC: *'Through wizard's eyes and red stone's stare*
*By Arioch's will and Arioch's glare...*
*By fiery crystal, blazing light...*
*Submit to me your giantly might!'*

GIANT: 'That is a powerful and dangerous spell, master. Hate thee as I do, I am bound to obey thee.'

*Elric clings to the giant's single scalp lock as he poises on the edge of the city wall, like a diver ready to dive into pool. Elric has the Actorios in his bag.*

GIANT: 'I have done you no wrong, Prince Elric. I shall die in agony but I can only obey...

*Dives –*

*Elric on the giant's head, clinging to the scalp lock, the giant swims through lava, his skin burning.*

*At edge of the lake of lava, White Crow jumps off the giant, who is dying, drowning as he is sucked back into the lava. White Crow begins to run, the raven flying overhead.*

GIANT: 'You will pay a price for your lack of mercy, Prince Elric. Mark my words...'

And then White Crow ran home.

# Chapter Five
## *The Swearing of Oaths*

WHITE CROW *is returning home, the sack over his back. It is summer.*

*The arrogant young rebel, Tvarim Kha, sees him approaching the camp and scowls in rage. He had expected White Crow to die on his quest.*

TVARIM KHA: 'So he survived the quest! We must end this prince's run of luck…'

*Elsewhere – Yyrkoon puts an enchantment on Tanglebones so that his men can go in and finish off Elric –*

YYRKOON: 'There! The oldster's enchanted. Now do your work…'

*Elric arrives at Varnik's wigwam. Varnik is almost as surprised to see him as Tvarim Kha.*

VARNIK: 'White Crow! You have it. And just in time!'

*Elric holds the sack back from Varnik's eager fingers. In his other hand Varnik holds what looks like a lance-blade with a half-moon female joint for the haft. But the Actorios will actually fit there.*

VARNIK: 'Give me the Actorios. I know what to do!'

ELRIC: 'Not until you have sworn the oath we agreed! After you have used it, you must return the blade to Grome.'

VARNIK: 'Quickly! Very well, I swear. I swear to do as you ask.'

*Enter Tvarim Kha.*

TVARIM KHA: 'There's no time left for the keeping of oaths. Your bloodline is about to end!'

*At the same time, Yyrkoon's bravos push into the dream chamber, ready to kill Elric as he lies helpless.*

*And meanwhile Tvarim Kha's men follow him into the tent as White Crow yells urgently to Varnik:*

ELRIC: 'Brother – the blade – to me!'

*A fraction of a second's hesitation and Varnik tosses the black blade to White Crow/Elric, while taking up another lance of his own.*

*The assassins press closer.*

*Elric fits the Actorios into the hilt. It still doesn't have a handle and cross-bar, but he can wield the lance blade like a sword, two-handed.*

*And now a bizarre light burns in White Crow/Elric's crimson eyes. The Actorios brings red runes to the black iron. They ripple up and down its length, unstable and dangerous.*

*Black Sword in his hands, White Crow engages the bravos.*

ELRIC/WHITE CROW: 'By great Arioch, I'll take you all with me!'

*In old-fashioned demonic glee, Elric lays about him with the sword and the wicked plotters go down like scythed wheat...*

*Weaponless, Varnik lies panting against the side of the tent as Elric finishes the last of the terrified attackers.*

*Elric finishes Tvarim Kha.*

*Meanwhile...*

*Tanglebones wakes from his enchantment to see with astonishment –*

*– the bodies of Yyrkoon's assassins, lying everywhere in the chamber.*

*And, in the prone Elric's right hand, the shadowy, fading shape of the Black Sword. Tanglebones reaches towards it, but it vanishes.*

TANGLEBONES: 'Wicked sorcery as I lay entranced – yet the danger's been averted! How –? Aha!'

*Tanglebones stands over the sleeping Elric. The sword has gone, but there are splashes of blood on his body from those he has killed.*

TANGLEBONES: 'The sword! That damnable sword preserves its own existence...'

*White Crow hands the sword to his brother, Prince Varnik, who has some very urgent business with it.*

VARNIK: 'Thanks, brother! The conjunction is almost over. There is so little time left if we're to bring our people through...'

*Out of sight of their camp, Varnik hurries out to a great slab of rock the same as the one Elric encountered 'earlier'. Other members of his tribe stand ready, uncertain, cheering as he holds up the black blade, with the Actorios in it, red runes rippling the length of that supernatural steel. Varnik takes a run at it and, calling out runes, brings the blade against the rock – which splits – **KRAK** (because I know you'll put one in, Walter ☺)... This rock goes on splitting – it splits upwards, then it splits the land, then the sky and through this sky, from the universe in which they have been trapped, fly the Phoorn – the great dragon brothers and sisters of the Mernii, who will one day be known as the Melnibonéans. It is DRAGONS, DRAGONS, DRAGONS... The human figures are thoroughly dwarfed by these huge beasts.*

VARNIK:'The Phoorn! Blood-kin to our folk!'

*The dragons fly down – down towards the great underground cave-system revealed by the fissure in the rock. There we see the same underground lake around which the dragons were settled earlier.*

*As one dragon passes he speaks to White Crow. The dragon is Flamefang, one of the oldest of the Phoorn.*

FLAMEFANG: 'Brother, in a million years... Flamefang will not have forgotten your help.'

*White Crow can only acknowledge the words, but not answer, he is so astonished at what has happened.*

*But White Crow has not forgotten his promise to King Grome. As the dragons continue to come through, Elric reaches his hand for the black blade.*

ELRIC:'Now give me the blade. We must keep our promise to Grome!'

*With the dwarves at his back, Elric gives the sword into Grome's keeping.*

GROME: 'You have done well, young silverskin. You can rely upon my help whenever your need is great.'

GROME: 'And I'll return this burdensome blade to the black rock which birthed it. It is cursed and would doom us all.'

GROME: 'Ready your folk. I will give them back their ships!'

*Elric and Varnik are standing on the flanks of the hill, just below the tent town of Elric's people. A great gathering. Some distance off, pulling himself up out of the ground, comes King Grome, hating the sunlight. He has two ships – one under each huge earthy arm.*

GROME: 'Here're the first two. Hmmm. Ye'll need something to float 'em on… Best get to higher ground.'

*Now we see King Grome at full strength – raising the Mernii ships from deep underground where he had dragged them – so that they come bursting up through the earth – while creating an island out of the camp and the mountain it sits on, so that sea runs around it and the ships are floated, like so many toys, by his huge, earthy hands…*

GROME: 'So now Pukwadji and Mernii will live in peace by my decree! I have rewarded you well for keeping your bargain with me. Let us all prosper.'

And so began the history of Melniboné…

*White Crow fades discreetly back into the frame which shows Elric asleep on the dream couch.*

*Tanglebones and Cymoril greet Elric as Tanglebones gives Elric potion as usual.*

*Tanglebones watches helplessly as Elric tosses the cup aside, puts his arm around Cymoril's shoulders and strides away.*

TANGLEBONES: 'You must rest, study…'

ELRIC: 'Farewell, Doctor Tanglebones. We have old friends to visit…'

*Main picture is Elric, Cymoril and Dyvim Tvar in Dragon Caves. Elric is communicating in runic with the old dragon we saw earlier. Cymoril and Dyvim Tvar (holding dragon lance which resembles the black blade in length and style but is fashioned into a tall spear, with a blue stone glowing where the haft meets the blade).*

ELRIC: '*()^^&&)))' *(in runic).*

FLAMEFANG: '%%%^^^^^&&**(()(' *(also in runic).*

CYMORIL: 'Now he speaks the language of the Phoorn!'

DYVIM TVAR: 'I told you. Phoorn is not learned – it's remembered…'

*Inset has King Sadric with Tanglebones:*

SADRIC: 'He's passed the first great test. But does he have the character to pass the next?'

*Then final inset is Yyrkoon with Arisand, whose expression is unreadable.*

YYRKOON (*glowering*): 'I was too crude. Strong sorcery protects my puny cousin. Now I know how and where to defeat him!'

# Book Two

*The Dream of Two Years:*
*The Dream of Water*

The Sea-King's Sister

# Chapter One

## *Return of the Prince*

Now Imrryr, the Dreaming City, stands at a node of the moonbeam roads.

Here the roads cross and re-cross the multiverse, taking travellers to worlds of every kind, all versions of our own.

Some worlds are substantial, others barely formed, the ghosts of realms unborn, of dying worlds and worlds who owe their existence only to our dreams.

Back and forth go the travellers on the moonbeam roads, making and destroying worlds, inhabiting dreams and desires, making real that which was unreal. Powerful dreams. Dreams of power. Of deep longing and wild desire.

Would one of these worlds, including our own, exist beyond our dreams? If we stopped dreaming would they fade into nothing? Would we fade with them?

Even old Tanglebones, administering the dream couch of his young master, the Sorcerer Prince Elric, dare not ask that question...

Meanwhile, Elric embarks on the second of his great dream-quests whose outcome will bring him enormous power and decide the fate of the multiverse, should, that is, it exist at all...

*A panorama of Melniboné at the centre of a criss-crossing network of the roads between the worlds. A sort of reprise of the moonbeam road sequence in Michael Moorcock's Multiverse. Elric, on his dream couch, sleeps and there is a suggestion that this is what he dreams... The black crow we have seen in the first book flies between Elric and the dream roads...*

*Tanglebones and Cymoril walk together in a hanging garden overlooking the harbour of Melniboné.*

CYMORIL: 'He's changing, Doctor Tanglebones. The dreams are changing him...'

TANGLEBONES: 'That's the nature of his education, my dear. Just pray that he is changed to your liking...'

*Sadric and the human girl, Arisand, stand on a balcony looking down on Tanglebones and Cymoril.*

SADRIC: 'I'll wager that, like us, old Tanglebones and Lady Cymoril are contemplating my son's fate. Well, what do *you* say, girl? Does my son become the stuff of emperors? Or should his cousin Yyrkoon be given the throne?'

ARISAND: 'He matures, my lord Sadric. Prince Elric grows in character if not in physical energy. Doctor Tanglebones's potions keep him strong.'

Elsewhere, deep within the tower, Prince Yyrkoon prepares to lie down on his own dream couch.

*His servant, gaunt and Heepish, readies the potion.*

SERVANT: 'Where would you go in your sleep, master?'

YYRKOON: 'I'll follow my weakling cousin, of course. I have business with him there in the Dream Realms...'

*The dream roads. Elric already walks them. In the dream chamber, Tanglebones looks down on Elric's troubled, dreaming face. Cymoril rushes in, concerned. She's just learned of Yyrkoon's decision.*

TANGLEBONES (*muses*): 'Now you dream the Dream of Two Years... the Dream of Water. You carry a great burden already, my lord, and it can only grow heavier on your journey.'

CYMORIL: 'Doctor Tanglebones! My brother Yyrkoon – he's taken to the dream couches. He can mean Elric only harm!'

TANGLEBONES (*sadly*): 'Then Elric's test will be all the harder. He must fend for himself in those dangerous realms...'

*In his dreams, Elric has come to a less magnificent but rather beautiful Melniboné. While he still sports braids and a vaguely Indian look, he is dressed in much more sophisticated clothing. The city itself has yet to grow in might or splendour but is a long way on from the wigwam dwellings we saw in the first book. Beached ships indicate low tides, however, as he walks on to be greeted, again, as White Crow, by the sailors hauling their ships up the beach.*

FIRST SAILOR: 'Why 'tis White Crow himself come back to us. The queen will be glad to see you.'

SECOND SAILOR: 'Perhaps not. They say she was furious at his leaving. He claimed to be plotting against our enemies, the Falkryn.'

ELRIC: 'The tide's so low. What's the cause?'

SECOND SAILOR: 'You have not heard? Our oceans shrink almost by the month. Some say a thirsty beast of Chaos is drinking all the world's water. Others blame the Falkryn.

ELRIC (*frowning*): 'My memory deserts me. Best take me to the queen. Her name?'

SECOND SAILOR (*laughing*): 'Ho, ho! You pretend not to know Queen Shyrix'x? You who were betrothed to her! You'd be advised to find your memory before you see her again! Come.'

*He's taken to Queen Shyrix'x IX – and she remembers him as a lover. He finds it hard to respond to her. She's angry, believing herself betrayed by him.*

QUEEN SHYRIX'X: 'Back from your quest, White Crow? Did you find the Falkryn sorcerer you sought?'

ELRIC: 'I have no memory of my past, madam, forgive me...'

SHYRIX'X: 'No memory? A lame excuse. You left to sulk because our love had died and I am due to wed Dyvim Mar!'

ELRIC: 'I fear that past is gone from me, madam... I was astonished to find the tide so low...'

*She responds angrily.*

SHYRIX'X: 'Rumour says some Chaos beast drinks the oceans. Caravans now cross where seas once were. You pretend not to know this, too?'

ELRIC: 'You must believe me, Queen Shyrix'x... I – I think I was under a sleeping charm...'

SHYRIX'X: 'No longer under *my* charm, that's evident! I refused your love – and you schemed against me, eh?'

*She whirls pettishly, but she is half won over. A little puzzled by this attitude, which she had not expected. But she's beginning to believe him.*

ELRIC: 'Madam – I assure you...'

*Elric and Queen Shyrix'x stand together looking out over the harbour. She puts a friendly hand on his shoulder.*

SHYRIX'X: 'Well, our cooled love and Imrryr's rebuilding must both wait. You know the sea levels fall –'

*A caravan of odd beasts of burden crosses a desert, once an ocean.*

SHYRIX'X: '– but our capital grows vulnerable to barbarian attack!'

*The sea-maze. Waters grow very low, exposing rocks and stranded sea creatures.*

SHYRIX'X: 'Our sea defences no longer protect us against our Falkryn foes. You are our nation's champion, White Crow. How will you help us?'

ELRIC: 'I see my task, sweet lady. As to its solution... how can I see what is happening in the world at large?'

SHYRIX'X: 'We must ask the Dragon Master... your rival, Dyvim Mar.'

*The Dragon Caves. Queen and Elric stand together observing the sleeping dragons. They are clearly in a very deep sleep, save for one younger dragon, who raises a sleepy eye to regard them. Dyvim Mar, the Dragon Master, greets them cheerfully. He wears a version, a little more primitive, of the clothing worn by the first Dragon Master Elric and Cymoril encountered when they visited the caves in Book One. He embraces Elric.*

DYVIM MAR: 'Ah, cousin! Our champion returns! Our need for you is great. You know of the seas receding?'

ELRIC: 'Aye, but not why. We must wake a dragon, cousin. Is that possible?'

DYVIM MAR: 'You'll recall we used all the Phoorn only some nine years past to defend ourselves against the Falkryn, who have long coveted us our power. But we held one back, as we always do. Snaptail! She's ready. And eager for the skies. Where would you go?'

ELRIC: 'Across the world, so that we can observe all the oceans. If some natural dam has raised itself, perhaps we can destroy it.'

DYVIM MAR: 'Good thinking, cousin. She'll be ready by morning...'

*Back at the palace, Queen Shyrix'x holds up her hands, believing that Elric means to follow her into the bedchamber...*

SHYRIX'X: 'If by feigning memory loss you hope to revive our love...'

ELRIC (*concerned*): 'Believe me, madam, I intend to serve you and Melniboné only as your champion.'

*A little disappointed, the queen accepts his refusal. She claps her hands. Servants enter. She gives orders:*

SHYRIX'X: 'Prepare our champion's quarters. Sleep well, White Crow. And may your memory soon be restored.'

And shortly after daybreak...

*Queen and some warriors stand by while Elric and Dyvim Mar get ready to mount the huge dragon which now crouches on the side of the harbour. Further away stands a crowd of Melnibonéans. Others hang from balconies to watch. She embraces Dyvim Mar.*

SHYRIX'X: 'May the gods of Melniboné go with you, and may you find the solution you seek.'

*Elric and his cousin Dyvim Mar bow.*

*They climb into the high dragon saddles:*

DYVIM MAR: 'I trust you do not hate me for what happened, cousin. You were betrothed, 'tis true. But we could not resist our love…'

ELRIC: 'Believe me, Dyvim Mar, I hold no ill will whatsoever…'

*The dragon is airborne. She flies on vast wings away from the city across an evidently dying ocean. Strange islands emerge where none should exist. The two men fly towards the sun, shielding their eyes as they scan the landscape and the sea below.*

DYVIM MAR: 'As you know, cousin, dragons sleep for years and then have a few days of activity at most. We must be careful not to tire our steed or she'll be unable to fly back home!'

*They are now flying over a butte-studded desert not unlike the Painted Desert. Great worn limestone cliffs emerge from glinting pools of water – the only water there is. Wild animals lap hungrily at the stuff, glancing up as the great shape of the dragon flies by overhead.*

ELRIC: 'These are not old deserts, but new-made. What sorcery could rob the world of her water?'

DYVIM: 'There's a small lake below. While we have the chance, we'd best land and let Mistress Snaptail drink.'

*They head towards the small lake where many other animals are already drinking, rearing away in panic when the shadow of the dragon passes over them. As they do so Elric spots something in the distance. It will prove to be a vast horde of warriors. Elric points.*

ELRIC: 'What's that?'

*The two have landed and, while worried animals watch from a safe distance, Snaptail drinks. Meanwhile Elric and Dyvim Mar climb a great slab of rock so that they can look without being seen at a great army riding and marching towards them. At the head of the army are two men. One of them is Yyrkoon, though we can't quite make that out yet, maybe. The other is a rider who is almost too big for his mount, armoured in spikes and scales, like a lizard. Try for a Vin Diesel look. This is Agras Ti, sorcerer of the Falkryn and partner to Yyrkoon, who here takes on another persona, unaware of his life in Melniboné…*

ELRIC: 'The Falkryn horde! Without doubt they ride toward Melniboné!!'

DYVIM MAR: 'When Snaptail's drunk her fill, we'll fly home to warn them…'

ELRIC: 'First we'll take their measure, cousin.'

*It is sunset. The light casts long shadows, but the horde is closer now and we can make out the leading figures. This time it's obvious that the mounted warrior is Melnibonéan. And, of course, it's Prince Yyrkoon.*

DYVIM MAR: 'Do you know him?'

ELRIC: 'Something in the back of my brain does. He means us no good, that's for certain…'

*Close-up of Prince Yyrkoon, smirking with triumph.*

*Behind, at the lake, the dragon looks with surprise as something surfaces at the centre of the water – it is the angry eyes of what will be one of Straasha the Sea-King's people…*

## Chapter Two
### *A Thirsty Chaos Lord*

*A* N ANGRY THRASHING *of the waters of the lake. Elric and Dyvim Mar turn to see Snaptail in a struggle with a huge water-creature. His fishy face identifies him as a water elemental.*

*The two beings wrestle each other while Elric and Dyvim Mar look helplessly from the shore.*

DYVIM MAR: 'A water elemental! Snaptail – break free!'

ELRIC: 'She's not strong enough! We've lost our steed, cousin!'

*But the dragon breaks free at last, beating up into the air as the elemental turns into a great water-spout, using up all the water in the lake, trying to reach the escaping monster.*

ELRIC: 'She's free!'

DYVIM MAR: 'Aye. But at what cost?'

*The water elemental falls back into the lake. But the dragon is falling, too. She's barely able to keep her height. Falling back to earth in a great spiral, she lands utterly exhausted far out across the wasteland.*

*Elric and Dyvim Mar race towards their fallen steed, reaching her at last. She is weary, barely able to keep her great eyes open.*

DYVIM MAR: 'She's exhausted. The fight took all her power. It will be days or weeks before she'll fly again!'

*Elric whirls – hearing a sound behind him. And here come a whole host of barbarians, of the same kind as Yyrkoon led...*

ELRIC: 'Barbarians. Look to your sword, cousin!'

*Elric and Dyvim Mar are swiftly embroiled in a heavy fight. Their swordsmanship is superior to that of the barbarians but there are a lot more barbarians...*

*Slowly but surely the barbarians get the upper hand.*

*Elric and Dyvim Mar are dragged before the two leaders of the barbarians – Yyrkoon and Agras Ti.*

AGRAS TI: 'Melnibonéans! Spying on us. Do you know them, Wild Dog?'

YYRKOON / WILD DOG: 'I've told you. My memory fails me in some ways. But that's a silver warrior – like me, he's of noble birth – perhaps a prince of the line – only certain emperors and their blood have that pallor and those ruby eyes. We have a fine prize, Agras Ti.'

*Elric and Dyvim Mar, chained and thrown into a glass-sided cage on wheels, become part of the barbarians' advance as a seashore comes in sight. Again, there are beached boats far up above the waterline, indicating that the ocean has receded. Wild Dog and Agras Ti bring their troops to a halt and rest on their saddle pommels looking away to sea.*

WILD DOG: 'Beyond that ocean lies Melniboné. Once the sea was her friend and she was impregnable. Now she'll fall like a ripe apple into our hands. All we must do is wait a little for the sea to recede. Then we attack.'

AGRAS TI: 'You're sure her dragons sleep and cannot harm us?'

WILD DOG: 'We have over a year before they can wake the mass of dragons. By that time we shall control both the city and, through me, the dragons, for we speak a common tongue. And through Melniboné's dragons – the whole world shall be ours!'

*A raven appears and flies towards the cage of transparent obsidian where Elric and Dyvim Mar are imprisoned.*

*It comes to perch on a tree, watching the sun set.*

*In the firelight, the raven hops down from the tree to where a guard relaxes, his keys on the ground beside him.*

*Miraculously the raven manages to separate a key from the ring and fly off with it.*

*The raven flies to the cage where a miserable Elric and Dyvim Mar sit talking in their cage.*

DYVIM MAR: 'So that's their plan. They must know why the waters are falling so quickly. Perhaps their sorcery is the cause? But if we cannot warn our people, they lack the resources to resist such a powerful army. The sea has always been our best defence...'

*Elric notices the raven hopping through the bars, the key in its beak. He frowns.*

ELRIC: 'Sorcery, you say? And what's this?'

RAVEN: 'This is all I can do for you now. Later, perhaps, I will be able to help more. But Chaos rules this whole realm and my magic's not yet strong enough to fight it. A boat awaits you on the shore. Use it to warn your people of their danger.'

DYVIM MAR: 'A loquacious bird. And a useful one. Is he yours, White Crow? Or merely some relative?'

*Elric is already unlocking his manacles.*

*He completes the job and passes the key to Dyvim Mar.*

ELRIC: 'Perhaps he is my totem, I do not know. Let's not question our fortune. Let's find that boat and warn the queen.'

*They make it to the shore and see the little skiff waiting for them.*

*They sail into the sunrise. The raven watches from his perch on a rock.*

*Elric and Dyvim Mar have a good wind behind them and they can see the slender buildings of Melniboné in the distance.*

DYVIM MAR: 'There! Imrryr's in sight! Now at last we can ready ourselves for the barbarian attack!'

*But now the sea begins to swirl and tremble. Soon it turns into strange, half-recognisable shapes. The two men stare around them in dismay as the sea around the boat forms itself into a giant watery hand and begins to lift them –*

*– then the massive, fishy face of King Straasha, the king of the water elementals, materialises above them. He holds the boat in the palm of his hand. His other hand holds a great fishing spear. He is in poor temper and glares down at the two tiny mortals and their boat. But he is also sad. He is reluctant to interfere. It seems something might even control him...*

KING STRAASHA: 'Little mortals, I have no argument with thee. But if you interfere with your enemy's plans, 'tis I who shall suffer. I have no choice but to do what I must do.'

*Elric attempts to persuade the sea-king.*

ELRIC: 'King Straasha! Lord of the Waters. We mean you no ill. We seek to discover why your realm is vanishing so rapidly...'

STRAASHA: 'Well, little mortal, I believe you. I can show you the source of our mutual danger. But I cannot let you fight it...'

*King Straasha speeds with his mortal captives through the waters. He needs water to take shape so he can't go too far into the shallows.*

STRAASHA: 'This is the closest I can take you...'

*He lifts his hand so that they can see further...*

*Standing in King Straasha's watery palm the two men look into the distance where a monstrous form can be seen. He is Artigkern, Lord of Chaos – bloated and disgusting. He has taken the form of a gigantic toad and is sucking up water through a great hollow tree.*

STRAASHA: 'He is Artigkern of Chaos. He has already sucked the fourth planet dry of all its water and he will do the same to us. Agras Ti of the Falkryn brought him here through sorcery and I fear to stop him. He is too powerful – and – and...'

ELRIC: 'Great lord of elementals. You fear nothing. He must have some other hold over you.'

*Straasha frowns, almost ashamed.*

STRAASHA: 'What if he does? I must do what he demands or he will take *all* the water. Through this bargain, he leaves me a little hope... But as the water drains, so does my power. Even if he died, he says he will spit all the water into the sun first. There is nothing I can do against him...'

*Elric is horrified, remonstrates with the great king of elementals.*

ELRIC: 'But, my lord king – this world will die as the last one did. Would you not help us to fight against him?'

STRAASHA (*truly shamefaced now*): 'I cannot.'

STRAASHA: 'He holds my sister hostage. If I resist him, she dies. Come now, I have kept my promise...'

*We see a cut of a beautiful merwoman, Straasha's sister, held in a gigantic semi-transparent clam shell.*

ELRIC: 'Upon my oath, King Straasha, if you take us to Melniboné, I promise you I shall do all I can to save your sister.'

STRAASHA: 'What can a little mortal do? But I thank thee for thy good intent. For that I'll not return thee to Agras Ti, but take thee to thy destination.'

*Straasha transports the two men back to Melniboné.*

*He deposits them on the shores near their home island, which is visible far away across the glistening mud-flats – all kinds of abandoned ships, sea creatures and so forth.*

STRAASHA: 'Thy heart is a good one, mortal. If only thou knew some way of saving my sister, I would be in thy debt for ever.'

ELRIC: 'I will think on it, sire. All our interests depend on defeating this Chaos creature!'

*The two men are exhausted by the time they get to Imrryr. They stagger through the streets, issuing warnings to any who pause to listen –*

ELRIC: 'Arm yourselves! The Falkryn march upon Melniboné!'

DYVIM MAR: 'They drain the sea – to remove our defences!'

*They come into the throne room where the queen sits on the traditional Ruby Throne of Melniboné. She scowls, scarcely believing what they have to say.*

ELRIC: 'Scarcely three days, your majesty, and the Falkryn horde's upon us! The dragons sleep. We have no walls against them!'

QUEEN SHYRIX'X: 'You clearly have no faith in the courage and skill of our warriors, White Crow. Melniboné can beat any barbarian horde, no matter how large!'

DYVIM MAR: 'A renegade Melnibonéan is with them, madam! They call him Wild Dog.'

SHYRIX'X: 'I know of no "Wild Dog". What I'd rather hear is how you came to lose one of our Phoorn. Where is the dragon on which you rode?'

*Dyvim Mar is embarrassed. He explains and we hear him at the end of his explanation…*

DYVIM MAR: '… then she was seized by a water elemental and exhausted. We were forced to abandon her in the drained lake. At that point we were captured by the Falkryn horde…'

SHYRIX'X: 'Cowards! You concoct a fantasy to explain your own incompetence. White Crow, you're no true champion, but a fraud. And you, of all people, Dyvim Mar, have lied to me!'

SHYRIX'X: 'Guards – to the oubliette with them!'

*The pair are taken and thrown down into the oubliette – a deep pit with steep sides from which there is no apparent escape. A grille is placed over the top.*

*At the bottom, Elric and Dyvim Mar are disconsolate to say the least…*

DYVIM MAR: 'Well, cousin, it's an old adage but a true one – the bringer of bad news is never welcome at Court. But I fear she believes herself betrayed by us. With luck she'll let us linger here for a few weeks and then forgive us.'

ELRIC: 'There'll be worse news soon. We must get out of here.'

DYVIM MAR: 'You know a spell to grant us wings?'

ELRIC: 'There's one thing we can try…'

*The two men have braced their backs against the walls of the oubliette, across from one another. They have twisted their legs together so that they create a kind of bridge between them. So long as they maintain this tension they can 'chimney' up the oubliette.*

*They are sweating by the time they get to the top and, using a narrow ridge for their toes, push up the grille.*

*Guards spot them and come running towards them.*

*Elric and Dyvim Mar take on the guards and, with superior fighting skills, disarm them and use their own weapons against them.*

*Then they go running through the tunnels.*

DYVIM MAR: 'This way. An old tunnel's a secret way to the Dragon Caves!'

*They hide in the maze of caverns while the guards fail to find them.*

*They arrive in the secret Dragon Caves where all the dragons sleep solidly.*

DYVIM MAR: 'If only we had not awakened all but Snaptail. It will be a full year before we can use them again.'

ELRIC: 'Is there no sorcery which will wake them sooner?'

DYVIM MAR: 'Sleep's the secret of their power. They restore their bodies and their venom. Even if they could fly, they would have no weapons against their enemies. They rely on our people to guard them while they sleep… All we can do is wait – and fight our enemies as best we can…'

# Chapter Three
## *The Year of the Barbarian*

T HEN THE FALKRYN came...

*A massive battle scene as the Falkryn attack the Melnibonéans, driving them back into their own streets. at the forefront is the demonic Yyrkoon/ Wild Dog while the sorcerer Agras Ti does not fight, but watches from safety, smirking to himself. In an inset he slips into the throne room.*

*Elric and Dyvim Mar have followed Agras Ti into the throne room as he attempts to kill the queen.*

AGRAS TI: 'Aha! The queen!'

*While Dyvim Mar tries to get the queen to leave, Elric engages Agras Ti.*

DYVIM MAR: 'My lady! 'Tis the Falkryn chief. Beware his sorcery!'

ELRIC: 'In his eagerness, he's left his bodyguards behind.'

*Under pressure, Agras Ti calls upon his protector, Lord Arioch of Chaos.*

AGRAS TI: 'Arioch! My lord Arioch, aid me now!'

ELRIC: 'So that foul Duke of Hell protects you! I should have guessed that's who helped you bring the drinker of oceans to this realm!'

*As Dyvim Mar helps the queen out of danger, they look in horror as Arioch of Chaos begins to manifest himself.*

*He first appears as a hideous creature of smoke and flame but slowly manifests himself as a gigantic golden youth of impossible beauty, wearing clothing exactly the same style as that worn by the Melnibonéans. A way of flattering them and putting them at their ease.*

*Agras Ti runs towards his master, begging for help as Elric recoils.*

AGRAS TI: 'Master! Save me. They mean to kill me!'

*Arioch smiles almost benignly down on his creature, Agras Ti. He reaches out one slender-fingered hand towards the sorcerer.*

ARIOCH: ''Twas thy sorcery brought me to this realm, Agras Ti. For that I repaid thee by inviting my brother Lord Artigkern, the drinker of oceans, to join us, even do thy bidding. But now he has what he wants and, indeed, I have exactly what I want. Thy purpose is fulfilled, mortal.'

AGRAS TI: 'P-purpose, lord?'

ARIOCH: 'I have a destiny to carry out, as have we all. There is a mortal here more important to my plans than ever you could be. Elric – Silverskin – do you know me? White Crow, is it?'

*As he speaks he casually raises the writhing, horrified Agras Ti towards his beautiful lips…*

ELRIC: 'I know thee not, Chaos Lord. Begone from this realm. We want none of your folk in Melniboné!'

*Agras Ti is screaming in terror, unnoticed by Arioch, who now parts his lips a little, preparing to eat him…*

ARIOCH: 'But I come to help thee. I could destroy all these foolish humans, if you will let me…'

ELRIC: 'Melniboné never makes bargains with Chaos. My destiny and thine have nothing in common!'

ARIOCH: 'Ah, my friend, but we could do so much for each other, thee and I…'

*Elric recoils as Arioch munches on half of the Falkryn sorcerer. The rest of him is still in his hands.*

ELRIC: 'Cruel monster! I'd rather die than make a compact with corrupted Chaos…'

ARIOCH: 'Well, I inhabit thy realm now, young mortal. I suspect the time will come when thou'll find it convenient to strike a bargain...'

*The golden youth begins to become the monster of smoke and flame again.*

ARIOCH: 'For the moment, farewell. To summon me, thou hast only to call for me by name. And all I'll ask for my help is a little blood, a few worthless souls...'

*Elric leads Dyvim Mar and the queen behind the throne and down a flight of secret steps as the Falkryn barbarians, led by Yyrkoon, all of them covered with blood and bearing booty, burst into the throne room.*

ELRIC: 'Quickly! We have only seconds!'

YYRKOON: 'Ha! She's fled. And left me the Ruby Throne. I'm Emperor of Melniboné now!'

*He seats himself on the throne, brooding.*

YYRKOON: 'But until that silverskin is dead, I shall not know peace of mind.'

Wild Dog spoke truth. Though he controlled Melniboné, he had poor control of the Falkryn, whose leader was now mysteriously vanished...

... and he maintained even less authority over his own people.

*A montage of guerrilla fighting. The occupying Falkryn, though cruel and vicious, have a poor time controlling the streets.*

*They are harassed, within Melniboné and in the Imrryrian countryside, by small bands of Melnibonéans led by Elric, Queen Shyrix'x and Dyvim Mar.*

Death comes to the conquerors by secret arrows, sudden strangulation, sword thrusts and spear casts.

*Artigkern has the sea-king's sister in the giant clam shell, semi-transparent. His horrible hands open the shell wide enough to reach in and caress her face... She recoils in horror.*

*Yyrkoon is riding out at night on a secret mission of his own.*

YYRKOON: 'Another few months... then the power of the dragons will be mine. Meanwhile those rebels shall be tamed...'

*Yyrkoon meets Artigkern, grown even fatter, slimier and grosser than ever, still sucking the oceans and leaving fish, ships and all stranded... Yyrkoon addresses him angrily.*

YYRKOON: 'Must you drink it all? I helped summon thee to this realm.'

ARTIGKERN: 'I leave a realm when there is nothing left to drink. The time will come when I'll spit all this water into the sun and set off to find new worlds with fresh seas for me to sup...'

YYRKOON: 'Then give up the sea-king's sister. He has no more power over you.'

ARTIGKERN (*grinning*): 'Give up my darling. Did I not tell thee, mortal? I'm in love. I'll take her with me when I go. Bring me a bride as beautiful and perhaps I'll give thee her and a little of thy water back...'

Months passed. The morale of the conquered people was maintained only by the activities of Elric and his companions.

While the rebels were free, the future held freedom...

*Montage of Elric, Dyvim Mar and the queen. They lead small parties of warriors on secret raids. They attack Falkryn in the streets. They steal from rich carpetbaggers. They are applauded by the Melnibonéans. They disappear down alleys. And Queen Shyrix'x and Dyvim Mar grow closer, become lovers with Elric's blessing.*

*A deputation of Falkryn knights stands before Yyrkoon. They and their soldiers are leaving.*

FALKRYN LEADER: 'You promised us booty and booty we have. You promised us power over the world, and that we do *not* have. Water grows scarce here. The people thirst.'

FALKRYN LEADER: 'We leave to find the fabled "lost ocean".'

Now Wild Dog's grip on the throne grew weaker...

*Yyrkoon/Wild Dog, surrounded by Melnibonéan guards who have a somewhat decadent look, sits brooding on the Ruby Throne.*

YYRKOON (*thinks*): I must consolidate my power or my plans come to nothing. Once the dragons wake, I rule the world. But until then...

MELNIBONÉAN GUARD: 'Our water runs low, Lord King. I understood you had a compact with Duke Artigkern...'

YYRKOON (*scowling*): 'So I do. He'll keep his bargain. I'll see to that! But these rebels must be tricked into submission...'

ANOTHER GUARD (*whispers in his ear*): 'Then, sire...'

A newly dry approach to Imrryr...

*We see a caravan coming in from the drained sea bottoms. The beasts have giant water jars and skins strapped over them. Queen Shyrix'x and Dyvim Mar lie hidden in wait with a small band of men, ready to raid it.*

... now a caravan route for that most precious of commodities...

SHYRIX'X: 'The people grow thirsty. This water will ease their misery...'

*She leads her men in an attack on the caravan.*

The canyons echo with battle cries...

... followed by an abrupt silence!

SHYRIX'X: '*It's a trap!*'

*From hiding all around them comes a large force of warriors. The queen fights bravely, but it's clear the soldiers want only her. Their men lie dead all around them. Dyvim Mar is badly wounded. She cries to him to escape:*

SHYRIX'X: 'Flee, Dyvim Mar! Warn White Crow and the others!'

*She's dragged before Yyrkoon who grins in pleasure.*

YYRKOON: 'You're mine now, lady.'

*They then drag in the wounded Dyvim Mar.*

YYRKOON: 'Become my queen and consolidate my power over Melniboné – or your paramour dies in exquisite agony!'

*Elric watches from cover as…*

The great ceremonial procession winds its way through the streets of Melniboné.

*Yyrkoon is very smug, but clearly Queen Shyrix'x is deeply miserable.*

The watching crowd is not exactly overjoyed, but they bow low before the passing parade, accepting the inevitable.

ELRIC (*thinks*): He has achieved some legitimacy. And soon the dragons will begin to wake. Wild Dog's power will be complete.

*Elric sneaks into the royal apartments to keep an assignation with Shyrix'x.*

*She fears Yyrkoon but risks all to speak to Elric.*

SHYRIX'X: 'Dyvim Mar is thrown into the oubliette. His life ensures my good behaviour – but the people grow unruly. Water is too scarce. They thirst.'

*Elric gets into the dungeons and sees Dyvim Mar, still wounded, down at the bottom of the oubliette. As Elric speaks he breaks a dagger trying to undo the padlock holding the grille in place.*

ELRIC: 'Hsssst! Dyvim Mar!'

DYVIM MAR: 'Cousin! Risk not your own liberty here. I'm too valuable. They'll not let me get free again.'

DYVIM MAR: 'While I'm his prisoner, the queen will do whatever he orders. Yet she's right – thirst will madden them enough to rise up and overthrow him…'

In the dragon caverns...

*Elric looks down on the sleeping dragons, some of whom are indeed stirring. He is thoughtful, trying to work out a plan.*

*Out of nowhere a black raven comes to settle on his shoulder. He addresses it.*

ELRIC: 'Ha, old friend. You saved my life once. But how can we save the folk of Melniboné from tyranny and the world from drought...?'

VOICE (*from outside the frame [it's Arioch]*): 'There's one way, my friend.'

# Chapter Four
## *Dealing with Darkness*

A FIGURE OF *smoke and flame gradually materialises into the golden youth who is Duke Arioch of Chaos.*

ARIOCH: 'I wish only to help you, young mortal...'

ELRIC (*reacts angrily*): 'Before I make bargains with Chaos, I'll risk everything!!!'

ARIOCH: 'A few more weeks and the dragons wake. The emperor will control them. He will have the power to set the whole world on fire. But if he were thwarted and Artigkern were dead, Melniboné would thrive again as a force for good...'

ELRIC: 'Good? What does Chaos know of good?'

ARIOCH: 'You simplify the multiverse. Neither Law nor Chaos are forces for good or evil in themselves. It is the use to which they are put by mortals that determines those qualities...'

ELRIC (*buries his head in his hands. He is baffled, tormented*): 'I don't know!'

*We cut to the dream couch in contemporary Melniboné. Elric lies on it clearly in the grip of a terrible nightmare. Cymoril looks at him and is alarmed, turning to Tanglebones.*

CYMORIL: 'See how tormented he is! What is happening to him? You *must* let me go to him, Doctor Tanglebones!'

TANGLEBONES: 'You would have no memory of this world and would be a stranger in his. You'd hinder rather than help him, I assure you, Lady Cymoril...'

CYMORIL: 'But...!'

TANGLEBONES (*also deeply concerned as he stares out of the panel at us*): 'Though I share your frustration, he must solve this problem for himself, risking life and mind... or defeat the point of his dream-quest...'

*Elric is back at the oubliette, trying to get Dyvim Mar out again.*

ELRIC: 'No good. It won't budge.'

DYVIM MAR: 'Forget me. He means to trade Shyrix'x for water. She's served her turn and he knows she plots against him... Save her, White Crow! for my sake!'

ELRIC: 'But how? I possess no power. No allies left...'

*Yyrkoon/Wild Dog appears snarling at the top of the steps:*

YYRKOON: 'So true, White Crow! And now I have all three of you! I baited my trap well.'

YYRKOON: 'As the dragons fly again, the world shall know Melniboné's might, and you two will not live long enough to see me trade my beautiful queen. Tomorrow she'll became Artigkern's bride and the people will thank me for restoring their water to them again! They'll follow me, and the dragons will grant us imperial power!'

YYRKOON: 'I outwit thee at every turn!'

*Elric is up against it, fighting off dozens of well-armed warriors who are bound to beat him. Yyrkoon snarls with triumph.*

YYRKOON: '*Kill him!* I would be rid of that vermin once and for all!'

And now the young albino made a decision which was to determine his fate and that of his people until the end of time...

ELRIC (*thinks*): I have no choice. Either we perish, or I betray my own principles – and can I let my friends die and my nation become a tyranny because I have a few scruples?

*As the guards close around him Elric lifts back his head and cries out:*

ELRIC: *'ARIOCH! ARIOCH! BLOOD AND SOULS FOR MY LORD ARIOCH!'*

*And the thing of smoke and flame begins to materialise in the darkness of the dungeon...*

*Clobbering time, Walter. You draw it. I'll go hide. Sound effects to taste.*

*Arioch remains in demonic form for this moment, rending and tearing, scattering body parts, and sending guards left and right before reaching for Yyrkoon, who runs for it.*

*Arioch tears off the grille of the oubliette. Elric throws Yyrkoon down into it. He survives by crawling away into a hole to hide.*

*As Arioch does his deadly work, Elric secures the grille, then helps Dyvim Mar towards the upper regions of the palace, fighting as he goes.*

ELRIC: 'Quickly, the queen...'

*Dyvim Mar finds Queen Shyrix'x already tied up ready for the trade with Artigkern. He releases her. They embrace.*

*The fighting's over in the dungeon. Elric looks sick as he reviews the carnage in the dungeon. Now Arioch has assumed the likeness of a golden youth, but he is grinning demoniacally, wiping the blood from his mouth. His hands, too, are bloody.*

ARIOCH: 'See, Elric. I keep my promises. What other help can I offer thee?'

ELRIC: 'None, demon. I have no stomach for this bargain. Thou hast thy blood and souls. Now begone...'

ARIOCH (*bows*): 'Very well, sweet mortal. But remember I am part of this plane from this day on – and always at thy service...'

*The black raven settles on Elric's shoulder as the Lord of Hell fades again into smouldering smoke. Elric scowls at the bird, which flaps up into the gloom of the cavern. Elric looks at it suspiciously, unable to work out what its function is.*

ELRIC: 'I have a premonition. Nothing but darkness and blood-shed can come of this bargain…'

*The day is won. The nobles of Melniboné bend the knee to Queen Shyrix'x and her consort Dyvim Mar.*

Shortly, in the queen's restored Court…

*Elric comes hurrying into the chamber.*

ELRIC: 'The dragons begin to wake. But how do we restore the oceans?'

SHYRIX'X: 'Wild Dog planned to trade me not only for water, but for the sea-king's sister, whom Artigkern holds captive.'

ELRIC: 'If Artigkern sees us coming in force, he'll know we plan to trick him. He'll spit the world's water into the sun and we'll all die of thirst…'

DYVIM MAR: 'And no doubt kill the sea-king's sister.'

ELRIC: 'Then here's what we must risk…'

*Artigkern, as large as a large island, glistening and bulging with all the water he has drunk, still keeps the sea-king's sister in the shell he has created for her.*

ARTIGKERN: 'The mortal's a fool if he thinks I'll give up satisfying my thirst for a fresh bride, no matter how beautiful. I'll take the new woman he offers, but if I give up the sea-king's sister, he'll take his vengeance on me if he can…'

*Elric, dressed like Yyrkoon, comes riding a deep-sided wagon over the drained ocean floor escorting an apparently bound and gagged Queen Shyrix'x. It's the same wagon he and Dyvim Mar were trapped in earlier.*

ELRIC: 'My Lord of Chaos! I come to keep our bargain. You will give me a ration of water and the sea-king's sister, and I'll give thee this mortal woman.'

ARTIGKERN: ''Tis a bargain. Bring her closer.'

*Elric, driving the wagon, approaches the impossibly huge bulk of the Chaos Lord.*

*As he gets close to where the sea-king's sister wallows in melancholy in her half-open shell, he whips up the horses!*

ELRIC: 'Faster, faster! Ha! Ya!'

*The draperies on the wagon fall back to reveal a near-transparent obsidian tank of water and Queen Shyrix'x throws back her cloak to reveal she's not bound. With a war-axe she smashes the clam shell, releasing the sea-king's sister and then half-hauls her into the tank of water the wagon is drawing.*

SHYRIX'X: 'Quickly, my lady – we must not hesitate!'

*Artigkern makes to reach towards them to stop them – then looks to the horizon.*

ARTIGKERN: 'What's this?'

*Over the horizon pours a huge flight of Phoorn dragons. (Inset is Dyvim Mar, with his long dragon-goad in his hand, riding the leading Phoorn.)*

*Suddenly the sky is black with dragons.*

*As the wagon hauls away, the first dragons dive on Artigkern, their venom striking his swollen body – and piercing the skin... bursting him so that water erupts from every wound...*

*... and Elric and Queen Shyrix'x, hauling the sea-king's sister, are pursued by a vast tidal wave of water released from Artigkern...*

*... which overwhelms them so it seems they must drown... The horses fight for their lives. Elric slashes their harness...*

*... until Dyvim Mar swoops down on the dragon to rescue Queen Shyrix'x...*

*... and the sea-king's sister, in open water now, catches up Elric and the horses, swimming with them to a high hill which is swiftly becoming an island...*

*... whereupon Straasha the Sea-King, clearly delighting in his watery kingdom again, comes swimming towards them to embrace his sister...*

STRAASHA: 'Against all odds you've kept your promise, mortal – henceforth thy people and mine shall be allied and I shall be forever in thy debt! Your nation shall prosper and become the strongest in the world!'

*In the distance, heading for Melniboné, Dyvim Mar and Queen Shyrix'x wave farewell from the back of the dragon.*

ELRIC: 'And sweet Melniboné shall know peace and security again...'

*In the dream chamber Elric stirs and wakes. He looks pretty wasted, but he's smiling as he's greeted with relief by Tanglebones and Cymoril, who hands him his reviving potion.*

CYMORIL: 'Thank Arioch! You survived!'

TANGLEBONES: 'Another dream-quest accomplished. Another lesson learned. Welcome back, young master!'

*Elric swings off the couch and begins to stride for the door. They follow him, puzzled.*

*He enters another dream chamber where Yyrkoon is also coming to. But Yyrkoon does not look at all happy. He glares at his cousin. He strikes away the offered potion.*

YYRKOON: 'So you wake, cousin. You still live... I recall – I recall – it was not a pleasant dream...'

ELRIC: 'For my part, cousin, I'm feeling all the better for my long slumber. Yours, it seems, has not entirely agreed with you!'

*Yyrkoon staggers away on the arm of his slave, snarling. Cymoril moves to embrace Elric.*

---

YYRKOON: 'There'll be other opportunities, I'm sure...'

*Meanwhile the brooding Sadric frowns as he looks down on the scene from a gallery high above the room... The mysterious Arisand stands beside him.*

SADRIC: 'So once again my enfeebled son survives. But for how long? How long? The crown's not yet decided...'

# Book Three

## *The Dream of Five Years: The Dream of Air*

## The South Wind's Soul

# Chapter One
## *Death from Above*

$S$ UNRISE IN MELNIBONÉ...

*Three small panels across the top of a large panel:*

*Yyrkoon is getting up from his bed, donning his robe and talking to the human woman Arisand.*

Prince Yyrkoon, Elric's rival, rises...

YYRKOON: 'The dream's done! Two more still to dream... And that weakling dog lives on. How to destroy my feeble cousin and make myself old Sadric's heir?'

*Sadric, brooding as always, stares into the rising sun from his balcony.*

... while Elric's father Sadric broods on...

SADRIC: 'Two dreams, two powerful allies gained. My son does well, but can his success be sustained?'

*Elric is about to mount the dream couch and is sipping a concoction handed him by Cymoril as he addresses Tanglebones.*

TANGLEBONES: 'You'll sleep, Lord Elric, for twenty hours. Each four hours represents a year in the dream lands of our common past.'

ELRIC: 'Thanks, Doctor Tanglebones.' *(Addresses Cymoril:)* 'Shall I find your brother lying in wait to murder me again, my dear Cymoril?'

CYMORIL: 'No doubt, in some guise. You can be killed as readily in your dream reality as you can here. You must take care, my love.'

And so the fresh dream begins.

It is some eight thousand years earlier, when Melniboné had achieved economic ascendancy over the peoples of the 'Old Kingdoms' but had not yet begun to build her empire...

*From the viewpoint of Melnibonéan King Feneric and his teenage son, Silverskin (Elric in this dream), we look out across a stylised map of the Old Kingdoms (which, believe it or not, preceded the Young Kingdoms). The map can be based on the Cawthorn map in the White Wolf editions, but many of the names will be different. I'll do a rough drawing of the map and send it to Walter and Joey* [Cavalieri, editor of the book at DC]. *It will show, among other things, the distant Mountains of the Myyrrhn, the port city (across the sea from Melniboné) of Port Norvaknol in the Kingdom of Forin'Shen and so on. The outlines of the main continent will be the same, of course, but many of the names will be different. These are the 'Old Kingdoms' which will disappear with the rise of Melniboné, replaced with the 'Young Kingdoms'.*

KING FENERIC: 'Our island nation grows in power and influence. We trade across the wide world. My son, you must learn diplomacy if you would rule in Melniboné's interest. You must ever respect the Old Kingdoms who were here before us...'

ELRIC/SILVERSKIN: 'You teach me my duty, Father, and my responsibilities. Respect, I think, is at the heart of all.'

FENERIC: 'Trade is the source of our power. If we are fair and honourable, our power is well earned and will never be threatened...'

*Feneric is taking his son through a market where Melnibonéans trade with strange-looking people from all over the Old Kingdoms, including the Pukwadji we saw in the first story. All are humanoid, but some are distinctly alien.*

FENERIC: 'But should we seek to maintain that power by the sword, Melniboné shall inevitably fall. That is the fate of all who would force their will upon the world. Our ancestors knew that and passed their wisdom down to us.'

ELRIC: 'I have learned that much, at least. If we remain adaptable, we remain strong. If we force others to accept our traditions and values, we ultimately grow weak...'

FENERIC (*smiles*): 'How well you learn the statecraft of Melniboné. You will make a great king one day...'

*His brother Ederic strides up, all arrogance and swaggering power.*

EDERIC: 'My lord Feneric!'

FENERIC: 'Ah, Ederic, brother! Well met!'

EDERIC (*laughs in a somewhat sinister way*): 'Kings are judged by the firmness of their fists, brother, not the sweetness of their tongues. Greedy hands reach for our wealth, young Silverskin. Greedy eyes burn with envy.'

*Young Silverskin scowls, finding this advice unpalatable.*

Weeks went by while the young Silverskin studied, oblivious of the rivalry between his father and his uncle. But then, one morning –

*Elric/Silverskin is at his lessons when he hears a shout from the street. Going to the window he sees people pointing skyward and out to sea. There is a great armada – ships sailing across the sky as they might sail across the sea. The ships are single-sailed, rather like Viking ships, with ugly carvings as figureheads and green-skinned, hairless men crowding their rails and rigging, as hideous a group of raiders as we've ever seen. Their sails billow with a mysterious wind as they approach the island of Melniboné and the city of Imrryr. Flying alongside these ships are a different breed – the Winged Men of Myyrrhn – who have appeared in the Elric books. They are armed with long spears and bows and arrows. They are handsome and strong and have huge, downy wings which make them resemble stereotypical angels...*

FIRST CITIZEN: 'Raiders! The green men of Karasim!'

SECOND CITIZEN: 'And the winged men of Myyrrhn are with them!'

ELRIC (*thinks*): 'The Karasim have long hated our power. And now they come to challenge it. But what sorcery drives those ships?'

FENERIC (*bursting into the room*): 'Lad, we must to arms. But whoever aids the Karasim and their allies cannot be defeated by swords alone...'

ELRIC: 'I'll seek Ivram Tvar, the Dragon Master...'

*Elric speeds off through the corridors of the palace, down the steps which lead to the secret passages in turn leading to the Dragon Caves...*

*A Melnibonéan captain has already reached the caves and addresses Ivram Tvar, the Dragon Master. Ivram Tvar spreads his hands helplessly:*

IVRAM TVAR: 'Their time to strike is well chosen. All the Phoorn sleep and cannot be wakened. Powerful sorcery aids the Karasim. I suspect Chaos itself has a hand in this!'

ELRIC: 'If the dragons cannot save us, what can?'

IVRAM TVAR: 'Only our courage and our weapons, young prince...'

*A sword in his hand, Elric emerges into the Imrryrian street, to find towers burning as skins of Greek fire are dropped from the ships above and green warriors slip down ropes dropped over the sides of the hovering ships.*

ELRIC: 'The winged men of Myyrrhn have never been our enemies. What makes them attack Melniboné now?'

*Attacked by several Karasim at once Elric defends himself well. From overhead his father sees him and cries encouragement. Elric shows considerable skill and ferocity in the fight.*

FENERIC: 'You fight well, my son!'

ELRIC (*to the raiders*): 'We have no quarrel with you! Why do you attack us?'

*A Karasim captain sees Elric fighting outside a burning building and calls from where he swings by a rope from his ship, pointing at Elric.*

CAPTAIN: 'He's the one! Capture him alive!'

*Elric fights well but is eventually captured. A winged man of Myyrrhn swoops down and carries him up towards the Karasim ship. Elric is bopped on the head and passes out.*

*Scene from the ground. The Karasim ships are swinging around to leave. Laden with booty, the green men climb back up into their ships. The Myyrrhn have no booty. They carry their dead or wounded with them in the air, disdaining the Karasim ships. It is as if they wish to have little to do with their green allies. Ederic watches, sweating in his armour. Could he be glad of what's happening?*

MELNIBONÉAN (*in burning ruin*): 'They retreat! We've driven them off.'

FENERIC: 'They've taken young Silverskin! They've stolen my son!'

IVRAM TVAR: 'They've gone beyond the Edge of the World. As soon as I can rouse a dragon, I'll follow.'

FENERIC: 'We'll need an army – and who knows what will have become of him by the time we get there...'

*Bowed with grief but looking grim Feneric turns back to his gutted palace.*

FENERIC: 'But we must do whatever we can to find him. Rally my captains. Harsh sorcery's at work here and I know not how to fight it.'

EDERIC: 'Go, brother, and good luck!'

# Chapter Two
## *Into the Middle March*

I N LESS THAN an hour, Melniboné was far behind and the young Silverskin grew tired of struggling...

*The invaders are now over the ocean, with Melniboné out of sight behind.*

*Elric is weary. He is now tied up and lying on the deck of one of the ships whose sails fill with a mysterious wind, blown by scarcely seen supernatural creatures.*

ELRIC (*thinks*): Wind spirits aid them and no doubt keep their ships airborne. How do the Karasim make allies of such supernaturals? If I escaped now I'd have an ocean to swim before I could reach home...

*The Karasim captain stands over Elric as his men lift him up off the deck.*

CAPTAIN: 'He's served his turn. We've no further use for him. Throw him overboard!'

*Elric is thrown overboard, falling down into the clouds below.*

*Elric is plunging helplessly through the clouds.*

*A handsome Myyrrhn warrior swoops in and snatches him up.*

*Flying with him away from the Karasim fleet.*

*Towards an horizon on which bleak, spikey mountains can be seen. This is the land of the Myyrrhn and others are flying towards the mountains.*

ELRIC: 'You saved me. Why?'

*Prince Vashntni offers Elric a grim smile.*

PRINCE VASHNTNI: 'I am Vashntni, Prince of the Myyrrhn. We are warriors, not murderers.'

*They have reached the vast, high, spikey mountains in which the Myyrrhn make their homes. On these peaks are built houses which bear some resemblance to eagles' nests. Prince Vashntni drops down towards an elaborate house of this kind and deposits Elric on a balcony.*

VASHNTNI: 'You are now my guest.'

ELRIC: 'I must return to Melniboné at once. My father...'

VASHNTNI: 'You will remain with us. I cannot anger the Karasim...'

ELRIC: 'Why would a people as honourable as yours ally themselves with corrupt thieves like the Karasim?'

VASHNTNI (*scowling*): 'We had no choice. Ask no further questions, young Silverskin. You are welcome to remain here, to move as freely as possible. Our famous libraries are yours. It is the best I can offer you.'

And so the Melnibonéan prince became an exiled prisoner, pining for his homeland, but determined to continue his studies – especially in the arts of sorcery...

*Time passes as Elric wanders the strange labyrinthine 'nests' of the Myyrrhn, befriended by young winged women in particular. He studies old manuscripts, stares yearningly over the mountains, and generally pines for his home...*

ELRIC (*thinks*): I yearn to know how my father fares. If I could get even a message to him... For now, I'll study what sorcery I can.

Meanwhile, there were diversions...

*The Myyrrhn girls and youths befriend Elric. High in the air they toss him from one to another, bearing him for miles over the wild peaks of the mountains.*

*Elric dallies with one of the winged girls. He asks her a question:*

ELRIC: 'I wonder why folk as fine as yours should aid the Karasim?'

*Girl drops her eyes, telling him a secret she shouldn't really tell.*

GIRL: 'The Karasim hold Vashntni's daughter hostage. We had no choice...'

Then, late one night, a visitor...

*Elric wearily pores over old scrolls in the library. Then through the window flies the black raven (Sepiriz) which perches on one of the old books and looks at him with wise, ancient eyes.*

ELRIC: 'The raven! It seems I recognise you... What book would you have me read?'

*Elric has discovered a spell in one of the old books. A breakthrough!*

ELRIC (*thinks*): Here's a means of creating a portal to return me home. If only I can remember all I learned in Melniboné, there could be a way. 'Tis dangerous magic...

*Referring to the scroll, Elric begins to make strange passes in the air and speaks in 'runic'...*

*He is blown back by a blast which effectively blows black light into the chamber. You can see from his face that the spell has gone wrong.*

ELRIC: 'NO! The spell failed! This is disaster!'

*A portal had been created – now it dragged the young albino into horrible darkness...*

*Elric is dragged, screaming, into a black hole. He falls backwards, deeper and deeper into darkness...*

*... to arrive not in Melniboné, but a chill landscape, grim and near-lightless...*

*Elric has landed on a black featureless plain. A little pale light comes down from a tiny moon high overhead. There are some distant stars, but unfamiliar.*

ELRIC: 'Those stars! They are like no constellations I've ever seen. This place – what have I done? Where am I?'

VOICE (*from outside the frame*): 'Welcome, young Silverskin. Welcome to limbo – the place some call "The Middle March" – the lands between the worlds.'

*Elric turns – and there stands the one we know as Arioch, who here calls himself The Unknown. His own light emanates from him. He is a golden, gorgeous youth. A dandy in strange, alien clothes. At his hip is a scabbarded black sword and in his right hand is a golden staff. He himself is of stunning appearance. He smiles a little sardonically.*

ARIOCH: 'Have you forgotten who I am, Silverskin?'

ELRIC: 'We've never met before!'

ARIOCH: 'Oh, we've met before and we'll meet again, for I am your supernatural mentor. Your interests and mine are the same. And shall be to the end of time...'

ELRIC: 'I've never seen you before, sir!'

ARIOCH: 'Perhaps you don't recognise me. I'll forgive your poor manners. After all, you are not very old.'

*Elric recovers himself and makes a short bow to the newcomer.*

ELRIC: 'Excuse me, my lord. Perhaps my memory has been affected by my fall...'

ARIOCH: 'I can tell I'm unwelcome. Call for me should you need my help. Farewell.'

*And Arioch vanishes in a golden flash. Leaving nothing but the dark, bleak, moonlit landscape.*

ELRIC: 'I suspect that creature. But I need a guide if I'm to return to Melniboné. What's that slithering, unwholesome sound?'

*He whirls at a sound behind him and catches a glimpse of a Night Worm. The Night Worms are huge, blind white worms. They crawl at the edge of the darkness, scenting for Elric's blood. They have vampire mouthparts.*

*Another voice whispers out of the darkness:*

FENKI: 'Heh, heh, heh – the Night Worms are sniffing for your blood, little Silverskin... They hunger so for such sweet, fresh sustenance...'

ELRIC: 'Who's that?'

*Fenki is sitting on a high rock looking down at Elric. The Night Worms slither in closer.*

FENKI: 'Only old Fenki, master. Just another poor lost soul like yourself... exiled to the Middle March through his own bad sorcery...'

ELRIC: 'Come down, sir, and declare yourself!'

FENKI: 'It would be rude to interrupt the Night Worms when they feast on your tasty blood...'

*Elric has no weapon, no means of defending himself. The worms slither in closer. He tries to scramble for the rocks and slips. Fenki capers above, enjoying Elric's predicament. Elric kicks futilely at the Night Worms.*

ELRIC: 'Filthy creatures... *Aarkkk!*'

FENKI: 'Hee, hee! You must learn to scramble faster than that, Silverskin!'

*There comes a blast from out of the darkness which sends Fenki hopping away in terror.*

FENKI: '*Eek!* No offence, my lord! Forgive me...'

*Arioch has reappeared. He is grinning at Fenki's discomfort and also at Elric's disgust. He throws Elric a black sword (it's Stormbringer).*

ARIOCH: 'Here, take this blade. See if you can use it!'

*Then the Night Worms have closed in on Elric and he is fighting for his life.*

ELRIC: 'This sword! It seems to lend me strength!'

*Slicing and stabbing around him.*

*Elric becomes demonic as he fights the Night Worms. Scores of them attack him, but he succeeds in fighting them off while Arioch, smiling with satisfaction, watches him beat them off. Fenki sits on his own bit of rock nearby, scared both of Arioch and Elric's sword.*

ARIOCH: 'He fights well, eh, Master Fenki?'

FENKI: 'Oh, aye, master – very well. But who could not, with that damned blade?'

*Arioch claps his hand on Fenki's shoulders.*

ARIOCH: 'Oh, come now, Master Fenki. You don't give the lad enough credit...'

FENKI (*shuddering*): 'Whatever you say, my lord.'

*Elric rests panting as the remaining Night Worms slither away to safety. He looks down at the bloody sword in his hands. He is somewhat aghast at the havoc he has been able to cause.*

ELRIC: 'How –? How could I have killed so many?'

*Arioch jumps down from the rock and approaches him.*

ARIOCH: 'See. You're more skilled than you thought, Master Silverskin, eh?'

*In revulsion, Elric flings the sword down.*

ELRIC: 'No! Some foul sorcery has aided me. That blade's enchanted!'

ARIOCH: 'Possibly. But you owe it your life, do you not?'

ELRIC: 'I thank you for your aid, sir. I fear that weapon. It seems alive...'

*Arioch stoops and picks up the sword.*

ARIOCH: 'I must admit, it has its sentient moments. Do you still resist my help?'

*Elric remains highly suspicious of Arioch.*

ELRIC: 'I suspect there are conditions to that help, my lord. Where is this place and how did you know when to expect me?'

*Arioch shrugs and spreads his hands, making a pantomime of his innocence. He sheathes the Black Sword in his own scabbard.*

ARIOCH: 'Merely a traveller between the worlds, like yourself, Sir Silverskin. Perhaps I'm a little more familiar with these marches. I could help you save your father and return to Melniboné... Meanwhile...

*He makes a passage in the air and we see a shadowy table and chairs appear.*

ARIOCH: '... let's eat! You must be tired of Myyrrhn's simple fare and long for the luxury of the life you left behind.'

*Arioch has conjured a table and two chairs. While Fenki looks on from a safe perch, Arioch produces delicious food for the table, a jug of wine. Fenki is hungry. As Arioch eats, he throws the creature scraps.*

*Elric is hungry and sets to. But he is still deeply suspicious.*

ELRIC: 'You are a sorcerer, that's plain. Can you get me back to my father in Melniboné?'

ARIOCH: 'Regrettably, your father is not in Melniboné. For the past two years he has been crossing the world to its very edge!'

*Arioch makes a passage in the air to show a scene of Elric's father's expedition. He heads a weary, battered army on bony horses in ragged armour.*

ARIOCH: 'Naturally, he saw the Karasim steal you. And it is to the Abyss of Karasim that he ventured. It has been a long, hard journey with many dangers on the way...'

ELRIC (*half-rising from the table*): 'Then I must go to his aid! I had no idea so many lives were at risk!'

ARIOCH (*lifts his goblet in a toast*): 'Sit down, young man. We are in limbo. Time has stopped here. But you must make up your mind. Would you return home – or aid your father? Your Uncle Ederic sits on his throne, ruling in his stead. If you were in Melniboné now, I could help you seize that power back...'

ELRIC (*puzzled*): 'Why should I do that? I'm sure my uncle rules well in my father's absence...'

*Arioch spirits them up from the ground to a rocky ledge where he throws scraps of food down to the Night Worms while Fenki hovers in fear below him.*

ARIOCH (*amused*) 'Ah, such innocence! Know you not that your uncle aided the Karasim raid just so that you could be captured, knowing your father would mount an expedition to find you?'

ELRIC (*angry*): 'Why would my uncle plot such infamy?'

ARIOCH: 'He believes with me that Melniboné will only maintain her power through strong magic and force of arms.'

ELRIC: 'My father sees such thinking as the ruin of all we stand for! If you share Ederic's opinion, why not aid *him*?'

ARIOCH: 'Because I cultivate the larger picture.'

ELRIC (*angry*): 'What mean you by that?'

ARIOCH: 'A few thousand years, and you'll learn my purpose. Never fear...'

*Elric reaches towards Arioch who backs away with a smile.*

ELRIC: 'Take me to my father! I'll thwart you yet, Sir Demon!'

*Arioch is amused and still dandified, unhurried. He smiles down at the snivelling Fenki.*

ARIOCH: 'Well, Fenki? Would you lead our young Silverskin out of here to join his father in defeat?'

FENKI (*grins in anticipation*): 'Oh, gladly, master. Gladly!'

*Arioch puts his hand on Elric's shoulder. The young albino scowls at him.*

ARIOCH: 'Then so be it!'

ELRIC: 'What cunning is this? Why would you help me?'

*Arioch smiles insouciantly:*

ARIOCH: 'Why? Because you asked! But now I grow tired of your callow rudeness. I'll leave you in Master Fenki's good hands...'

*Again Arioch vanishes.*

FENKI: 'Come, then, young master, let's be on our way before the Night Worms sense you're weaponless again...'

*Fenki leads Elric across a glinting peatbog from which sinister mist rises and in which sinister shapes shift and shamble...*

*And then, suddenly, the sun begins to rise over the bog until Elric sees figures in the distance. Fenki points and grins. The ruined, weary army of King Feneric can be seen trailing its way over the wasteland.*

FENKI: 'There. You are back in your own world. And there's your wretched father. Join him in his misery!'

*Elric begins to run towards the distant warriors.*

ELRIC: 'FATHER!'

# Chapter Three
## *To the World's Edge*

*E*LRIC RUNS TOWARDS *the ribbon of soldiery on the horizon, but as he draws closer he realises that this is a defeated army. Their armour is dented, their clothes in rags, their mounts and the horses which draw their chariots are exhausted, as are the soldiers themselves. They look up as Elric approaches and there is only misery in their faces. Elric's father is not among them.*

ELRIC: 'Melnibonéans, yes... But where's my father?'

SOLDIER: 'My prince! You live still! But you are too late!'

*A captain conveys the terrible news to Elric.*

CAPTAIN: 'Great Feneric fought heroically as a true king of Melni-boné. All around him were killed and he, too, could be dead. We had no choice but to retreat...'

SOLDIER: 'They have wind demons to aid them, and they hide deep in an abyss. Feneric's courage and skills were not enough.'

*Elric scowls and clenches his fists.*

ELRIC: 'You abandoned my father! Well I shall not.'

*He reaches towards the soldier.*

ELRIC: 'Give me weapons and I'll return to the Karasim Abyss alone!'

*Equipped with armour and weapons, mounted on a horse, Elric sets off in the opposite direction to the battered army. One warrior shouts after him –*

WARRIOR: 'Prince, your courage is not doubted. But they have sorcerous help.'

*Elric flings back over his shoulder:*

ELRIC: 'As I have, captain. As I have!'

Weeks later...

*Elric reins in his horse on a ridge, looking out across a wide plain. The plain ends at the edge of a vast abyss. The other side of the abyss is invisible. Great dark clouds obscure the far side, giving the impression, indeed, that we have reached the edge of the world.*

*The other strange sight is that of the Karasim fleet, at rest on the edge of the abyss as if they were beached in harbour. Their sails are furled and their oars shipped. These are the same ships which attacked Melniboné, but are not moored on water. They are not moored at all.*

ELRIC (*thinks*): That can only be the Karasim Abyss. I recognise their ships. And they appear to have no guards. Doubtless they take confidence from the defeat of our soldiers.

*Elric leaves his horse and weapons, and approaches the ships, using what cover he can.*

*There is no sign of the Karasim.*

ELRIC (*thinks*): They say the Karasim favour darkness to daylight. Could they all be down below the Edge of the World?

*Under cover of darkness, Elric sneaks amongst the Karasim warships. There are a few of the green men sleeping on the decks but it is easy for him to reach the 'edge of the world' and lying on his belly peer down into the gorge.*

*What he sees there astonishes him. A long stairway, occasionally becoming steps, which winds down the side of the abyss. There are brands guttering in holders every few feet. Unsuspecting Karasim come and go. But there is no sign of his father.*

ELRIC (*thinks*): I've no choice but to go down there. If my father's alive, I must find him...

*Elric begins to descend into the abyss.*

ELRIC (*thinks*): ... and save him...

Soon the young Silverskin was deep into the abyss...

ELRIC (*thinks*): Their city is carved into the living rock. Somewhere here they'll have my father, if he still lives.

*Elric sneaks past a group of Karasim warriors. They seem very cheer-
ful, having just won a great victory and captured some important
prisoners.*

*The city is huge and gloomy, full of ancient carved obsidian pillars and
walls. Carved stairways, galleries and halls. Elric sneaks through these,
avoiding green Karasim warriors and womenfolk at every turn. Great
brands flare everywhere and he uses the shadows to conceal himself.*

ELRIC (*thinks*): The Karasim celebrate their victory. But where in
  this vast warren...?

*He finds himself in a huge hall where clearly the Karasim are celebrating.
On his carved obsidian throne sits King Minak, chief of the Karasim. He
drinks from an upturned Melnibonéan helmet and two dead Melnibonéans hang in chains on the wall beside him. A scene of barbaric
horror and cruelty.*

ELRIC (*thinks*): If I only had a weapon...

*Suddenly an old woman hisses and points at him. He tries to turn and
flee but he is surrounded by Karasim warriors. He knocks one out and
grabs his sword and puts up a good fight but –*

*– he's overwhelmed and dragged before the gleeful King Minak.*

KING MINAK: 'Ha! One we overlooked. Like the silverskin we
  killed, he's pale enough to resemble those creatures who live in
  our city's depths. We'll skin him when we're done with our
  entertainment. Put him with the others!'

ELRIC (*thinks*): At least he doesn't recognise me...

*Elric is dragged through more corridors, deeper into the city, into a cham-
ber which is a kind of wide pit. Around the edges are a number of iron
cages, fancifully worked. In the centre of the pit is a block of rock and on*

*the rock is perched a sealed wine jug. Most of these cages are filled with Melnibonéan prisoners, some of them wounded. A sorry sight. Elric's father is in one of these and stifles an exclamation as Elric is thrown into the cage next to his.*

*The green warriors depart.*

FENERIC: 'My son! We are reunited in sorry circumstance. Where did they keep you?'

ELRIC: 'I was saved from death by a prince of the Myyrrhn. He told me by what infamy the Karasim employed his people...'

FENERIC: 'I know. His daughter is here with us...'

*Elric looks around in surprise. A voice comes from overhead.*

PRINCESS: 'I am Dela-Fwaar. You have seen my father?'

*Elric looks up and sees a beautiful winged girl clinging to the roof of a nearby cage. She flies down towards him and clings to the bars of the cage.*

ELRIC: 'He saved my life. But could not let me go. I escaped with supernatural help.'

FENERIC: 'How so?'

*Elric turns to his father.*

ELRIC: 'By a poorly cast spell and then with the aid of a Lord of Chaos...'

FENERIC (*brow clouds*): 'Help from Chaos always has a price.'

ELRIC (*sceptically*): 'Well, his seemed low enough.'

FENERIC: 'Our legends tell how Chaos has sought to trick us in the past.'

ELRIC: 'Without that help, I'd not be here with you, Father. Have you considered a means of escape?'

MELNIBONÉAN: 'Even if we could get out of their city, they'd hunt us down with those flying ships of theirs.'

*Elric turns to the princess:*

ELRIC: 'I owe my life to your father, lady. And my escape I owe to his library. How did you come to be captured?'

*We see a flashback scene. The princess is flying with some of her maidens when wind elementals seize them.*

PRINCESS: 'I was flying one day with my maidens when we were ambushed by wind sprites. They have always been our friends in the past.'

*The wind elementals carry the struggling princess to the Karasim Abyss.*

PRINCESS: 'They brought me here and I've been a prisoner ever since.'

*Elric's father is deep in thought.*

FENERIC (*broodingly*): 'I cannot work out the logic behind these plots.'

ELRIC (*points to wine jar*): 'It's simple, Father. Uncle Ederic seeks to rule in your stead. Secretly he's studied sorcery.'

ELRIC: ''Twas he who captured the South Wind's soul and imprisoned it in yonder jar. That gave him control over the wind elementals who in turn helped the Karasim, who were commissioned to kidnap me so that you would take those loyal to you and try to rescue me.'

FENERIC: 'But why would my brother go to such lengths?'

ELRIC: 'No doubt he believes you are too soft. That Melniboné should rule the world, attacking all potential enemies before they attack us.'

FENERIC: 'That goes against all our traditions.'

ELRIC: 'Which is why he'd be rid of all those who support those traditions...'

FENERIC (*slumps in despair*): 'So 'tis not merely our own deaths we anticipate, but the death of everything we hold dear.'

ELRIC: 'Aye, I heard their plans for us. Our torture will be their entertainment.'

FENERIC: 'We have no hope of escape.'

ELRIC: 'There is one hope, Father. All I have to do to summon the Chaos Lord is call his name.'

FENERIC: 'No! Better a few of us die than the whole world be tormented by unchecked Chaos!'

*Feneric is horrified. He reaches through the bars to grab at Elric's clothing.*

FENERIC: 'Chaos Lords can enter our world only if we invite them. That's his trick to ensnare you – and put Melniboné in his power. Believe me, my son, I have read the old books. More than once they have tried, but we have resisted. Best we perish than make alliances with Chaos!'

ELRIC (*angry*): 'Let me decide! I'll not watch my own father tortured and killed, knowing I could have helped him!'

*King Minak and some of his nobles appear on the steps above the cages. Minak is gloating with his power.*

MINAK: 'What's this? Quarrelling amongst yourselves? Well, your shouts will be louder still tonight, when our entertainments begin.'

*Minak caresses the wine jug in which is kept the soul of the South Wind.*

MINAK: 'You upstart Melnibonéans thought you could lord it over the Old Kingdoms, but now you know how foolish you were to challenge us.'

ELRIC: 'So you make alliances with our traitors and expect them to be less of a threat? You don't deserve to survive.'

*Minak is angry. He pokes at Elric through the bars with his cutlass.*

MINAK: 'That tongue will beg me for mercy before it's torn from your mouth!' (*He turns to his guards:*) 'Take the old king first. We'll show our guests what torments to expect tonight!'

ELRIC (*in rage*): 'No! Leave him or I'll –'

MINAK (*grins*): 'You'll do what? Beg me for mercy?'

*In desperation Elric throws back his head and shouts for the help of the Chaos Lord –*

ELRIC: 'ARIOCH! AID ME NOW, I BEG THEE! ARIOCH! BLOOD AND SOULS! BLOOD AND SOULS!'

MINAK (*laughs at him*): 'You pray to your useless gods. They'll not help you here.'

*But already a thick, black smoke is beginning to roil over in one corner of the cage. Minak and his men look startled.*

ELRIC: 'Arioch! Bring me the Black Sword!'

*Elric's father shouts out in one last attempt to stop his son.*

FENERIC: 'My son! No! Please do not do this!'

*But the black roiling smoke is forming a demonic, hideous shape. Already Minak is retreating up the stairs leaving his men to deal with it.*

MINAK: 'Some conjuring trick. Deal with it, men. I have business elsewhere…'

*The hideous shape gradually becomes the beautiful youth, the form Arioch always prefers on Earth. Soon he stands there, smiling, drawing the Black Sword from his scabbard.*

FENERIC: 'That sword was banished from our world centuries ago. Only evil can come of its return.'

ELRIC: 'And only evil will befall us if I do not use it now!'

*And with a single mighty blow he has cut through the bars of the cage and is already advancing upon the Karasim who ready their weapons.*

*Watched by an elegant Arioch, twice the size of a normal man, who leans against a wall, applauding, Elric takes on the whole pack of Karasim warriors who come at him from all sides. They are no match for the black blade, nor with Elric's demonic energy as he moves about the prison pit killing man after man.*

ELRIC: 'So... are you still entertained by the sight of dying men, my friends?'

*The work done, he hacks away the bars of the cages. Arioch grins in cynical delight at all this mayhem.*

ELRIC: 'There, my countrymen! You are free. Take what weapons are here and follow me.'

*Still perturbed, Feneric stoops to pick up a fallen sword then helps the princess through the mangled bars of her cage.*

ARIOCH: 'Well, Feneric, would you rather be martyred or free to be avenged on your brother?'

FENERIC: 'Why help us when Ederic serves your cause better than I ever could?'

ARIOCH: 'Ah, I am a patient demon, you see. I look to the long term. Well, I have done all I can for you here and I'll say farewell.'

*Arioch turns into fading smoke, only his cynical smile remaining for a moment. Scowling back at him, Feneric helps one of the wounded Melnibonéans up the steps of the pit. Elric, too, helps a wounded man, while the princess hovers in the air overhead.*

*In the passage outside, King Minak has assembled more warriors, but he has taken care not to be in the forefront.*

MINAK: 'That demon's abandoned them. Slay them all. Don't let one escape!'

*Elric, his father and the Melnibonéans fight their way to the outside and eventually make it to the top of the abyss, no longer pursued by the Karasim. Elric pauses on the edge of the abyss and looks down. The battle light is still in his eyes and he laughs almost like a demon himself.*

ELRIC: 'The cowards have had enough. They're reluctant to pursue us now.'

*Elric looks around but can't see the Princess Dela-Fwaar.*

ELRIC: 'Where's the princess?'

MELNIBONÉAN: 'There – there she goes – flying home!'

*They see Princess Dela-Fwaar in outline against the sky as she heads for home.*

FENERIC: 'Get rid of that blade now, my son, I beg thee. The thing's addictive. Abandon it before it's too late!'

*Elric finds this amusing but is prepared to humour his father.*

ELRIC: 'I'll not become so easily dependent on a mere sword, however powerful…' *(He looks at his father's frightened eyes.)* 'But if it pleases you, Father –'

*He hurls the black blade out over the abyss. It falls, turning and twisting, down into the clouded darkness.*

ELRIC: 'There! It's gone. It will never perturb you again.'

ELRIC: 'And now…'

*He signs to his men. Using the 'firebags' which the Karasim had used against Melniboné, they ignite brands and start setting fire to the ships.*

ELRIC: 'They'll never use these ships to pursue us.'

*His father is looking back, still perturbed, but says nothing of his thoughts.*

*The Melnibonéans, with their worst wounded on the back of Elric's horse, are now leaving the World's Edge. The ships are all blazing and they are not pursued by the Karasim.*

*Elric grins as he turns his eyes away from the scene.*

ELRIC: 'Let's for home, Father – to confront your ambitious brother.'

## Chapter Four

### *The Long Way Home*

*T*HE DREAM COUCHES. *Cymoril and Tanglebones look down on a disturbed Elric who frowns and moans in his sleep.*

TANGLEBONES: 'I fear his dream-quest does not go easily for him.'

CYMORIL: 'Does he know that he is one person in this life and another in his dream?'

TANGLEBONES: 'He is almost certainly unconscious of his two lives – just the same as your brother Yyrkoon... But some instinct drives them both to fulfil a destiny which mirrors the life they inhabit in this world.'

*They walk through the dream chambers until they find Arisand, the human girl, together with Sadric, looking down on Yyrkoon who, in contrast to Elric, has a satisfied smirk on his sleeping features.*

TANGLEBONES: 'Your brother's dream persona seems to be somewhat happier than your cousin's, Lady Cymoril.'

*They leave Yyrkoon's chamber.*

CYMORIL: 'Is there nothing we can do to help Elric?'

TANGLEBONES: 'Nothing. That, after all, is the point of dream-quests.'

*He pauses, drawing his brows together.*

TANGLEBONES: 'We can only pray to the powers of fate that Prince Elric has the resources to defeat what dangers and temptations wait for him in his dreams...'

Though there was no immediate threat from the Karasim, the Melnibonéans had fled without provisions or mounts and the march home was to be long and gruelling, while King Minak was eventually to overcome his caution as well as the loss of his sky ships and raise an army of pursuit...

By the following winter, King Feneric, his son and his warriors had reached the Melmane Marshes and Minak had their scent...

*Elric and the Melnibonéans are hiding in a forest of peculiar trees on the edge of a desolate peatbog criss-crossed by waterways. The Melnibonéans are watching the far horizon where King Minak and a large army of Karasim, mounted on ugly, white hippopotamus-like beasts, ride in pursuit.*

*Elric turns to his father.*

ELRIC: 'Father, they're catching up with us. Another few days and there will be no more than half a mile between us.'

FENERIC: 'At least our wounded are in better condition and we need fear no attack from above...'

FENERIC: '... but I agree our chances of staying ahead of them are slim unless we can lose them in the marshes ahead.'

ELRIC: 'I'm beginning to wish I had not given up that sword so readily.'

*Feneric becomes intense. He seizes his son by the shoulder and turns him round so that they are face to face...*

FENERIC: 'Believe me, my son, that blade is cursed, and cursed is any man who makes a compact with Chaos. As it is, Lord Arioch now inhabits our world by your invitation. And that can only mean disaster for some, if not for Melniboné.'

ELRIC (*grins*): 'Then let's hope it is for King Minak and the Karasim who reap Chaos.'

*The little band is now in the wide marshland. Marsh birds fly overhead and the place has a desolate beauty. The tiny figures of the Melnibonéans*

*make their difficult way from one piece of relatively dry land to another
and, very close behind, with tracker beasts of a reptilian appearance,
who can swim easily through the swamps as well as run over dry
land, comes Minak and his great army of Karasim.*

ELRIC: 'Perhaps I was hasty in ridding myself of that sword,
Father. After all, you said yourself the damage is done and
Arioch already in our world.'

FENERIC: 'No need to compound the folly, my son. We can only
hope – and press on...'

MINAK: 'There! Ahead! They'll soon be paying the price of incon-
veniencing the Karasim...'

*Soon there was nothing for it but to make a stand and prepare to fight.*

*The grim-faced band of Melnibonéans has found some relatively high
ground surrounded by a natural moat with only a narrow causeway leading to it. Here they will make their stand against the whole Karasim army.*

FENERIC: 'Here's a natural fort we can defend. At least we'll take
a good many of our enemies with us!'

*A full scale battle scene as the Karasim attack from all sides, wading or
swimming through the water, using the corpses of their own slain men
and animals to get to the mound on which the Melnibonéans stand. Elric,
Feneric and their men give good account of themselves, through the
course of the day.*

But as night falls...

MINAK: 'Fall back! The darkness only aids them. We'll attack again
at dawn!'

*The Karasim fall back. Leaving the battle-weary men of Melniboné to
count their losses – four dead and twelve wounded – and be rallied by
Elric's praise.*

ELRIC: 'Well, done, warriors of Melniboné! Each of you has sent
at least a score of Karasim down to hell!'

FENERIC: 'But can we last another night, my son?'

ELRIC: 'Only by calling on supernatural aid, Father.'

*Close-up of a weary, angry Feneric clutching at Elric.*

FENERIC: 'No! Future generations will curse us if we rely on the aid of Arioch of Chaos and that damned black blade!'

ELRIC: 'And I will curse myself if, by not summoning Chaos, I see my father die under Karasim steel!'

FIRST MELNIBONÉAN SOLDIER (*points*): 'Dawn is almost upon us and the Karasim advance!'

*Elric, scowling, backs away from where his father stands, sword in hand, rallying the weary remnants of his army.*

FENERIC: 'Stand ready!'

ELRIC (*slips down behind a rock*): 'Arioch! Bring me back the black blade, I beg thee!'

*We get a glimpse of a triumphantly smiling face as Arioch causes the Black Sword to materialise.*

ARIOCH: 'There, little mortal. Do your worst with it.'

*The Melnibonéan soldiers are forced into a tighter and tighter knot as the Karasim gain the islet and close in on them.*

FENERIC: 'They close for the kill! Where's my son? Dead already?'

*Elric, his face a mask of terrible vengeful glee, the Black Sword in both hands, suddenly appears to deal death to the astonished Karasim.*

MINAK: 'No! He wields the Chaos sword again! But he still cannot defeat so many of us. Destroy him and make the sword our own!'

*Feneric looks over his shoulder at Elric and is horrified:*

FENERIC: 'Foolish youth! You have no idea what monstrous terror that blade will bring upon the world!'

SECOND MELNIBONÉAN SOLDIER (*points into the rising sun. Out of it comes a swarm of flying soldiers. The men of Myyrrhn, led by their prince*): 'We're finished. Those are the warriors of Myyrrhn, come to join their allies!'

But the Prince of Myyrrhn was no longer in King Minak's power – and brought him not help but revenge...

*The flying warriors of Myyrrhn descend upon the Karasim with wild ferocity, so the Karasim and their king are now trapped between two groups of warriors.*

FENERIC: 'They side with us! We are saved! And you, foolish son, summoned the sword too soon!'

*Elric's crimson eyes still glow with berserk bloodlust and the sword in his hands gives off a black glow.*

ELRIC: 'You call me foolish, yet I have saved thee once, Father!'

*Then, to his astonishment, the sword twists in his hand and, against Elric's will, attempts to stab Feneric...*

FENERIC: 'What? You'd kill your own father now?'

ELRIC: 'No! The sword moves by itself! *No!*'

*With all his strength, the young Silverskin was barely able to stop the sword's movement...*

*In horror at what he had almost done, Elric hurled the Black Sword far into the marsh...*

ELRIC: 'Oh, Father! You are right! I should never have called on Chaos. I almost killed you! There, damned sword, go – never again will I seek the aid of Chaos!'

*Almost sobbing, he falls into his father's arms. The old man still looks grim as he comforts his son.*

FENERIC: 'My son, you have learned a good lesson. But even now it could be too late...'

ELRIC: 'I promise you, Father, not even at my moments of great-est trial will I summon either Arioch or the sword. From now on I will listen to your wisdom and obey...'

FENERIC: 'I hope so, my boy. There are many great trials still ahead of you. And we have yet to face the usurper who sits on my throne.'

*The winged men of Myyrrhn have routed the Karasim. King Minak is dead, his body, still with a spear in its side, is being carried off by the ragged remnants of the Karasim army. They are thoroughly defeated and getting away as fast as they can. Prince Vashntni is smiling as he puts his hand on young Elric's shoulder.*

PRINCE VASHNTNI: 'I am glad to see thee again, young Silverskin. And my daughter sends you her affectionate greetings. What now? Do you return to Melniboné to claim the throne from that traitor Ederic?'

ELRIC: 'That is for my father to decide, but I hope he will decide to go back to our homeland.'

FENERIC: 'It will be dangerous, but we must make the journey. I cannot allow Ederic to corrupt the heart of our great nation. But knowing he has studied sorcery, I am unsure if we will be successful.'

VASHNTNI: 'We can help –'

FENERIC: 'Thanks, great prince, but we Melnibonéans alone should be present when we confront my brother. Soon we'll reach Port Ishagd, where our friends the Pukwadji rule. They will lend us a ship. When we reach Melniboné we can only hope the people will rise to place me back upon my throne.'

VASHNTNI: 'You are a man of wisdom and faith, King Feneric, and I honour your decision. However, it is possible my daughter will want to visit your son. Will you permit that?'

FENERIC: 'Of course, she will always be welcome at our court.' *(He turns his head towards the north. It is time to think of the last stage of their journey.)* 'But many weeks will pass before we get there...'

# Chapter Five

## *A Gift from the Heavens*

*T*HE DREAM COUCHES *again. Cymoril and Tanglebones look down on Elric with considerable pity and frustration as he writhes in his sleep.*

CYMORIL: 'Still he is in torment. What can be happening to him, Doctor Tanglebones?'

TANGLEBONES: 'An inner conflict fills him, clearly. We can only hope he has the sense and the resources to save himself.'

*They look in on the next chamber. Sadric is leaving Yyrkoon's dream chamber but the human girl remains at his side. Yyrkoon looks decidedly happy.*

SADRIC: 'By the look of satisfaction on his face, my nephew has been thoroughly successful in his ambitions. Does this mean my son is dead?'

TANGLEBONES: 'No, sire. But clearly Prince Yyrkoon feels no threat from Prince Elric...'

*Sadric takes Tanglebones aside.*

SADRIC: 'I would not have my son die – is there nothing you can do to ensure he lives on?'

TANGLEBONES: 'I fear not, sire. For it is his soul which travels the Dream Realms, if his memory and his body do not...'

SADRIC: 'Soul and memory? Are they not the same?'

TANGLEBONES: 'The soul's memory is not the same as the mind's, my emperor...'

*Sadric walks sadly up the stairs towards his own apartments. Cymoril and Tanglebones watch him leave.*

CYMORIL: 'He would deny it, I know. But I think there is something in that old man which loves the son he claims to spurn.'

TANGLEBONES: 'He puts his nation first, however. And that is his duty...'

*The Melnibonéans are on a ship about to leave the harbour. They are saying farewell to their Pukwadji friends (see Book One) who have also attained a much greater level of sophistication than when we first met them. Feneric has his hand on his son's shoulders.*

FENERIC: 'Farewell, friend. We thank thee for the loan of this ship. It will be returned when we get to Melniboné.'

PUKWADJI MERCHANT: 'May your brother give up the throne with good grace, sire.'

ELRIC: 'I suspect Uncle Ederic will not be so generous, Father. After all, he must think us dead these many moons!'

FENERIC (*looks up at the filling sail*): 'It will be his duty to give the throne back to me, my son. And most Melnibonéans will support us in that.'

*The ship makes good speed.*

In a few days, the towers of Melniboné came in sight...

*From the deck of the ship we see the towers of Melniboné in the distance. Some are still burned out, some are restored, many have scaffolding still around them. There is a bleak, dark mood about the city.*

ELRIC: 'There she is, Father. After almost five years, she seems like a different city. So bleak and ravaged.'

FENERIC: 'Yet there must have been treasure aplenty in the public coffers to rebuild her.'

ELRIC: 'Unless Uncle Ederic keeps that treasure for himself and his cronies.'

*In the great throne room of Melniboné there is a dark, brooding, atro-phied air to all. The throne is surrounded by harsh-faced, cruel men and women, some of whom are slaves, wearing neck rings and other mana-cles. There is a barbaric feel about the place.*

*A soldier comes running in and prostrates himself before King Ederic, who half-starts from his throne, scowling...*

SOLDIER: 'My lord! My lord, the king! The rumours are true. I have come from the harbour. Your brother, his son and their warriors have just disembarked. They are returned from the quest to rescue young Silverskin!'

EDERIC: 'By Chaos! This cannot be!'

*We switch to the dockside. Feneric and Elric are waving to the cheering crowds who throng the harbour. There is no doubt that they are popular with the people.*

FIRST MELNIBONÉAN ON QUAYSIDE: 'Hurrah! The king and his son return!'

SECOND MELNIBONÉAN: 'Now prosperity, peace and justice will be restored and Ederic deposed!!!'

*The returning Melnibonéans are embraced by their friends and fellow nobles. One noble speaks to Feneric:*

NOBLE: 'Oh, lord king, you are most welcome. Your brother has taxed and tyrannised us almost since the day you left!'

FENERIC: 'Fear not, my friend, we are here to re-establish the gravity and dignity of the State.'

*News spreads throughout the city...*

*... while, back at the palace...*

EDERIC (*murmurs to one of his minions*): 'The two must die. We shall do it with poison at the welcoming feast tonight. Put out the word that they brought a disease with them from foreign parts...'

*As Elric and Feneric enter the throne room, Ederic rushes down the steps of his throne, arms spread to greet them.*

EDERIC: 'My brother! My nephew! We heard you were dead, that you had contracted a foreign disease while fighting abroad.'

*He grins a sinister welcome:*

EDERIC: 'How good it is to see you. You look as if your hardships have wearied you. Please rest. Tonight we hold a feast in your honour, to celebrate your safe return. Slaves! Take the king and the prince to their apartments!'

*Cringing slaves take Feneric and Elric through gloomy passages to their own rooms, which are dusty and poorly maintained. They pause in Feneric's apartments first...*

FENERIC: 'These rooms are so badly kept. Slaves? We had nought to do with such barbarism. An air of terror hangs over the whole palace. There is much work to be done here, my son, though I fear we'll prove little if we accuse my brother.'

ELRIC: 'First we must begin rebuilding. Justice for Uncle Ederic must wait, Father.'

*Back in the throne room, Ederic whispers to another minion:*

EDERIC: 'Ensure every dish they eat is thoroughly poisoned. Meanwhile, spread the rumour that they are sickly, fearing death...'

*Later, freshly dressed, Feneric and Elric and the surviving Melnibonéan warriors come down the stairs into the great banqueting hall where again Ederic greets them, ushering Feneric to his place at the top of the table. Elric will sit on his father's right side, Ederic on the left.*

The dinner hour, in the great banqueting hall...

EDERIC: 'Returning heroes, all! You are doubtless famished. Our chefs have prepared their best for you, dear relatives.'

*The returned heroes seat themselves at the table. They are just about to be served with the first course when the doors of the hall fly open and through them flies a newcomer. It is Princess Dela-Fwaar and she carries a sack in her hands. Ederic rises, startled from his chair, eyes wide –*

EDERIC: 'What? A new attack from the air? Guards! To arms!'

*Feneric stays Ederic with his hand, smiling.*

FENERIC: 'No, no, brother! She is our friend. The Myyrrhn aided us. Without them we should not be sitting down to meat with you tonight!'

ELRIC: 'Greetings, princess. This is unexpected but a welcome honour. Will you dine with us?'

*The princess alights on a nearby plinth, reaching into the sack as she does so.*

PRINCESS: 'Thank you, Prince Silverskin. I should be glad to accept your hospitality. But first I have a gift for your uncle… which I have carried all the way from the Edge of the World!'

*She pulls out of the sack the simple wine jar in which Ederic had imprisoned the South Wind's soul!*

EDERIC (*starts backward in terror*): 'No! It cannot be! That jar's in safe-keeping with King Minak!'

PRINCESS: 'King Minak's dead and most of his warriors with him. I took this from his prison when Silverskin rescued us from the Karasim who had captured us at your instigation!'

EDERIC: 'No! Kill her. The Myyrrhn bitch lies!'

FENERIC: 'Do not harm our guest. She tells the truth.'

*King Feneric rises from the table, pointing at Ederic:*

FENERIC: 'My brother condemns himself. That whole attack on Imrryr was his contrivance! He has enslaved you while pretending to protect you!'

EDERIC: 'This is just another trick by those who would bring terror and grief to Melniboné. Guards! Obey me. I am your true king!'

*The guards look uncertainly from one to another. Around Elric and Feneric their old guard assemble. None of them has swords or other weapons, however, whereas Ederic's guards are heavily armed.*

EDERIC (*grins in his certain power*): 'Seize them at once. They are traitors!'

ELRIC: 'We are not the traitors! It must be plain to anyone that my uncle planned this disaster! He had his own folk killed and imprisoned so he could take the throne!'

*As the armed guards close in on the little band of Melnibonéans, the winged princess flies up and hovers above them, the wine jar held over her head.*

PRINCESS: 'Fear not, friend Silverskin. I know exactly how to settle this dispute!'

*And she flings down the wine jar...*

*... which shatters on the flagstones of the hall...*

EDERIC: '*NOOOOOO!*'

*... and from it begins to pour a dense, white cloud...*

*It is Shaarnasaa, Queen of the South Wind, her soul released from the wine jar where Ederic's sorcery had kept it...*

PRINCESS: 'I free Shaarnasaa, Queen of the South Wind, whose soul was imprisoned by Ederic's foul sorcery!'

*The cloud grows and grows until it becomes the outline of a huge and lovely creature, whose hair curls around her like trees streaming in a powerful wind. Everything about her is reminiscent of the South Wind of which she is ruler.*

SHAARNASAA: 'So there is my captor, who by his bleak enchantments did trap me in a jar! I was foolish to trust him, as I had learned to trust the folk of Melniboné. But he tricked me as no doubt he has tricked you all. My imprisonment meant my servants were forced to obey him and his allies. But now I am free and shall not be tricked again!'

*Shaarnasaa moves towards the terrified Ederic, who cringes backwards.*

EDERIC: 'Men! Protect me. I command thee!'

*But the looks on the faces of his guards are hard and their eyes are like ice.*

*Shaarnasaa picks up Ederic who begins to beg her for his life.*

EDERIC: 'Spare me, I beg thee! Do not kill me, gentle queen!'

SHAARNASAA: 'It is not the habit of the South Wind's queen to kill. I am sworn to bless and to heal. But you, little mortal, are an evil thing which pollutes the earth and stains it with every breath you take.'

EDERIC: 'Th-then have mercy, gentle queen!'

SHAARNASAA: 'Oh, I am not always gentle, as you shall discover. I will carry you off to the tall peaks of the world where you can never harm immortal or mortal again!'

FENERIC: 'It is just he should be banished.'

SHAARNASAA (*looks down at Elric*): 'And you, young Silverskin, shall be remembered by all the spirits of the air. When you or your descendants need our aid, you must call on us and we shall come.'

*With this the Queen of the South Wind leaves the hall. Elric and Feneric and the winged princess all watch from the steps of the palace as she goes up into the air, bearing the shrieking Ederic with her. Black clouds boil high on the horizon…*

SHAARNASAA: 'Farewell, mortals. I go to fulfil this creature's punishment!'

*They watch as she disappears out over the water. King Feneric embraces his son, then turns to take the princess's hand:*

FENERIC: 'Princess, I thank thee most gladly for all thine aid…'

PRINCESS: ''Tis your brave son you should thank, O king. Without him, all our lives would be ended bloodily and dark villainy a shadow on our worlds and souls.'

FENERIC: 'Now, instead, this island city shall rise again in glory and beauty, to shine her light upon our lives and harmonise our destinies.' *(He turns again to Elric:)* 'And you, my son, shall continue that work when I am gone, making Melniboné's name a synonym for justice and integrity...'

ELRIC *(smiling with joy, thinks)*: Aye, but in future I shall trust fewer mortals or immortals and bring a sterner hand to our rule, lest our nation be threatened again with the doom we've so narrowly avoided.

*The sun suddenly breaks through the black clouds on the horizon, sending deep shadows across the scene as the three all turn to go back into the tower and continue the feast.*

FENERIC: 'Let's continue our celebration feast, content in knowing our enemy has met his just deserts!'

ELRIC: 'Father, with respect to Uncle Ederic's feast, perhaps we should give his chefs the first taste. Of everything.'

*We see a close-up of Silverskin as he frowns, turning away from his father and looking out towards the harbour where Melniboné's ships are at anchor.*

ELRIC *(thinks)*: While my father lives, I'll honour my vow to him. But the time might come when I shall need the help of Chaos and that black blade. It's helped us once, and saved us, too. Mayhap it will save us again in years to come.

*We make a transition now from Elric in the palace to Elric lying on the dream couch. Cymoril points at his face and Tanglebones is astonished:*

CYMORIL: 'Doctor Tanglebones! Look! His face!'

TANGLEBONES: 'The gods bless us!'

*We see Elric's face. The torment has gone from it and now he smiles.*

While in the nearby chamber...

*Sadric is bending over Yyrkoon's dream couch and the human maiden is herself deeply concerned with something, though she seems to nurse a small, secret smile...*

SADRIC: 'What ails my nephew? His expression changes!'

ARISAND: 'It seems, my lord emperor, that Prince Yyrkoon has met with an unexpected reversal in the other life.'

*Yyrkoon sits up on his bench, frowning and cursing and reaching for a goblet Arisand holds out for him.*

YYRKOON: '*Aark!* I have a miserable headache. My dream fades, as they always do. What's happened to my cousin? Did he die?'

*Tanglebones appears in the doorway, bowing to emperor and prince.*

TANGLEBONES: 'Good news, my lord. The young Prince Elric lives and is well.'

YYRKOON: 'What! How is it that he survives every dream-quest? Everyone knows how full of danger they are.'

SADRIC: 'He's well, you say. I must congratulate him on his success...'

TANGLEBONES: 'He has left already, lord emperor.'

SADRIC: 'What? Where does he go?'

TANGLEBONES: 'He told me he planned to take the Princess Cymoril – sailing...'

*Elric is steering a small boat out of the harbour. He has already passed through the great sea-maze. He has his other arm around Cymoril and she is laughing with delight – for the wind elementals are puffing the sails and making the boat scud across the harbour, leaving the great warships of Melniboné's secret harbour far behind.*

CYMORIL: 'And what did you learn in your dream, my lord?'

ELRIC: 'As usual, I don't remember. But now I command the *h'Haarshanns*, so I must have learned something, eh? More sorcerous wisdom to help me carry the burden of my destiny on the day when I become Emperor of Melniboné.'

*Yyrkoon glowers in his apartments eating voraciously from a plate of food.*

YYRKOON: 'Today my cousin delights in his survival and goes out to play, but the powerful poison of my ambition shall destroy him yet. I swear...'

*The boat is caught by a shaft of sunlight piercing the clouds and Elric laughs in his delight as the* h'Haarshanns *continue to fill his sail with air and Cymoril trails her hand in the water.*

ELRIC: 'Meanwhile, sweet Cymoril, let's enjoy the remains of the evening while we may.'

# Book Four

## *The Dream of Ten Years: The Dream of Fire*

## Dragon Lord's Destiny

# Chapter One

## *Two Ways to Forge an Empire*

*T*HE GREAT THRONE *room of Melniboné. Ancient, brooding Sadric sits slumped in the great Ruby Throne, staring with melancholy eyes down at his son and nephew who stand, at odds, before him. Elric on one side, Yyrkoon on the other. By Yyrkoon's side stands Arisand, the human woman; by Elric's side stand Cymoril and Tanglebones. On Tanglebones's shoulder sits the black raven, our old friend. Elric and Yyrkoon have almost come to blows and their companions touch their sleeves, hoping to restrain them.*

ELRIC: 'We must settle this soon, cousin Yyrkoon. I challenge you to confront me here, and not in the shadows of the Dream Realms!'

YYRKOON: 'Your physical weakness now infects your mind, cousin Elric. Surely my Uncle Sadric notices how his son grows daily less fit for power? 'Tis I who own all the qualities demanded of an emperor.'

SADRIC: 'Silence, nephew. You, too, my son. I am still Emperor and not yet dead. My concern is for Melniboné and what is best for the nation. You are tested now on the dream couches. That is where your destinies will be resolved.'

*Sadric rises from his throne.*

*As he speaks we see a panorama of Melnibonéan history. Kings and emperors in the battle armour of their calling lead men and demons to victory over human fighters.*

*We see the golden battle-barges, the flying dragons. With both of these Melniboné established her great empire.*

SADRIC: 'Our ancestors fought to establish this empire. They made the pacts with Chaos allowing us to rule for ten thousand years. For too long have the Chaos Lords been absent from that compact.'

SADRIC: 'The one who'll rule best is he who revives our power – who proves the best sorcerer!'

*Sadric sweeps from the throne room, summoning Arisand to come with him. With a backward look at Yyrkoon, she follows. Tanglebones plucks at Elric's urgent sleeve.*

TANGLEBONES: 'Come, young master. Your father is right. Your destiny will be determined on the dream couches. It is time for your last dream – your most crucial dream – the Dream of Ten Years...'

CYMORIL: 'Doctor Tanglebones speaks wisely, dear Elric.'

*Yyrkoon is already striding, grim-faced, from the throne room. He snarls one last retort behind him as he leaves.*

YYRKOON: 'You all disgust me. You stink of weakness and compromise. Aye, to the dream couches – and battle!!!'

ELRIC: 'Very well. I am ready.'

It had become obvious to all now that a kind of duel was being fought on the dream couches of Melniboné. Each party went to its own chamber. A crucial battle was about to commence, while the two chief combatants lay asleep...

*In Elric's chamber, the black crow flies from Tanglebones's shoulder to Elric's.*

ELRIC: 'So our destiny truly does lie in our dreams, Doctor Tanglebones?'

TANGLEBONES: 'So it seems, my lord. But your education will be accomplished there, also.'

CYMORIL: 'I fear you are in great danger, dear Elric...!'

ELRIC: 'Aye, I smell it in the air, Cymoril. But we must do what conscience and circumstance demands...'

While, in Yyrkoon's chamber...

*The mysterious human girl, Arisand, is diffidently suggesting something to Yyrkoon, who listens with haughty interest.*

YYRKOON: 'Bah! The weakling has so far engineered his victories by tricks and luck. How am I to ensure his defeat in this, the final dream of his initiation?'

ARISAND: 'If I can offer some simple human magic to aid you, my lord...'

YYRKOON: 'Human magic? Unsophisticated and crude compared with ours. How can that help me?'

ARISAND: 'Sometimes, my lord, the simpler spell can be more effective...'

YYRKOON (*coming round to the idea*): 'I take your meaning. What do you suggest?'

ARISAND: 'I know a way which will not make you vulnerable to dying with your avatar. And I can accompany you, if you will permit...'

*Yyrkoon drinks his potion and lies down on his couch as Arisand lays herself down beside him.*

YYRKOON: 'After all, what do I risk?'

*Meanwhile Elric's limp hand falls from Cymoril's. She looks up, her eyes filled with fear.*

CYMORIL: 'Be lucky, my lord. For I suspect luck is all you'll have on your side in this long dream...'

Then the dream roads of the multiverse opened before them...

*Both Elric and Yyrkoon set their feet on the dream roads of the multiverse. A ghostly Arisand is with Yyrkoon as both set off.*

ARISAND: 'Stay close with me, Lord Yyrkoon. I'll help your soul occupy a perfect vessel, while you yourself will be invulnerable. And be patient... for we must stay a little behind Elric if we're to be successful anon...'

*They pass along the great roads, with Elric a little ahead of Yyrkoon and Arisand, unaware that they are behind him. And behind them all flies the black crow.*

Thus all three walked the moonbeam roads, with Elric unaware of Yyrkoon and his companion, until at last the towers of ancient Melniboné lay ahead, thousands of years in their past...

*These Melnibonéan towers are not so high nor as elaborate as the ones we've left. But they are still pretty impressive.*

... when the power of the Bright Empire had reached a peak of magnificent strength.

Then Elric's dreaming soul had occupied that of his avatar, King Elrik, brother to his beautiful 'silverskin' Queen Asrid, joint ruler of this other, ancient Melniboné...

*Elric merges into King Elrik who stands hand in hand with his sister Queen Asrid, observing a great golden sailing quireme being built. These are the early types of the battle-barges which, with the dragons, form the basis of 'modern' Melniboné's power.*

ASRID: 'Another ship is added to our fleet, brother Elrik. Her holds will carry our goods far abroad, and bring back the wealth of all the world!'

ELRIK: 'Aye, dear sister Asrid. Melniboné grows rich on her trade. We have much to be grateful for. Though I once chose a more direct route to power, I know you will rule with gentle and effective wisdom while I am gone.'

*Asrid turns to Elrik/Elric embracing him with sisterly concern. The golden barge is still behind them, still being worked on.*

ASRID : 'You seek to educate yourself abroad, learning all you can from the emerging humans of the new, civilised tribes... But I cannot help fear for you, sweet brother. There are so many unknown dangers...'

ELRIK : 'The new tribes still remain wary of us. They see us as alien interlopers. Not only will I learn their customs and condition, sister... but I will act as ambassador, making friends and creating new trade for Melniboné. Such knowledge and diplomacy is worth gold in Melniboné's coffers. We shall be rich in wisdom as well as money!'

ASRID : 'I myself persuaded you to this idea, I know. The new tribes covet our wealth. We must always be ready to defend against any attack. But it is far better for our security to be liked than feared. By venturing abroad on this exploratory journey, you will forge alliances and friendships. You'll secure our strength at every point...'

*An interior chamber.*

ELRIK (*in close-up, indicates a map*): 'I leave in the morning for Pukwadji, our old ally. From there I head inland. We all know the rumours of entire civilisations to be found there, some more ancient than our own. While I am gone, you must rule here alone, wisely... as you have always done. Together we will lay the foundations of a great, peaceful trading empire...'

*The map is of the same land area as other maps we've seen, but it shows the worlds of The 'New Tribes', mostly mountains, forests, rivers and plains, with large parts marked as unknown territory. Pukwadji is plainly marked, as a territory on the coast nearest to Melniboné.*

ASRID : 'Farewell, dear Elrik. When you return, our whole fleet will be complete...'

And so the young king went forth...

... to complete his education...

… in the lands of the new tribes…

… the people who one day would emerge…

… as 'the Young Kingdoms'…

*Elric/Elrik aboard a Melnibonéan ship. He stares forward, dreaming of the adventures he is likely to have.*

*The ship docks. Elrik rides his horse off the ship onto a dock where Pukwadji people greet him with pleasure, as an old friend.*

*We see him leaving the Pukwadji city and heading off into the interior. The black crow follows him.*

*He meets friendly tribespeople (some black, some white) in simple villages and towns. He sees strange animals, some of them gigantic mammals (such as riding giraffes with black warriors on their backs), some transporting people. In one village, he sits down with a Wise Woman. Black crow perches in distant tree.*

WISE WOMAN: 'There is an ancient city, far from here, which has the same name in every human tongue. Tanelorn is a city of peace…'

WISE WOMAN (*voice*): '… there all peoples can meet and know tranquillity. There is no fighting there. Few own weapons. She has no king, but is administered by a council known as the Grey Lords… They say past, present and future come together there…'

ELRIK: 'I think I'll search out this city and see what I can learn from it…'

And so, some four years later…

*Elrik rides out over a verdant plain. It's sunrise.*

*Next panel and it's sunset. Black crow flies against the setting sun.*

ELRIK (thinks): It's time I found a good place to camp.

*Suddenly the earth begins to rise and bulge under his horse's hoofs. Elrik fights to control his horse.*

ELRIK: '? The earth! It's moving beneath me!'

# Chapter Two
## *The Heart of Creation*

Massive movement of earth as King Grome (from Book One) bursts up out of the ground.

GROME: 'Aha! Ho, little mortal! It has been a few thousand years since we last met!'

ELRIK: 'Wha –?'

*The horse throws Elric and gallops off. Elrik picks himself up as Grome reaches towards him. He draws his sword, backing away. Grome looks puzzled.*

GROME: 'Do you not recognise me, mortal? We have a compact, you and I!'

*Elrik frowns, his hand going to his brow.*

ELRIK: 'I – I – remember something – a dream, perhaps...'

GROME: 'I am Grome, king of all that is of the earth and below it. You once did me a service...'

ELRIK: 'Not I, King Grome...'

GROME *(suddenly realising he's made a mistake)*: 'Ah! What a fool I am. I forget how short-lived your folk are. No doubt I made the pact with your ancestor! Still, that pact remains...'

*Grome bears Elric/Elrik down into a great wonderful cave, full of glinting jewels.*

*He frowns trustingly down at the albino.*

GROME: 'The Black Sword has been stolen again. Uprooted from the rock in which I secured it. I suspect grave sorcery was involved. I need you to find it again...'

ELRIK: 'Again? Why should I know where it is?'

*Grome places a vast finger against Elrik's chest and smiles –*

GROME: 'Because you have an affinity for the blade. Among mortals, only a "silverskin" of your blood can handle it. If it is not returned to me, then great harm will fall upon our world.'

ELRIK: 'Doubtless, 'tis my duty to seek it. Yet how could I begin...?'

GROME: 'You must go to the city of Tanelorn and ask the Grey Lords. They will help you.'

ELRIK: 'Very well, sire. That's the city I seek, even now. Tell me how to find Tanelorn.'

GROME: ''Tis hard to find, mortal. Best I take you there myself.'

*Grome picks up Elric and starts off through the night, but now the black crow flies ahead of them. Grome pauses at one point when he sees Elric's horse.*

GROME: 'Hmm. You'll be needing him...'

*Grome picks up the startled horse and tucks it under his other arm.*

Next morning...

*Elrik is astonished by what Grome reveals to him. It is an incredibly beautiful city, with a somewhat medieval appearance, the sun rising behind it. It is Tanelorn, the beautiful. The mythical city where all warriors are said to find peace, where there is no conflict and which exists on every plane of the multiverse, perhaps in every person's heart. The black crow flies away into the city.*

GROME: 'Not all can find Tanelorn. I am blessed. And now you are also blessed.'

GROME: 'Go in peace, young mortal. Discover what you need in holy Tanelorn...'

*Grome lopes away over the horizon.*

GROME: 'Farewell. Find the Black Sword and return it to where it belongs.'

*Elric/Elrik walks through the peaceful streets of Tanelorn, leading his horse.*

ELRIK: 'I've never known a more beautiful, nor more civilised place. A man could settle here and know peace for ever...'

*A big, hearty fellow, clearly a warrior, but without weapons, grins down at Elric as the albino asks him a question.*

HEARTY: 'How can I help you, friend?'

ELRIK: 'Where shall I find the Grey Lords?'

HEARTY: 'Ho! Ho! You'll not find them! But they'll find you, friend.'

HEARTY: 'Go to any tavern and ask.'

*We see Elric entering a tavern and speaking to the landlord, who also smiles in reply, pointing behind him to a bench at which sit five old, grey men, playing chess and drinking porter.*

*Elric approaches the table and politely addresses the five old men.*

ELRIK: 'Pardon me, gentlemen. I gather you are the rulers of this city...'

FIRST GREY MAN: 'Not us, young sir. We rule nothing and no-one. In Tanelorn, citizens rule themselves.'

ELRIK: 'I'm sorry. I understood you were the Grey Lords...'

SECOND GREY MAN: 'So we are, young sir. So we are.'

THIRD GREY MAN: 'But we merely counsel – to maintain the peace of Tanelorn.'

FOURTH GREY MAN: 'Whatever is necessary, my boy. That's our only calling – to be called...'

FIFTH GREY MAN: 'How can we help you?'

ELRIK: 'I seek the Black Sword.'

FIRST GREY MAN: 'In the one place it is least likely to exist?'

FOURTH GREY MAN: 'A pretty irony. Who sent you, my boy?'

ELRIK: 'King Grome.'

FIRST: 'Our old friend.'

SECOND: 'If he trusts you, then so shall we.'

THIRD: 'You must look for the Chasm of Nihrain, far, far from here.'

FOURTH: 'Then ask the black crow...'

FIFTH: 'Only he will know...'

ELRIK: 'How will I find this place?'

LANDLORD: 'I have a map. But it is on the world's farthest edge.'

More years were to pass until...

... on the far side of the world...

*Elrik is riding through black mountains, whose peaks rise to spikes all around him.*

*A dreary, morbid place, with no apparent life. He is weary, battered and no longer has his horse. There are no arrows left in his quiver and it is clear he has been through the wars in order to get here. He has only a drop of water left in his flask.*

ELRIK (*thinks*): Food gone. Horse gone. Water almost gone. I've followed the map to the letter... Those grey ones joked with me. They sent me to my death.

*As he thinks this, he looks up and there, perched on a rock, staring at him with what appears to be amusement, is the black crow.*

CROW/SEPIRIZ: 'Good evening, Lord Elrik. And welcome to the land of Nihrain.'

*Elrik is astonished.*

ELRIK: 'You speak! Has my weariness turned my brain?'

*The crow begins to change before him –*

*– and becomes a huge black man – Sepiriz, leader of the ten Nihrainian brothers. And while you should do your best, Walter, to make him look as different from the guy in* The Matrix *as possible, it's not my fault that I thought Sepiriz up looking like this in 1963 or whenever it was. OK. Give him long hair. He was bald in the original. He's wearing a simple yellow toga. He's smiling.*

SEPIRIZ: 'I have awaited this moment for a thousand years. I am Sepiriz, leader of the ten Nihrainian brothers and the servant of the Balance. Welcome, young silverskin.'

*Sepiriz claps his hands, and around the great black rock comes a chariot pulled by a single black horse, whose hoofs do not quite touch the ground. This is one of the famous stallions of Nihrain, whose hoofs tread the space of another time and place, and can thus traverse almost any terrain in this world.*

*Helping the astonished young man into the chariot beside him, Sepiriz sets off at a wild gallop through the mountains – to the Chasm of Nihrain – which lies at the heart of the mountains and from which, from time to time, bursts flame and smoke.*

SEPIRIZ: 'Behold! My home. The great Chasm of Nihrain!'

*Elrik sits drinking wine, a finished plate of food pushed back, as he begins to tell Sepiriz why he is here. But Sepiriz raises a hand.*

SEPIRIZ: 'You need tell me nothing, young man. I know why you are here. You seek the Black Sword which Lord Arioch stole.'

ELRIK: 'It's true, Lord Sepiriz. Do you know where I can find it?'

SEPIRIZ: 'First you must come with me... to the heart of creation...'

*Sepiriz rises and leads Elrik from the cave room, out into a vaster cave, which is black glassy rock reflecting the fires which are burning far below. A series of steps and walkways leading deeper and deeper downwards.*

SEPIRIZ: '... where the Fire Elders await us.'

*The two tiny figures are dwarfed by the vast walls of the dark cavern.*

SEPIRIZ: 'The entire multiverse is ruled by Law and Chaos, the two forces held in check by the power of the Cosmic Balance... and those who serve it.'

*They have descended until they stand before a great roaring wall of fire. Elric/Elrik looks wonderingly at his flesh and clothing.*

ELRIK: 'I do not burn. Why?'

SEPIRIZ: 'This is the fire which creates life... but does not take it – look –!!!'

*The flames part to show a vision of the Cosmic Balance. It is shadowy, clearly only a representation. The shaft of the Balance consists of a black sword. The crosspiece supports a long, slender staff, imbedded with every kind of jewel. This is the Runestaff. From the jewelled ends of the Runestaff depend the two cups of the Balance.*

SEPIRIZ: 'The Balance consists of the Black Sword and the Runestaff. One is a negation of life. The other is the essence of life. Yet neither can exist without the other. The two cups of the Balance represent Law and Chaos. If one tips too far we shall have nothing but sterile Law. Too far the other way and we have unchecked Chaos. It is your destiny and the destiny of all those we call "The Champion" to fight not for Law or Chaos, but for the Balance itself.'

ELRIK: 'So one is good and the other evil?'

SEPIRIZ: 'No. The uses to which mortals and immortals put them determine whether they are used in the service of good or evil. Just as it is not possible to have life without death, so one can only exist if the other exists. It is the eternal paradox. The eternal truth.'

ELRIK: 'Why burden me with this weighty secret?'

*Suddenly a beautiful flame elemental appears in the fire, speaking to Elrik.*

FLAME ELEMENTAL: 'Because it is your destiny to serve both. You, or your descendants, will learn more in the course of the next few thousand years, but now you must find the sword which Arioch of Chaos stole from King Grome... and which we, with Grome's compliance, will place on another plane, where it will be safe for as long as need be...'

ELRIK: 'I don't understand...'

ELEMENTAL: 'You are not asked to understand. You must make the journey back towards Melniboné. There you will find the rest of your destiny and the Black Sword. When you hold the sword, a word we have placed in your mind will summon us. If you need our help, you'll receive it...'

*The flame elemental begins to fade back into the common fire. Elrik turns to Sepiriz –*

ELRIK: 'My destiny? The Black Sword? I want only to be a good and wise ruler of Melniboné...'

*Sepiriz turns away, half smiling, half in grief.*

SEPIRIZ: 'That will become a matter of opinion, King Elrik...'

*They are back in Sepiriz's chamber. Elrik looks a bit scared and distinctly puzzled.*

ELRIK: 'I did not ask you to make me a servant of the Balance, Lord Sepiriz!'

SEPIRIZ: 'None of us asks that, young king. It is fate which selects us, in spite of our wishes.'

*He raises an arm to show Elrik out of the chamber.*

*They return to Sepiriz's quarters.*

ELRIK: 'How am I supposed to seize a sword from a Chaos Lord?'

SEPIRIZ: 'You must take it from the one Arioch has given it to. Come. I'll set you on your way home.'

*Sepiriz drives his great chariot. He and Elrik occupy the chariot, which goes at a great pace, not quite touching the ground. Tethered to it is a great Nihrainian stallion, the match of the horse which pulls the chariot.*

ELRIK: 'Tell me, Lord Sepiriz. To whom did Arioch give the Black Sword?'

SEPIRIZ: 'The one who even now brings the power of your kingdom against the new tribes.'

*Elrik is astonished as Sepiriz drags on the reins to bring the chariot to a halt.*

ELRIK: '**What??**'

*Sepiriz hands the reins of the stallion to Elrik who stands bewildered beside the chariot now.*

SEPIRIZ: 'Go home. You'll discover what I mean. I can tell you no more.'

*Elrik, still baffled, mounts the stallion.*

*Sepiriz looks at him in sympathy and sadness.*

SEPIRIZ: 'Farewell, Elrik. Forgive me. I do not envy you your destiny…'

## Chapter Three
### *Changing Destinies*

B ACK THROUGH THE lands of the new tribes rode King Elrik, his mind heavy with questions, his heart full of uncertainty...

*People in the fields look up in surprise as the haunted figure rides past on the great black Nihrain steed. He is a driven creature, his red eyes blazing as he stares ahead of him.*

PEASANT: 'Greetings, master – where dost thou –? *Miggea!* He rides as if hell's horde pursues him!'

*Elrik reins in his horse as he comes upon the town where he spoke to the Wise Woman. The place has been burned to the ground.*

*The Wise Woman, wounded and half-burned herself, comes hobbling out of cover to confront him.*

WISE WOMAN: '*You!* You're the Melnibonéan! May you and your kind be cursed for ten thousand years!'

ELRIK: 'Believe me, mother, I know nothing of what you speak!'

WISE WOMAN: 'You lie! You came scouting here all those years ago. Your aim was to discover our defences. Then your war-dogs and their flying allies came upon us, taking all we owned! Kill me, if you will, Whiteface. I have nothing left to love and no loved one left to mourn me!'

Elrik rode on while the old woman hurled curses at his back.

*He is deeply troubled.*

ELRIK (*thinks*): How can Melnibonéans have done this? My gentle sister would never have permitted it.

The hills above Pukwadji Port, where the young king first came ashore so many years before...

*Elrik reins in the great Nihrain horse in the hills above the port town where he came ashore [on page eight]. The whole place has been razed to the ground. All are dead.*

*He is even more horrified. On these ruins squat the weary dragons of Imrryr, the Phoorn. They look sleepy, sated. A little venom drips from the mouths of one or two of them. From gibbets hang the bodies of Pukwadji men and women. In the harbour are golden Melnibonéan barges onto which Melnibonéan soldiers are loading their loot.*

ELRIK (*thinks*): So, it's the same here, as it has been across all their lands. Every Pukwadji dead. Every city razed and looted. I left Melniboné with my sister sworn to pursue the peace she persuaded me of. Now I find nothing but death. It can only mean she has been usurped, perhaps killed, and another ruling in her place.

ELRIK (*thinks*): But how?

*Elrik has waited until night. He sneaks past the roving Melnibonéan soldiers and the dragons and reaches the water, remounting his stallion on the beach.*

ELRIK (*thinks*): Now to see if this steed can gallop over the ocean, as Sepiriz promised –

*He rides the great black stallion over the moonlit water. The towers of Melniboné can be seen in the distance.*

ELRIK (*thinks*): Soon I'll reach my home and confront the destiny I was warned I'd find.

*Elric/Elrik has dismounted from the horse and with the reins in his hands creeps towards the towers of Melniboné.*

ELRIK (*thinks*): What possesses my Melniboné? Even here it stinks of blood and fire.

*He leaves the horse and sneaks into the city. Melnibonéan soldiers are dragging slaves ashore from ships and carrying bundles of booty home. Melnibonéans triumph in their victories, all quite mad with their filthy glory.*

ELRIK (*thinks*): The hidden passage will bring me out in the Tower of Kings where I last saw Asrid.

*Elrik sneaks up towards the Tower of Kings, where he last left his sister. He sneaks into the tower and into the great throne room. Here is a figure in black armour, face hidden by a wonderfully elaborate visor which resembles the face of a snarling dragon. It lounges in the throne, a massive black sword held in its gauntleted hands. Beside the throne is none other than the figure of Arisand, the beautiful human woman who accompanied Yyrkoon here. She is smiling in evil pleasure. A tribal king is dragged before the figure.*

FIGURE: 'So, little chief. You've seen the power of Melniboné. Swear loyalty to us. Promise the empire half your wealth, or die at the point of my blade!'

CHIEF: 'Melnibonéans were once fair and honourable people. We traded with you because we chose to. Now you are nought but thieves and murderers, using your dragons and your ships against weaker foes. I'll promise you nothing!'

*Figure rises from the throne and holds the great black battle-blade out by the blade, offering the hilt to the barbarian.*

BLACK ARMOUR: 'Would you kill me, little mortal? I offer you the opportunity...'

*Hesitantly, knowing he is being tricked, but feeling he has nothing to lose, the mortal stretches his hand towards the hilt of the blade...*

*He grasps the hilt and then yells in pain and terror.*

CHIEF: 'Aaaaaaaaaaaaah! Oh, no, the thing sucks my very soul from my body. Aahhh. P-please – n-no...!'

*He writhes, unable to release his hand from the sword as the blade sucks his soul from him.*

BLACK ARMOUR: 'Ha! Ha! Only I can handle that black blade and live! You shall die, little mortal! Your body will feed my dogs. Your soul will feed my sword!'

*Chief sobs as the sword drinks his soul. Not every Melnibonéan can stand watching this. Some, who seemed hardened, now turn away.*

CHIEF: 'Aach! My soul – n-not my s-soul...'

BLACK ARMOUR: 'Ha! Ha! Ha! The reality's worse than you could imagine, eh? It always was!'

*And Elrik, horrified, sneaks away, back into the shadows.*

ELRIK: 'I can do nothing against such evil sorcery. I must discover what has happened to my sister... surely Dyvim Karm, Lord of the Dragons, will know...'

*Melnibonéan guards spot Elrik. He begins to run.*

GUARD: 'Who's that? Some spy?'

ELRIK: 'If they've killed my sister, then I'll share her fate.'

*Elrik is pursued through the corridors by the soldiers. At one point he's surrounded by guards and fights them. He gets to his horse and rides as fast as the great Nihrain stallion will carry him, the pursuing guards in disarray.*

GUARD: '*STOP HIM!*'

*He's riding across the island when he looks back and sees a great shape rise into the sky behind him. It is one of the Melnibonéan dragons.*

ELRIK: 'And now they send a dragon against me! This is a nightmare!'

*He lies flat across his horse's neck as overhead one of the huge Melnibonéan dragons flies in rapid pursuit. He's riding over the ocean again, the dragon getting closer and closer.*

*They have reached land. The horse rears up as the dragon lands in front of it.*

*It opens its maw, poison and fiery venom bubbling from it and falling with a fiery splash to the ground.*

ELRIK: 'I cannot defeat a dragon. But I can die like a Melnibonéan king!'

*The dragon pauses, surprised.*

DRAGON: *'You speak the language of the Phoorn? You are our kin?'*

ELRIK: 'Aye. I expect no mercy from you. I have seen what you have done to the mainland tribes...'

DRAGON: *'You are the Silverskin. We have a bond, you and I. I am Flamefang, oldest of the Phoorn.'*

*Elrik dismounts and reaches a hand to Flamefang's snout.*

ELRIK: 'Bond?'

FLAMEFANG: *'The silverskins saved us from limbo. Our loyalty is to you first. Many Phoorn now sleep in our caves. They are weary of their work. But I have slept longest and am ready to serve my brother. How can Flamefang help?'*

ELRIK: 'I do not yet know. Return to your cave. I will call you if you are needed. Now I go to seek allies amongst the new tribes...'

*The dragon turns to leave, but Elrik stays it for a moment –*

ELRIK: 'Stay, brother. Tell me what has become of my sister Asrid. Less than ten years ago I left her ruling a peaceful kingdom – and now that black-armoured creature rules in her place...'

*Flamefang pauses.*

FLAMEFANG: *'I cannot help you, brother. I know nothing of the court politics. We merely serve whoever rules – unless, like me, we remember certain loyalties...'*

ELRIK: 'Is Dyvim Karm still Lord of the Dragon Caves?'

FLAMEFANG: *'He fled when he refused to lead us against the new tribes. His brother Dyvim Nir now commands us. But most already sleep. We have become weary with all this warfare. And now – farewell! Call me when you need me!'*

*The great shape of the dragon ascends into the dawn sky, leaving Elrik puzzled, confused and dismayed.*

Only a few days later...

*Elrik comes upon a Melnibonéan, ragged and starving, and greets him with joy.*

ELRIK: *'Dyvim Karm!* I've sought you everywhere. I feared you killed.'

*The two men embrace with some joy.*

*We next see them sitting beside a fire while Dyvim Karm eats part of a rabbit with some gusto.*

DYVIM KARM: 'It happened so swiftly. One moment your sweet sister enjoined us all to peace. The next, this creature in black armour, wielding that filthy sword, was on the throne. Those who refused to serve the Black Armour lost their souls to the sword. Your sister, I fear, is murdered. All I could rescue in my flight was my Dragon Horn...'

ELRIK: 'We must find allies to attack and reconquer Melniboné. What's more, I am sworn to take that black sword back to its rightful keepers.'

Through the coming months, King Elrik sought the remnants of the mainland tribes, trying to create an alliance powerful enough to defeat the usurper...

*Elrik is in the mountains again. He is meeting with the remnants of various barbarian tribes who have been attacked and defeated by the Melnibonéan forces.*

*One of the tribal leaders, the most striking and forceful, is Queen Bisrana, who is Queen of the Shazaar. She steps forward to confront Elrik.*

QUEEN BISRANA: 'I am Bisrana, Queen of the Shazaar. Why should we trust one of your blood?'

ELRIK: 'Because we have common cause. My cousin, Dyvim Karm, has told you how Melnibonéan power was stolen from my sister.'

*Chief Thokor of the Jharks now springs up.*

THOKOR: 'I, Thokor of the Jharks, would know what you offer us.'

ELRIK: 'A pact between our nations. I played no part in my people's attack on yours.'

*King Ralyn of the Dhar tribe now speaks:*

KING RALYN: 'I am Ralyn of the Dhars. You promise us loot, which will repay us for what has been stolen.'

ELRIK: 'I want none of my people needlessly killed. He who wears the black armour is responsible for what has happened. I do not believe he is of my blood.'

*The chiefs are in conference, talking amongst themselves while Elrik waits to one side.*

*Eventually Queen Bisrana steps forward from the gathering and addresses Elrik.*

BISRANA: 'We'll join you in this attack. But we want our fair share of the booty.'

ELRIK: 'You promise you'll leave the population and the buildings unscathed?'

BISRANA: 'Only those who threaten us will be harmed.'

*Elrik embraces Queen Bisrana.*

ELRIK: 'Then we are agreed. One dragon at least will aid us in the attack. We must strike suddenly and soon, before word of our plans gets back to Imrryr.'

# Chapter Four
## *Bitter Vengeance*

*E*LRIK, BISRANA AND *the other leaders of the barbarians look down on a secret bay as the ships assemble. it is a large fleet of miscellaneous ships, including a captured golden battle-barge.*

BISRANA: 'We are ready. Let us take our revenge!'

ELRIK: 'The majority of the dragons now sleep, exhausted. It is the best time to strike. We'll have one dragon to aid us – whom Dyvim Karm here will summon with his horn.'

BISRANA: 'This captured battle-barge will lead our fleet. We'll deceive their watchmen long enough to breach their defences.'

DYVIM KARM: 'The last thing they'll be expecting is a counter-attack.'

*Elrik turns to Queen Bisrana and addresses her fiercely –*

ELRIK: 'But remember – I will confront the thing in black armour. I have a strange instinct… I believe I know who he is.'

*The ships sail out to sea towards the distant towers of Melniboné. Inset of Elrik on the deck of the golden battle-barge, staring fiercely towards the towers.*

*From the POV of Melnibonéans. In astonishment they watch the ragged navy approach (this is in the years before the sea-maze). Hastily they scramble to defensive positions, some rubbing sleep-filled eyes, some buckling on bits of armour.*

*A Melnibonéan soldier runs into the throne room where Black Armour sits, his black sword still with him.*

SOLDIER: 'Sire! A fleet attacks us!'

BLACK ARMOUR: 'What? I thought those savages had learned their lesson.'

FIRST CAPTAIN: 'It's too late to ready the battle-barges. We must fight them as they come ashore.'

SECOND CAPTAIN: 'We expected no attack. We have no defences ready.'

BLACK ARMOUR: 'We'll defeat them easily enough...'

*And then the barbarian invaders are pouring ashore, led by Queen Bisrana and the other chieftains...*

*Behind them, offshore, the golden barge lies at anchor.*

*On it, Dyvim Karm raises the Dragon Horn to his lips. Elrik beside him speaks grimly.*

ELRIK: 'Now, Dyvim Karm. Blow the note to summon my brother Flamefang!'

*The barbarians clash with the startled Melnibonéans. They pursue them into their towers. Black Armour has sneaked away into the highest tower while his men are fighting.*

BLACK ARMOUR: 'NO!'

*He climbs the steps to the throne room, where Arisand stands, smiling slightly.*

BLACK ARMOUR: 'You promised me triumph! Now we face defeat.'

ARISAND: 'Come now, mortal – you must keep your nerve. I made you the gift of the Black Sword. You know how to use it best.'

BLACK ARMOUR: 'If this body is killed, then I die also!'

ARISAND: 'I promised you I would save you from that fate. I keep my promises.'

*A great shadow passes against the window outside. Black Armour turns when he sees it.*

BLACK ARMOUR: 'What's that?'

*Outside, flying around the Tower of Kings is Flamefang, with Elric on his back.*

*Black Armour runs out to the balcony and looks down. In the streets the barbarians are driving the Melnibonéans back into the tower. One of the chieftains flourishes a brand.*

FIRST CHIEFTAIN: 'Burn the cursed city to the ground!'

BISRANA: 'We swore we'd not fire Imrryr.'

SECOND CHIEFTAIN: 'You think he'll keep his word to us? Burn the whole foul place and every Melnibonéan with it!'

*Queen Bisrana makes an effort to stop the chieftain but she's held by some of his men as he and other warriors throw burning brands through windows where women and children can be seen drawing back in terror.*

*Elrik sees this from the back of his dragon and is horrified.*

ELRIK: 'The barbarians break their word!'

*He sees Black Armour staring up at him from the balcony and, in a wild leap, sword in hand, jumps from the back of the dragon to the balcony.*

ELRIK: 'Flamefang! Go! Aid my people! Go! Help them drive off the barbarians if you can!'

BARBARIANS: 'KILL!'
  'Kill them all!'
  'Above us! Look to your lives!'

*Flamefang swoops down on the barbarians and their fleet, his fiery venom destroying everything it touches.*

BARBARIANS: 'He circles again!'
  'Fly, brothers! To the ships while we can!'
  'The monster comes too late to save their precious city, anyway!'

*Meanwhile, back on the balcony of the Tower of Kings, Elrik confronts Black Armour...*

ELRIK: 'You! One thing I can do – and that is kill the one who has betrayed everything Melniboné stood for!'

*So fierce is Elrik's attack that he drives the black-armoured figure back into the throne room where Arisand still watches, her face full of nervous glee.*

*Black Armour pauses at the throne.*

BLACK ARMOUR: 'You are more powerful than I guessed.'

*He flings the sword at Elrik's feet.*

BLACK ARMOUR: 'There. The sword is yours. Kill me if you will...'

ELRIK (*thinks*): I know this trick – and yet...

*He stoops to pick up the sword.*

ELRIK (*thinks*): I have no choice but to take the risk and kill this foul being who has brought my sister and my kingdom to disgrace!

*His hand reaches towards the sword.*

*Elrik's hand closes on the grip.*

*He is astonished. The sword does not harm him.*

ELRIK: 'The sword. It does not harm me!'

BLACK ARMOUR: 'What??'

*Black Armour's head whirls to where Arisand still stands.*

BLACK ARMOUR: 'Arioch! You swore only I could handle the sword!'

*Arisand smiles quietly, her great eyes full of malice and a kind of triumph.*

ARISAND: 'No, mortal – I swore only that one of *your blood* could handle the sword.'

*Then Elrik lunges forward, driving the sword towards the heart of Black Armour.*

ARISAND: 'But fear not. It suits my plan to save you before this vessel dies...'

*We see a ghostly human form pulled out of the armoured figure by Arisand, who shows enormous, supernatural strength as she does so.*

*Just as Elrik plunges the blade deep into the armour. To terrible effect.*

*As the ghostly form escapes, a great scream comes from the black helmet.*

ELRIK: 'There, usurper! Die as you deserve!'

*He lets his grip on the sword fall away as he stands listening in astonishment.*

ELRIK: 'That scream! It was a woman's scream. What's this? More sorcery?'

*The figure in black armour collapses, the black blade still sticking into the breastplate where its heart should be.*

*Unnoticed, Arisand opens a path to the moonbeam roads, all of which are ghostly.*

*Leading her ghostly charge, she steps out onto one of the roads. Elrik kneels beside the fallen figure, pulling off the helmet.*

ELRIK: 'Let's see the face of this filthy creature!'

*Arisand and the other figure disappear out onto the moonbeam roads.*

*Elrik pulls off the helmet.*

*There is the sweet face of his sister. Her eyes of full of tears and she is clearly dying.*

ELRIK: 'Asrid! My sister! This cannot be!'

ASRID: 'The sword takes my soul, brother. I was possessed by a demon. It was not I did those terrible deeds... Aaah. My soul! My soul!'

ELRIK (*in rage and agony*): 'No! **No!!!**'

ELRIK: 'I have killed my beloved sister! I have murdered my kin!'

*Dyvim Karm comes running up the steps into the throne room.*

DYVIM KARM: 'My lord Elrik! The barbarians have fired the city. They have broken their oath to you!'

*Elrik is in tears. He pulls the sword from his sister's body. She is dead.*

ELRIK: 'I have killed my sister. What care I if oaths are made and broken? They are meaningless sounds in the empty void…'

DYVIM KARM: 'Imrryr burns, my lord. There are women and children in those buildings.'

*Elrik looks up, his eyes full of grief.*

ELRIK: 'I want this black blade gone. I wish it banished forever from this realm. Where are the Fire Elders? They said they would come when I held the Black Sword!'

ELRIK: 'Well here it is! Now, Fire Elders, keep your word! Abolish this filthy thing to where no mortal hand can ever find it again!'

*Dyvim Karm backs away in awe as the Fire Elders, creatures of pure flame, manifest themselves in the room, reaching out to take the blade from Elrik.*

FIRE ELDER: 'Here we are, King Elrik. You have done us a great service which we shall not forget.'

*Elrik hands a Fire Elder the black blade.*

ELRIK: 'Take it. Make sure it is never again seen in Melniboné.'

FIRE ELDER: 'As long as one of your blood never holds it, it will do no further harm in this realm.'

ELRIK: 'None of mine will ever touch such a filthy thing, I swear! But this, too, I swear – that I shall keep no bargains with humans. Henceforth I shall rule by blood and fire, making Arioch and the Dukes of Hell my allies! All others shall bow the knee in vassalage to Melniboné!'

*Dyvim Karm speaks urgently:*

DYVIM KARM: 'My lord! The towers still burn. Is there nothing these allies can do against those flames?'

*The Flame Elder turns to look at Dyvim Karm.*

FLAME ELDER: 'Fear not, mortal. We shall gather the flames to our own bodies and take them with us when we leave.' (*He turns to Elrik:*) 'Farewell, young King Elrik. We sorrow for your lost sister. But I fear your own destiny is not a happy one...'

*Elrik's face screws up with pain and anger as he watches the Flame Elders fade and leave.*

ELRIK: 'Happiness? That's no longer a quality we of Melniboné shall seek. I'll keep the compact made with Arioch. He shall have his share of blood and souls! Henceforth we shall be strong and merciless and our pleasures will be of the cruellest kind!'

*Dyvim Karm goes to the balcony and looks down. He turns with astonishment to address King Elrik –*

DYVIM KARM: 'My lord king! The fires are out. The barbarians retreat. Imrryr is saved!'

*We see a close-up as Dyvim Karm's face goes from astonished delight to horrified surprise –*

DYVIM KARM: 'Elrik? My lord?'

*Elrik has collapsed on the flagstones of the throne room, beside his sister.*

*A black crow perches on the throne itself, looking down at them.*

*Then it spreads its wings and flies out of the window.*

*Dyvim Karm looks up as Melnibonéan soldiers rush into the throne room.*

DYVIM KARM: 'Quickly... our king has fainted from exhaustion...!'

MELNIBONÉAN SOLDIER: 'And our queen?'

DYVIM KARM: 'She's dead. And her soul, I fear, is forever in limbo. This is the end of the Melniboné she hoped to create. From this day on, our history darkens...'

*Dyvim Karm returns to the window and looks out across the blackened streets towards the harbour where the battle-barges lie at anchor.*

DYVIM KARM: '... from this day on, we begin the making of an empire.'

# Epilogue

T HE DREAM HAS ended, but the dreamers have yet to wake...

*We are back at the dream couches. Tanglebones is distraught. He tries to lift Elric's head. He takes a cup from Cymoril's hand.*

TANGLEBONES: 'This is what I feared, Lady Cymoril.'

CYMORIL: 'What is it, Sir Tanglebones?'

*Tanglebones can't get the still-sleeping Elric to take the potion.*

TANGLEBONES: 'If he was killed in the dream, the chances are he is dead – or at least in limbo. Yet this is strange.'

TANGLEBONES (*looks up, frowning*): 'He still breathes. It's as if he refuses to wake. As if something happened in his dream adventure which was so terrible, he has no will to come back to life!'

*Cymoril turns as a shout comes from the nearby dream chamber, where Yyrkoon went at about the same time as Elric.*

UNSEEN VOICE: 'Dead! No question of it!'

CYMORIL: 'Yyrkoon – dead? But –'

*Cymoril leaves Elric's chamber – and enters Yyrkoon's.*

*Her eyes widen in astonishment. Yyrkoon has a goblet in one hand and is leaning heavily on his elbow, clearly groggy, but definitely not dead.*

YYRKOON: 'He – she – Arioch can't be...'

*But it is Arisand who lies sprawled on the flagstones.*

*And Yyrkoon rises weakly, in horror.*

YYRKOON: 'He promised me triumph –'

*Yyrkoon sits on the bench, his hand to his chest, exactly on the spot where Elrik plunged the Black Sword into Black Armour's body.*

YYRKOON: '– and brought me death…'

*Yyrkoon puts his hand to his head.*

YYRKOON: 'Ah. Memory fades. The dream – I no longer recall it…'

CYMORIL: 'Whatever scheme you and this human woman concocted, brother, it clearly failed again.'

*Cymoril hurries from the room, back to Elric's chamber.*

*Where Tanglebones is reviving a very faint, weak Elric, whose eyes will scarcely open.*

TANGLEBONES: 'He revives – but barely…'

ELRIC: 'Arioch. He possessed my sister. No – two beings possessed her – who was the other…?'

*Tanglebones tries to soothe his master.*

TANGLEBONES: 'My lord, you must not tax yourself. It was but a bad dream.'

*Elric glares up at Tanglebones.*

ELRIC: 'No! It was all too real. All too dark and terrible. It was how we let ourselves become what we are today. Creatures bereft of mercy or real happiness…'

*Cymoril speaks soothingly to him:*

CYMORIL: 'Some of us feel it is a mercy you are saved from oblivion, my lord. And some of us are happy that you live.'

*Elric softens as he takes Cymoril's hand.*

ELRIC: 'Oh, sweet love. Yet you and I are still Melnibonéans. Still what our history has made of us…'

CYMORIL: 'Cannot our will overcome such things, my lord?'

ELRIC: 'I do not know. That terrible dream. It fades now. Yet I seem to have learned lessons which permeate my very bones. No matter what our will, we must always be thwarted by dark destiny.'

CYMORIL: 'No, Elric. No, my lord. Our love will overcome any so-called "destiny". We can carve a new fate for ourselves. One that allows our love to flourish.'

ELRIC: 'I hope so, sweet Cymoril. I hope so.'

*But when we look into his face, into his brooding eyes, it is clear he holds no such hope.*

*There is a step in the corridor. We catch a glimpse of Sadric as he comes towards the dream chambers.*

Emperor Sadric stared at his son without speaking.

He seemed to be reading something there.

It was as if he understood what had happened in that dream...

*Sadric enters, pausing at the entrance to the dream chamber.*

Pausing for only a moment, he made his way to the next dream chamber, occupied by his nephew...

*Sadric looks down at Yyrkoon, who is snarling, though still very groggy. He looks at the body of Arisand still sprawled there.*

SADRIC: 'What happened here?'

YYRKOON: 'The bitch – or whatever the creature was – betrayed me. She said she'd aid me against that bloodless weakling. Instead, she died. I – I cannot remember how...'

SADRIC: 'You killed her? You killed my only consolation?'

*Yyrkoon simply cannot remember what happened. He tries to explain himself to Sadric, but cannot.*

YYRKOON: 'N-no, my lord – at least, I d-do not think so...'

Wordlessly, the emperor turned his back on his nephew and returned to where his son still tried to rid himself of his last, long dream...

*Sadric looks down on Elric. He is not smiling. It is almost as if he is reluctant to voice the words he speaks. But speak them he does...*

SADRIC: 'The tests are complete. The duel is done. You have won, my son. Though it will bring you scant satisfaction, you will be the next emperor of Melniboné.'

There was no more to be said. Sadric returned to his books and his solitary misery.

Elric's eyes still carried the shadows of that terrible dream.

He felt no triumph in his father's decision. Yet there was some comfort in the embrace of the beautiful young woman beside him...

*Cymoril embraces Elric, who is now pretty much recovered, though there are still shadows in his eyes as he tries to forget, rather than recall, the dream he has emerged from.*

CYMORIL: 'It means we can be wed, my lord. As emperor and empress we shall bring a new era of prosperity and power to Melniboné. We'll learn, as you say, to live with the humans of the Young Kingdoms, to win their friendship and offer them ours...'

ELRIC: 'Yet we shall still be Melnibonéans, my darling. We shall still be what we are. For Chaos remains our ally.'

*Tanglebones turns his head suddenly, for he thinks he sees something behind him.*

*There, hanging like smoke in the far corner of the chamber, is a triumphantly smiling face. It is the face of Arioch, but what we can see of the body seems to bear the clothes of Arisand.*

*Tanglebones frowns, lost in his own thoughts, and a black raven comes to perch again on his shoulder.*

*Elric turns to look at the old seer.*

ELRIC: 'But I brood too much, eh, Doctor Tanglebones?'

Then the young prince was on his feet, shrugging off his melancholy as the dreams of doom faded from his memory.

*Elric is smiling again. He has risen and has his arm around the delighted Cymoril.*

ELRIC: 'Come, my dear Cymoril. Let's to our horses and the clean sweet air again. I have a fancy to taste the simple pleasures.'

*He and Cymoril leave the room, laughing joyfully.*

*Leaving Tanglebones who, in his thoughtful wisdom, watches them go.*

TANGLEBONES: 'Aye, my lord. Taste them while you may. And pray they last – as I shall also pray.'

For the old man feared that tragedy and death would soon fall upon Melniboné, and when they came, they must surely signify…

*The End*

# And So the Great Emperor
# Received His Education...

LEARNING HIS WIZARD'S craft on the dream couches, where one might live a thousand years in a single night, Elric was trained in the ancient traditions of Melniboné's Sorcerer Kings.

No mortal could learn all there was to learn in a single lifetime, and thus it was that the lords of the Bright Empire conceived a means by which their sons might gain all their inherited wisdom. A wisdom of millennia.

These sons (and sometimes daughters) dreamed the long dreams of Imrryr the Beautiful, the Dreaming City. They made pacts with the great elementals of fire, water, air and earth.

In these dreams, while they lay upon the dream couches of the Dreaming City, they consorted with demons, with angels and with violent, desperate men, with cruel warlocks, powerful witches and all manner of supernatural beings.

In these dreams they walked with the denizens of hell and made bargains with the Lords of Chaos, even indulged in compacts with the Dukes and Duchesses of Law.

In sublime terror they made love to the undying. With horrible joy they made war against the never-to-be-born. They explored the corridors of measureless palaces and wandered through unmappable landscapes without horizon or end.

They journeyed beneath the earth, into the lands of sunless, crystalline beauty, where vast, glowing rivers roared and strange, unhuman beings ruled.

They walked the moonbeam roads, the astral roads between the worlds. They fell into burning suns and froze on silver moons. They learned the histories of all their pasts and all their futures.

In these dreams no pain was unfamiliar to them. No pleasure

went untasted. Dream followed dream. Knowledge was heaped on knowledge. Terror on terror and joy on joy. And by this means they learned their magic, their power over all men and all the forces of nature. They learned to summon great winds, to throw fire, to raise the waters, to break open the very surface of the earth. They learned to destroy the living and to resurrect the dead. They learned to survive dangers no ordinary mortal might ever hope to experience and live...

Not all survived. Many died on the dream couches, trapped in some nameless spell, victims of some voracious immortal, torn apart by unimaginable creatures, destroyed by some appalling force.

Of course, no mortal brain could absorb so many experiences or hold so many memories and remain sane and it was frequently argued that there were few sane emperors of Melniboné.

Was Elric sane?

Elric of Melniboné, son of Sadric, would never be certain of his own sanity, nor indeed of his own moral choices. These were questions forever in his conscious mind, filling his waking hours, just as the terrors and wisdom of his dream-quests remained in his *un*conscious mind, to disturb his sleeping hours.

Elric of Melniboné had received the most rigorous education of all. For almost every hour of his lifetime he had lived ten years upon the dream couches. Those who saw a young man, just reaching maturity, could not possibly know, unless they had experienced it themselves, what an ancient near-immortal dwelled within.

Yet in some ways, the ordinary ways of the world, its certainties and its deceits, Elric *was* a young man. He had a young man's ambitions, a young man's ideals, a young man's need for spontaneous action, for love and for adventure.

Elric's dreams had not dulled his taste for life. They had taught him sorcery more than teaching him conventional manners. Though he had the courtliness and grace taught to all Melnibonéan aristocrats, though his own stock of irony was not small and his own powers of observation not minor, yet he was still an untried creature, whose vast sorcerous power was balanced by his own moral uncertainties.

Elric's dream-quests were recalled as nightmares, the vaguest of disturbing memories, interruptions of the sleeping mind. But what he had learned on those quests remained – sorcerous and military arts of complex depth and variety. Arts which something in him feared to use, for he instinctively understood their destructive power.

When one day Elric's father died suddenly, brought low by deep melancholy and too many disappointments, having failed to reinvigorate an empire which had grown lazy with its own great might, Elric was forced to consider his inheritance.

He was now natural successor to the throne of ancient Imrryr. A responsibility he was not sure he could fulfil.

And Elric was not the only one to doubt his own abilities. Some said he was not suited for the task, that he had deficient blood, impaired strength, weak eyes and an unstable mind, such as marked earlier, so-called 'Silver Emperors', the white-haired, crimson-eyed albinos whose strange condition marked them out in the long line of sorcerer emperors and empresses.

Some, who supported another contender for the throne, said this 'Silver Emperor' who conversed with humans as if they were equals, who had human friends as well as alliances with demons, would bring the empire down. It was predicted, they said (though these predications, when challenged, proved to be somewhat numinous). Elric's succession would cause the defences of Imrryr to tumble, they said. He would allow the human hordes to flood in. These hordes had grown powerful and longed to sack the city of the Dragon Lords. They hated these lords, who had ruled them for so many millennia. They longed to loot, to destroy, to rape. These voices warned that Elric was fated to be the very last of his ancient line, a prince of ruins and desolation.

Even Melniboné's greatest power, the Phoorn, asleep in the dragon caves far below the Dreaming City, dragons who dripped fiery venom upon their enemies, even these would not defend the Bright Empire against the threat of those nations they called the

Young Kingdoms, the upstart nations of a new and changing world.

Some of Elric's own party, often the wisest, argued that Melniboné had grown too certain of herself, too proud to make alliances with those who refused vassalage, too arrogant to call upon the emergent nations and respect them as brothers, rather than clients. In her lofty pride lay the seeds of her own doom. Even as she rose to her greatest power, Melniboné was already facing destruction. But this was not talk Elric's enemies cared to hear. Rather, they blamed him alone for any dangers Melniboné might face. And they championed his cousin, the swaggering warrior prince Yyrkoon, who promised them glory, who promised them new wealth, who promised them a kind of immortality.

Yyrkoon, too, had learned his sorcerous craft upon the dream couches, though not with Elric's patience. He saw that his power lay not in wisdom but in strength. He placed all his ambitions in the blade of his sword.

And so they schemed, these various parties – some for Elric, some for Yyrkoon, some for themselves. There were those who loved their strange country as passionately as any patriot loved their country, there were some who cared little for Melniboné, but sought personal advancement. There were others who calculated the security of their nation and saw Elric as too weak to defend them, while loving the man himself. Some hated him and his dependence on drugs to survive at all, yet revered his lineage as the true blood of ancient Melniboné. They would support him no matter what arguments were brought against him. Still others spoke of ridding Melniboné of kings and aristocrats and founding a fresh republic, as had once ruled the Dreaming City.

And all of these and more gathered at the great Court of Emperors, to scheme behind their hands, to whisper of betrayal and support, of wisdom and folly, and plot the dominance of this party or that. Over all of them, the young emperor must preside, with due ceremony and pride. Over all of them he must appear dispassionate and distant, as his blood demanded. Over all he must exert his enormous power, a power he did not even understand as yet.

Soon he would begin to learn of that power. But meanwhile, a great Masque must be played out, for the entertainment of the fresh-crowned emperor, for the satisfaction of tradition. A masque which, some would later say, predicted much that was to occur to bring about the doom of Elric's long line and the destruction of the Dreaming City...

*Elric of Melniboné*

*To the late Poul Anderson for* The Broken Sword *and* Three Hearts and Three Lions. *To the late Fletcher Pratt for* The Well of the Unicorn. *To the late Bertolt Brecht for* The Threepenny Opera *which, for obscure reasons, I link with the other books as being one of the chief influences on the first Elric stories.*

# Prologue

This is the tale of Elric before he was called Womanslayer, before the final collapse of Melniboné. This is the tale of his rivalry with his cousin Yyrkoon and his love for his cousin Cymoril, before that rivalry and that love brought Imrryr, the Dreaming City, crashing in flames, raped by the reavers from the Young Kingdoms. This is the tale of the two black swords, Stormbringer and Mournblade, and how they were discovered and what part they played in the destiny of Elric and Melniboné – a destiny which was to shape a larger destiny: that of the world itself. This is the tale of when Elric was a king, the commander of dragons, fleets and all the folk of that half-human race which had ruled the world for ten thousand years.

This is a tale of tragedy, this tale of Melniboné, the Dragon Isle. This is a tale of monstrous emotions and high ambitions. This is a tale of sorceries and treacheries and worthy ideals, of agonies and fearful pleasures, of bitter love and sweet hatred. This is the tale of Elric of Melniboné. Much of it Elric himself was to remember only in his nightmares.

– The Chronicle of the Black Sword

# Book One

On the island kingdom of Melniboné all the old rituals are still observed, though the nation's power has waned for five hundred years, and now her way of life is maintained only by her trade with the Young Kingdoms and by the fact that the city of Imrryr has become the meeting place of merchants. Are those rituals no longer useful; can the rituals be denied and doom avoided? One who would rule in Emperor Elric's stead prefers to think not. He says that Elric will bring destruction to Melniboné by his refusal to honour all the rituals (Elric honours many). And now opens the tragedy which will close many years from now and precipitate the destruction of this world.

# Chapter One

## A Melancholy King: A Court Strives
## to Honour Him

I T IS THE colour of a bleached skull, his flesh; and the long hair
which flows below his shoulders is milk-white. From the tapering, beautiful head stare two slanting eyes, crimson and moody,
and from the loose sleeves of his yellow gown emerge two slender
hands, also the colour of bone, resting on each arm of a seat
which has been carved from a single, massive ruby.

The crimson eyes are troubled and sometimes one hand
will rise to finger the light helm which sits upon the white locks:
a helm made from some dark, greenish alloy and exquisitely
moulded into the likeness of a dragon about to take wing. And
on the hand which absently caresses the crown there is a ring in
which is set a single rare Actorios stone whose core sometimes
shifts sluggishly and reshapes itself, as if it were sentient smoke
and as restless in its jewelled prison as the young albino on his
Ruby Throne.

He looks down the long flight of quartz steps to where his
Court disports itself, dancing with such delicacy and whispering
grace that it might be a court of ghosts. Mentally he debates
moral issues and in itself this activity divides him from the great
majority of his subjects, for these people are not human.

These are the people of Melniboné, the Dragon Isle, which
ruled the world for ten thousand years and has ceased to rule it for
less than five hundred years. And they are cruel and clever and to
them 'morality' means little more than a proper respect for the
traditions of a hundred centuries.

To the young man, four hundred and twenty-eighth in direct
line of descent from the first Sorcerer Emperor of Melniboné,
their assumptions seem not only arrogant but foolish; it is plain

that the Dragon Isle has lost most of her power and will soon be threatened, in another century or two, by a direct conflict with the emerging human nations whom they call, somewhat patronisingly, the Young Kingdoms. Already pirate fleets have made unsuccessful attacks on Imrryr the Beautiful, the Dreaming City, capital of the Dragon Isle of Melniboné.

Yet even the emperor's closest friends refuse to discuss the prospect of Melniboné's fall. They are not pleased when he mentions the idea, considering his remarks not only unthinkable, but also a singular breach of good taste.

So, alone, the emperor broods. He mourns that his father, Sadric the Eighty-Sixth, did not sire more children, for then a more suitable monarch might have been available to take his place on the Ruby Throne. Sadric has been dead a year; seeming to whisper glad welcome to that which came to claim his soul. Through most of his life Sadric had never known another woman than his wife, for the empress had died bringing her sole thin-blooded issue into the world. But, with Melnibonéan emotions (oddly different from those of the human newcomers), Sadric had loved his wife and had been unable to find pleasure in any other company, even that of the son who had killed her and who was all that was left of her. By magic potions and the chanting of runes, by rare herbs had her son been nurtured, his strength sustained artificially by every art known to the Sorcerer Kings of Melniboné. And he had lived – still lives – thanks to sorcery alone, for he is naturally lassitudinous and, without his drugs, would barely be able to raise his hand from his side through most of a normal day.

If the young emperor has found any advantage in his lifelong weakness it must be in that, perforce, he has read much. Before he was fifteen he had read every book in his father's library, some more than once. His sorcerous powers, learned initially from Sadric, are now greater than any possessed by his ancestors for many a generation. His knowledge of the world beyond the shores of Melniboné is profound, though he has as yet had little direct experience of it. If he wished he could resurrect the Dragon

Isle's former might and rule both his own land and the Young Kingdoms as an invulnerable tyrant. But his reading has also taught him to question the uses to which power is put, to question his motives, to question whether his own power should be used at all, in any cause. His reading has led him to this 'morality', which, still, he barely understands. Thus, to his subjects, he is an enigma and, to some, he is a threat, for he neither thinks nor acts in accordance with their conception of how a true Melnibonéan (and a Melnibonéan emperor, at that) should think and act. His cousin Yyrkoon, for instance, has been heard more than once to voice strong doubts concerning the emperor's right to rule the people of Melniboné. 'This feeble scholar will bring doom to us all,' he said one night to Dyvim Tvar, Lord of the Dragon Caves.

Dyvim Tvar is one of the emperor's few friends and he had duly reported the conversation, but the youth had dismissed the remarks as 'only a trivial treason', whereas any of his ancestors would have rewarded such sentiments with a very slow and exquisite public execution.

The emperor's attitude is further complicated by the fact that Yyrkoon, who is even now making precious little secret of his feelings that he should be emperor, is the brother of Cymoril, a girl whom the albino considers the closest of his friends, and who will one day become his empress.

Down on the mosaic floor of the court Prince Yyrkoon can be seen in all his finest silks and furs, his jewels and his brocades, dancing with a hundred women, all of whom are rumoured to have been mistresses of his at one time or another. His dark features, at once handsome and saturnine, are framed by long black hair, waved and oiled, and his expression, as ever, is sardonic while his bearing is arrogant. The heavy brocade cloak swings this way and that, striking other dancers with some force. He wears it almost as if it is armour or, perhaps, a weapon. Amongst many of the courtiers there is more than a little respect for Prince Yyrkoon. Few resent his arrogance and those who do keep silent, for Yyrkoon is known to be a considerable sorcerer himself. Also his behaviour is what the Court expects and welcomes in a Melnibonéan noble; it is what they would welcome in their emperor.

The emperor knows this. He wishes he could please his Court as it strives to honour him with its dancing and its wit, but he cannot bring himself to take part in what he privately considers a wearisome and irritating sequence of ritual posturings. In this he is, perhaps, somewhat more arrogant than Yyrkoon who is, at least, a conventional boor.

From the galleries, the music grows louder and more complex as the slaves, specially trained and surgically operated upon to sing but one perfect note each, are stimulated to more passionate efforts. Even the young emperor is moved by the sinister harmony of their song which in few ways resembles anything previously uttered by the human voice. Why should their pain produce such marvellous beauty? he wonders. Or is all beauty created through pain? Is that the secret of great art, both human and Melnibonéan?

The Emperor Elric closes his eyes.

There is a stir in the hall below. The gates have opened and the dancing courtiers cease their motion, drawing back and bowing low as soldiers enter. The soldiers are clad all in light blue, their ornamental helms cast in fantastic shapes, their long, broad-bladed lances decorated with jewelled ribbons. They surround a young woman whose blue dress matches their uniforms and whose bare arms are encircled by five or six bracelets of diamonds, sapphires and gold. Strings of diamonds and sapphires are wound into her hair. Unlike most of the women of the Court, her face has no designs painted upon the eyelids or cheekbones. Elric smiles. This is Cymoril. The soldiers are her personal ceremonial guard who, according to tradition, must escort her into the court. They ascend the steps leading to the Ruby Throne. Slowly Elric rises and stretches out his hands.

'Cymoril. I thought you had decided not to grace the Court tonight.'

She returns his smile. 'My emperor, I found that I was in the mood for conversation, after all.'

Elric is grateful. She knows that he is bored and she knows, too, that she is one of the few people of Melniboné whose conversation interests him. If protocol allowed, he would offer her the throne, but as it is she must sit on the topmost step at his feet.

'Please sit, sweet Cymoril.' He resumes his place upon the throne and leans forward as she seats herself and looks into his eyes with a mixed expression of humour and tenderness. She speaks softly as her guard withdraws to mingle at the sides of the steps with Elric's own guard. Her voice can be heard only by Elric.

'Would you ride out to the wild region of the island with me tomorrow, my lord?'

'There are matters to which I must give my attention...' He is attracted by the idea. It is weeks since he left the city and rode with her, their escort keeping a discreet distance away.

'Are they urgent?'

He shrugs. 'What matters are urgent in Melniboné? After ten thousand years, most problems may be seen in a certain perspective.' His smile is almost a grin, rather like that of a young scholar who plans to play truant from his tutor. 'Very well – early in the morning, we'll leave, before the others are up.'

'The air beyond Imrryr will be clear and sharp. The sun will be warm for the season. The sky will be blue and unclouded.'

Elric laughs. 'Such sorcery you must have worked!'

Cymoril lowers her eyes and traces a pattern on the marble of the dais. 'Well, perhaps a little. I am not without friends among the weakest of the elementals...'

Elric stretches down to touch her fine, dark hair. 'Does Yyrkoon know?'

'No.'

Prince Yyrkoon has forbidden his sister to meddle in magical matters. Prince Yyrkoon's friends are only among the darker of the supernatural beings and he knows that they are dangerous to deal with; thus he assumes that all sorcerous dealings bear a similar element of danger. Besides this, he hates to think that others possess the power that he possesses. Perhaps this is what, in Elric, he hates most of all.

'Let us hope that all Melniboné needs fine weather for tomorrow,' says Elric. Cymoril stares curiously at him. She is still a Melnibonéan. It has not occurred to her that her sorcery might prove unwelcome to some. Then she shrugs her lovely shoulders and touches her lord lightly upon the hand.

'This "guilt",' she says. 'This searching of the conscience. Its purpose is beyond my simple brain.'

'And mine, I must admit. It seems to have no practical function. Yet more than one of our ancestors predicted a change in the nature of our earth. A spiritual as well as a physical change. Perhaps I have glimmerings of this change when I think my stranger, un-Melnibonéan, thoughts?'

The music swells. The music fades. The courtiers dance on, though many eyes are upon Elric and Cymoril as they talk at the top of the dais. There is speculation. When will Elric announce Cymoril as his empress-to-be? Will Elric revive the custom that Sadric dismissed, of sacrificing twelve brides and their bridegrooms to the Lords of Chaos in order to ensure a good marriage for the rulers of Melniboné? It was obvious that Sadric's refusal to allow the custom to continue brought misery upon him and death upon his wife; brought him a sickly son and threatened the very continuity of the monarchy. Elric must revive the custom. Even Elric must fear a repetition of the doom which visited his father. But some say that Elric will do nothing in accordance with tradition and that he threatens not only his own life, but the existence of Melniboné itself and all it stands for. And those who speak thus are often seen to be on good terms with Prince Yyrkoon who dances on, seemingly unaware of their conversation or, indeed, unaware that his sister talks quietly with the cousin who sits on the Ruby Throne; who sits on the edge of the seat, forgetful of his dignity, who exhibits none of the ferocious and disdainful pride which has, in the past, marked virtually every other emperor of Melniboné; who chats animatedly, forgetful that the Court is supposed to be dancing for his entertainment.

And then suddenly Prince Yyrkoon freezes in mid-pirouette and raises his dark eyes to look up at his emperor. In one corner

of the hall, Dyvim Tvar's attention is attracted by Yyrkoon's calculated and dramatic posture and the Lord of the Dragon Caves
frowns. His hand falls to where his sword would normally be, but
no swords are worn at a court ball. Dyvim Tvar looks warily and
intently at Prince Yyrkoon as the tall nobleman begins to ascend
the stairs to the Ruby Throne. Many eyes follow the emperor's
cousin and now hardly anyone dances, though the music grows
wilder as the masters of the music slaves goad their charges to
even greater exertions.

Elric looks up to see Yyrkoon standing one step below that on
which Cymoril sits. Yyrkoon makes a bow which is subtly insulting.

'I present myself to my emperor,' he says.

J·CAWTHORN·78

# Chapter Two

## *An Upstart Prince: He Confronts His Cousin*

'AND HOW DO you enjoy the ball, cousin?' Elric asked, aware that Yyrkoon's melodramatic presentation had been designed to catch him off-guard and, if possible, humiliate him. 'Is the music to your taste?'

Yyrkoon lowered his eyes and let his lips form a secret little smile. 'Everything is to my taste, my liege. But what of yourself? Does something displease you? You do not join the dance.'

Elric raised one pale finger to his chin and stared at Yyrkoon's hidden eyes. 'I enjoy the dance, cousin, nonetheless. Surely it is possible to take pleasure in the pleasure of others?'

Yyrkoon seemed genuinely astonished. His eyes opened fully and met Elric's. Elric felt a slight shock and then turned his own gaze away, indicating the music galleries with a languid hand. 'Or perhaps it is the pain of others which brings me pleasure. Fear not, for my sake, cousin. I am pleased. I am pleased. You may dance on, assured that your emperor enjoys the ball.'

But Yyrkoon was not to be diverted from his object. 'Surely, if his subjects are not to go away saddened and troubled that they have not pleased their ruler, the emperor should demonstrate his enjoyment...?'

'I would remind you, cousin,' said Elric quietly, 'that the emperor has no duty to his subjects at all, save to rule them. Their duty is to him. That is the tradition of Melniboné.'

Yyrkoon had not expected Elric to use such arguments against him, but he rallied with his next retort. 'I agree, my lord. The emperor's duty is to rule his subjects. Perhaps that is why so many of them do not, themselves, enjoy the ball as much as they might.'

'I do not follow you, cousin.'

Cymoril had risen and stood with her hands clenched on the step above her brother. She was tense and anxious, worried by her brother's bantering tone, his disdainful bearing.

'Yyrkoon...' she said.

He acknowledged her presence. 'Sister. I see you share our emperor's reluctance to dance.'

'Yyrkoon,' she murmured, 'you are going too far. The emperor is tolerant, but...'

'Tolerant? Or is he careless? Is he careless of the traditions of our great race? Is he contemptuous of that race's pride?'

Dyvim Tvar was now mounting the steps. It was plain that he, too, sensed that Yyrkoon had chosen this moment to test Elric's power.

Cymoril was aghast. She said urgently: 'Yyrkoon. If you would live...'

'I would not care to live if the soul of Melniboné perished. And the guardianship of our nation's soul is the responsibility of the emperor. And what if we should have an emperor who failed in that responsibility? An emperor who was weak? An emperor who cared nothing for the greatness of the Dragon Isle and its folk?'

'A hypothetical question, cousin.' Elric had recovered his composure and his voice was an icy drawl. 'For such an emperor has never sat upon the Ruby Throne and such an emperor never shall.'

Dyvim Tvar came up, touching Yyrkoon on the shoulder. 'Prince, if you value your dignity and your life...'

Elric raised his hand. 'There is no need for that, Dyvim Tvar. Prince Yyrkoon merely entertains us with an intellectual debate. Fearing that I was bored by the music and the dance – which I am not – he thought he would provide the subject for a stimulating discourse. I am certain that we are most stimulated, Prince Yyrkoon.' Elric allowed a patronising warmth to colour his last sentence.

Yyrkoon flushed with anger and bit his lips.

'But go on, dear cousin Yyrkoon,' Elric said. 'I am interested. Enlarge further on your argument.'

Yyrkoon looked around him, as if for support. But all his

supporters were on the floor of the hall. Only Elric's friends, Dyvim Tvar and Cymoril, were nearby. Yet Yyrkoon knew that his supporters were hearing every word and that he would lose face if he did not retaliate. Elric could tell that Yyrkoon would have preferred to have retired from this confrontation and choose another day and another ground on which to continue the battle, but that was not possible. Elric, himself, had no wish to continue the foolish banter which was, no matter how disguised, a little better than the quarrelling of two little girls over who should play with the slaves first. He decided to make an end of it.

Yyrkoon began: 'Then let me suggest that an emperor who was physically weak might also be weak in his will to rule as befitted...'

And Elric raised his hand. 'You have done enough, dear cousin. More than enough. You have wearied yourself with this conversation when you would have preferred to dance. I am touched by your concern. But now I, too, feel weariness steal upon me.' Elric signalled for his old servant Tanglebones who stood on the far side of the throne dais, amongst the soldiers. 'Tanglebones! My cloak.'

Elric stood up. 'I thank you again for your thoughtfulness, cousin.' He addressed the Court in general. 'I was entertained. Now I retire.'

Tanglebones brought the cloak of white fox fur and placed it around his master's shoulders. Tanglebones was very old and much taller than Elric, though his back was stooped and all his limbs seemed knotted and twisted back on themselves, like the limbs of a strong, old tree.

Elric walked across the dais and through the door which opened onto a corridor which led to his private apartments.

Yyrkoon was left fuming. He whirled round on the dais and opened his mouth as if to address the watching courtiers. Some, who did not support him, were smiling quite openly. Yyrkoon clenched his fists at his sides and glowered. He glared at Dyvim Tvar and opened his thin lips to speak. Dyvim Tvar coolly returned the glare, daring Yyrkoon to say more.

Then Yyrkoon flung back his head so that the locks of his hair, all curled and oiled, swayed against his back. And Yyrkoon laughed.

The harsh sound filled the hall. The music stopped. The laughter continued.

Yyrkoon stepped up so that he stood on the dais. He dragged his heavy cloak round him so that it engulfed his body.

Cymoril came forward. 'Yyrkoon, please do not...' He pushed her back with a motion of his shoulder.

Yyrkoon walked stiffly towards the Ruby Throne. It became plain that he was about to seat himself in it and thus perform one of the most traitorous actions possible in the code of Melniboné. Cymoril ran the few steps to him and pulled at his arm.

Yyrkoon's laughter grew. 'It is Yyrkoon they would wish to see on the Ruby Throne,' he told his sister. She gasped and looked in horror at Dyvim Tvar whose face was grim and angry.

Dyvim Tvar signed to the guards and suddenly there were two ranks of armoured men between Yyrkoon and the throne.

Yyrkoon glared back at the Lord of the Dragon Caves. 'You had best hope you perish with your master,' he hissed.

'This guard of honour will escort you from the hall,' Dyvim Tvar said evenly. 'We were all stimulated by your conversation this evening, Prince Yyrkoon.'

Yyrkoon paused, looked about him, then relaxed. He shrugged. 'There's time enough. If Elric will not abdicate, then he must be deposed.'

Cymoril's slender body was rigid. Her eyes blazed. She said to her brother:

'If you harm Elric in any way, I will slay you myself, Yyrkoon.'

He raised his tapering eyebrows and smiled. At that moment he seemed to hate his sister even more than he hated his cousin. 'Your loyalty to that creature has ensured your own doom, Cymoril. I would rather you died than that you should give birth to any progeny of his. I will not have the blood of our house diluted, tainted – even touched – by his blood. Look to your own life, sister, before you threaten mine.'

And he stormed down the steps, pushing through those who came up to congratulate him. He knew that he had lost and the murmurs of his sycophants only irritated him further.

The great doors of the hall crashed together and closed. Yyrkoon was gone from the hall.

Dyvim Tvar raised both his arms. 'Dance on, courtiers. Pleasure yourselves with all that the hall provides. It is what will please the emperor most.'

But it was plain there would be little more dancing done tonight. Courtiers were already deep in conversation as, excitedly, they debated the events.

Dyvim Tvar turned to Cymoril. 'Elric refuses to understand the danger, Princess Cymoril. Yyrkoon's ambition could bring disaster to all of us.'

'Including Yyrkoon.' Cymoril sighed.

'Aye, including Yyrkoon. But how can we avoid this, Cymoril, if Elric will not give orders for your brother's arrest?'

'He believes that such as Yyrkoon should be allowed to say what they please. It is part of his philosophy. I can barely understand it, but it seems integral to his whole belief. If he destroys Yyrkoon, he destroys the basis on which his logic works. That at any rate, Dragon Master, is what he has tried to explain to me.'

Dyvim Tvar sighed and he frowned. Unable to understand Elric, he was afraid that he could sometimes sympathise with Yyrkoon's viewpoint. At least Yyrkoon's motives and arguments were relatively straightforward. He knew Elric's character too well, however, to believe that Elric acted from weakness or lassitude. The paradox was that Elric tolerated Yyrkoon's treachery because he was strong, because he had the power to destroy Yyrkoon whenever he cared. And Yyrkoon's own character was such that he must constantly be testing that strength of Elric's, for he knew instinctively that if Elric did weaken and order him slain, then he would have won. It was a complicated situation and Dyvim Tvar dearly wished that he was not embroiled in it. But his loyalty to the royal line of Melniboné was strong and his personal loyalty to Elric was great. He considered the idea of having Yyrkoon secretly assassinated, but he knew that such a plan would almost certainly come to nothing. Yyrkoon was a sorcerer of immense power and doubtless would be forewarned of any attempt on his life.

'Princess Cymoril,' said Dyvim Tvar, 'I can only pray that your brother swallows so much of his rage that it eventually poisons him.'

'I will join you in that prayer, Lord of the Dragon Caves.'

Together, they left the hall.

## Chapter Three

### *Riding Through the Morning:*
### *A Moment of Tranquillity*

T HE LIGHT OF the early morning touched the tall towers of
Imrryr and made them scintillate. Each tower was of a different hue; there were a thousand soft colours. There were rose
pinks and pollen yellows, there were purples and pale greens,
mauves and browns and oranges, hazy blues, whites and powdery
golds, all lovely in the sunlight. Two riders left the Dreaming City
behind them and rode away from the walls, over the green turf
towards a pine forest where, among the shadowy trunks, a little
of the night seemed to remain. Squirrels were stirring and foxes
crept homeward; birds were singing and forest flowers opened
their petals and filled the air with delicate scent. A few insects
wandered sluggishly aloft. The contrast between life in the nearby
city and this lazy rusticity was very great and seemed to mirror
some of the contrasts existing in the mind of at least one of the
riders who now dismounted and led his horse, walking knee-deep
through a mass of blue flowers. The other rider, a girl, brought
her own horse to a halt but did not dismount. Instead, she leaned
casually on her high Melnibonéan pommel and smiled at the man,
her lover.

'Elric? Would you stop so near to Imrryr?'

He smiled back at her, over his shoulder. 'For the moment. Our
flight was hasty. I would collect my thoughts before we ride on.'

'How did you sleep last night?'

'Well enough, Cymoril, though I must have dreamed without
knowing it, for there were – there were little intimations in my
head when I awoke. But then, the meeting with Yyrkoon was not
pleasant...'

'Do you think he plots to use sorcery against you?'

Elric shrugged. 'I would know if he brought a large sorcery against me. And he knows my power. I doubt if he would dare employ wizardry.'

'He has reason to believe you might not use your power. He has worried at your personality for so long – is there not a danger he will begin to worry at your skills? Testing your sorcery as he has tested your patience?'

Elric frowned. 'Yes, I suppose there is that danger. But not yet, I should have thought.'

'He will not be happy until you are destroyed, Elric.'

'Or is destroyed himself, Cymoril.' Elric stooped and picked one of the flowers. He smiled. 'Your brother is inclined to absolutes, is he not? How the weak hate weakness.'

Cymoril took his meaning. She dismounted and came towards him. Her thin gown matched, almost perfectly, the colour of the flowers through which she moved. He handed her the flower and she accepted it, touching its petals with her perfect lips. 'And how the strong hate strength, my love. Yyrkoon is my kin and yet I give you this advice – use your strength against him.'

'I could not slay him. I have not the right.' Elric's face fell into familiar, brooding lines.

'You could exile him.'

'Is not exile the same as death to a Melnibonéan?'

'You, yourself, have talked of travelling in the lands of the Young Kingdoms.'

Elric laughed somewhat bitterly. 'But perhaps I am not a true Melnibonéan. Yyrkoon has said as much – and others echo his thoughts.'

'He hates you because you are contemplative. Your father was contemplative and no-one denied that he was a fitting emperor.'

'My father chose not to put the results of his contemplation into his personal actions. He ruled as an emperor should. Yyrkoon, I must admit, would also rule as an emperor should. He, too, has the opportunity to make Melniboné great again. If he were emperor, he would embark on a campaign of conquest to restore our trade to its former volume, to extend our power across the earth. And that is what the majority of our folk would wish. Is it my right to deny that wish?'

'It is your right to do what you think, for you are the emperor. All who are loyal to you think as I do.'

'Perhaps their loyalty is misguided. Perhaps Yyrkoon is right and I will betray that loyalty, bring doom to the Dragon Isle.' His moody, crimson eyes looked directly into hers. 'Perhaps I should have died as I left my mother's womb. Then Yyrkoon would have become emperor. Has Fate been thwarted?'

'Fate is never thwarted. What has happened has happened because Fate willed it thus – if, indeed, there is such a thing as Fate and if men's actions are not merely a response to other men's actions.'

Elric drew a deep breath and offered her an expression tinged with irony. 'Your logic leads you close to heresy, Cymoril, if we are to believe the traditions of Melniboné. Perhaps it would be better if you forgot your friendship with me.'

She laughed. 'You begin to sound like my brother. Are you testing my love for you, my lord?'

He began to remount his horse. 'No, Cymoril, but I would advise you to test your love yourself, for I sense there is tragedy implicit in our love.'

As she swung herself back into her saddle she smiled and shook her head. 'You see doom in all things. Can you not accept the good gifts granted you? They are few enough, my lord.'

'Aye. I'll agree with that.'

They turned in their saddles, hearing hoofbeats behind them. Some distance away they saw a company of yellow-clad horsemen riding about in confusion. It was their guard, which they had left behind, wishing to ride alone.

'Come!' cried Elric. 'Through the woods and over yonder hill and they'll never find us!'

They spurred their steeds through the sun-speared wood and up the steep sides of the hill beyond, racing down the other side and away across a plain where *noidel* bushes grew, their lush, poison fruit glimmering a purplish blue, a night-colour which even

the light of day could not disperse. There were many such peculiar berries and herbs on Melniboné and it was to some of them
that Elric owed his life. Others were used for sorcerous potions
and had been sown generations before by Elric's ancestors. Now
few Melnibonéans left Imrryr even to collect these harvests. Only
slaves visited the greater part of the island, seeking the roots and
the shrubs which made men dream monstrous and magnificent
dreams, for it was in their dreams that the nobles of Melniboné
found most of their pleasures; they had ever been a moody,
inward-looking race and it was for this quality that Imrryr had
come to be named the Dreaming City. There, even the meanest
slaves chewed berries to bring them oblivion and thus were easily
controlled, for they came to depend on their dreams. Only Elric
himself refused such drugs, perhaps because he required so many
others simply to ensure his remaining alive.

The yellow-clad guards were lost behind them and once across
the plain where the *noidel* bushes grew they slowed their flight
and came at length to cliffs and then the sea.

The sea shone brightly, and languidly washed the white beaches
below the cliffs. Seabirds wheeled in the clear sky and their cries
were distant, serving only to emphasise the sense of peace which
both Elric and Cymoril now had. In silence the lovers guided their
horses down steep paths to the shore and there they tethered the
steeds and began to walk across the sand, their hair – his white,
hers jet-black – waving in the wind which blew from the east.

They found a great, dry cave which caught the sounds the sea
made and replied in a whispering echo. They removed their silken
garments and made love tenderly in the shadows of the cave.
They lay in each other's arms as the day warmed and the wind
dropped. Then they went to bathe in the waters, filling the empty
sky with their laughter.

When they were dry and were dressing themselves they noticed a
darkening of the horizon and Elric said: 'We shall be wet again
before we return to Imrryr. No matter how fast we ride, the storm
will catch us.'

'Perhaps we should remain in the cave until it is past?' she suggested, coming close and holding her soft body against him.

'No,' he said. 'I must return soon, for there are potions in Imrryr I must take if my body is to retain its strength. An hour or two longer and I shall begin to weaken. You have seen me weak before, Cymoril.'

She stroked his face and her eyes were sympathetic. 'Aye. I've seen you weak before, Elric. Come, let's find the horses.'

By the time they reached the horses the sky was grey overhead and full of boiling blackness not far away in the east. They heard the grumble of thunder and the crash of lightning. The sea was threshing as if infected by the sky's hysteria. The horses snorted and pawed at the sand, anxious to return. Even as Elric and Cymoril climbed into their saddles large spots of rain began to fall on their heads and spread over their cloaks.

Then, suddenly, they were riding at full tilt back to Imrryr while the lightning flashed around them and the thunder roared like a furious giant, like some great old Lord of Chaos attempting to break through, unbidden, into the Realm of Earth.

Cymoril glanced at Elric's pale face, illuminated for a moment by a flash of sky-fire, and she felt a chill come upon her then and the chill had nothing to do with the wind or the rain, for it seemed to her in that second that the gentle scholar she loved had been transformed by the elements into a hell-driven demon, into a monster with barely a semblance of humanity. His crimson eyes had flared from the whiteness of his skull like the very flames of the Higher Hell; his hair had been whipped upward so that it had become the crest of a sinister war-helm and, by a trick of the stormlight, his mouth had seemed twisted in a mixture of rage and agony.

And suddenly Cymoril knew.

She knew, profoundly, that their morning's ride was the last moment of peace the two of them would ever experience again. The storm was a sign from the gods themselves – a warning of storms to come.

She looked again at her lover. Elric was laughing. He had turned his face upward so that the warm rain fell upon it, so that the water splashed into his open mouth. The laughter was the easy, unsophisticated laughter of a happy child.

Cymoril tried to laugh back, but then she had to turn her face away so that he should not see it. For Cymoril had begun to weep.

She was weeping still when Imrryr came in sight – a black and grotesque silhouette against a line of brightness which was the as yet untainted western horizon.

# Chapter Four

## *Prisoners: Their Secrets Are Taken from Them*

THE MEN IN yellow armour saw Elric and Cymoril as the two approached the smallest of the eastern gates.

'They have found us at last,' smiled Elric through the rain, 'but somewhat belatedly, eh, Cymoril?'

Cymoril, still embattled with her sense of doom, merely nodded and tried to smile in reply.

Elric took this as an expression of disappointment, nothing more, and called to his guards: 'Ho, men! Soon we shall all be dry again!'

But the captain of the guard rode up urgently, crying: 'My lord emperor is needed at Monshanjik Tower where spies are held.'

'Spies?'

'Aye, my lord.' The man's face was pale. Water cascaded from his helm and darkened his thin cloak. His horse was hard to control and kept sidestepping through pools of water, which had gathered wherever the road was in disrepair. 'Caught in the maze this morning. Southern barbarians, by their chequered dress. We are holding them until the emperor himself can question them.'

Elric waved his hand. 'Then lead on, captain. Let's see the brave fools who dare Melniboné's sea-maze.'

The Tower of Monshanjik had been named for the wizard-architect who had designed the sea-maze millennia before. The maze was the only means of reaching the great harbour of Imrryr and its secrets had been carefully guarded, for it was their greatest protection against sudden attack. The maze was complicated and pilots had to be specially trained to steer ships through it. Before the maze had been built, the harbour had been a kind of inland lagoon, fed by the sea which swept in through a system of natural caverns in the towering cliff which rose between lagoon and ocean. There were five separate routes through the sea-maze and any individual pilot knew but one. In the outer wall of the cliff there were five entrances. Here Young Kingdom ships waited until a pilot came aboard. Then one of the gates to one of the entrances would be lifted, all aboard the ship would be blind-folded and sent below save for the oar-master and the steersman who would also be masked in heavy steel helms so that they could see nothing, do nothing but obey the complicated instructions of the pilot. And if a Young Kingdom ship should fail to obey any of those instructions and should crush itself against the rock walls, Melniboné did not mourn for it and any survivors from the crew would be taken as slaves. All who sought to trade with the Dreaming City understood the risks, but scores of merchants came every month to dare the dangers of the maze and trade their own poor goods for the splendid riches of Melniboné.

The Tower of Monshanjik stood overlooking the harbour and the massive mole which jutted out into the middle of the lagoon. It was a sea-green tower and was squat compared with most of those in Imrryr, though still a beautiful and tapering construction, with wide windows so that the whole of the harbour could be seen from it. From Monshanjik Tower most of the business of the harbour was done and in its lower cellars were kept any prisoners who had broken any of the myriad rules governing the functioning of the harbour. Leaving Cymoril to return to the palace with a guard, Elric entered the tower, riding through the great archway at the base, scattering not a few merchants who were waiting for per-mission to begin their bartering, for the whole of the ground floor was full of sailors, merchants and Melnibonéan officials engaged in the business of trade, though it was not here that the actual wares were displayed. The great echoing babble of a thousand voices engaged in a thousand separate aspects of bargaining slowly stilled as Elric and his guard rode arrogantly through to another dark arch at the far end of the hall. This arch opened onto a ramp which sloped and curved down into the bowels of the tower.

Down this ramp clattered the horsemen, passing slaves, servants and officials who stepped hastily aside, bowing low as they recognised the emperor. Great brands illuminated the tunnel, guttering and smoking and casting distorted shadows onto the smooth obsidian walls. A chill was in the air now, and a dampness, for water washed about the outer walls below the quays of Imrryr. And still the emperor rode on and still the ramp struck lower through the glassy rock. And then a wave of heat rose to meet them and shifting light could be seen ahead and they passed into a chamber that was full of smoke and the scent of fear. From the low ceiling hung chains and from eight of the chains, swinging by their feet, hung four people. Their clothes had been torn from them, but their bodies were clothed in blood from tiny wounds, precise but severe, made by the artist who stood, scalpel in hand, surveying his handiwork.

The artist was tall and very thin, almost like a skeleton in his stained, white garments. His lips were thin, his eyes were slits, his fingers were thin, his hair was thin and the scalpel he held was thin, too, almost invisible save when it flashed in the light from the fire which erupted from a pit on the far side of the cavern. The artist was named Doctor Jest and the art he practised was a performing art rather than a creative one (though he could argue otherwise with some conviction): the art of drawing secrets from those who kept them. Doctor Jest was the Chief Interrogator of Melniboné. He turned sinuously as Elric entered, the scalpel held between the thin thumb and the thin forefinger of his right hand; he stood poised and expectant, almost like a dancer, and then bowed from the waist.

'My sweet emperor!' His voice was thin. It rushed from his thin throat as if bent on escape and one was inclined to wonder if one had heard the words at all, so quickly had they come and gone.

'Doctor. Are these the southlanders caught this morning?'

'Indeed they are, my lord.' Another sinuous bow. 'For your pleasure.'

Coldly Elric inspected the prisoners. He felt no sympathy for them. They were spies. Their actions had led them to this pass.

They had known what would happen to them if caught. But one of them was a boy and another a woman, it appeared, though they writhed so in their chains it was quite difficult to tell at first. It seemed a shame. Then the woman snapped what remained of her teeth at him and hissed: 'Demon!' And Elric stepped back, saying:

'Have they informed you of what they were doing in our maze, doctor?'

'They still tantalise me with hints. They have a fine sense of drama. I appreciate that. They are here, I would say, to map a route through the maze which a force of raiders might then follow. But they have so far withheld the details. That is the game. We all understand how it must be played.'

'And when will they tell you, Doctor Jest?'

'Oh, very soon, my lord.'

'It would be best to know if we are to expect attackers. The sooner we know, the less time we shall lose dealing with the attack when it comes. Do you not agree, doctor?'

'I do, my lord.'

'Very well.' Elric was irritated by this break in his day. It had spoiled the pleasure of the ride, it had brought him face to face with his duties too quickly.

Doctor Jest returned to his charges and, reaching out with his free hand, expertly seized the genitals of one of the male prisoners. The scalpel flashed. There was a groan. Doctor Jest tossed something onto the fire. Elric sat in the chair prepared for him. He was bored rather than disgusted by the rituals attendant upon the gathering of information and the discordant screams, the clash of the chains, the thin whisperings of Doctor Jest, all served to ruin the feeling of well-being he had retained even as he reached the chamber. But it was one of his kingly duties to attend such rituals and attend this one he must until the information was presented to him and he could congratulate his Chief Interrogator and issue orders as to the means of dealing with any attack and even when that was over he must confer with admirals and with generals, probably through the rest of the night, choosing between arguments, deciding on the deposition of men and ships. With a poorly disguised yawn he leaned back and watched as Doctor Jest ran fingers and scalpel, tongue, tongs and pincers over the bodies. He was soon thinking of other matters: philosophical problems which he had still failed to resolve.

It was not that Elric was inhumane; it was that he was, still, a Melnibonéan. He had been used to such sights since childhood. He could not have saved the prisoners, even if he had desired, without going against every tradition of the Dragon Isle. And in this case it was a simple matter of a threat being met by the best methods available. He had become used to shutting off those feelings which conflicted with his duties as emperor. If there had been any point in freeing the four who danced now at Doctor Jest's pleasure he would have freed them, but there was no point and the four would have been astonished if they had received any other treatment than this. Where moral decisions were concerned Elric was, by and large, practical. He would make his decision in the context of what action he could take. In this case, he could take no action. Such a reaction had become second nature to him. His desire was not to reform Melniboné but to reform himself, not to initiate action but to know the best way of responding to the actions of others. Here, the decision was easy to make. A spy was an aggressor. One defended oneself against aggressors in the best possible way. The methods employed by Doctor Jest were the best methods.

'My lord?'

Absently, Elric looked up.

'We have the information now, my lord.' Doctor Jest's thin voice whispered across the chamber. Two sets of chains were now empty and slaves were gathering things up from the floor and flinging them on the fire. The two remaining shapeless lumps reminded Elric of meat carefully prepared by a chef. One of the lumps still quivered a little, but the other was still.

Doctor Jest slid his instruments into a thin case he carried in a pouch at his belt. His white garments were almost completely covered in stains.

'It seems there have been other spies before these,' Doctor Jest told his master. 'These came merely to confirm the route. If they do not return in time, the barbarians will still sail.'

'But surely they will know that we expect them?' Elric said.

'Probably not, my lord. Rumours have been spread amongst the Young Kingdom merchants and sailors that four spies were seen in the maze and were speared – slain whilst trying to escape.'

'I see.' Elric frowned. 'Then our best plan will be to lay a trap for the raiders.'

'Aye, my lord.'

'You know the route they have chosen?'

'Aye, my lord.'

Elric turned to one of his guards. 'Have messages sent to all our generals and admirals. What's the hour?'

'The hour of sunset is just past, my liege.'

'Tell them to assemble before the Ruby Throne at two hours past sunset.'

Wearily, Elric rose. 'You have done well, as usual, Doctor Jest.'

The thin artist bowed low, seeming to fold himself in two. A thin and somewhat unctuous sigh was his reply.

# Chapter Five

## *A Battle: The King Proves His War-Skill*

YRKOON WAS THE first to arrive, all clad in martial finery, accompanied by two massive guards, each holding one of the prince's ornate war-banners.

'My emperor!' Yyrkoon's shout was proud and disdainful. 'Would you let me command the warriors? It will relieve you of that care when, doubtless, you have many other concerns with which to occupy your time.'

Elric replied impatiently: 'You are most thoughtful, Prince Yyrkoon, but fear not for me. I shall command the armies and the navies of Melniboné, for that is the duty of the emperor.'

Yyrkoon glowered and stepped to one side as Dyvim Tvar, Lord of the Dragon Caves, entered. He had no guard whatsoever with him and it seemed he had dressed hastily. He carried his helmet under his arm.

'My emperor – I bring news of the dragons...'

'I thank you, Dyvim Tvar, but wait until all my commanders are assembled and impart that news to them, too.'

Dyvim Tvar bowed and went to stand on the opposite side of the hall to that on which Prince Yyrkoon stood.

Gradually the warriors arrived until a score of great captains waited at the foot of the steps which led to the Ruby Throne where Elric sat. Elric himself still wore the clothes in which he had gone riding that morning. He had not had time to change and had until a little while before been consulting maps of the mazes – maps which only he could read and which, at normal times, were hidden by magical means from any who might attempt to find them.

'Southlanders would steal Imrryr's wealth and slay us all,' Elric began. 'They believe they have found a way through our sea-maze. A fleet of a hundred warships sails on Melniboné even now. Tomorrow it will wait below the horizon until dusk, then it will sail to the maze and enter. By midnight it expects to reach the harbour and to have taken the Dreaming City before dawn. Is that possible, I wonder?'

'No!' Many spoke the single word.

'No.' Elric smiled. 'But how shall we best enjoy this little war they offer us?'

Yyrkoon, as ever, was first to shout. 'Let us go to meet them now, with dragons and with battle-barges. Let us pursue them to their own land and take their war to them. Let us attack their nations and burn their cities! Let us conquer them and thus ensure our own security!'

Dyvim Tvar spoke up again:

'No dragons,' he said.

'What?' Yyrkoon whirled. 'What?'

'No dragons, prince. They will not be awakened. The dragons sleep in their caverns, exhausted by their last engagement on your behalf.'

'Mine?'

'You would use them in our conflict with the Vilmirian pirates. I told you that I would prefer to save them for a larger engagement. But you flew them against the pirates and you burned their little boats and now the dragons sleep.'

Yyrkoon glowered. He looked up at Elric. 'I did not expect...'

Elric raised his hand. 'We need not use our dragons until such a time as we really need them. This attack from the southlander fleet is nothing. But we will conserve our strength if we bide our time. Let them think we are unready. Let them enter the maze. Once the whole hundred are through, we close in, blocking off all routes in or out of the maze. Trapped, they will be crushed by us.'

Yyrkoon looked pettishly at his feet, evidently wishing he could think of some flaw in the plan. Tall, old Admiral Magum Colim in his sea-green armour stepped forward and bowed. 'The golden battle-barges of Imrryr are ready to defend their city, my liege. It will take time, however, to manoeuvre them into position. It is doubtful if all will fit into the maze at once.'

'Then sail some of them out now and hide them around the coast, so that they can wait for any survivors that may escape our attack,' Elric instructed him.

'A useful plan, my liege.' Magum Colim bowed and sank back into the crowd of his peers.

The debate continued for some time and then they were ready and about to leave. But then Prince Yyrkoon bellowed once more:

'I repeat my offer to the emperor. His person is too valuable to risk in battle. My person – it is worthless. Let me command the warriors of both land and sea while the emperor may remain at the palace, untroubled by the battle, confident that it will be won and the southlanders trounced – perhaps there is a book he wishes to finish?'

Elric smiled. 'Again I thank you for your concern, Prince Yyrkoon. But an emperor must exercise his body as well as his mind. I will command the warriors tomorrow.'

When Elric arrived back at his apartments it was to discover that Tanglebones had already laid out his heavy, black war-gear. Here was the armour which had served a hundred Melnibonéan emperors; an armour which was forged by sorcery to give it a strength unequalled on the Realm of Earth, which could, so rumour went, even withstand the bite of the mythical runeblades, Stormbringer and Mournblade, which had been wielded by the wickedest of Melniboné's many wicked rulers before being seized by the Lords of the Higher Worlds and hidden for ever in a realm where even those lords might rarely venture.

The face of the tangled man was full of joy as he touched each piece of armour, each finely balanced weapon, with his long, gnarled fingers. His seamed face looked up to regard Elric's care-ravaged features. 'Oh, my lord! Oh, my king! Soon you will know the joy of the fight!'

'Aye, Tanglebones – and let us hope it will be a joy.'

'I taught you all the skills – the art of the sword and the poignard – the art of the bow – the art of the spear, both mounted and on foot. And you learned well, for all they say you are weak. Save one, there's no better swordsman in Melniboné.'

'Prince Yyrkoon could be better than me,' Elric said reflectively. 'Could he not?'

'I said "save one", my lord.'

'And Yyrkoon is that one. Well, one day perhaps we'll be able to test the matter. I'll bathe before I don all that metal.'

'Best make speed, master. From what I hear, there is much to do.'

'And I'll sleep after I've bathed.' Elric smiled at his old friend's consternation. 'It will be better thus, for I cannot personally direct the barges into position. I am needed to command the fray – and that I will do better when I've rested.'

'If you think it good, lord king, then it is good.'

'And you are astonished. You are too eager, Tanglebones, to get me into all that stuff and see me strut about in it as if I were Arioch himself...'

Tanglebones's hand flew to his mouth as if he had spoken the words, not his master, and he was trying to block them. His eyes widened.

Elric laughed. 'You think I speak bold heresies, eh? Well, I've spoken worse without any ill befalling me. On Melniboné, Tanglebones, the emperors control the demons, not the reverse.'

'So you say, my liege.'

'It is the truth.' Elric swept from the room, calling for his slaves. The war-fever filled him and he was jubilant.

Now he was in all his black gear: the massive breastplate, the padded jerkin, the long greaves, the mail gauntlets. At his side was a five-foot broadsword which, it was said, had belonged to a human hero called Aubec. Resting on the deck against the golden rail of the bridge was the great round war-board, his shield, bearing the sign of the swooping dragon. And a helm was on his head; a black helm, with a dragon's head craning over the peak, and dragon's wings flaring backward above it, and a dragon's tail curling down the back. All the helm was black, but within the helm there was a white shadow from which glared two crimson orbs, and from the sides of the helm strayed wisps of milk-white hair, almost like smoke escaping from a burning building. And, as the helm turned in what little light came from the lantern hanging at the base of the mainmast, the white shadow sharpened to reveal features – fine, handsome features – a straight nose, curved lips, up-slanting eyes. The face of Emperor Elric of Melniboné peered into the gloom of the maze as he listened for the first sounds of the sea-raiders' approach.

He stood on the high bridge of the great golden battle-barge which, like all its kind, resembled a floating ziggurat equipped with masts and sails and oars and catapults. The ship was called *The Son of the Pyaray* and it was the flagship of the fleet. The Grand Admiral Magum Colim stood beside Elric. Like Dyvim Tvar, the admiral was one of Elric's few close friends. He had known Elric all his life and had encouraged him to learn all he could concerning the running of fighting ships and fighting fleets. Privately Magum Colim might fear that Elric was too scholarly and introspective to rule Melniboné, but he accepted Elric's right to rule and was made angry and impatient by the talk of the likes of Yyrkoon. Prince Yyrkoon was also aboard the flagship, though at this moment he was below, inspecting the war-engines.

*The Son of the Pyaray* lay at anchor in a huge grotto, one of hundreds built into the walls of the maze when the maze itself was built, and designed for just this purpose – to hide a battle-barge. There was just enough height for the masts and enough width for the oars to move freely. Each of the golden battle-barges was equipped with banks of oars, each bank containing between twenty and thirty oars on either side. The banks were four, five or six decks high and, as in the case of *The Son of the Pyaray*, might have three independent steering systems, fore and aft. Being armoured all in gold, the ships were virtually indestructible, and, for all their massive size, they could move swiftly and manoeuvre delicately when occasion demanded. It was not the first time they had waited for their enemies in these grottoes. It would not be the last (though when next they waited it would be in greatly different circumstances).

The battle-barges of Melniboné were rarely seen on the open seas these days, but once they had sailed the oceans of the world like fearsome floating mountains of gold and they had brought terror whenever they were sighted. The fleet had been larger then, comprising hundreds of craft. Now there were less than forty ships. But forty would suffice. Now, in damp darkness, they awaited their enemies.

Listening to the hollow slap of the water against the sides of the ship, Elric wished that he had been able to conceive a better plan than this. He was sure that this one would work, but he regretted the waste of lives, both Melnibonéan and barbarian. It would have been better if some way could have been devised of frightening the barbarians away rather than trapping them in the sea-maze. The southlander fleet was not the first to have been attracted by Imrryr's fabulous wealth. The southlander crews were not the first to entertain the belief that the Melnibonéans, because they never now ventured far from the Dreaming City, had become decadent and unable to defend their treasures. And so the southlanders must be destroyed in order to make the lesson clear. Melniboné was still strong. She was strong enough, in Yyrkoon's view, to resume her former dominance of the world – strong in sorcery if not in soldiery.

'Hist!' Admiral Magum Colim craned forward. 'Was that the sound of an oar?'

Elric nodded. 'I think so.'

Now they heard regular splashes, as of rows of oars dipping in and out of the water, and they heard the creak of timbers. The southlanders were coming. *The Son of the Pyaray* was the ship nearest to the entrance and it would be the first to move out, but only when the last of the southlanders' ships had passed them. Admiral Magum Colim bent and extinguished the lantern, then, quickly, quietly, he descended to inform his crew of the raiders' coming.

Not long before, Yyrkoon had used his sorcery to summon a peculiar mist, which hid the golden barges from view, but through which those on the Melnibonéan ships could peer. Now Elric saw torches burning in the channel ahead as carefully the reavers negotiated the maze. Within the space of a few minutes ten of the galleys had passed the grotto. Admiral Magum Colim rejoined Elric on the bridge and now Prince Yyrkoon was with him. Yyrkoon, too, wore a dragon helm, though less magnificent than Elric's, for Elric was chief of the few surviving Dragon Princes of Melniboné. Yyrkoon was grinning through the gloom and his eyes gleamed in anticipation of the bloodletting to come. Elric wished that Prince Yyrkoon had chosen another ship than this, but it was Yyrkoon's right to be aboard the flagship and he could not deny it.

Now half the hundred vessels had gone past.

Yyrkoon's armour creaked as, impatiently, he waited, pacing the bridge, his gauntleted hand on the hilt of his broadsword. 'Soon,' he kept saying to himself. 'Soon.'

And then their anchor was groaning upwards and their oars were plunging into the water as the last southland ship went by and they shot from the grotto into the channel ramming the enemy galley amidships and smashing it in two.

A great yell went up from the barbarian crew. Men were flung in all directions. Torches danced erratically on the remains of the deck as men tried to save themselves from slipping into the dark, chill waters of the channel. A few brave spears rattled against the sides of the Melnibonéan flag-galley as it began to turn amongst the débris it had created. But Imrryrian archers returned the shots and the few survivors went down.

The sound of this swift conflict was the signal to the other battle-barges. In perfect order they came from both sides of the high rock walls and it must have seemed to the astonished barbarians that the great golden ships had actually emerged from solid stone – ghost ships filled with demons who rained spears, arrows and brands upon them. Now the whole of the twisting channel was confusion and a medley of war-shouts echoed and boomed and the clash of steel upon steel was like the savage hissing of some monstrous snake, and the raiding fleet itself resembled a snake which had been broken into a hundred pieces by the tall, implacable golden ships of Melniboné. These ships seemed almost serene as they moved against their enemies, their grappling irons flashing out to catch wooden decks and rails and draw the galleys nearer so that they might be destroyed.

But the southlanders were brave and they kept their heads after their initial astonishment. Three of their galleys headed directly for *The Son of the Pyaray*, recognising it as the flagship. Fire arrows sailed high and dropped down into the decks which were wooden and not protected by the golden armour, starting fires wherever they fell, or else bringing blazing death to the men they struck.

Elric raised his shield above his head and two arrows struck it, bouncing, still flaring, to a lower deck. He leapt over the rail, following the arrows, jumping down to the widest and most exposed deck where his warriors were grouping, ready to deal with the attacking galleys. Catapults thudded and balls of blue fire swished through the blackness, narrowly missing all three galleys. Another volley followed and one mass of fire struck the far galley's mast and then burst upon the deck, scattering huge flames wherever it touched. Grapples snaked out and seized the first galley, dragging it close and Elric was amongst the first to leap down onto the deck, rushing forward to where he saw the southland captain, dressed all in crude, chequered armour, a chequered surcoat over that, a big sword in both his huge hands, bellowing at his men to resist the Melnibonéan dogs.

As Elric approached the bridge three barbarians armed with curved swords and small, oblong shields ran at him. Their faces were full of fear, but there was determination there as well, as if they knew they must die but planned to wreak as much destruction as they could before their souls were taken.

Shifting his war-board onto his arm, Elric took his own broadsword in both hands and charged the sailors, knocking one off his feet with the lip of the shield and smashing the collarbone of another. The remaining barbarian skipped aside and thrust his curved sword at Elric's face. Elric barely escaped the thrust and the sharp edge of the sword grazed his cheek, bringing out a drop or two of blood. Elric swung the broadsword like a scythe and it bit deep into the barbarian's waist, almost cutting him in two. He struggled for a moment, unable to believe that he was dead but then, as Elric yanked the sword free, he closed his eyes and dropped. The man who had been struck by Elric's shield was staggering to his feet as Elric whirled, saw him, and smashed the broadsword into his skull. Now the way was clear to the bridge. Elric began to climb the ladder, noting that the captain had seen him and was waiting for him at the top.

Elric raised his shield to take the captain's first blow. Through all the noise he thought he heard the man shouting at him.

'Die, you white-faced demon! Die! You have no place on this earth any longer!'

Elric was almost diverted from defending himself by these words. They rang true to him. Perhaps he really had no place on the earth. Perhaps that was why Melniboné was slowly collapsing, why fewer children were born every year, why the dragons themselves were no longer breeding. He let the captain strike another blow at the shield, then he reached under it and swung at the man's legs. But the captain had anticipated the move and jumped backwards. This, however, gave Elric time to run up the few remaining steps and stand on the deck, facing the captain.

The man's face was almost as pale as Elric's. He was sweating and he was panting and his eyes had misery in them as well as a wild fear.

'You should leave us alone,' Elric heard himself saying. 'We offer you no harm, barbarian. When did Melniboné last sail against the Young Kingdoms?'

'You offer us harm by your very presence, Whiteface. There is your sorcery. There are your customs. And there is your arrogance.'

'Is that why you came here? Was your attack motivated by disgust for us? Or would you help yourselves to our wealth? Admit it, captain – greed brought you to Melniboné.'

'At least greed is an honest quality, an understandable one. But you creatures are not human. Worse – you are not gods, though you behave as if you were. Your day is over and you must be wiped out, your city destroyed, your sorceries forgotten.'

Elric nodded. 'Perhaps you are right, captain.'

'I am right. Our holy men say so. Our seers predict your downfall. The Chaos Lords whom you serve will themselves bring about that downfall.'

'The Chaos Lords no longer have any interest in the affairs of Melniboné. They took away their power nearly a thousand years since.' Elric watched the captain carefully, judging the distance between them. 'Perhaps that is why our own power waned. Or perhaps we merely became tired of power.'

'Be that as it may,' the captain said, wiping his sweating brow, 'your time is over. You must be destroyed once and for all.' And then he groaned, for Elric's broadsword had come under his chequered breastplate and gone up through his stomach and into his lungs.

One knee bent, one leg stretched behind him, Elric began to withdraw the long sword, looking up into the barbarian's face which had now assumed an expression of reconciliation. 'That was unfair, Whiteface. We had barely begun to talk and you cut the conversation short. You are most skilful. May you writhe for ever in the Higher Hell. Farewell.'

Elric hardly knew why, after the captain had fallen face down on the deck, he hacked twice at the neck until the head rolled off the body, rolled to the side of the bridge and was then kicked over the side so that it sank into the cold, deep water.

And then Yyrkoon came up behind Elric and he was still grinning.

'You fight fiercely and well, my lord emperor. That dead man was right.'

'Right?' Elric glared at his cousin. 'Right?'

'Aye – in his assessment of your prowess.' And, chuckling, Yyrkoon went to supervise his men who were finishing off the few remaining raiders.

Elric did not know why he had refused to hate Yyrkoon before. But now he did hate Yyrkoon. At that moment he would gladly have slain him. It was as if Yyrkoon had looked deeply into Elric's soul and expressed contempt for what he had seen there.

Suddenly Elric was overwhelmed by an angry misery and he wished with all his heart that he was not a Melnibonéan, that he was not an emperor and that Yyrkoon had never been born.

# Chapter Six

## *Pursuit: A Deliberate Treachery*

L IKE HAUGHTY LEVIATHANS the great golden battle-barges swam through the wreckage of the reaver fleet. A few ships burned and a few were still sinking, but most had sunk into the unplumbable depths of the channel. The burning ships sent strange shadows dancing against the dank walls of the sea-caverns, as if the ghosts of the slain offered a last salute before departing to the sea-depths where, it was said, a Chaos king still ruled, crewing his eery fleets with the souls of all who died in conflict upon the oceans of the world. Or perhaps they went to a gentler doom, serving Straasha, Lord of the Water Elementals, who ruled the upper reaches of the sea.

But a few had escaped. Somehow the southland sailors had got past the massive battle-barges, sailed back through the channel and must even now have reached the open sea. This was reported to the flagship where Elric, Magum Colim and Prince Yyrkoon now stood together again on the bridge, surveying the destruction they had wreaked.

'Then we must pursue them and finish them,' said Yyrkoon. He was sweating and his dark face glistened; his eyes were alight with fever. 'We must follow them.'

Elric shrugged. He was weak. He had brought no extra drugs with him to replenish his strength. He wished to go back to Imr-ryr and rest. He was tired of bloodletting, tired of Yyrkoon and tired, most of all, of himself. The hatred he felt for his cousin was draining him still further – and he hated the hatred; that was the worst part. 'No,' he said. 'Let them go.'

'Let them go? Unpunished? Come now, my lord king! That is

not our way!' Prince Yyrkoon turned to the ageing admiral. 'Is that our way, Admiral Magum Colim?'

Magum Colim shrugged. He, too, was tired, but privately he agreed with Prince Yyrkoon. An enemy of Melniboné should be punished for daring even to think of attacking the Dreaming City. Yet he said: 'The emperor must decide.'

'Let them go,' said Elric again. He leaned heavily against the rail. 'Let them carry the news back to their own barbarian land. Let them say how the Dragon Princes defeated them. The news will spread. I believe we shall not be troubled by raiders again for some time.'

'The Young Kingdoms are full of fools,' Yyrkoon replied. 'They will not believe the news. There will always be raiders. The best way to warn them will be to make sure that not one southlander remains alive or uncaptured.'

Elric drew a deep breath and tried to fight the faintness which threatened to overwhelm him. 'Prince Yyrkoon, you are trying my patience...'

'But, my emperor, I think only of the good of Melniboné. Surely you do not want your people to say that you are weak, that you fear a fight with but five southland galleys?'

This time Elric's anger brought him strength. 'Who will say that Elric is weak? Will it be you, Yyrkoon?' He knew that his next statement was senseless, but there was nothing he could do to stop it. 'Very well, let us pursue these poor little boats and sink them. And let us make haste. I am weary of it all.'

There was a mysterious light in Yyrkoon's eyes as he turned away to relay the orders.

The sky was turning from black to grey when the Melnibonéan fleet reached the open sea and turned its prows south towards the Boiling Sea and the Southern Continent beyond. The barbarian ships would not sail through the Boiling Sea – no mortal ship could do that, it was said – but would sail around it. Not that the barbarian ships would even reach the edges of the Boiling Sea, for the huge battle-barges were fast-sailing vessels. The slaves who pulled the oars were full of a drug which increased their speed and their strength for a score or so of hours, before it slew them. And now the sails billowed out, catching the breeze. Golden mountains, skimming rapidly over the sea, these ships; their method of construction was a secret lost even to the Melnibonéans (who had forgotten so much of their lore). It was easy to imagine how men of the Young Kingdoms hated Melniboné and its inventions, for it did seem that the battle-barges belonged to an older, alien age, as they bore down upon the fleeing galleys now sighted on the horizon.

*The Son of the Pyaray* was in the lead of the rest of the fleet and was priming its catapults well before any of its fellows had seen the enemy. Perspiring slaves gingerly manhandled the viscous stuff of the fireballs, getting them into the bronze cups of the catapults by means of long, spoon-ended tongs. It flickered in the pre-dawn gloom.

Now slaves climbed the steps to the bridge and brought wine and food on platinum platters for the three Dragon Princes who had remained there since the pursuit had begun. Elric could not summon the strength to eat, but he seized a tall cup of yellow wine and drained it. The stuff was strong and revived him a trifle. He had another cup poured and drank that as swiftly as the other. He peered ahead. It was almost dawn. There was a line of purple light on the horizon. 'At the first sign of the sun's disc,' Elric said, 'let loose the fireballs.'

'I will give the order,' said Magum Colim, wiping his lips and putting down the meat bone on which he had been chewing. He left the bridge. Elric heard his feet striking the steps heavily. All at once the albino felt surrounded by enemies. There had been something strange in Magum Colim's manner during the argument with Prince Yyrkoon. Elric tried to shake off such foolish thoughts. But the weariness, the self-doubt, the open mockery of his cousin, all succeeded in increasing the feeling that he was alone and without friends in the world. Even Cymoril and Dyvim Tvar were, finally, Melnibonéans and could not understand the peculiar concerns which moved him and dictated his actions.

Perhaps it would be wise to renounce everything Melnibonéan and wander the world as an anonymous soldier of fortune, serving whoever needed his aid?

The dull red semicircle of the sun showed above the black line of the distant water. There came a series of booming sounds from the forward decks of the flagship as the catapults released their fiery shot; there was a whistling scream, fading away, and it seemed that a dozen meteors leapt through the sky, hurtling towards the five galleys which were now little more than thirty ship-lengths away.

Elric saw two galleys flare, but the remaining three began to sail a zigzag course and avoided the fireballs which landed on the water and burned fitfully for a while before sinking (still burning) into the depths.

More fireballs were prepared and Elric heard Yyrkoon shout from the other side of the bridge, ordering the slaves to greater exertions. Then the fleeing vessels changed their tactics, evidently realising that they could not save themselves for long, and, spreading out, sailed towards *The Son of the Pyaray*, just as the other ships had done in the sea-maze. It was not merely their courage that Elric admired but their manoeuvring skill and the speed at which they had arrived at this logical, if hopeless, decision.

The sun was behind the southland ships as they turned. Three brave silhouettes drew nearer to the Melnibonéan flagship as scarlet stained the sea, as if in anticipation of the bloodletting to come.

Another volley of fireballs was flung from the flagship and the leading galley tried to tack round and avoid it, but two of the fiery globes spattered directly on its deck and soon the whole ship was alive with flame. Burning men leapt into the water. Burning men shot arrows at the flagship. Burning men fell slowly from their positions in the rigging. The burning men died, but the burning ship came on; someone had lashed the steering arm and directed the galley at *The Son of the Pyaray*. It crashed into the golden side of the battle-barge and some of the fire splashed on the deck where the main catapults were in position. A cauldron containing the fire-stuff caught and immediately men were running from all quarters of the ship to try to douse the flame. Elric grinned as he saw what the barbarians had done. Perhaps that ship had deliberately allowed itself to be fired. Now the majority of the flagship's complement was engaged with putting out the blaze – while the southland ships drew alongside, threw up their own grapples, and began to board.

"Ware boarders!' Elric shouted, long after he might have warned his crew. 'Barbarians attack.'

He saw Yyrkoon whirl round, see the situation, and rush down the steps from the bridge. 'You stay there, my lord king,' he flung at Elric as he disappeared. 'You are plainly too weary to fight.'

And Elric summoned all that was left of his strength and stumbled after his cousin, to help in the defence of the ship.

The barbarians were not fighting for their lives – they knew those to be taken already. They were fighting for their pride. They wanted to take one Melnibonéan ship down with them and that ship must be the flagship itself. It was hard to be contemptuous of such men. They knew that even if they took the flagship the other ships of the golden fleet would soon overwhelm them.

But the other ships were still some distance away. Many lives would be lost before they reached the flagship.

On the lowest deck Elric found himself facing a pair of tall barbarians, each armed with a curved blade and a small, oblong shield. He lunged forward, but his armour seemed to drag at his limbs, his own shield and sword were so heavy that he could barely lift them. Two swords struck his helm, almost simultaneously. He lunged back and caught a man in the arm, rammed the other with his shield. A curved blade clanged on his backplate and he all but lost his footing. There was choking smoke everywhere, and heat, and the tumult of battle. Desperately he swung about him and felt his broadsword bite deep into flesh. One of his opponents fell, gurgling, with blood spouting from his mouth and nose. The other lunged. Elric stepped backwards, fell over the corpse of the man he had slain, and went down, his broadsword held out before him in one hand. And as the triumphant barbarian leapt forward to finish the albino, Elric caught him on the point of the broadsword, running him through. The dead man fell towards Elric who did not feel the impact, for he had already fainted. Not for the first time had his deficient blood, no longer enriched by drugs, betrayed him.

He tasted salt and thought at first it was blood. But it was sea water. A wave had risen over the deck and momentarily revived him. He struggled to crawl from under the dead man and then he heard a voice he recognised. He twisted his head and looked up.

Prince Yyrkoon stood there. He was grinning. He was full of glee at Elric's plight. Black, oily smoke still drifted everywhere, but the sounds of the fight had died.

'Are – are we victorious, cousin?' Elric spoke painfully.

'Aye. The barbarians are all dead now. We are about to sail for Imrryr.'

Elric was relieved. He would begin to die soon if he could not get to his store of potions.

His relief must have been evident, for Yyrkoon laughed. 'It is as well the battle did not last longer, my lord, or we should have been without our leader.'

'Help me up, cousin.' Elric hated to ask Prince Yyrkoon any favour, but he had no choice. He stretched out his empty hand. 'I am fit enough to inspect the ship.'

Yyrkoon came forward as if to take the hand, but then he hesitated, still grinning. 'But, my lord, I disagree. You will be dead by the time this ship turns eastward again.'

'Nonsense. Even without the drugs I can live for a considerable time, though movement is difficult. Help me up, Yyrkoon, I command you.'

'You cannot command me, Elric. I am emperor now, you see.'

'Be wary, cousin. I can overlook such treachery, but others will not. I shall be forced to…'

Yyrkoon swung his legs over Elric's body and went to the rail. Here were bolts which fixed one section of the rail in place when it was not used for the gangplank. Yyrkoon slowly released the bolts and kicked the section of rail into the water.

Now Elric's efforts to free himself became more desperate. But he could hardly move at all.

Yyrkoon, on the other hand, seemed possessed of unnatural strength. He bent and easily flung the corpse away from Elric.

'Yyrkoon,' said Elric, 'this is unwise of you.'

'I was never a cautious man, cousin, as well you know.' Yyrkoon placed a booted foot against Elric's ribs and began to shove. Elric slid towards the gap in the rail. He could see the black sea heaving below. 'Farewell, Elric. Now a true Melnibonéan shall sit upon the Ruby Throne. And, who knows, might even make Cymoril his queen? It has not been unheard of...'

And Elric felt himself rolling, felt himself fall, felt himself strike the water, felt his armour pulling him below the surface. And Yyrkoon's last words drummed in Elric's ears like the persistent booming of the waves against the sides of the golden battle-barge.

# Book Two

Less certain of himself or his destiny than ever, the albino king must perforce bring his powers of sorcery into play, conscious of embarking on actions which will make of his life something other than he might have wished it to be. And now matters must be settled. He must begin to rule. He must become cruel. But even in this he will find himself thwarted.

# Chapter One

## *The Caverns of the Sea-King*

ELRIC SANK RAPIDLY, desperately trying to keep the last of his breath in his body. He had no strength to swim and the weight of the armour denied any hope of his rising to the surface and being sighted by Magum Colim or one of the others still loyal to him.

The roaring in his ears gradually faded to a whisper so that it sounded as if little voices were speaking to him, the voices of the water elementals with whom, in his youth, he had had a kind of friendship. and the pain in his lungs faded; the red mist cleared from his eyes and he thought he saw the face of his father, Sadric, of Cymoril and, fleetingly, of Yyrkoon. Stupid Yyrkoon: for all that he prided himself that he was a Melnibonéan, he lacked the Melnibonéan subtlety. He was as brutal and direct as some of the Young Kingdom barbarians he so much despised. And now Elric began to feel almost grateful to his cousin. His life was over. The conflicts which tore his mind would no longer trouble him. His fears, his torments, his loves and his hatreds all lay in the past and only oblivion lay before him. As the last of his breath left his body, he gave himself wholly to the sea; to Straasha, Lord of all the Water Elementals, once the comrade of the Melnibonéan folk. And as he did this he remembered the old spell which his ancestors had used to summon Straasha. The spell came unbidden into his dying brain.

> *Waters of the sea, thou gave us birth*
> *And were our milk and mother both*
> *In days when skies were overcast*
> *You who were first shall be the last.*

*Sea-rulers, fathers of our blood,*
*Thine aid is sought, thine aid is sought,*
*Your salt is blood, our blood your salt,*
*Your blood the blood of Man.*

*Straasha, eternal king, eternal sea*
*Thine aid is sought by me;*
*For enemies of thine and mine*
*Seek to defeat our destiny, and drain away our sea.*

Either the words had an old, symbolic meaning or they referred to some incident in Melnibonéan history which even Elric had not read about. The words meant very little to him and yet they continued to repeat themselves as his body sank deeper and deeper into the green waters. Even when blackness overwhelmed him and his lungs filled with water, the words continued to whisper through the corridors of his brain. It was strange that he should be dead and still hear the incantation.

It seemed a long while later that his eyes opened and revealed swirling water and, through it, huge, indistinct figures gliding towards him. Death, it appeared, took a long time to come and, while he died, he dreamed. The leading figure had a turquoise beard and hair, pale green skin that seemed made of the sea itself and, when he spoke, a voice that was like a rushing tide. He smiled at Elric.

'*Straasha answers thy summons, mortal. Our destinies are bound together. How may I aid thee, and, in aiding thee, aid myself?*'

Elric's mouth was filled with water and yet he still seemed capable of speech (thus proving he dreamed).

He said:

'King Straasha. The paintings in the Tower of D'a'rputna – in the library. When I was a boy I saw them, King Straasha.'

The sea-king stretched out his sea-green hands. '*Aye. You sent the summons. You need our aid. We honour our ancient pact with your folk.*'

'No. I did not mean to summon you. The summons came unbidden to my dying mind. I am happy to drown, King Straasha.'

'*That cannot be. If your mind summoned us it means you wish to*

live. *We will aid you.*' King Straasha's beard streamed in the tide and his deep, green eyes were gentle, almost tender, as they regarded the albino.

Elric closed his own eyes again. 'I dream,' he said. 'I deceive myself with fantasies of hope.' He felt the water in his lungs and he knew he no longer breathed. It stood to reason, therefore, that he was dead. 'But if you were real, old friend, and you wished to aid me, you would return me to Melniboné so that I might deal with the usurper, Yyrkoon, and save Cymoril, before it is too late. That is my only regret – the torment which Cymoril will suffer if her brother becomes Emperor of Melniboné.'

'*Is that all you ask of the water elementals?*' King Straasha seemed almost disappointed.

'I do not even ask that of you. I only voice what I would have wished, had this been reality and I was speaking, which I know is impossible. Now I shall die.'

'*That cannot be, Lord Elric, for our destinies are truly intertwined and I know that it is not yet your destiny to perish. Therefore I will aid you as you have suggested.*'

Elric was surprised at the sharpness of detail of this fantasy. He said to himself, 'What a cruel torment I subject myself to. Now I must set about admitting my death...'

'*You cannot die. Not yet.*'

Now it was as if the sea-king's gentle hands had picked him up and bore him through twisting corridors of a delicate coral-pink texture, slightly shadowed, no longer in water. And Elric felt the water vanish from his lungs and stomach and he breathed. Could it be that he had actually been brought to the legendary plane of the elemental folk – a plane which intersected that of the earth and in which they dwelled, for the most part?

In a huge, circular cavern, which shone with pink and blue mother-of-pearl, they came to rest at last. The sea-king laid Elric down upon the floor of the cavern, which seemed to be covered with fine, white sand which was yet not sand for it yielded and then sprang back when he moved.

When King Straasha moved, it was with a sound like the tide

drawing itself back over shingle. The sea-king crossed the white sand, walking towards a large throne of milky jade. He seated himself upon this throne and placed his green head on his green fist, regarding Elric with puzzled, yet compassionate, eyes.

Elric was still physically weak, but he could breathe. It was as if the sea water had filled him and then cleansed him when it was driven out. He felt clear-headed. And now he was much less sure that he dreamed.

'I still find it hard to know why you saved me, King Straasha,' he murmured from where he lay on the sand.

'*The rune. We heard it on this plane and we came. That is all.*'

'Aye. But there is more to sorcery-working than that. There are chants, symbols, rituals of all sorts. Previously that has always been true.'

'*Perhaps the rituals take the place of urgent need of the kind which sent out your summons to us. Though you say you wished to die, it was evident that this was not your true desire or the Summoning would not have been so clear nor reached us so swiftly. Forget all this now. When you have rested, we shall do what you have requested of us.*'

Painfully, Elric raised himself into a sitting position. 'You spoke earlier of "intertwined destinies". Do you, then, know something of my destiny?'

'*A little, I think. Our world grows old. Once the elementals were powerful on your plane and the people of Melniboné all shared that power. But now our power wanes, as does yours. Something is changing. There are intimations that the Lords of the Higher Worlds are again taking an interest in your world. Perhaps they fear that the folk of the Young Kingdoms have forgotten them. Perhaps the folk of the Young Kingdoms threaten to bring in a new age, where gods and beings such as myself no longer shall have a place. I suspect there is a certain unease upon the planes of the Higher Worlds.*'

'You know no more?'

King Straasha raised his head and looked directly into Elric's eyes. '*There is no more I can tell you, son of my old friends, save that you would be happier if you gave yourself up entirely to your destiny when you understand it.*'

Elric sighed. 'I think I know of what you speak, King Straasha. I shall try to follow your advice.'

'*And now that you have rested, it is time to return.*'

The sea-king rose from his throne of milky jade and flowed towards Elric, lifting him up in strong, green arms.

'*We shall meet again before your life ends, Elric. I hope that I shall be able to aid you once more. And remember that our brothers of the air and of fire will try to aid you also. And remember the beasts – they, too, can be of service to you. There is no need to suspect their help. But beware of gods, Elric. Beware of the Lords of the Higher Worlds and remember that their aid and their gifts must always be paid for.*'

These were the last words Elric heard the sea-king speak before they rushed again through the sinuous tunnels of this other plane, moving at such a speed that Elric could distinguish no details and, at times, did not know whether they remained in King Straasha's kingdom or had returned to the depths of his own world's sea.

# Chapter Two

## *A New Emperor and an Emperor Renewed*

S TRANGE CLOUDS FILLED the sky and the sun hung heavy and huge and red behind them and the ocean was black as the golden galleys swept homeward before their battered flagship *The Son of the Pyaray* which moved slowly with dead slaves at her oars and her tattered sails limp at their masts and smoke-begrimed men on her decks and a new emperor upon her war-wrecked bridge. The new emperor was the only jubilant man in the fleet and he was jubilant indeed. It was his banner now, not Elric's, which took pride of place on the flagmast, for he had lost no time in proclaiming Elric slain and himself ruler of Melniboné.

To Yyrkoon, the peculiar sky was an omen of change, of a return to the old ways and the old power of the Dragon Isle. When he issued orders, his voice was a veritable croon of pleasure, and Admiral Magum Colim, who had ever been wary of Elric but who now had to obey Yyrkoon's orders, wondered if, perhaps, it would not have been preferable to have dealt with Yyrkoon in the manner in which (he suspected) Yyrkoon had dealt with Elric.

Dyvim Tvar leaned on the rail of his own ship, *Terhali's Particular Satisfaction*, and he also paid attention to the sky, though he saw omens of doom, for he mourned for Elric and considered how he might take vengeance on Prince Yyrkoon, should it emerge that Yyrkoon had murdered his cousin for possession of the Ruby Throne.

Melniboné appeared on the horizon, a brooding silhouette of crags, a dark monster squatting in the sea, calling her own back to the heated pleasures of her womb, the Dreaming City of Imrryr. The great cliffs loomed, the central gate to the sea-maze opened, water slapped and gasped as the golden prows disturbed it and the golden ships were swallowed into the murky dankness of the tunnels where bits of wreckage still floated from the previous night's encounter; where white, bloated corpses could still be seen when the brandlight touched them. The prows nosed arrogantly through the remains of their prey, but there was no joy aboard the golden battle-barges, for they brought news of their old emperor's death in battle (Yyrkoon had told them what had happened). Next night and for seven nights in all the Wild Dance of Melniboné would fill the streets. Potions and petty spells would ensure that no-one slept, for sleep was forbidden to any Melnibonéan, old or young, while a dead emperor was mourned. Naked, the Dragon Princes would prowl the city, taking any young woman they found and filling her with their seed for it was traditional that if an emperor died then the nobles of Melniboné must create as many children of aristocratic blood as was possible. Music-slaves would howl from the top of every tower. Other slaves would be slain and some eaten. It was a dreadful dance, the Dance of Misery, and it took as many lives as it created. A tower would be pulled down and a new one erected during those seven days and the tower would be called for Elric VIII, the Albino Emperor, slain upon the sea, defending Melniboné against the southland pirates.

Slain upon the sea and his body taken by the waves. That was not a good portent, for it meant that Elric had gone to serve Pyaray, the Tentacled Whisperer of Impossible Secrets, the Chaos Lord who commanded the Chaos Fleet – dead ships, dead sailors, forever in his thrall – and it was not fitting that such a fate should befall one of the royal line of Melniboné. Ah, but the mourning would be long, thought Dyvim Tvar. He had loved Elric, for all that he had sometimes disapproved of his methods of ruling the Dragon Isle. Secretly he would go to the Dragon Caves that night and spend the period of mourning with the sleeping dragons who, now that Elric was dead, were all he had left to love. And Dyvim Tvar then thought of Cymoril, awaiting Elric's return.

The ships began to emerge into the half-light of the evening. Torches and braziers already burned on the quays of Imrryr which were deserted save for a small group of figures who stood around a chariot which had been driven out to the end of the central mole. A cold wind blew. Dyvim Tvar knew that it was the Princess Cymoril who waited, with her guards, for the fleet.

Though the flagship was the last to pass through the maze, the rest of the ships had to wait until it could be towed into position and dock first. If this had not been the required tradition, Dyvim Tvar would have left his ship and gone to speak to Cymoril, escort her from the quay and tell her what he knew of the circumstances of Elric's death. But it was impossible. Even before *Terhali's Particular Satisfaction* had dropped anchor, the main gangplank of *The Son of the Pyaray* had been lowered and the Emperor Yyrkoon, all swaggering pride, had stepped down it, his arms raised in triumphant salute to his sister who could be seen, even now, searching the decks of the ships for a sign of her beloved albino.

Suddenly Cymoril knew that Elric was dead and she suspected that Yyrkoon had, in some way, been responsible for Elric's death. Either Yyrkoon had allowed Elric to be borne down by a group of southland reavers or else he had managed to slay Elric himself. She knew her brother and she recognised his expression. He was pleased with himself as he always had been when successful in some form of treachery or another. Anger flashed in her tear-filled eyes and she threw back her head and shouted at the shifting, ominous sky:

'Oh! Yyrkoon has destroyed him!'

Her guards were startled. The captain spoke solicitously. 'Madam?'

'He is dead – and that brother slew him. Take Prince Yyrkoon, captain. Kill Prince Yyrkoon, captain.'

Unhappily, the captain put his right hand on the hilt of his sword. A young warrior, more impetuous, drew his blade, murmuring: 'I will slay him, princess, if that is your desire.' The young warrior loved Cymoril with considerable and unthinking intensity.

The captain offered the warrior a cautionary glance, but the warrior was blind to it. Now two others slid swords from scabbards as Yyrkoon, a red cloak wound about him, his dragon crest catching the light from the brands guttering in the wind, stalked forward and cried:

'Yrrkoon is emperor now!'

'No!' shrieked Yyrkoon's sister. 'Elric! Elric! Where are you?'

'Serving his new master, Pyaray of Chaos. His dead hands pull at the sweep of a Chaos ship, sister. His dead eyes see nothing at all. His dead ears hear only the crack of Pyaray's whips and his dead flesh cringes, feeling nought but that unearthly scourge. Elric sank in his armour to the bottom of the sea.'

'Murderer! Traitor!' Cymoril began to sob.

The captain, who was a practical man, said to his warriors in a low voice: 'Sheathe your weapons and salute your new emperor.'

Only the young guardsman who loved Cymoril disobeyed. 'But he slew the emperor! My lady Cymoril said so!'

'What of it? He is emperor now. Kneel or you'll be dead within the minute.'

The young warrior gave a wild shout and leapt towards Yyrkoon, who stepped back, trying to free his arms from the folds of his cloak. He had not expected this.

But it was the captain who leapt forward, his own sword drawn, and hacked down the youngster so that he gasped, half-turned, then fell at Yyrkoon's feet.

This demonstration of the captain's was confirmation of his real power and Yyrkoon almost smirked with satisfaction as he looked down at the corpse. The captain fell to one knee, the bloody sword still in his hand. 'My emperor,' he said.

'You show a proper loyalty, captain.'

'My loyalty is to the Ruby Throne.'

'Quite so.'

Cymoril shook with grief and rage, but her rage was impotent. She knew now that she had no friends.

Leering, the Emperor Yyrkoon presented himself before her. He reached out his hand and he caressed her neck, her cheek, her mouth. He let his hand fall so that it grazed her breast. 'Sister,' he said, 'thou art mine entirely now.'

And Cymoril was the second to fall at his feet, for she had fainted.

'Pick her up,' Yyrkoon said to the guard. 'Take her back to her own tower and there be sure she remains. Two guards will be with her at all times, in even her most private moments they must observe her, for she may plan treachery against the Ruby Throne.'

The captain bowed and signed to his men to obey the emperor. 'Aye, my lord. It shall be done.'

Yyrkoon looked back at the corpse of the young warrior. 'And feed that to her slaves tonight, so that he can continue serving her.' He smiled.

The captain smiled, too, appreciating the joke. He felt it was good to have a proper emperor in Melniboné again. An emperor who knew how to behave, who knew how to treat his enemies and who accepted unswerving loyalty as his right. The captain fancied that fine, martial times lay ahead for Melniboné. The golden battle-barges and the warriors of Imrryr could go a-spoiling again and instil in the barbarians of the Young Kingdoms a sweet and satisfactory sense of fear. Already, in his mind, the captain helped himself to the treasures of Lormyr, Argimiliar and Pika-rayd, of Ilmiora and Jadmar. He might even be made governor, say, of the Isle of the Purple Towns. What luxuries of torment would he bring to those upstart sea-lords, particularly Count Smiorgan Baldhead who was even now beginning to try to make the isle a rival to Melniboné as a trading port! As he escorted the limp body of the Princess Cymoril back to her tower, the captain looked on that body and felt the swellings of lust within him. Yyrkoon would reward his loyalty, there was no doubt of that. Despite the cold wind, the captain began to sweat in his anticipation. He, himself, would guard the Princess Cymoril. He would relish it.

Marching at the head of his army, Yyrkoon strutted for the Tower of D'a'rputna, the Tower of Emperors, and the Ruby Throne within. He preferred to ignore the litter which had been brought for him and to go on foot, so that he might savour every small moment of his triumph. He approached the tower, tall among its fellows at the very centre of Imrryr, as he might approach a beloved woman. He approached it with a sense of delicacy and without haste, for he knew that it was his.

He looked about him. His army marched behind him. Magum Colim and Dyvim Tvar led the army. People lined the twisting streets and bowed low to him. Slaves prostrated themselves. Even the beasts of burden were made to kneel as he strode by. Yyrkoon could almost taste the power as one might taste a luscious fruit. He drew deep breaths of the air. Even the air was his. All Imrryr was his. All Melniboné. Soon would all the world be his. And he would squander it all. How he would squander it! Such a grand terror would he bring back to the earth; such a munificence of fear! In ecstasy, almost blindly, did the Emperor Yyrkoon enter the tower. He hesitated at the great doors of the throne room. He signed for the doors to be opened and as they opened he deliberately took in the scene tiny bit by tiny bit. The walls, the banners, the trophies, the galleries, all were his. The throne room was empty now, but soon he would fill it with colour and celebration and true, Melnibonéan entertainments. It had been too long since blood had sweetened the air of this hall. Now he let his eyes linger upon the steps leading up to the Ruby Throne itself, but, before he looked at the throne, he heard Dyvim Tvar gasp behind him and his gaze went suddenly to the Ruby Throne and his jaw slackened at what he saw. His eyes widened in incredulity.

'An illusion!'

'An apparition,' said Dyvim Tvar with some satisfaction.

'Heresy!' cried the Emperor Yyrkoon, staggering forward, finger pointing at the robed and cowled figure which sat so still upon the Ruby Throne. 'Mine! Mine!'

The figure made no reply.

'Mine! Begone! The throne belongs to Yyrkoon. Yyrkoon is emperor now! What are you? Why would you thwart me thus?'

The cowl fell back and a bone-white face was revealed, surrounded by flowing, milk-white hair. Crimson eyes looked coolly down at the shrieking, stumbling thing which came towards them.

'You are dead, Elric! I know that you are dead!'

The apparition made no reply, but a thin smile touched the white lips.

'You *could* not have survived. You drowned. You cannot come back. Pyaray owns your soul!'

'There are others who rule in the sea,' said the figure on the Ruby Throne. 'Why did you slay me, cousin?'

Yyrkoon's guile had deserted him, making way for terror and confusion. 'Because it is my right to rule! Because you were not strong enough, nor cruel enough, nor humorous enough...'

'Is this not a good joke, cousin?'

'Begone! Begone! Begone! I shall not be ousted by a spectre! A dead emperor cannot rule Melniboné!'

'We shall see,' said Elric, signing to Dyvim Tvar and his soldiers.

# Chapter Three

## *A Traditional Justice*

'Now indeed I shall rule as you would have had me rule, cousin.' Elric watched as Dyvim Tvar's soldiers surrounded the would-be usurper and seized his arms, relieving him of his weapons.

Yyrkoon panted like a captured wolf. He glared around him as if hoping to find support from the assembled warriors, but they stared back at him either neutrally or with open contempt.

'And you, Prince Yyrkoon, will be the first to benefit from this new rule of mine. Are you pleased?'

Yyrkoon lowered his head. He was trembling now. Elric laughed. 'Speak up, cousin.'

'May Arioch and all the Dukes of Hell torment you for eternity,' growled Yyrkoon. He flung back his head, his wild eyes rolling, his lips curling: 'Arioch! Arioch! Curse this feeble albino! Arioch! Destroy him or see Melniboné fall!'

Elric continued to laugh. 'Arioch does not hear you. Chaos is weak upon the earth now. It needs a greater sorcery than yours to bring the Chaos Lords back to aid you as they aided our ancestors. And now, Yyrkoon, tell me – where is the Lady Cymoril?'

But Yyrkoon had lapsed, again, into a sullen silence.

'She is at her own tower, my emperor,' said Magum Colim.

'A creature of Yyrkoon's took her there,' said Dyvim Tvar. 'The captain of Cymoril's own guard, he slew a warrior who tried to defend his mistress against Yyrkoon. It could be that Princess Cymoril is in danger, my lord.'

'Then go quickly to the tower. Take a force of men. Bring both Cymoril and the captain of her guard to me.'

'And Yyrkoon, my lord?' asked Dyvim Tvar.

'Let him remain here until his sister returns.'

Dyvim Tvar bowed and, selecting a body of warriors, left the throne room. All noticed that Dyvim Tvar's step was lighter and his expression less grim than when he had first approached the throne room at Prince Yyrkoon's back.

Yyrkoon straightened his head and looked about the court. For a moment he seemed like a pathetic and bewildered child. All the lines of hate and anger had disappeared and Elric felt sympathy for his cousin growing again within him. But this time Elric quelled the feeling.

'Be grateful, cousin, that for a few hours you were totally powerful, that you enjoyed domination over all the folk of Melniboné.'

Yyrkoon said in a small, puzzled voice: 'How did you escape? You had no time for making a sorcery, no strength for it. You could barely move your limbs and your armour must have dragged you deep to the bottom of the sea so that you should have drowned. It is unfair, Elric. You should have drowned.'

Elric shrugged, 'I have friends in the sea. They recognise my royal blood and my right to rule if you do not.'

Yyrkoon tried to disguise the astonishment he felt. Evidently his respect for Elric had increased, as had his hatred for the albino emperor. 'Friends.'

'Aye,' said Elric, with a thin grin.

'I – I thought, too, you had vowed not to use your powers of sorcery.'

'But you thought that a vow which was unbefitting for a Melnibonéan monarch to make, did you not? Well, I agree with you. You see, Yyrkoon, you have won a victory, after all.'

Yyrkoon stared narrowly at Elric, as if trying to divine a secret meaning behind Elric's words. 'You will bring back the Chaos Lords?'

'No sorcerer, however powerful, can summon the Chaos Lords or, for that matter, the Lords of Law, if they do not wish to be summoned. That you know. You must know it, Yyrkoon. Have you not, yourself, tried? And Arioch did not come, did he? Did he bring you the gift you sought – the gift of the two black swords?'

'You know that?'

'I did not. I guessed. Now I know.'

Yyrkoon tried to speak but his voice would not form words, so angry was he. Instead, a strangled growl escaped his throat and for a few moments he struggled in the grip of his guards.

Dyvim Tvar returned with Cymoril. The girl was pale but she was smiling. She ran into the throne room. 'Elric!'

'Cymoril! Are you harmed?'

Cymoril glanced at the crestfallen captain of her guard who had been brought with her. A look of disgust crossed her fine face. Then she shook her head. 'No. I am not harmed.'

The captain of Cymoril's guard was shaking with terror. He looked pleadingly at Yyrkoon as if hoping that his fellow prisoner could help him. But Yyrkoon continued to stare at the floor.

'Have that one brought closer.' Elric pointed at the captain of the guard. The man was dragged to the foot of the steps leading to the Ruby Throne. He moaned. 'What a petty traitor you are,' said Elric. 'At least Yyrkoon had the courage to attempt to slay me. And his ambitions were high. Your ambition was merely to become one of his pet curs. So you betrayed your mistress and slew one of your own men. What is your name?'

The man had difficulty speaking, but at last he murmured, 'It is Valharik, my name. What could I do? I serve the Ruby Throne, whoever sits upon it.'

'So the traitor claims that loyalty motivated him. I think not.'

'It was, my lord. It was.' The captain began to whine. He fell to his knees. 'Slay me swiftly. Do not punish me more.'

Elric's impulse was to heed the man's request, but he looked at Yyrkoon and then remembered the expression on Cymoril's face when she had looked at the guard. He knew that he must make a point now, whilst making an example of Captain Valharik. So he shook his head. 'No. I will punish you more. Tonight you will die here according to the traditions of Melniboné, while my nobles feast to celebrate this new era of my rule.'

Valharik began to sob. Then he stopped himself and got slowly to his feet, a Melnibonéan again. He bowed low and stepped backward, giving himself into the grip of his guards.

'I must consider a way in which your fate may be shared with the one you wished to serve,' Elric went on. 'How did you slay the young warrior who sought to obey Cymoril?'

'With my sword. I cut him down. It was a clean stroke. But one.'

'And what became of the corpse.'

'Prince Yyrkoon told me to feed it to Princess Cymoril's slaves.'

'I understand. Very well, Prince Yyrkoon, you may join us at the feast tonight while Captain Valharik entertains us with his dying.'

Yyrkoon's face was almost as pale as Elric's. 'What do you mean?'

'The little pieces of Captain Valharik's flesh which our Doctor Jest will carve from his limbs will be the meat on which you feast. You may give instructions as to how you wish the captain's flesh prepared. We should not expect you to eat it raw, cousin.'

Even Dyvim Tvar looked astonished at Elric's decision. Certainly it was in the spirit of Melniboné and a clever irony improving on Prince Yyrkoon's own idea, but it was unlike Elric – or at least, it was unlike the Elric he had known up until a day earlier.

As he heard his fate, Captain Valharik gave a great scream of terror and glared at Prince Yyrkoon as if the would-be usurper were already tasting his flesh. Yyrkoon tried to turn away, his shoulders shaking.

'And that will be the beginning of it,' said Elric. 'The feast will start at midnight. Until that time, confine Yyrkoon to his own tower.'

After Prince Yyrkoon and Captain Valharik had been led away, Dyvim Tvar and Princess Cymoril came and stood beside Elric who had sunk back in his great throne and was staring bitterly into the middle distance.

'That was a clever cruelty,' Dyvim Tvar said.

Cymoril said: 'It is what they both deserve.'

'Aye,' murmured Elric. 'It is what my father would have done. It is what Yyrkoon would have done had our positions been reversed. I but follow the traditions. I no longer pretend that I am my own man. Here I shall stay until I die, trapped upon the Ruby Throne – serving the Ruby Throne as Valharik claimed to serve it.'

'Could you not kill them both quickly?' Cymoril asked. 'You know that I do not plead for my brother because he is my brother. I hate him most of all. But it might destroy you, Elric, to follow through with your plan.'

'What if it does? Let me be destroyed. Let me merely become an unthinking extension of my ancestors. The puppet of ghosts and memories, dancing to strings which extend back through time for ten thousand years.'

'Perhaps if you slept…' Dyvim Tvar suggested.

'I shall not sleep, I feel, for many nights after this. But your brother is not going to die, Cymoril. After his punishment – after he has eaten the flesh of Captain Valharik – I intend to send him into exile. He will go alone into the Young Kingdoms and he will not be allowed to take his grimoires with him. He must make his way as best he can in the lands of the barbarian. That is not too severe a punishment, I think.'

'It is too lenient,' said Cymoril. 'You would be best advised to slay him. Send soldiers now. Give him no time to consider counterplots.'

'I do not fear his counterplots.' Elric rose wearily. 'Now I should like it if you would both leave me, until an hour or so before the feasting begins. I must think.'

'I will return to my tower and prepare myself for tonight,' said Cymoril. She kissed Elric lightly upon his pale forehead. He looked up, filled with love and tenderness for her. He reached out and touched her hair and her cheek. 'Remember that I love you, Elric,' she said.

'I will see that you are safely escorted homeward,' Dyvim Tvar said to her. 'And you must choose a new commander of your guard. Can I assist in that?'

'I should be grateful, Dyvim Tvar.'

They left Elric still upon the Ruby Throne, still staring into space. The hand that he lifted from time to time to his pale head shook a little and now the torment showed in his strange, crimson eyes.

Later, he rose up from the Ruby Throne and walked slowly, head bowed, to his own apartments, followed by his guards. He hesitated at the door which led onto the steps going up to the library. Instinctively he sought the consolation and forgetfulness of a certain kind of knowledge, but at that moment he suddenly hated his scrolls and his books. He blamed them for his ridiculous concerns regarding 'morality' and 'justice'; he blamed them for the feelings of guilt and despair which now filled him as a result of his decision to behave as a Melnibonéan monarch was expected to behave. So he passed the door to the library and went on to his apartments, but even his apartments displeased him now. They were austere. They were not furnished according to the luxurious tastes of all Melnibonéans (save for his father) with their delight in lush mixtures of colour and bizarre design. He would have them changed as soon as possible. He would give himself up to those ghosts who ruled him. For some time he stalked from room to room, trying to push back that part of him which demanded he be merciful to Valharik and to Yyrkoon – at very least to slay them and be done with it or, better, to send them both into exile. But it was impossible to reverse his decision now.

At last he lowered himself to a couch which rested beside a window looking out over the whole of the city. The sky was still full of turbulent cloud, but now the moon shone through, like the yellow eye of an unhealthy beast. It seemed to stare with a certain triumphant irony at him, as if relishing the defeat of his conscience. Elric sank his head into his arms.

Later the servants came to tell him that the courtiers were assembling for the celebration feast. He allowed them to dress him in his yellow robes of state and to place the dragon crown upon his head and then he returned to the throne room to be greeted by a mighty cheer, more wholehearted than any he had ever received before. He acknowledged the greeting and then seated himself in the Ruby Throne, looking out over the banqueting tables which now filled the hall. A table was brought and set before him and two extra seats were brought, for Dyvim Tvar and Cymoril would sit beside him. But Dyvim Tvar and Cymoril were not yet here and neither had the renegade Valharik been brought. And where was Yyrkoon? They should, even now, be at the centre of the hall – Valharik in chains and Yyrkoon seated beneath him. Doctor Jest was there, heating his brazier on which rested his cooking pans, testing and sharpening his knives. The hall was filled with excited talk as the Court waited to be entertained. Already the food was being brought in, though no-one might eat until the emperor ate first.

Elric signed to the commander of his own guard. 'Has the Princess Cymoril or Lord Dyvim Tvar arrived at the tower yet?'

'No, my lord.'

Cymoril was rarely late and Dyvim Tvar never. Elric frowned. Perhaps they did not relish the entertainment.

'And what of the prisoners?'

'They have been sent for, my lord.'

Doctor Jest looked up expectantly, his thin body tensed in anticipation.

And then Elric heard a sound above the din of the conversation. A groaning sound which seemed to come from all around the tower. He bent his head and listened closely.

Others were hearing it now. They stopped talking and also listened intently. Soon the whole hall was in silence and the groaning increased.

Then, all at once, the doors of the throne room burst open and there was Dyvim Tvar, gasping and bloody, his clothes slashed and his flesh gashed. And following him in came a mist – a swirling mist of dark purples and unpleasant blues and it was this mist that groaned.

Elric sprang from his throne and knocked the table aside. He leapt down the steps towards his friend. The groaning mist began to creep further into the throne room, as if reaching out for Dyvim Tvar.

Elric took his friend in his arms. 'Dyvim Tvar! What is this sorcery?'

Dyvim Tvar's face was full of horror and his lips seemed frozen until at last he said:

'It is Yyrkoon's sorcery. He conjured the groaning mist to

aid him in his escape. I tried to follow him from the city but the mist engulfed me and I lost my senses. I went to his tower to bring him and his accessory here, but the sorcery had already been accomplished.'

'Cymoril? Where is she?'

'He took her, Elric. She is with him. Valharik is with him and so are a hundred warriors who remained secretly loyal to him.'

'Then we must pursue him. We shall soon capture him.'

'You can do nothing against the groaning mist. Ah! It comes!'

And sure enough the mist was beginning to surround them. Elric tried to disperse it by waving his arms, but then it had gathered thickly around him and its melancholy groaning filled his ears, its hideous colours blinded his eyes. He tried to rush through it, but it remained with him. And now he thought he heard words amongst the groans. 'Elric is weak. Elric is foolish. Elric must die!'

'Stop this!' he cried. He bumped into another body and fell to his knees. He began to crawl, desperately trying to peer through the mist. Now faces formed in the mist – frightful faces, more terrifying than any he had ever seen, even in his worst nightmares.

'Cymoril!' he cried. 'Cymoril!'

And one of the faces became the face of Cymoril – a Cymoril who leered at him and mocked him and whose face slowly aged until he saw a filthy crone and, ultimately, a skull on which the flesh rotted. He closed his eyes, but the image remained.

'Cymoril,' whispered the voices. 'Cymoril.'

And Elric grew weaker as he became more desperate. He cried out for Dyvim Tvar, but heard only a mocking echo of the name, as he had heard Cymoril's. He shut his lips and he shut his eyes and, still crawling, tried to free himself from the groaning mist. But hours seemed to pass before the groans became whines and the whines became faint strands of sound and he tried to rise, opening his eyes to see the mist fading, but then his legs buckled and he fell down against the first step which led to the Ruby Throne. Again he had ignored Cymoril's advice concerning her brother – and again she was in danger. Elric's last thought was a simple one:

'I am not fit to live,' he thought.

# Chapter Four

## *To Call the Chaos Lord*

A s soon as he recovered from the blow which had knocked him unconscious and thus wasted even more time, Elric sent for Dyvim Tvar. He was eager for news. But Dyvim Tvar could report nothing. Yyrkoon had summoned sorcerous aid to free him, sorcerous aid to effect his escape. 'He must have had some magical means of leaving the island, for he could not have gone by ship,' said Dyvim Tvar.

'You must send out expeditions,' said Elric. 'Send a thousand detachments if you must. Send every man in Melniboné. Strive to wake the dragons that they might be used. Equip the golden battle-barges. Cover the world with our men if you must, but find Cymoril.'

'All those things I have already done,' said Dyvim Tvar, 'save that I have not yet found Cymoril.'

A month passed and Imrryrian warriors marched and rode through the Young Kingdoms seeking news of their renegade countrymen.

'I worried more for myself than for Cymoril and I called that "morality",' thought the albino. 'I tested my sensibilities, not my conscience.'

A second month passed and Imrryrian dragons sailed the skies to South and East, West and North, but though they flew across mountains and seas and forests and plains and, unwittingly, brought terror to many a city, they found no sign of Yyrkoon and his band.

'For, finally, one can only judge oneself by one's actions,' thought Elric. 'I have looked at what I have done, not at what I meant to do or thought I would like to do, and what I have done has, in the main, been foolish, destructive and with little point. Yyrkoon was right to despise me and that was why I hated him so.'

A fourth month came and Imrryrian ships stopped in remote ports and Imrryrian sailors questioned other travellers and explorers for news of Yyrkoon. But Yyrkoon's sorcery had been strong and none had seen him (or remembered seeing him).

'I must now consider the implications of all these thoughts,' said Elric to himself.

Wearily, the swiftest of the soldiers began to return to Melniboné, bearing their useless news. And as faith disappeared and hope faded, Elric's determination increased. He made himself strong, both physically and mentally. He experimented with new drugs which would increase his energy. He read much in the library, though this time he read only certain grimoires and he read those over and over again.

These grimoires were written in the High Speech of Melniboné – the ancient language of sorcery with which Elric's ancestors had been able to communicate with the supernatural beings they had summoned. And at last Elric was satisfied that he understood them fully, though what he read sometimes threatened to stop him in his present course of action.

And when he was satisfied – for the dangers of misunderstanding the implications of the things described in the grimoires were catastrophic – he slept for three nights in a drugged slumber.

And then Elric was ready. He ordered all slaves and servants from his quarters. He placed guards at the doors with instructions to admit no-one, no matter how urgent their business. He cleared one great chamber of all furniture so that it was completely empty save for one grimoire which he had placed in the very centre of the room. Then he seated himself beside the book and began to think.

When he had meditated for more than five hours Elric took a brush and a jar of ink and began to paint both walls and floor with complicated symbols, some of which were so intricate that they seemed to disappear at an angle to the surface on which they had been laid. At last this was done and Elric spreadeagled himself in the

very centre of his huge rune, face down, one hand upon his grimoire, the other (with the Actorios upon it) stretched palm down.
The moon was full. A shaft of its light fell directly upon Elric's head,
turning the hair to silver. And then the Summoning began.

Elric sent his mind into twisting tunnels of logic, across endless
plains of ideas, through mountains of symbolism and endless universes of alternate truths; he sent his mind out further and further
and as it went he sent with it the words which issued from his
writhing lips – words that few of his contemporaries would understand, though their very sound would chill the blood of any
listener. And his body heaved as he forced it to remain in its original position and from time to time a groan would escape him.
And through all this a few words came again and again.

One of these words was a name. 'Arioch'.

Arioch, the patron demon of Elric's ancestors; one of the most
powerful of all the Dukes of Hell, who was called Knight of the
Swords, Lord of the Seven Darks, Lord of the Higher Hell and
many more names besides.

'Arioch!'

It was on Arioch whom Yyrkoon had called, asking the Lord of
Chaos to curse Elric. It was Arioch whom Yyrkoon had sought to
summon to aid him in his attempt upon the Ruby Throne. It was
Arioch who was known as the Keeper of the Two Black Swords –
the swords of unearthly manufacture and infinite power which
had once been wielded by emperors of Melniboné.

'Arioch! I summon thee.'

Runes, both rhythmic and fragmented, howled now from
Elric's throat. His brain had reached the plane on which Arioch
dwelt. Now it sought Arioch himself.

'Arioch! It is Elric of Melniboné who summons thee.'

Elric glimpsed an eye staring down at him. The eye floated,
joined another. The two eyes regarded him.

'Arioch! My Lord of Chaos! Aid me!'

The eyes blinked – and vanished.

'Oh, Arioch! Come to me! Come to me! Aid me and I will
serve you.'

A silhouette that was not a human form turned slowly until a black, faceless head looked down upon Elric. A halo of red light gleamed behind the head.

Then that, too, vanished.

Exhausted, Elric let the image fade. His mind raced back through plane upon plane. His lips no longer chanted the runes and the names. He lay exhausted upon the floor of his chamber, unable to move, in silence.

He was certain that he had failed.

There was a small sound. Painfully he raised his weary head.

A fly had come into the chamber. It buzzed about erratically, seeming almost to follow the lines of the runes Elric had so recently painted.

The fly settled first upon one rune and then on another.

It must have come in through the window, thought Elric. He was annoyed by the distraction but still fascinated by it.

The fly settled on Elric's forehead. It was a large, black fly and its buzz was loud, obscene. It rubbed its forelegs together, and it seemed to be taking a particular interest in Elric's face as it moved over it. Elric shuddered, but he did not have the strength to swat it. When it came into his field of vision, he watched it. When it was not visible he felt its legs covering every inch of his face. Then it flew up and, still buzzing loudly, hovered a short distance from Elric's nose. And then Elric could see the fly's eyes and recognise something in them. They were the eyes – and yet not the eyes – he had seen on that other plane.

It began to dawn on him that this fly was no ordinary creature. It had features that were in some way faintly human.

The fly smiled at him.

From his hoarse throat and through his parched lips Elric was able to utter but one word:

'Arioch?'

And a beautiful youth stood where the fly had hovered. The beautiful youth spoke in a beautiful voice – soft and sympathetic and yet manly. He was clad in a robe that was like a liquid jewel and yet which did not dazzle Elric, for in some way no light seemed to come from it. There was a slender sword at the youth's belt and he wore no helm, but a circlet of red fire. His eyes were wise and his eyes were old and when they were looked at closely they could be seen to contain an ancient and confident evil.

'Elric.'

That was all the youth said, but it revived the albino so that he could raise himself to his knees.

'Elric.'

And Elric could now stand. He was filled with energy.

The youth was taller, now, than Elric. He looked down at the Emperor of Melniboné and he smiled the smile that the fly had smiled. 'You alone are fit to serve Arioch. It is long since I was invited to this plane, but now that I am here I shall aid you, Elric. I shall become your patron. I shall protect you and give you strength and the source of strength, though master I be and slave you be.'

'How must I serve you, Duke Arioch?' Elric asked, having made a monstrous effort of self-control, for he was filled with terror by the implications of Arioch's words.

'You will serve me by serving yourself for the moment. Later a time will come when I shall call upon you to serve me in specific ways, but (for the moment) I ask little of you, save that you swear to serve me.'

Elric hesitated.

'You must swear that,' said Arioch reasonably, 'or I cannot help you in the matter of your cousin Yyrkoon or his sister Cymoril.'

'I swear to serve you,' said Elric. And his body was flooded with ecstatic fire and he trembled with joy and he fell to his knees.

'Then I can tell you that, from time to time, you can call on my aid and I will come if your need is truly desperate. I will come in whichever form is appropriate, or no form at all if that should prove appropriate. And now you may ask me one question before I depart.'

'I need the answers to two questions.'

'Your first question I cannot answer. I will not answer. You must accept that you have now sworn to serve me. I will not tell you what the future holds. But you need not fear, if you serve me well.'

'Then my second question is this: Where is Prince Yyrkoon?'

'Prince Yyrkoon is in the South, in a land of barbarians. By sorcery and by superior weapons and intelligence he has effected the conquest of two mean nations, one of which is called Oin and the other of which is called Yu. Even now he trains the men of Oin and the men of Yu to march upon Melniboné, for he knows that your forces are spread thinly across the earth, searching for him. Ask a third.'

'How has he hidden?'

'He has not. But he has gained possession of the Mirror of Memory – a magical device whose hiding place he discovered by his sorceries. Those who look into this mirror have their memories taken. The mirror contains a million memories: the memories of all who have looked into it. Thus anyone who ventures into Oin or Yu or travels by sea to the capital which serves both is confronted by the mirror and forgets that he has seen Prince Yyrkoon and his Imrryrians in those lands. It is the best way of remaining undiscovered.'

'It is.' Elric drew his brows together. 'Therefore it might be wise to consider destroying the mirror. But what would happen then, I wonder?'

Arioch raised his beautiful hand. 'Although I have answered further questions which are, one could argue, part of the same question, I will answer no more. It could be in your interest to destroy the mirror, but it might be better to consider other means of countering its effects, for it does, I remind you, contain many memories, some of which have been imprisoned for thousands of years. Now I must go. And you must go – to the lands of Oin and Yu which lie several months' journey from here, to the South and well beyond Lormyr. They are best reached by the Ship Which Sails Over Land and Sea. Farewell, Elric.'

And a fly buzzed for a moment upon the wall before vanishing.

Elric rushed from the room, shouting for his slaves.

# Chapter Five

## *The Ship Which Sails Over Land and Sea*

'A ND HOW MANY dragons still sleep in the caverns?' Elric paced the gallery overlooking the city. It was morning, but no sun came through the dull clouds which hung low upon the towers of the Dreaming City. Imrryr's life continued unchanged in the streets below, save for the absence of the majority of her soldiers who had not yet returned home from their fruitless quests and would not be home for many months to come.

Dyvim Tvar leaned on the parapet of the gallery and stared unseeingly into the streets. His face was tired and his arms were folded on his chest as if he sought to contain what was left of his strength.

'Two perhaps. It would take a great deal to wake them and even then I doubt if they'd be useful to us. What is this "Ship Which Sails Over Land and Sea" which Arioch spoke of?'

'I've read of it before – in the Silver Grimoire and in other tomes. A magic ship. Used by a Melnibonéan hero even before there was Melniboné and the empire. But where it exists, and if it exists, I do not know.'

'Who would know?' Dyvim Tvar straightened his back and turned it on the scene below.

'Arioch?' Elric shrugged. 'But he would not tell me.'

'What of your friends the water elementals? Have they not promised you aid? And would they not be knowledgeable in the matter of ships?'

Elric frowned, deepening the lines which now marked his face. 'Aye – Straasha might know. But I'm loath to call on his aid again. The water elementals are not the powerful creatures that the Lords of Chaos are. Their strength is limited and, moreover, they

are inclined to be capricious, in the manner of the elements. What
is more, Dyvim Tvar, I hesitate to use sorcery, save where abso-
lutely imperative...'

'You are a sorcerer, Elric. You have but lately proved your greatness in that respect, involving the most powerful of all sorceries,
the summoning of a Chaos Lord – and you still hold back? I would
suggest, my lord king, that you consider such logic and that you
judge it unsound. You decided to use sorcery in your pursuit of
Prince Yyrkoon. The die is already cast. It would be wise to use
sorcery now.'

'You cannot conceive of the mental and physical effort
involved...'

'I can conceive of it, my lord. I am your friend. I do not wish to
see you pained – and yet...'

'There is also the difficulty, Dyvim Tvar, of my physical weakness,' Elric reminded his friend. 'How long can I continue in the
use of these overstrong potions that now sustain me? They supply
me with energy, aye – but they do so by using up my few resources.
I might die before I find Cymoril.'

'I stand rebuked.'

But Elric came forward and put his white hand on Dyvim
Tvar's butter-coloured cloak. 'But what have I to lose, eh? No. You
are right. I am a coward to hesitate when Cymoril's life is at stake.
I repeat my stupidities – the stupidities which first brought this
pass upon us all. I'll do it. Will you come with me to the ocean?'

'Aye.'

Dyvim Tvar began to feel the burden of Elric's conscience settling
upon him also. It was a peculiar feeling to come to a Melnibonéan
and Dyvim Tvar knew very well that he liked it not at all.

Elric had last ridden these paths when he and Cymoril were happy.
It seemed a long age ago. He had been a fool to trust that happiness. He turned his white stallion's head towards the cliffs and the
sea beyond them. A light rain fell. Winter was descending swiftly
on Melniboné.

They left their horses on the cliffs, lest they be disturbed by

Elric's sorcery-working, and clambered down to the shore. The rain fell into the sea. A mist hung over the water little more than five ship-lengths from the beach. It was deathly still and, with the tall, dark cliffs behind them and the wall of mist before them, it seemed to Dyvim Tvar that they had entered a silent netherworld where might easily be encountered the melancholy souls of those who, in legend, had committed suicide by a process of slow self-mutilation. The sound of the two men's boots on shingle was loud and yet was at once muffled by the mist which seemed to suck at noise and swallow it greedily as if it sustained its life on sound.

'Now,' Elric murmured. He seemed not to notice the brooding and depressive surroundings. 'Now I must recall the rune which came so easily, unsummoned, to my brain not many months since.' He left Dyvim Tvar's side and went down to the place where the chill water lapped the land and there, carefully, he seated himself, cross-legged. His eyes stared, unseeingly, into the mist.

To Dyvim Tvar the tall albino appeared to shrink as he sat down. He seemed to become like a vulnerable child and Dyvim Tvar's heart went out to Elric as it might go out to a brave, nervous boy, and he had it in mind to suggest that the sorcery be done with and they seek the lands of Oin and Yu by ordinary means.

But Elric was already lifting his head as a dog lifts its head to the moon. And strange, thrilling words began to tumble from his lips and it became plain that, even if Dyvim Tvar did speak now, Elric would not hear him.

Dyvim Tvar was no stranger to the High Speech – as a Melnibonéan noble he had been taught it as a matter of course – but the words seemed nonetheless strange to him, for Elric used peculiar inflections and emphases, giving the words a special and secret weight and chanting them in a voice which ranged from bass groan to falsetto shriek. It was not pleasant to listen to such noises coming from a mortal throat and now Dyvim Tvar had some clear understanding of why Elric was reluctant to use sorcery. The Lord of the Dragon Caves, Melnibonéan though he was, found himself inclined to step backward a pace or two, even to retire to the cliff-tops and watch over Elric from there, and he had to force himself to hold his ground as the Summoning continued.

For a good space of time the rune-chanting went on. The rain beat harder upon the pebbles of the shore and made them glisten. It dashed most ferociously into the still, dark sea, lashed about the fragile head of the chanting, pale-haired figure, and caused Dyvim Tvar to shiver and draw his cloak more closely about his shoulders.

'Straasha – Straasha – Straasha...'

The words mingled with the sound of the rain. They were now barely words at all but sounds which the wind might make or a language which the sea might speak.

'Straasha...'

Again Dyvim Tvar had the impulse to move, but this time he desired to go to Elric and tell him to stop, to consider some other means of reaching the lands of Oin and Yu.'

'Straasha!'

There was a cryptic agony in the shout.

'Straasha!'

Elric's name formed on Dyvim Tvar's lips, but he found that he could not speak it.

'Straasha!'

The cross-legged figure swayed. The word became the calling of the wind through the Caverns of Time.

'Straasha!'

It was plain to Dyvim Tvar that the rune was, for some reason, not working and that Elric was using up all his strength to no effect. And yet there was nothing the Lord of the Dragon Caves could do. His tongue was frozen. His feet seemed frozen to the ground.

He looked at the mist. Had it crept closer to the shore? Had it taken on a strange, almost luminous, green tinge? He peered closely.

There was a massive disturbance of the water. The sea rushed up the beach. The shingle crackled. The mist retreated. Vague lights flickered in the air and Dyvim Tvar thought he saw the

shining silhouette of a gigantic figure emerging from the sea and
he realised that Elric's chant had ceased.

'King Straasha,' Elric was saying in something approaching his
normal tone. 'You have come. I thank you.'

The silhouette spoke and the voice reminded Dyvim Tvar of
slow, heavy waves rolling beneath a friendly sun.

'*We elementals are concerned, Elric, for there are rumours that you
have invited Chaos Lords back to your plane and the elementals have
never loved the Lords of Chaos. Yet I know that if you have done this it
is because you are fated to do it and therefore we hold no enmity
against you.*'

'The decision was forced upon me, King Straasha. There was
no other decision I could make. If you are therefore reluctant to
aid me, I shall understand that and call on you no more.'

'*I will help you, though helping you is harder now, not for what happens in the immediate future but what is hinted will happen in years to
come. Now you must tell me quickly how we of the water can be of service to you.*'

'Do you know aught of the Ship Which Sails Over Land and
Sea? I need to find that ship if I am to fulfil my vow to find my
love, Cymoril.'

'*I know much of that ship, for it is mine. Grome also lays claim to it.
But it is mine. Fairly, it is mine.*'

'Grome of the Earth?'

'*Grome of the Land Below the Roots. Grome of the Ground and all
that lives under it. My brother. Grome. Long since, even as we elementals
count time, Grome and I built that ship so that we could travel between
the realms of Earth and Water whenever we chose. But we quarrelled
(may we be cursed for such foolishness) and we fought. There were earth-
quakes, tidal waves, volcanic eruptions, typhoons and battles in which
all the elementals joined, with the result that new continents were flung
up and old ones drowned. It was not the first time we had fought each
other, but it was the last. And finally, lest we destroy each other completely, we made a peace. I gave Grome part of my domain and he gave
me the Ship Which Sails Over Land and Sea. But he gave it somewhat
unwillingly and thus it sails the sea better than it sails the land, for*

*Grome thwarts its progress whenever he can. Still, if the ship is of use to you, you shall have it.'*

'I thank you, King Straasha. Where shall I find it?'

*'It will come. And now I grow weary, for the further from my own realm I venture, the harder it is to sustain my mortal form. Farewell, Elric – and be cautious. You have a greater power than you know and many would make use of it to their own ends.'*

'Shall I wait here for the Ship Which Sails Over Land and Sea?'

*'No...'* the sea-king's voice was fading as his form faded. Grey mist drifted back where the silhouette and the green lights had been. The sea again was still. *'Wait. Wait in your tower... It will come...'*

A few wavelets lapped the shore and then it was as if the king of the water elementals had never been there at all. Dyvim Tvar rubbed his eyes. Slowly at first he began to move to where Elric still sat. Gently he bent down and offered the albino his hand. Elric looked up in some surprise. 'Ah, Dyvim Tvar. How much time has passed?'

'Some hours, Elric. It will soon be night. What little light there is begins to wane. We had best ride back for Imrryr.'

Stiffly Elric rose to his feet, with Dyvim Tvar's assistance. 'Aye...' he murmured absently. 'The sea-king said...'

'I heard the sea-king, Elric. I heard his advice and I heard his warning. You must remember to heed both. I like too little the sound of this magic boat. Like most things of sorcerous origin, the ship appears to have vices as well as virtues, like a double-bladed knife which you raise to stab your enemy and which, instead, stabs you...'

'That must be expected where sorcery is concerned. It was you who urged me on, my friend.'

'Aye,' said Dyvim Tvar almost to himself as he led the way up the cliff-path towards the horses. 'Aye. I have not forgotten that, my lord king.'

Elric smiled wanly and touched Dyvim Tvar's arm. 'Worry not. The Summoning is over and now we have the vessel we need to take us swiftly to Prince Yyrkoon and the lands of Oin and Yu.'

'Let us hope so.' Dyvim Tvar was privately sceptical about the benefits they would gain from the Ship Which Sails Over Land and Sea. They reached the horses and he began to wipe the water off the flanks of his own roan. 'I regret,' he said, 'that we have once again allowed the dragons to expend their energy on a use-less endeavour. With a squadron of my beasts, we could do much against Prince Yyrkoon. And it would be fine and wild, my friend, to ride the skies again, side by side, as we used to.'

'When all this is done and Princess Cymoril brought home, we shall do that,' said Elric, hauling himself wearily into the saddle of his white stallion. 'You shall blow the Dragon Horn and our dragon brothers will hear it and you and I shall sing the Song of the Dragon Masters and our goads shall flash as we straddle Flamefang and his mate Sweetclaw. Ah, that will be like the days of old Melniboné, when we no longer equate freedom with power, but let the Young Kingdoms go their own way and be certain that they let us go ours!'

Dyvim Tvar pulled on his horse's reins. His brow was clouded. 'Let us pray that day will come, my lord. But I cannot help this nagging thought which tells me that Imrryr's days are numbered and that my own life nears its close…'

'Nonsense, Dyvim Tvar. You'll survive me. There's little doubt of that, though you be my elder.'

Dyvim Tvar said, as they galloped back through the closing day: 'I have two sons. Did you know that, Elric?'

'You have never mentioned them.'

'They are by old mistresses.'

'I am happy for you.'

'They are fine Melnibonéans.'

'Why do you mention this, Dyvim Tvar?' Elric tried to read his friend's expression.

'It is that I love them and would have them enjoy the pleasures of the Dragon Isle.'

'And why should they not?'

'I do not know.' Dyvim Tvar looked hard at Elric. 'I could sug-gest that it is your responsibility, the fate of my sons, Elric.'

'Mine?'

'It seems to me, from what I gathered from the water elemental's words, that your decisions could decide the fate of the Dragon Isle. I ask you to remember my sons, Elric.'

'I shall, Dyvim Tvar. I am certain they shall grow into superb Dragon Masters and that one of them shall succeed you as Lord of the Dragon Caves.'

'I think you miss my meaning, my lord emperor.'

And Elric looked solemnly at his friend and shook his head. 'I do not miss your meaning, old friend. But I think you judge me harshly if you fear I'll do aught to threaten Melniboné and all she is.'

'Forgive me, then.' Dyvim Tvar lowered his head. But the expression in his eyes did not change.

In Imrryr they changed their clothes and drank hot wine and had spiced food brought. Elric, for all his weariness, was in better spirits than he had been for many a month. And yet there was still a tinge of something behind his surface mood which suggested he encouraged himself to speak gaily and put vitality into his movements. Admittedly, thought Dyvim Tvar, the prospects had improved and soon they would be confronting Prince Yyrkoon. But the dangers ahead of them were unknown, the pitfalls probably considerable. Still, he did not, out of sympathy for his friend, want to dispel Elric's mood. He was glad, in fact, that Elric seemed in a more positive frame of mind. There was talk of the equipment they would need in their expedition to the mysterious lands of Yu and Oin, speculation concerning the capacity of the Ship Which Sails Over Land and Sea – how many men it would take, what provisions they should put aboard and so on.

When Elric went to his bed, he did not walk with the dragging tiredness which had previously accompanied his step and again, bidding him goodnight, Dyvim Tvar was struck by the same emotion which had filled him on the beach, watching Elric begin his rune. Perhaps it was not by chance that he had used the example of his sons when speaking to Elric earlier that day, for he had a feeling that was almost protective, as if Elric were a boy looking forward to some treat which might not bring him the joy he expected.

Dyvim Tvar dismissed the thoughts, as best he could, and went to his own bed. Elric might blame himself for all that had occurred in the question of Yyrkoon and Cymoril, but Dyvim Tvar wondered if he, too, were not to blame in some part. Perhaps he should have offered his advice more cogently – more vehemently, even – earlier and made a stronger attempt to influence the young emperor. And then, in the Melnibonéan manner, he dismissed such doubts and questions as pointless. There was only one rule – seek pleasure however you would. But had that always been the Melnibonéan way? Dyvim Tvar wondered suddenly if Elric might not have regressive rather than deficient blood. Could Elric be a reincarnation of one of their most distant ancestors? Had it always been in the Melnibonéan character to think only of one-self and one's own gratification?

And again Dyvim Tvar dismissed the questions. What use was there in questions, after all? The world was the world. A man was a man. Before he sought his own bed he went to visit both his old mistresses, waking them up and insisting that he see his sons, Dyvim Slorm and Dyvim Mav, and when his sons, sleepy-eyed, bewildered, had been brought to him, he stared at them for a long while before sending them back. He had said nothing to either, but he had brought his brows together frequently and rubbed at his face and shaken his head and, when they had gone, had said to Niopal and Saramal, his mistresses, who were as bewildered as their offspring, 'Let them be taken to the Dragon Caves tomorrow and begin their learning.'

'So soon, Dyvim Tvar?' said Niopal.

'Aye. There's little time left, I fear.'

He would not amplify on this remark because he could not. It was merely a feeling he had. But it was a feeling that was fast becoming an obsession with him.

In the morning Dyvim Tvar returned to Elric's tower and found the emperor pacing the gallery above the city, asking eagerly for any news of a ship sighted off the coast of the island. But no such ship had been seen. Servants answered earnestly that if their emperor could describe the ship, it would be easier for them to know for what to look, but he could not describe the ship, and could only hint that it might not be seen on water at all, but might appear on land. He was all dressed up in his black war-gear and it was plain to Dyvim Tvar that Elric was indulging in even larger quantities of the potions which replenished his blood. The crimson eyes gleamed with a hot vitality, the speech was rapid and the bone-white hands moved with unnatural speed when Elric made even the lightest gesture.

'Are you well this morning, my lord?' asked the Dragon Master.

'In excellent spirits, thank you, Dyvim Tvar.' Elric grinned. 'Though I'd feel even better if the Ship Which Sails Over Land and Sea were here now.' He went to the balustrade and leaned upon it, peering over the towers and beyond the city walls, looking first to the sea and then to the land. 'Where can it be? I wish that King Straasha had been able to be more specific.'

'I'll agree with that.' Dyvim Tvar, who had not breakfasted, helped himself from the variety of succulent foods laid upon the table. It was evident that Elric had eaten nothing.

Dyvim Tvar began to wonder if the volume of potions had not affected his old friend's brain; perhaps madness, brought about by his involvement with complicated sorcery, his anxiety for Cymoril, his hatred of Yyrkoon, had begun to overwhelm Elric.

'Would it not be better to rest and to wait until the ship is sighted?' he suggested quietly as he wiped his lips.

'Aye – there's reason in that,' Elric agreed. 'But I cannot. I have an urge to be off, Dyvim Tvar, to come face to face with Yyrkoon, to have my revenge on him, to be united with Cymoril again.'

'I understand that. Yet, still…'

Elric's laugh was loud and ragged. 'You fret like Tanglebones over my well-being. I do not need two nursemaids, Lord of the Dragon Caves.'

With an effort Dyvim Tvar smiled. 'You are right. Well, I pray that this magical vessel – what is that?' He pointed out across the island. 'A movement in yonder forest. As if the wind passes through it. But there is no sign of wind elsewhere.'

Elric followed his gaze. 'You are right. I wonder...'

And then they saw something emerge from the forest and the land itself seemed to ripple. It was something which glinted white and blue and black. It came closer.

'A sail,' said Dyvim Tvar. 'It is your ship, I think, my lord.'

'Aye,' Elric whispered, craning forward. 'My ship. Make yourself ready, Dyvim Tvar. By midday we shall be gone from Imrryr.'

# Chapter Six
## *What the Earth God Desired*

T HE SHIP WAS tall and slender and she was delicate. Her rails, masts and bulwarks were exquisitely carved and obviously not the work of a mortal craftsman. Though built of wood, the wood was not painted but naturally shone blue and black and green and a kind of deep smoky red; and her rigging was the colour of seaweed and there were veins in the planks of her polished deck, like the roots of trees, and the sails on her three tapering masts were as fat and white and light as clouds on a fine summer day. The ship was everything that was lovely in nature; few could look upon her and not feel a delight like that which comes from sighting a perfect view. In a word, the ship radiated harmony, and Elric could think of no finer vessel in which to sail against Prince Yyrkoon and the dangers of the lands of Oin and Yu.

The ship sailed gently in the ground as if upon the surface of a river and the earth beneath the keel rippled as if turned momentarily to water. Wherever the keel of the ship touched, and a few feet around it, this effect became evident, though, after the ship had passed, the ground would return to its usual stable state. This was why the trees of the forest had swayed as the ship passed through them, parting before the keel as the ship sailed towards Imrryr.

The Ship Which Sails Over Land and Sea was not particularly large. Certainly she was considerably smaller than a Melnibonéan battle-barge and only a little bigger than a southern galley. But the grace of her; the curve of her line; the pride of her bearing – in these, she had no rival at all.

Already her gangplanks had been lowered to the ground and she was being made ready for her journey. Elric, hands on his slim hips, stood looking up at King Straasha's gift. From the gates

of the city wall slaves were bearing provisions and arms and carrying them up the gangways. Meanwhile Dyvim Tvar was assembling the Imrryrian warriors and assigning them their ranks and duties while on the expedition. There were not many warriors. Only half the available strength could come with the ship, for the other half must remain behind under the command of Admiral Magum Colim and protect the city. It was unlikely that there would be any large attack on Melniboné after the punishment meted out to the barbarian fleet, but it was wise to take precautions, particularly since Prince Yyrkoon had vowed to conquer Imrryr. Also, for some strange reason that none of the onlookers could divine, Dyvim Tvar had called for volunteers – veterans who shared a common disability – and made up a special detachment of these men who, so the onlookers thought, could be of no use at all on the expedition. Still, neither were they of use when it came to defending the city, so they might as well go. These veterans were led aboard first.

Last to climb the gangway was Elric himself. He walked slowly, heavily, a proud figure in his black armour, until he reached the deck. Then he turned, saluted his city, and ordered the gangplank raised.

Dyvim Tvar was waiting for him on the poop deck. The Lord of the Dragon Caves had stripped off one of his gauntlets and was running his naked hand over the oddly coloured wood of the rail. 'This is not a ship made for war, Elric,' he said. 'I should not like to see it harmed.'

'How can it be harmed?' Elric asked lightly as Imrryrians began to climb the rigging and adjust the sails. 'Would Straasha let it be destroyed? Would Grome? Fear not for the Ship Which Sails Over Land and Sea, Dyvim Tvar. Fear only for our own safety and the success of our expedition. Now, let us consult the charts. Remembering Straasha's warning concerning his brother Grome, I suggest we travel by sea for as far as possible, calling in here...' he pointed to a sea-port on the western coast of Lormyr – 'to get our bearings and learn what we can of the lands of Oin and Yu and how those lands are defended.'

'Few travellers have ever ventured beyond Lormyr. It is said that the edge of the world lies not far from that country's most southerly borders.' Dyvim Tvar frowned. 'Could not this whole mission be a trap, I wonder? Arioch's trap? What if he is in league with Prince Yyrkoon and we have been completely deceived into embarking upon an expedition which will destroy us?'

'I have considered that,' said Elric. 'But there is no other choice. We must trust Arioch.'

'I suppose we must.' Dyvim Tvar smiled ironically. 'Another matter now occurs to me. How does the ship move? I saw no anchors we could raise and there are no tides that I know of that sweep across the land. The wind fills the sails – see.' It was true. The sails were billowing and the masts creaked slightly as they took the strain.

Elric shrugged and spread his hands. 'I suppose we must tell the ship,' he suggested. 'Ship – we are ready to sail.'

Elric took some pleasure in Dyvim Tvar's expression of astonishment as, with a lurch, the ship began to move. It sailed smoothly, as over a calm sea, and Dyvim Tvar instinctively clutched the rail, shouting: 'But we are heading directly for the city wall!'

Elric crossed quickly to the centre of the poop deck where a large lever lay, horizontally attached to a ratchet which in turn was attached to a spindle. This was almost certainly the steering gear. Elric grasped the lever as one might grasp an oar and pushed it round a notch or two. Immediately the ship responded – and turned towards another part of the wall! Elric hauled back on the lever and the ship leaned, protesting a little as she yawed around and began to head out across the island. Elric laughed in delight. 'You see, Dyvim Tvar, it is easy. A slight effort of logic was all it took!'

'Nonetheless,' said Dyvim Tvar suspiciously, 'I'd rather we rode dragons. At least they are beasts and may be understood. But this sorcery, it troubles me.'

'Those are not fitting words for a noble of Melniboné!' Elric shouted above the sound of the wind in the rigging, the creaking of the ship's timbers, the slap of the great white sails.

'Perhaps not,' said Dyvim Tvar. 'Perhaps that explains why I stand beside you now, my lord.'

Elric darted his friend a puzzled look before he went below to find a helmsman whom he could teach how to steer the ship.

The ship sped swiftly over rocky slopes and up gorse-covered hills; she cut her way through forests and sailed grandly over grassy plains. She moved like a low-flying hawk which keeps close to the ground but progresses with incredible speed and accuracy as it searches for its prey, altering its course with an imperceptible flick of a wing. The soldiers of Imrryr crowded her decks, gasping in amazement at the ship's progress over the land, and many of the men had to be clouted back to their positions at the sails or elsewhere about the ship. The huge warrior who acted as bosun seemed the only member of the crew unaffected by the miracle of the ship. He was behaving as he would normally behave aboard one of the golden battle-barges; going solidly about his duties and seeing to it that all was done in a proper seamanly manner. The helmsman Elric had selected was, on the other hand, wide-eyed and somewhat nervous of the ship he handled. You could see that he felt he was, at any moment, going to be dashed against a slab of rock or smash the ship apart in a tangle of thick-trunked pines. He was forever wetting his lips and wiping sweat from his brow, even though the air was sharp and his breath steamed as it left his throat. Yet he was a good helmsman and gradually he became used to handling the ship, though his movements were, perforce, more rapid, for there was little time to deliberate upon a decision, the ship travelled with such speed over the land. The speed was breathtaking; they sped more swiftly than any horse – were swifter, even, than Dyvim Tvar's beloved dragons. Yet the motion was exhilarating, too, as the expressions on the faces of all the Imrryrians told.

Elric's delighted laughter rang through the ship and infected many another member of the crew.

'Well, if Grome of the Roots is trying to block our progress, I hesitate to guess how fast we shall travel when we reach water!' he called to Dyvim Tvar.

Dyvim Tvar had lost some of his earlier mood. His long, fine hair streamed around his face as he smiled at his friend. 'Aye – we shall all be whisked off the deck and into the sea!'

And then, as if in answer to their words, the ship began suddenly to buck and at the same time sway from side to side, like a ship caught in powerful cross-currents. The helmsman went white and clung to his lever, trying to get the ship back under control. There came a brief, terrified yell and a sailor fell from the highest crosstree in the mainmast and crashed onto the deck, breaking every bone in his body. And then the ship swayed once or twice and the turbulence was behind them and they continued on their course.

Elric stared at the body of the fallen sailor. Suddenly the mood of gaiety left him completely and he gripped the rail in his black-gauntleted hands and he gritted his strong teeth and his crimson eyes glowed and his lips curled in self-mockery. 'What a fool I am. What a fool I am to tempt the gods so!'

Still, though the ship moved almost as swiftly as it had done, there seemed to be something dragging at it, as if Grome's minions clung on to the bottom as barnacles might cling in the sea. And Elric sensed something around him in the air, something in the rustling of the trees through which they passed, something in the movement of the grass and the bushes and the flowers over which they crossed, something in the weight of the rocks, of the angle of the hills. And he knew that what he sensed was the presence of Grome of the Ground – Grome of the Land Below the Roots – Grome, who desired to own what he and his brother Straasha had once owned jointly, what they had made as a sign of the unity between them and over which they had then fought. Grome wanted very much to take back the Ship Which Sails Over Land and Sea. And Elric, staring down at the black earth, became afraid.

# Chapter Seven
## *King Grome*

B UT AT LAST, with the land tugging at their keel, they reached the sea, sliding into the water and gathering speed with every moment, until Melniboné was gone behind them and they were sighting the thick clouds of steam which hung forever over the Boiling Sea. Elric thought it unwise to risk even this magic vessel in those peculiar waters, so the vessel was turned and headed for the coast of Lormyr, sweetest and most tranquil of the Young Kingdom nations, and the port of Ramasaz on Lormyr's western shore. If the southern barbarians with whom they had so recently fought had been from Lormyr, Elric would have considered making for some other port, but the barbarians had almost certainly been from the south-east on the far side of the continent, beyond Pikarayd. The Lormyrians, under their fat, cautious King Fadan, were not likely to join a raid unless its success was completely assured. Sailing slowly into Ramasaz, Elric gave instructions that their ship be moored in a conventional way and treated like any ordinary ship. It attracted attention, nonetheless, for its beauty, and the inhabitants of the port were astonished to find Melnibonéans crewing the vessel. Though Melnibonéans were disliked throughout the Young Kingdoms, they were also feared. Thus, outwardly at any rate, Elric and his men were treated with respect and were served reasonably good food and wine in the hostelries they entered.

In the largest of the waterfront inns, a place called Heading Outward and Coming Safely Home Again, Elric found a garrulous host who had, until he bought the inn, been a prosperous fisherman and who knew the southernmost shores reasonably well. He certainly knew the lands of Oin and Yu, but he had no respect for them at all.

'You think they could be massing for war, my lord.' He raised his eyebrows at Elric before hiding his face in his wine-mug. Wiping his lips, he shook his red head. 'Then they must war against sparrows. Oin and Yu are barely nations at all. Their only halfway decent city is Dhoz-Kam – and that is shared between them, half being on one side of the River Ar and half being on the other. As for the rest of Oin and Yu – it is inhabited by peasants who are for the most part so ill-educated and superstition-ridden that they are poverty stricken. Not a potential soldier among 'em.'

'You've heard nothing of a Melnibonéan renegade who has conquered Oin and Yu and set about training these peasants to make war?' Dyvim Tvar leaned on the bar next to Elric. He sipped fastidiously from a thick cup of wine. 'Prince Yyrkoon is the renegade's name.'

'Is that whom you seek?' The innkeeper became more interested. 'A dispute between the Dragon Princes, eh?'

'That's our business,' said Elric haughtily.

'Of course, my lords.'

'You know nothing of a great mirror which steals men's memories?' Dyvim Tvar asked.

'A magical mirror!' The innkeeper threw back his head and laughed heartily. 'I doubt if there's one decent mirror in the whole of Oin or Yu! No, my lords, I think you are misled if you fear danger from those lands!'

'Doubtless you are right,' said Elric, staring down into his own untasted wine. 'But it would be wise if we were to check for ourselves – and it would be in Lormyr's interests, too, if we were to find what we seek and warn you accordingly.'

'Fear not for Lormyr. We can deal easily with any silly attempt to make war from that quarter. But if you'd see for yourselves, you must follow the coast for three days until you come to a great bay. The River Ar runs into that bay and on the shores of the river lies Dhoz-Kam – a seedy sort of city, particularly for a capital serving two nations. The inhabitants are corrupt, dirty and disease-ridden, but fortunately they are also lazy and thus afford little trouble, especially if you keep a sword by you. When you have spent an hour in Dhoz-Kam, you will realise the impossibility of such folk becoming a menace to anyone else, unless they should get close enough to you to infect you with one of their several plagues!' Again the innkeeper laughed hugely at his own wit. As he ceased shaking, he added: 'Or unless you fear their navy. It consists of a dozen or so filthy fishing boats, most of which are so unseaworthy they dare only fish the shallows of the estuary.'

Elric pushed his wine-cup aside. 'We thank you, landlord.' He placed a Melnibonéan silver piece upon the counter.

'This will be hard to change,' said the innkeeper craftily.

'There is no need to change it on our account,' Elric told him.

'I thank you, masters. Would you stay the night at my establishment? I can offer you the finest beds in Ramasaz.'

'I think not,' Elric told him. 'We shall sleep aboard our ship tonight, that we might be ready to sail at dawn.'

The landlord watched the Melnibonéans depart. Instinctively he bit at the silver piece and then, suspecting he tasted something odd about it, removed it from his mouth. He stared at the coin, turning it this way and that. Could Melnibonéan silver be poisonous to an ordinary mortal? he wondered. It was best not to take risks. He tucked the coin into his purse and collected up the two wine-cups they had left behind. Though he hated waste, he decided it would be wiser to throw the cups out lest they should have become tainted in some way.

The Ship Which Sails Over Land and Sea reached the bay at noon on the following day and now it lay close inshore, hidden from the distant city by a short isthmus on which grew thick, near-tropical foliage. Elric and Dyvim Tvar waded through the clear, shallow water to the beach and entered the forest. They had decided to be cautious and not make their presence known until they had determined the truth of the innkeeper's contemptuous description of Dhoz-Kam. Near the tip of the isthmus was a reasonably high hill and growing on the hill were several good-sized trees. Elric and Dyvim Tvar used their swords to clear a path through the undergrowth and made their way up the hill until they stood under the trees, picking out the one most easily climbed. Elric selected a tree whose trunk bent and then straightened out again. He sheathed his sword, got his hands onto the trunk and hauled himself up, clambering along until he reached a succession of thick branches which would bear his weight. In the meantime Dyvim Tvar climbed another nearby tree until at last both men could get a good view across the bay where the city of Dhoz-Kam could be clearly seen. Certainly the city itself deserved the innkeeper's description. It was squat and grimy and evidently poor. Doubtless this was why Yyrkoon had chosen it, for the lands of Oin and Yu could not have been hard to conquer with the help of a handful of well-trained Imrryrians and some of Yyrkoon's sorcerous allies. Indeed, few would have bothered to conquer such a place, since its wealth was plainly virtually non-existent and its geographical position of no strategic importance. Yyrkoon had chosen well, for purposes of secrecy if nothing else. But the landlord had been wrong about Dhoz-Kam's fleet. Even from here Elric and Dyvim Tvar could make out at least thirty good-sized warships in the harbour and there seemed to be more anchored upriver. But the ships did not interest them as much as the thing which flashed and glittered above the city – something which had been mounted on huge pillars which supported an axle which, in turn, supported a vast, circular mirror set in a frame whose workmanship was as plainly non-mortal as that of the ship which had brought the Melnibonéans here. There was no doubt that they looked upon the Mirror of Memory and that any who had sailed into the harbour after it had been erected must have had their memory of what they had seen stolen from them instantly.

'It seems to me, my lord,' said Dyvim Tvar from his perch a yard or two away from Elric, 'that it would be unwise of us to sail directly into the harbour of Dhoz-Kam. Indeed, we could be in danger if we entered the bay. I think that we look upon the mirror, even now, only because it is not pointed directly at us. But you notice there is machinery to turn it in any direction its user chooses – save one. It cannot be turned inland, behind the city.

There is no need for it, for who would approach Oin and Yu from the wastelands beyond their borders and who but the inhabitants of Oin or Yu would need to come overland to their capital?'

'I think I take your meaning, Dyvim Tvar. You suggest that we would be wise to make use of the special properties of our ship and...'

'... and go overland to Dhoz-Kam, striking suddenly and making full use of those veterans we brought with us, moving swiftly and ignoring Prince Yyrkoon's new allies – seeking the prince himself, and his renegades. Could we do that, Elric? Dash into the city – seize Yyrkoon, rescue Cymoril – then speed out again and away?'

'Since we have too few men to make a direct assault, it is all we can do, though it's dangerous. The advantage of surprise would be lost, of course, once we had made the attempt. If we failed in our first attempt it would become much harder to attack a second time. The alternative is to sneak into the city at night and hope to locate Yyrkoon and Cymoril alone, but then we should not be making use of our one important weapon, the Ship Which Sails Over Land and Sea. I think your plan is the best one, Dyvim Tvar. Let us turn the ship inland, now, and hope that Grome takes his time in finding us – for I still worry lest he try seriously to wrest the ship from our possession.' Elric began to climb down towards the ground.

Standing once more upon the poop deck of the lovely ship, Elric ordered the helmsman to turn the vessel once again towards the land. Under half-sail the ship moved gracefully through the water and up the curve of the bank and the flowering shrubs of the forest parted before its prow and then they were sailing through the green dark of the jungle, while startled birds cawed and shrilled and little animals paused in astonishment and peered down from the trees at the Ship Which Sails Over Land and Sea and some almost lost their balance as the graceful boat progressed calmly over the floor of the forest, turning aside for only the thickest of the trees.

And thus they made their way to the interior of the land called Oin, which lay to the north of the River Ar, which marked the border between Oin and the land called Yu with which Oin shared a single capital.

Oin was a country consisting largely of unforested jungle and infertile plains where the inhabitants farmed, for they feared the forest and would not go into it, even though that was where Oin's wealth might be found.

The ship sailed well enough through the forest and out over the plain and soon they could see a large river glinting ahead of them and Dyvim Tvar, glancing at the crude map with which he had furnished himself in Ramasaz, suggested that they begin to turn towards the south again and approach Dhoz-Kam by means of a wide semicircle. Elric agreed and the ship began to tack round.

It was then that the land began to heave again and huge waves of grassy earth this time rolled around the ship and blotted out the surrounding view. The ship pitched wildly up and down and from side to side. Two more Imrryrians fell from the rigging and were killed on the deck below. The bosun was shouting loudly – though in fact all this upheaval was happening in silence – and the silence made the situation seem that much more menacing. The bosun yelled to his men to tie themselves to their positions. 'And all those not doing anything – get below at once!' he added.

Elric had wound a scarf around the rail and tied the other end to his wrist. Dyvim Tvar had used a long belt for the same purpose. But still they were flung in all directions, often losing their footing as the ship bucked this way and that, and every bone in Elric's body seemed about to crack and every inch of his flesh seemed bruised. And the ship was creaking and protesting and threatening to break up under the awful strain of riding the heaving land.

'Is this Grome's work, Elric?' Dyvim Tvar panted. 'Or is it some sorcery of Yyrkoon's?'

Elric shook his head. 'Not Yyrkoon. It is Grome. And I know no way to placate him. Not Grome, who thinks least of all the kings of the elements, yet, perhaps, is the most powerful.'

'But surely he breaks his bargain with his brother by doing this to us?'

'No. I think not. King Straasha warned us this might happen. We can only hope that Grome expends all his energy and that the ship survives, as it might survive a natural storm at sea.'

'This is worse than a sea-storm, Elric!'

Elric nodded his agreement but could say nothing, for the deck was tilting at a crazy angle and he had to cling to the rails with both hands in order to retain any kind of footing.

And now the silence stopped.

Instead they heard a rumbling and a roaring that seemed to have something of the character of laugher.

'King Grome!' Elric shouted. 'King Grome! Let us be! We have done you no harm!'

But the laughter increased and it made the whole ship quiver as the land rose and fell around it, as trees and hills and rocks rushed towards the ship and then fell away again, never quite engulfing them, for Grome doubtless wanted his ship intact.

'Grome! You have no quarrel with mortals!' Elric cried again. 'Let us be! Ask a favour of us if you must, but grant us this favour in return!'

Elric was shouting almost anything that came into his head. Really, he had no hope of being heard by the earth god and he did not expect King Grome to bother to listen even if the elemental did hear. But there was nothing else to do.

'Grome! Grome! Grome! Listen to me!'

Elric's only response was in the louder laughter which made every nerve in him tremble. And the earth heaved higher and dropped lower and the ship spun round and round until Elric was sure he would lose his senses entirely.

'King Grome! King Grome! Is it just to slay those who have never done you harm?'

And then, slowly, the heaving earth subsided and the ship was still and a huge, brown figure stood looking down at the ship. The figure was the colour of earth and looked like a vast, old oak. His hair and his beard were the colour of leaves and his eyes were the colour of gold ore and his teeth were the colour of granite and his feet were like roots and his skin seemed covered in tiny green shoots in place of hair and he smelled rich and musty and good and he was King Grome of the Earth Elementals. He sniffed and he frowned and he said in a soft, mighty voice that was yet coarse and grumpy: 'I want my ship.'

'It is not our ship to give, King Grome,' said Elric.

Grome's tone of petulance increased. 'I want my ship,' he said slowly. 'I want the thing. It is mine.'

'Of what use is it to you, King Grome?'

'Use? It is mine.'

Grome stamped and the land rippled.

Elric said desperately: 'It is your brother's ship, King Grome. It is King Straasha's ship. He gave you part of his domain and you allowed him to keep the ship. That was the bargain.'

'I know nothing of a bargain. The ship is mine.'

'You know that if you take the ship then King Straasha will have to take back the land he gave you.'

'I want my ship.' The huge figure shifted its position and bits of earth fell from it, landing with distinctly heard thuds on the ground below and on the deck of the ship.

'Then you must kill us to obtain it,' Elric said.

'Kill? Grome does not kill mortals. He kills nothing. Grome builds. Grome brings to life.'

'You have already killed three of our company,' Elric pointed out. 'Three are dead, King Grome, because you made the land-storm.'

Grome's great brows drew together and he scratched his great head, causing an immense rustling noise to sound. 'Grome does not kill,' he said again.

'King Grome has killed,' said Elric reasonably. 'Three lives lost.'

Grome grunted. 'But I want my ship.'

'The ship is lent to us by your brother. We cannot give it to you. Besides, we sail in it for a purpose – a noble purpose, I think. We...'

'I know nothing of "purposes" – and care nothing for you.

I want my ship. My brother should not have lent it to you. I had almost forgotten it. But now that I remember it, I want it.'

'Will you not accept something else in place of the ship, King Grome?' said Dyvim Tvar suddenly. 'Some other gift.'

Grome shook his monstrous head. 'How could a mortal give me something? It is mortals who take from me all the time. They steal my bones and my blood and my flesh. Could you give me back all that your kind has taken?'

'Is there not one thing?' Elric said.

Grome closed his eyes.

'Precious metals? Jewels?' suggested Dyvim Tvar. 'We have many such in Melniboné.'

'I have plenty,' said King Grome.

Elric shrugged in despair. 'How can we bargain with a god, Dyvim Tvar?' He gave a bitter smile. 'What can the Lord of the Soil desire? More sun, more rain? These are not ours to give.'

'I am a rough sort of god,' said Grome, 'if indeed god I am. But I did not mean to kill your comrades. I have an idea. Give me the bodies of the slain. Bury them in my earth.'

Elric's heart leapt. 'That is all you wish of us?'

'It would seem much to me.'

'And for that you will let us sail on?'

'On water, aye,' growled Grome. 'But I do not see why I should allow you to sail over my land. It is too much to expect of me. You can go to yonder river, but from now this ship will only possess the properties bestowed upon it by my brother Straasha. No longer shall it cross my domain.'

'But, King Grome, we need this ship. We are upon urgent business. We need to sail to the city yonder.' Elric pointed in the direction of Dhoz-Kam.

'You may go to the river, but after that the ship will sail only on water. Now give me what I ask.'

Elric called down to the bosun who, for the first time, seemed amazed by what he was witnessing. 'Bring up the bodies of the three dead men.'

The bodies were brought up from below. Grome stretched out one of his great, earthy hands and picked them up.

'I thank you,' he growled. 'Farewell.'

And slowly Grome began to descend into the ground, his whole huge frame becoming, atom by atom, absorbed with the earth until he was gone.

And then the ship was moving again, slowly towards the river, on the last short voyage it would ever make upon the land.

'And thus our plans are thwarted,' said Elric.

Dyvim Tvar looked miserably towards the shining river. 'Aye. So much for that scheme. I hesitate to suggest this to you, Elric, but I fear we must resort to sorcery again if we are to stand any chance of achieving our goal.'

Elric sighed.

'I fear we must,' he said.

# Chapter Eight

## *The City and the Mirror*

PRINCE YYRKOON WAS pleased. His plans went well. He peered through the high fence which enclosed the flat roof of his house (three storeys high and the finest in Dhoz-Kam); he looked out towards the harbour at his splendid, captured fleet. Every ship which had come to Dhoz-Kam and which had not flown the standard of a powerful nation had been easily taken after its crew had looked upon the great mirror which squatted on its pillars above the city. Demons had built those pillars and Prince Yyrkoon had paid them for their work with the souls of all those in Oin and Yu who had resisted him. Now there was one last ambition to ful- fil and then he and his new followers would be on their way to Melniboné...

He turned and spoke to his sister. Cymoril lay on a wooden bench, staring unseeingly at the sky, clad in the filthy tatters of the dress she had been wearing when Yyrkoon abducted her from her tower.

'See our fleet, Cymoril! While the golden barges are scattered we shall sail unhampered into Imrryr and declare the city ours. Elric cannot defend himself against us now. He fell so easily into my trap. He is a fool! And you were a fool to give him your affection!'

Cymoril made no response. Through all the months she had been away, Yyrkoon had drugged her food and drink and pro- duced in her a lassitude which rivalled Elric's undrugged condition. Yyrkoon's own experiments with his sorcerous powers had turned him gaunt, wild-eyed and somewhat mangey; he ceased to take any pains with his physical appearance. But Cymoril had a wasted, haunted look to her, for all that beauty remained. It was as if

Dhoz-Kam's run-down seediness had infected them both in different ways.

'Fear not for your own future, however, my sister,' Yyrkoon continued. He chuckled. 'You shall still be empress and sit beside the emperor on his Ruby Throne. Only I shall be emperor and Elric shall die for many days and the manner of his death will be more inventive than anything he thought to do to me.'

Cymoril's voice was hollow and distant. She did not turn her head when she spoke. 'You are insane, Yyrkoon.'

'Insane? Come now, sister, is that a word that a true Melnibonéan should use? We Melnibonéans judge nothing sane or insane. What a man is – he is. What he does – he does. Perhaps you have stayed too long in the Young Kingdoms and its judgements are becoming yours. But that shall soon be righted. We shall return to the Dragon Isle in triumph and you will forget all this, just as if you yourself had looked into the Mirror of Memory.' He darted a nervous glance upwards, as if he half-expected the mirror to be turned on him.

Cymoril closed her eyes. Her breathing was heavy and very slow; she was bearing this nightmare with fortitude, certain that Elric must eventually rescue her from it. That hope was all that had stopped her from destroying herself. If the hope went altogether, then she would bring about her own death and be done with Yyrkoon and all his horrors.

'Did I tell you that last night I was successful? I raised demons, Cymoril. Such powerful, dark demons. I learned from them all that was left for me to learn. And I opened the Shade Gate at last. Soon I shall pass through it and there I shall find what I seek. I shall become the most powerful mortal on earth. Did I tell you all this, Cymoril?'

He had, in fact, repeated himself several times that morning, but Cymoril had paid no more attention to him then than she did now. She felt so tired. She tried to sleep. She said slowly, as if to remind herself of something: 'I hate you, Yyrkoon.'

'Ah, but you shall love me soon, Cymoril. Soon.'

'Elric will come...'

'Elric! Ha! He sits twiddling his thumbs in his tower, waiting for news that will never come – save when I bring it to him!'

'Elric will come,' she said.

Yyrkoon snarled. A brute-faced Oinish girl brought him his morning wine. Yyrkoon seized the cup and sipped the stuff. Then he spat it at the girl who, trembling, ducked away. Yyrkoon took the jug and emptied it onto the white dust of the roof. 'This is Elric's thin blood. This is how it will flow away!'

But again Cymoril was not listening. She was trying to remember her albino lover and the few sweet days they had spent together since they were children.

Yyrkoon hurled the empty jug at the girl's head, but she was adept at dodging him. As she dodged, she murmured her standard response to all his attacks and insults. 'Thank you, Demon Lord,' she said. 'Thank you, Demon Lord.'

Yyrkoon laughed. 'Aye. Demon Lord. Your folk are right to call me that, for I rule more demons than I rule men. My power increases every day!'

The Oinish girl hurried away to fetch more wine, for she knew he would be calling for it in a moment. Yyrkoon crossed the roof to stare through the slats in the fence at the proof of his power, but as he looked upon his ships he heard sounds of confusion from the other side of the roof. Could the Yurits and the Oinish be fighting amongst themselves? Where were their Imrryrian centurions? Where was Captain Valharik?

He almost ran across the roof, passing Cymoril who appeared to be sleeping, and peered down into the streets.

'Fire?' he murmured. 'Fire?'

It was true that the streets appeared to be on fire. And yet it was not an ordinary fire. Balls of fire seemed to drift about, igniting rush-thatched roofs, doors, anything which would easily burn – as an invading army might put a village to the torch.

Yyrkoon scowled, thinking at first that he had been careless and some spell of his had turned against him, but then he looked over the burning houses at the river and he saw a strange ship sailing there, a ship of great grace and beauty, that somehow seemed more a creation of nature than of man – and he knew they were under attack. But who would attack Dhoz-Kam? There was no loot worth the effort. It could not be Imrryrians…

It could not be Elric.

'It must not be Elric,' he growled. 'The mirror. It must be turned upon the invaders.'

'And upon yourself, brother?' Cymoril had risen unsteadily and leaned against a table. She was smiling. 'You were too confident, Yyrkoon. Elric comes.'

'Elric! Nonsense! Merely a few barbarian raiders from the interior. Once they are in the centre of the city, we shall be able to use the Mirror of Memory upon them.' He ran to the trapdoor which led down into his house. 'Captain Valharik! Valharik, where are you?'

Valharik appeared in the room below. He was sweating. There was a blade in his gloved hand, though he did not seem to have been in any fighting as yet.

'Make the mirror ready, Valharik. Turn it upon the attackers.'

'But, my lord, we might…'

'Hurry! Do as I say. We'll soon have these barbarians added to our own strength – along with their ships.'

'Barbarians, my lord? Can barbarians command the fire elementals? These things we fight are flame spirits. They cannot be slain any more than fire itself can be slain.'

'Fire can be slain by water,' Prince Yyrkoon reminded his lieutenant. 'By water, Captain Valharik. Have you forgotten?'

'But, Prince Yyrkoon, we have tried to quench the spirits with water – and the water will not move from our buckets. Some powerful sorcerer commands the invaders. He has the aid of the spirits of fire *and* water.'

'You are mad, Captain Valharik,' said Yyrkoon firmly. 'Mad. Prepare the mirror and let us have no more of these stupidities.'

Valharik wetted his dry lips. 'Aye, my lord.' He bowed his head and went to do his master's bidding.

Again Yyrkoon went to the fence and looked through. There were men in the streets now, fighting his own warriors, but smoke

289

obscured his view, he could not make out the identities of any of the invaders. 'Enjoy your petty victory,' Yyrkoon chuckled, 'for soon the mirror will take away your minds and you will become my slaves.'

'It is Elric,' said Cymoril quietly. She smiled. 'Elric comes to take vengeance on you, brother.'

Yyrkoon sniggered. 'Think you? Think you? Well, should that be the case, he'll find me gone, for I still have a means of evading him – and he'll find you in a condition which will not please him (though it will cause him considerable anguish). But it is not Elric. It is some crude shaman from the steppes to the east of here. He will soon be in my power.'

Cymoril, too, was peering through the fence.

'Elric,' she said. 'I can see his helm.'

'What?' Yyrkoon pushed her aside. There, in the streets, Imrryrian fought Imrryrian, there was no longer any doubt of that. Yyrkoon's men – Imrryrian, Oinish and Yurit – were being pushed back. And at the head of the attacking Imrryrians could be seen a black dragon helm such as only one Melnibonéan wore. It was Elric's helm. And Elric's sword, that had once belonged to Earl Aubec of Malador, rose and fell and was bright with blood which glistened in the morning sunshine.

For a moment Yyrkoon was overwhelmed with despair. He groaned. 'Elric. Elric. Elric. Ah, how we continue to underestimate each other! What curse is on us?'

Cymoril had flung back her head and her face had come to life again. 'I said he would come, brother!'

Yyrkoon whirled on her. 'Aye – he has come – and the mirror will rob him of his brain and he will turn into my slave, believing anything I care to put in his skull. This is even sweeter than I planned, sister. Ha!' He looked up and then flung his arms across his eyes as he realised what he had done. 'Quickly – below – into the house – the mirror begins to turn.' There came a great creaking of gears and pulleys and chains as the terrible Mirror of Memory began to focus on the streets below. 'It will be only a little while before Elric has added himself and his men to my

strength. What a splendid irony!' Yyrkoon hurried his sister down the steps leading from the roof and he closed the trapdoor behind him. 'Elric himself will help in the attack on Imrryr. He will destroy his own kind. He will oust himself from the Ruby Throne!'

'Do you not think that Elric has anticipated the threat of the Mirror of Memory, brother?' Cymoril said with relish.

'Anticipate it, aye – but resist it he cannot. He must see to fight. He must either be cut down or open his eyes. No man with eyes can be safe from the power of the mirror.' He glanced around the crudely furnished room. 'Where is Valharik? Where is the cur?'

Valharik came running in. 'The mirror is being turned, my lord, but it will affect our own men, too. I fear...'

'Then cease to fear. What if our own men are drawn under its influence? We can soon feed what they need to know back into their brains – at the same time as we feed our defeated foes. You are too nervous, Captain Valharik.'

'But Elric leads them...'

'And Elric's eyes *are* eyes – though they look like crimson stones. He will fare no better than his men.'

In the streets around Prince Yyrkoon's house Elric, Dyvim Tvar and their Imrryrians pushed on, forcing back their demoralised opponents. The attackers had lost barely a man, whereas many Oinish and Yurits lay dead in the streets, beside a few of their renegade Imrryrian commanders. The flame elementals, whom Elric had summoned with some effort, were beginning to disperse, for it cost them dear to spend so much time entirely within Elric's plane, but the necessary advantage had been gained and there was now little question of who would win as a hundred or more houses blazed throughout the city, igniting others and requiring attention from the defenders lest the whole squalid place burn down about their ears. In the harbour, too, ships were burning.

Dyvim Tvar was the first to notice the mirror beginning to swing into focus on the streets. He pointed a warning finger, then turned, blowing on his war-horn and ordering forward the troops who, up to now, had played no part in the fighting. 'Now you must lead us!' he cried, and he lowered his helm over his face. The eye-holes of the helm had been blocked so that he could not see through.

Slowly Elric lowered his own helm until he was in darkness. The sound of fighting continued however, as the veterans who had sailed with them from Melniboné set to work in their place and the other troops fell back. The leading Imrryrians had not blocked their eye-holes.

Elric prayed that the scheme would work.

Yyrkoon, peeking cautiously through a chink in a heavy curtain, said querulously: 'Valharik? They fight on. Why is that? Is not the mirror focused?'

'It should be, my lord.'

'Then, see for yourself, the Imrryrians continue to forge through our defenders – and our men are beginning to come under the influence of the mirror. What is wrong, Valharik? What is wrong?'

Valharik drew air between his teeth and there was a certain admiration in his expression as he looked upon the fighting Imrryrians.

'They are blind,' he said. 'They fight by sound and touch and smell. They are blind, my lord emperor – and they lead Elric and his men whose helms are so designed they can see nothing.'

'Blind?' Yyrkoon spoke almost pathetically, refusing to understand. 'Blind?'

'Aye. Blind warriors – men wounded in earlier wars, but good fighters nonetheless. That is how Elric defeats our mirror, my lord.'

'Agh! No! No!' Yyrkoon beat heavily on his captain's back and the man shrank away. 'Elric is not cunning. He is not cunning. Some powerful demon gives him these ideas.'

'Perhaps, my lord. But are there demons more powerful than those who have aided you?'

'No,' said Yyrkoon. 'There are none. Oh, that I could summon some of them now! But I have expended my powers in opening

the Shade Gate. I should have anticipated... I could not anticipate... Oh Elric! I shall yet destroy you, when the runeblades are
mine!' Then Yyrkoon frowned. 'But how could he have been prepared? What demon...? Unless he summoned Arioch himself? But
he has not the power to summon Arioch. I could not summon
him...'

And then, as if in reply, Yyrkoon heard Elric's battle-song
sounding from the nearby streets. And that song answered the
question.

'Arioch! Arioch! Blood and souls for my lord Arioch!'

'Then I must have the runeblades. I must pass through the Shade
Gate. There I still have allies – supernatural allies who shall deal
easily with Elric, if need be. But I need time...' Yyrkoon mumbled
to himself as he paced about the room. Valharik continued to
watch the fighting.

'They come closer,' said the captain.

Cymoril smiled. 'Closer, Yyrkoon? Who is the fool now? Elric?
Or you?'

'Be still! I think. I think...' Yyrkoon fingered his lips.

Then a light came into his eye and he looked cunningly at
Cymoril for a second before turning his attention to Captain
Valharik.

'Valharik, you must destroy the Mirror of Memory.'

'Destroy it? But it is our only weapon, my lord?'

'Exactly – but is it not useless now?'

'Aye.'

'Destroy it and it will serve us again.' Yyrkoon flicked a long
finger in the direction of the door. 'Go. Destroy the mirror.'

'But, Prince Yyrkoon – emperor, I mean – will that not have the
effect of robbing us of our only weapon?'

'Do as I say, Valharik! Or perish!'

'But how shall I destroy it, my lord?'

'Your sword. You must climb the column *behind* the face of the
mirror. Then, without looking into the mirror itself, you must
swing your sword against it and smash it. It will break easily. You

know the precautions I have had to take to make sure that it was not harmed.'

'Is that all I must do?'

'Aye. Then you are free from my service – you may escape or do whatever else you wish to do.'

'Do we not sail against Melniboné?'

'Of course not. I have devised another method of taking the Dragon Isle.'

Valharik shrugged. His expression showed that he had never really believed Yyrkoon's assurances. But what else had he to do but follow Yyrkoon, when fearful torture awaited him at Elric's hands? With shoulders bowed, the captain slunk away to do his prince's work.

'And now, Cymoril...' Yyrkoon grinned like a ferret as he reached out to grab his sister's soft shoulders. 'Now to prepare you for your lover, Elric.'

One of the blind warriors cried: 'They no longer resist us, my lord. They are limp and allow themselves to be cut down where they stand. Why is this?'

'The mirror has robbed them of their memories,' Elric called, turning his own blind head towards the sound of the warrior's voice. 'You can lead us into a building now – where, with luck, we shall not glimpse the mirror.'

At last they stood within what appeared to Elric, as he lifted his helm, to be a warehouse of some kind. Luckily it was large enough to hold their entire force and when they were all inside Elric had the doors shut while they debated their next action.

'We should find Yyrkoon,' Dyvim Tvar said. 'Let us interrogate one of those warriors...'

'There'll be little point in that, my friend,' Elric reminded him. 'Their minds are gone. They'll remember nothing at all. They do not at present remember even what they are, let alone who. Go to the shutters yonder, where the mirror's influence cannot reach, and see if you can see the building most likely to be occupied by my cousin.'

Dyvim Tvar crossed swiftly to the shutters and looked cautiously out. 'Aye – there's a building larger than the rest and I see some movement within, as if the surviving warriors were regrouping. It's likely that's Yyrkoon's stronghold. It should be easily taken.'

Elric joined him. 'Aye. I agree with you. We'll find Yyrkoon there. But we must hurry, lest he decides to slay Cymoril. We must work out the best means of reaching the place and instruct our blind warriors as to how many streets, how many houses and so forth, we must pass.'

'What is that strange sound?' One of the blind warriors raised his head. 'Like the distant ringing of a gong.'

'I hear it too,' said another blind man.

And now Elric heard it. A sinister noise. It came from the air above them. It shivered through the atmosphere.

'The mirror!' Dyvim Tvar looked up. 'Has the mirror some property we did not anticipate?'

'Possibly…' Elric tried to remember what Arioch had told him. But Arioch had been vague. He had said nothing of this dreadful, mighty sound, this shattering clangour as if… 'He is breaking the mirror!' he said. 'But why?' There was something more now, something brushing at his brain. As if the sound were, itself, sentient.

'Perhaps Yyrkoon is dead and his magic dies with him,' Dyvim Tvar began. And then he broke off with a groan.

The noise was louder, more intense, bringing sharp pain to his ears.

And now Elric knew. He blocked his ears with his gauntleted hands. The memories in the mirror. They were flooding into his mind. The mirror had been smashed and was releasing all the memories it had stolen over the centuries – the aeons, perhaps. Many of those memories were not mortal. Many were the memories of beasts and intelligent creatures which had existed even before Melniboné. And the memories warred for a place in Elric's skull – in the skulls of all the Imrryrians – in the poor, tortured skulls of the men outside whose pitiful screams could be heard rising from the streets – and in the skull of Captain Valharik, the turncoat, as he lost his footing on the great column and fell with the shards from the mirror to the ground far below.

But Elric did not hear Captain Valharik scream and he did not hear Valharik's body crash first to a rooftop and then into the street where it lay all broken beneath the broken mirror.

Elric lay upon the stone floor of the warehouse and he writhed, as his comrades writhed, trying to clear his head of a million memories that were not his own – of loves, of hatreds, of strange experiences and ordinary experiences, of wars and journeys, of the faces of relatives who were not his relatives, of men and women and children, of animals, of ships and cities, of fights, of love-making, of fears and desires – and the memories fought each other for possession of his crowded skull, threatening to drive his own memories (and thus his own character) from his head. And as Elric writhed upon the ground, clutching at his ears, he spoke a word over and over again in an effort to cling to his own identity.

'Elric. Elric. Elric.'

And gradually, by an effort which he had experienced only once before when he had summoned Arioch to the plane of the Earth, he managed to extinguish all those alien memories and assert his own until, shaken and feeble, he lowered his hands from his ears and no longer shouted his own name. And then he stood up and looked about him.

More than two thirds of his men were dead, blind or otherwise. The big bosun was dead, his eyes wide and staring, his lips frozen in a scream, his right eye-socket raw and bleeding from where he had tried to drag his eye from it. All the corpses lay in unnatural positions, all had their eyes open (if they had eyes) and many bore the marks of self-mutilation, while others had vomited and others had dashed their brains against a wall. Dyvim Tvar was alive, but curled up in a corner, mumbling to himself and Elric thought he might be mad. Some of the other survivors were, indeed, mad, but they were quiet, they afforded no danger. Only five, including Elric, seemed to have resisted the alien memories and retained their own sanity. It seemed to Elric, as he stumbled from corpse to corpse, that most of the men had had their hearts fail.

'Dyvim Tvar?' Elric put his hand on his friend's shoulder. 'Dyvim Tvar?'

Dyvim Tvar took his head from his arm and looked into Elric's eyes. In Dyvim Tvar's own eyes was the experience of a score of millennia and there was irony there, too. 'I live, Elric.'

'Few of us live now.'

A little later they left the warehouse, no longer needing to fear the mirror, and found that all the streets were full of the dead who had received the mirror's memories. Stiff bodies reached out hands to them. Dead lips formed silent pleas for help. Elric tried not to look at them as he pressed through them, but his desire for vengeance upon his cousin was even stronger now.

They reached the house. The door was open and the ground floor was crammed with corpses. There was no sign of Prince Yyrkoon.

Elric and Dyvim Tvar led the few Imrryrians who were still sane up the steps, past more imploring corpses, until they reached the top floor of the house.

And here they found Cymoril.

She was lying upon a couch and she was naked. There were runes painted on her flesh and the runes were, in themselves, obscene. Her eyelids were heavy and she did not at first recognise them. Elric rushed to her side and cradled her body in his arms. The body was oddly cold.

'He – he makes me – sleep…' said Cymoril. 'A sorcerous sleep – from which – only he can wake me…' She gave a great yawn. 'I have stayed awake – this long – by an effort of – will – for Elric comes…'

'Elric is here,' said her lover, softly. 'I am Elric, Cymoril.'

'Elric?' She relaxed in his arms. 'You – you must find Yyrkoon – for only he can wake me…'

'Where has he gone?' Elric's face had hardened. His crimson eyes were fierce. 'Where?'

'To find the two black swords – the runeswords – of – our ancestors – Mournblade…'

'And Stormbringer,' said Elric grimly. 'Those swords are cursed. But where has he gone, Cymoril? How has he escaped us?'

'Through – through – through the – Shade Gate – he conjured it – he made the most fearful pacts with demons to go through… The – other – room…'

Now Cymoril slept, but there seemed to be a certain peace on her face.

Elric watched as Dyvim Tvar crossed the room, sword in hand, and flung the door open. A dreadful stench came from the next room, which was in darkness. Something flickered on the far side.

'Aye – that's sorcery, right enough,' said Elric. 'And Yyrkoon has thwarted me. He conjured the Shade Gate and passed through it into some netherworld. Which one, I'll never know, for there is an infinity of them. Oh, Arioch, I would give much to follow my cousin!'

'*Then follow him you shall,*' said a sweet, sardonic voice in Elric's head.

At first the albino thought it was a vestige of a memory still fighting for possession of his head, but then he knew that Arioch spoke to him.

'*Dismiss your followers that I may speak with thee,*' said Arioch.

Elric hesitated. He wished to be alone – but not with Arioch. He wished to be with Cymoril, for Cymoril was making him weep. Tears already flowed from his crimson eyes.

'*What I have to say could result in Cymoril being restored to her normal state,*' said the voice. '*And, moreover, it will help you defeat Yyrkoon and be revenged upon him. Indeed, it could make you the most powerful mortal there has ever been.*'

Elric looked up at Dyvim Tvar, 'Would you and your men leave me alone for a few moments?'

'Of course.' Dyvim Tvar led his men away and shut the door behind him.

Arioch stood leaning against the same door. Again he had assumed the shape and poise of a handsome youth. His smile was friendly and open and only the ancient eyes belied his appearance.

'It is time to seek the black swords yourself, Elric,' said Arioch.

'Lest Yyrkoon reach them first. I warn you of this – with the rune-blades Yyrkoon will be so powerful he will be able to destroy half the world without thinking of it. That is why your cousin risks the dangers of the world beyond the Shade Gate. If Yyrkoon possesses those swords before you find them, it will mean the end of you, of Cymoril, of the Young Kingdoms and, quite possibly, the destruction of Melniboné, too. I will help you enter the netherworld to seek for the twin runeswords.'

Elric said musingly: 'I have often been warned of the dangers of seeking the swords – and the worse dangers of owning them. I think I must consider another plan, my lord Arioch.'

'There is no other plan. Yyrkoon desires the swords, if you do not. With Mournblade in one hand and Stormbringer in the other, he will be invincible, for the swords give their user power. Immense power.' Arioch paused.

'You must do as I say. It is to your advantage.'

'And to yours, Lord Arioch?'

'Aye – to mine. I am not entirely selfless.'

Elric shook his head. 'I am confused. There has been too much of the supernatural about this affair. I suspect the gods of manipulating us…'

'The gods serve only those who are willing to serve them. And the gods serve destiny, also.'

'I like it not. To stop Yyrkoon is one thing, to assume his ambitions and take the swords myself – that is another thing.'

'It is your destiny.'

'Cannot I change my destiny?'

Arioch shook his head. 'No more than can I.'

Elric stroked sleeping Cymoril's hair. 'I love her. She is all I desire.'

'You shall not wake her if Yyrkoon finds the blades before you do.'

'And how shall I find the blades?'

'Enter the Shade Gate – I have kept it open, though Yyrkoon thinks it closed – then you must seek the Tunnel Under the Marsh which leads to the Pulsing Cavern. In that chamber the runeswords are kept. They have been kept there ever since your ancestors relinquished them...'

'Why were they relinquished?'

'Your ancestors lacked courage.'

'Courage to face what?'

'Themselves.'

'You are cryptic, my lord Arioch.'

'That is the way of the Lords of the Higher Worlds. Hurry. Even I cannot keep the Shade Gate open long.'

'Very well. I will go.'

And Arioch vanished immediately.

Elric called in a hoarse, cracking voice for Dyvim Tvar who entered at once.

'Elric? What has happened in here? Is it Cymoril? You look...'

'I am going to follow Yyrkoon – alone, Dyvim Tvar. You must make your way back to Melniboné with those of our men who remain. Take Cymoril with you. If I do not return in reasonable time, you must declare her empress. If she still sleeps, then you must rule as regent until she wakes.'

Dyvim Tvar said softly. 'Do you know what you do, Elric?'

Elric shook his head.

'No, Dyvim Tvar, I do not.'

He got to his feet and staggered towards the other room where the Shade Gate waited for him.

# Book Three

And now there is no turning back at all. Elric's destiny has been forged and fixed as surely as the hellswords were forged and fixed aeons before. Was there ever a point where he might have turned off this road to despair, damnation and destruction? Or has he been doomed since before his birth? Doomed through a thousand incarnations to know little else but sadness and struggle, loneliness and remorse – eternally the champion of some unknown cause?

# Chapter One
## *Through the Shade Gate*

AND ELRIC STEPPED into a shadow and found himself in a world of shadows. He turned, but the shadow through which he had entered now faded and was gone. Old Aubec's sword was in Elric's hand, the black helm and the black armour were upon his body and only these were familiar, for the land was dark and gloomy as if contained in a vast cave whose walls, though invisible, were oppressive and tangible. And Elric regretted the hysteria, the weariness of brain, which had given him the impulse to obey his patron demon Arioch and plunge through the Shade Gate. But regret was useless now, so he forgot it.

Yyrkoon was nowhere to be seen. Either Elric's cousin had had a steed awaiting him or else, more likely, he had entered this world at a slightly different angle (for all the planes were said to turn about each other) and was thus either nearer or farther from their mutual goal. The air was rich with brine – so rich that Elric's nostrils felt as if they had been packed with salt – it was almost like walking under water and just being able to breathe the water itself. Perhaps this explained why it was so difficult to see any great distance in any direction, why there were so many shadows, why the sky was like a veil which hid the roof of a cavern. Elric sheathed his sword, there being no evident danger present at that moment, and turned slowly, trying to get some kind of bearing.

It was possible that there were jagged mountains in what he judged the east, and perhaps a forest to the west. Without sun, or stars, or moon, it was hard to gauge distance or direction. He stood on a rocky plain over which whistled a cold and sluggish wind, which tugged at his cloak as if it wished to possess it. There were a few stunted, leafless trees standing in a clump about a hundred paces away. It was all that relieved the bleak plain, save for a large, shapeless slab of rock which stood a fair way beyond the trees. It was a world which seemed to have been drained of all life, where Law and Chaos had once battled and, in their conflict, destroyed all. Were there many planes such as this one? Elric wondered. And for a moment he was filled with a dreadful presentiment concerning the fate of his own rich world. He shook this mood off at once and began to walk towards the trees and the rock beyond.

He reached the trees and passed them, and the touch of his cloak on a branch broke the brittle thing which turned almost at once to ash which was scattered on the wind. Elric drew the cloak closer about his body.

As he approached the rock he became conscious of a sound which seemed to emanate from it. He slowed his pace and put his hand upon the pommel of his sword.

The noise continued – a small, rhythmic noise. Through the gloom Elric peered carefully at the rock, trying to locate the source of the sound.

And then the noise stopped and was replaced by another – a soft scuffle, a padding footfall, and then silence. Elric took a pace backward and drew Aubec's sword. The first sound had been that of a man sleeping. The second sound was that of a man waking and preparing himself either for attack or to defend himself.

Elric said: 'I am Elric of Melniboné. I am a stranger here.'

And an arrow slid past his helm almost at the same moment as a bowstring sounded. Elric flung himself to one side and sought about for cover, but there was no cover save the rock behind which the archer hid.

And now a voice came from behind the rock. It was a firm, rather bleak voice. It said:

'That was not meant to harm you but to display my skill in case you considered harming me. I have had my fill of demons in this world and you look like the most dangerous demon of all, Whiteface.'

'I am mortal,' said Elric, straightening up and deciding that if he must die it would be best to die with some sort of dignity.

'You spoke of Melniboné. I have heard of the place. An isle of demons.'

'Then you have not heard enough of Melniboné. I am mortal as are all my folk. Only the ignorant think us demons.'

'I am not ignorant, my friend. I am a Warrior Priest of Phum, born to that caste and the inheritor of all its knowledge and, until recently, the Lords of Chaos themselves were my patrons. Then I refused to serve them any longer and was exiled to this plane by them. Perhaps the same fate befell you, for the folk of Melniboné serve Chaos, do they not?'

'Aye. And I know of Phum - it lies in the Unmapped East - beyond the Weeping Waste, beyond the Sighing Desert, beyond even Elwher. It is one of the oldest of the Young Kingdoms.'

'All that is so - though I dispute that the East is unmapped, save by the savages of the West. So you are, indeed, to share my exile, it seems.'

'I am not exiled. I am upon a quest. When the quest is done, I shall return to my own world.'

'Return, say you? That interests me, my pale friend. I had thought return impossible.'

'Perhaps it is and I have been tricked. And if your own powers have not found you a way to another plane, perhaps mine will not save me either.'

'Powers? I have none since I relinquished my servitude to Chaos. Well, friend, do you intend to fight me?'

'There is only one upon this plane I would fight and it is not you, Warrior Priest of Phum.' Elric sheathed his sword and at the same moment the speaker rose from behind the rock, replacing a scarlet-fletched arrow in a scarlet quiver.

'I am Rackhir,' said the man. 'Called the Red Archer for, as you see, I affect scarlet dress. It is a habit of the Warrior Priests of Phum to choose but a single colour to wear. It is the only loyalty to tradition I still possess.' He had on a scarlet jerkin, scarlet breeks, scarlet shoes and a scarlet cap with a scarlet feather in it. His bow was scarlet and the pommel of his sword glowed ruby-red. His face, which was aquiline and gaunt, as if carved from fleshless bone, was weather-beaten, and that was brown. He was tall and he was thin, but muscles rippled on his arms and torso. There was irony in his eyes and something of a smile upon his thin lips, though the face showed that it had been through much experience, little of it pleasant.

'An odd place to choose for a quest,' said the Red Archer, standing with hands on hips and looking Elric up and down. 'But I'll strike a bargain with you if you're interested.'

'If the bargain suits me, archer, I'll agree to it, for you seem to know more of this world than do I.'

'Well – you must find something here and then leave, whereas I have nothing at all to do here and wish to leave. If I help you in your quest, will you take me with you when you return to our own plane?'

'That seems a fair bargain, but I cannot promise what I have no power to give. I will say only this – if it is possible for me to take you back with me to our own plane, either before or after I have finished my quest, I will do it.'

'That is reasonable,' said Rackhir the Red Archer. 'Now – tell me what you seek.'

'I seek two swords, forged millennia ago by immortals, used by my ancestors but then relinquished by them and placed upon this plane. The swords are large and heavy and black and they have cryptic runes carved into their blades. I was told that I would find them in the Pulsing Cavern which is reached through the Tunnel Under the Marsh. Have you heard of either of these places?'

'I have not. Nor have I heard of the two black swords.' Rackhir rubbed his bony chin. 'Though I remember reading something in one of the Books of Phum and what I read disturbed me…'

'The swords are legendary. Many books make some small reference to them – almost always mysterious. There is said to be one tome which records the history of the swords and all who have used them – and all who will use them in the future – a timeless book which contains all time. Some call it the Chronicle of the Black Sword and in it, it is said, men may read their whole destinies.'

'I know nothing of that, either. It is not one of the Books of Phum. I fear, Comrade Elric, that we shall have to venture to the City of Ameeron and ask your questions of the inhabitants there.'

'There is a city upon this plane?'

'Aye – a city. I stayed but a short time in it, preferring the wilderness. But with a friend, it might be possible to bear the place a little longer.'

'Why is Ameeron unsuited to your taste?'

'Its citizens are not happy. Indeed, they are a most depressed and depressing group, for they are all, you see, exiles or refugees or travellers between the worlds who lost their way and never found it again. No-one lives in Ameeron by choice.'

'A veritable City of the Damned.'

'As the poet might remark, aye.' Rackhir offered Elric a sardonic wink. 'But I sometimes think all cities are that.'

'What is the nature of this plane where there are, as far as I can tell, no planets, no moon, no sun? It has something of the air of a great cavern.'

'There is, indeed, a theory that it is a sphere buried in an infinity of rock. Others say that it lies in the future of our own Earth – a future where the universe has died. I heard a thousand theories during the short space of time I spent in the City of Ameeron. All, it seemed to me, were of equal value. All, it seemed to me, could be correct. Why not? There are some who believe that everything is a Lie. Conversely, everything could be the Truth.'

It was Elric's turn to remark ironically: 'You are a philosopher, then, as well as an archer, friend Rackhir of Phum?'

Rackhir laughed. 'If you like! It is such thinking that weakened my loyalty to Chaos and led me to this pass. I have heard that there is a city called Tanelorn which may sometimes be found on the shifting shores of the Sighing Desert. If I ever return to our own world, Comrade Elric, I shall seek that city, for I have heard that peace may be found there – that such debates as the nature of Truth are considered meaningless. That men are content merely to exist in Tanelorn.'

'I envy those who dwell in Tanelorn,' said Elric.

Rackhir sniffed. 'Aye. But it would probably prove a disappointment, if found. Legends are best left as legends and attempts to make them real are rarely successful. Come – yonder lies Ameeron and that, sad to say, is more typical of most cities one comes across – on any plane.'

The two tall men, both outcasts in their different ways, began to trudge through the gloom of that desolate wasteland.

# Chapter Two

## *In the City of Ameeron*

T HE CITY OF Ameeron came in sight and Elric had never seen such a place before. Ameeron made Dhoz-Kam seem like the cleanest and most well-run settlement there could be. The city lay below the plain of rocks, in a shallow valley over which hung perpetual smoke: a filthy, tattered cloak meant to hide the place from the sight of men and gods.

The buildings were mostly in a state of semi-ruin or else were wholly ruined and shacks and tents erected in their place. The mixture of architectural styles – some familiar, some most alien – was such that Elric was hard put to see one building which resembled another. There were shanties and castles, cottages, towers and forts, plain, square villas and wooden huts heavy with carved ornamentation. Others seemed merely piles of rock with a jagged opening at one end for a door. But none looked well – could not have looked well in that landscape under that perpetually gloomy sky.

Here and there red fires sputtered, adding to the smoke, and the smell as Elric and Rackhir reached the outskirts was rich with a great variety of stinks.

'Arrogance, rather than pride, is the paramount quality of most of Ameeron's residents,' said Rackhir, wrinkling his hawklike nose. 'Where they have any qualities of character left at all.'

Elric trudged through filth. Shadows scuttled amongst the close-packed buildings. 'Is there an inn, perhaps, where we can enquire after the Tunnel Under the Marsh and its whereabouts?'

'No inn. By and large the inhabitants keep themselves to themselves...'

'A city square where folk meet?'

'This city has no centre. Each resident or group of residents

311

built their own dwelling where they felt like it, or where there was space, and they come from all planes and all ages, thus the confusion, the decay and the oldness of many of the places. Thus the filth, the hopelessness, the decadence of the majority.'

'How do they live?'

'They live off each other, by and large. They trade with demons who occasionally visit Ameeron from time to time…'

'Demons?'

'Aye. And the bravest hunt the rats which dwell in the caverns below the city.'

'What demons are these?'

'Just creatures, mainly minor minions of Chaos, who want something that the Ameeronese can supply – a stolen soul or two, a baby, perhaps (though few are born here) – you can imagine what else, if you've knowledge of what demons normally demand from sorcerers.'

'Aye. I can imagine. So Chaos can come and go on this plane as it pleases?'

'I'm not sure it's quite as easy. But it is certainly easier for the demons to travel back and forth here than it would be for them to travel back and forth in our plane.'

'Have you seen any of these demons?'

'Aye. The usual bestial sort. Coarse, stupid and powerful – many of them were once human before electing to bargain with Chaos. Now they are mentally and physically warped into foul, demon shapes.'

Elric found Rackhir's words not to his taste. 'Is that ever the fate of those who bargain with Chaos?' he said.

'You should know, if you come from Melniboné. I know that in Phum it is rarely the case. But it seems that the higher the stakes the subtler are the changes a man undergoes when Chaos agrees to trade with him.'

Elric sighed. 'Where shall we enquire of our Tunnel Under the Marsh?'

'There was an old man…' Rackhir began, and then a grunt behind him made him pause.

Another grunt.

A face with tusks in it emerged from a patch of darkness formed by a fallen slab of masonry. The face grunted again.

'Who are you?' said Elric, his sword-hand ready.

'Pig,' said the face with tusks in it. Elric was not certain whether he was being insulted or whether the creature was describing himself.

'Pig.'

Two more faces with tusks in them came out of the patch of darkness. 'Pig,' said one.

'Pig,' said another.

'Snake,' said a voice behind Elric and Rackhir. Elric turned while Rackhir continued to watch the pigs. A tall youth stood there. Where his head would have been sprouted the bodies of about fifteen good-sized snakes. The head of each snake glared at Elric. The tongues flickered and they all opened their mouths at exactly the same moment to say again:

'Snake.'

'Thing,' said another voice. Elric glanced in that direction, gasped, drew his sword and felt nausea sweep through him.

Then Pigs, Snake and Thing were upon them.

Rackhir took one Pig before it could move three paces. His bow was off his back and strung and a red-fletched arrow nocked and shot, all in a second. He had time to shoot one more Pig and then drop his bow to draw his sword. Back to back he and Elric prepared to defend themselves against the demons' attack. Snake was bad enough, with its fifteen darting heads hissing and snapping with teeth which dripped venom, but Thing kept changing its form – first an arm would emerge, then a face would appear from the shapeless, heaving flesh which shuffled implacably closer.

'Thing!' it shouted. Two swords slashed at Elric who was dealing with the last Pig and missed his stroke so that instead of running the Pig through the heart, he took him in a lung. Pig staggered backward and slumped to the ground in a pool of muck. He crawled for a moment, but then collapsed. Thing had produced a spear and Elric barely managed to deflect the cast with the flat of

his sword. Now Rackhir was engaged with Snake and the two demons closed on the men, eager to make a finish of them. Half the heads of Snake lay writhing on the ground and Elric had managed to slice one hand off Thing, but the demon still seemed to have three other hands ready. It seemed to be created not from one creature but from several. Elric wondered if, through his bargaining with Arioch, this would ultimately be his fate, to be turned into a demon – a formless monster. But wasn't he already something of a monster? Didn't folk already mistake him for a demon?

These thoughts gave him strength. He yelled as he fought. 'Elric!'

And: 'Thing!' replied his adversary, also eager to assert what he regarded as the essence of his being.

Another hand flew off as Aubec's sword bit into it. Another javelin jabbed out and was knocked aside; another sword appeared and came down on Elric's helm with a force which dazed him and sent him reeling back against Rackhir who missed his thrust at Snake and was almost bitten by four of the heads. Elric chopped at the arm and the tentacle which held the sword and saw them part from the body but then become reabsorbed again. The nausea returned. Elric thrust his sword into the mass and the mass screamed: 'Thing! Thing! Thing!'

Elric thrust again and four swords and two spears waved and clashed and tried to deflect Aubec's blade.

'Thing!'

'This is Yyrkoon's work,' said Elric, 'without a doubt. He has heard that I have followed him and seeks to stop us with his demon allies.' He gritted his teeth and spoke through them. 'Unless one of these is Yyrkoon himself! Are you my cousin Yyrkoon, Thing?'

'Thing...' The voice was almost pathetic. The weapons waved and clashed but they no longer darted so fiercely at Elric.

'Or are you some other old, familiar friend?'

'Thing...'

Elric stabbed again and again into the mass. Thick, reeking blood spurted and fell upon his armour. Elric could not understand why it had become so easy to take the attack to the demon.

'Now!' shouted a voice from above Elric's head. 'Quickly!'

Elric glanced up and saw a red face, a white beard, a waving arm. 'Don't look at me, you fool! Now – strike!'

And Elric put his two hands above his sword hilt and drove the blade deep into the shapeless creature which moaned and wept and said in a small whisper 'Frank...' before it died.

Rackhir thrust at the same moment and his blade went under the remaining snake heads and plunged into the chest and thence into the heart of the youth-body and his demon died, too.

The white-haired man came clambering down from the ruined archway on which he had been perched. He was laughing. 'Niun's sorcery still has some effect, even here, eh? I heard the tall one call his demon friends and instruct them to set upon you. It did not seem fair to me that five should attack two – so I sat upon that wall and I drew the many-armed demon's strength out of it. I still can. I still can. And now I have his strength (or a fair part of it) and feel considerably better than I have done for many a moon (if such a thing exists).'

'It said "Frank",' said Elric frowning. 'Was that a name, do you think? Its name before?'

'Perhaps,' said old Niun, 'perhaps. Poor creature. But still, it is dead now. You are not of Ameeron, you two – though I've seen you here before, red one.'

'And I've seen you,' said Rackhir with a smile. He wiped Snake's blood from his blade, using one of Snake's heads for the purpose. 'You are Niun Who Knew All.'

'Aye. Who Knew All but who now knows very little. Soon it will be over, when I have forgotten everything. Then I may return from this awful exile. It is the pact I made with Orland of the Staff. I was a fool who wished to know everything and my curiosity led me into an adventure concerning this Orland. Orland showed me the error of my ways and sent me here to forget. Sadly, as you noticed, I still remember some of my powers and my knowledge from time to time. I know you seek the black swords. I know you are Elric of Melniboné. I know what will become of you.'

'You know my destiny?' said Elric eagerly. 'Tell me what it is, Niun Who Knew All.'

Niun opened his mouth as if to speak but then firmly shut it again. 'No,' he said. 'I have forgotten.'

'No!' Elric made as if to seize the old man. 'No! You remember! I can see that you remember!'

'I have forgotten.' Niun lowered his head.

Rackhir took hold of Elric's arm. 'He has forgotten, Elric.'

Elric nodded. 'Very well.' Then he said, 'But have you remembered where lies the Tunnel Under the Marsh?'

'Yes. It is only a short distance from Ameeron, the marsh itself. You go that way. Then you look for a monument in the shape of an eagle carved in black marble. At the base of the monument is the entrance to the tunnel.' Niun repeated this information parrot-fashion and when he looked up his face was clearer. 'What did I just tell you?'

Elric said: 'You gave us instructions on how to reach the entrance to the Tunnel Under the Marsh.'

'Did I?' Niun clapped his old hands. 'Splendid. I have forgotten that now, too. Who are you?'

'We are best forgotten,' said Rackhir with a gentle smile. 'Farewell, Niun and thanks.'

'Thanks for what?'

'Both for remembering and for forgetting.'

They walked on through the miserable City of Ameeron, away from the happy old sorcerer, sighting the odd face staring at them from a doorway or a window, doing their best to breathe as little of the foul air as possible.

'I think perhaps that I envy Niun alone of all the inhabitants of this desolate place,' said Rackhir.

'I pity him,' said Elric.

'Why so?'

'It occurs to me that when he has forgotten everything, he may well forget that he is allowed to leave Ameeron.'

Rackhir laughed and slapped the albino upon his black-armoured back. 'You are a gloomy comrade, friend Elric. Are all your thoughts so hopeless?'

'They tend in that direction, I fear,' said Elric with a shadow of a smile.

# Chapter Three

## *The Tunnel Under the Marsh*

A ND ON THEY travelled through that sad and murky world until at last they came to the marsh.

The marsh was black. Black spikey vegetation grew in clumps here and there upon it. It was cold and it was dank; a dark mist swirled close to the surface and through the mist sometimes darted low shapes. From the mist rose a solid black object which could only be the monument described by Niun.

'The monument,' said Rackhir, stopping and leaning on his bow. 'It's well out into the marsh and there's no evident pathway leading to it. Is this a problem, do you think, Comrade Elric?'

Elric waded cautiously into the edge of the marsh. He felt the cold ooze drag at his feet. He stepped back with some difficulty.

'There must be a path,' said Rackhir, fingering his bony nose. 'Else how would your cousin cross?'

Elric looked over his shoulder at the Red Archer and he shrugged. 'Who knows? He could be travelling with sorcerous companions who have no difficulty where marshes are concerned.'

Suddenly Elric found himself sitting down upon the damp rock. The stink of brine from the marsh seemed for a moment to have overwhelmed him. He was feeling weak. The effectiveness of his drugs, last taken just as he stepped through the Shade Gate, was beginning to fade.

Rackhir came and stood by the albino. He smiled with a certain amount of bantering sympathy. 'Well, Sir Sorcerer, cannot you summon similar aid?'

Elric shook his head. 'I know little that is practical concerning the raising of small demons. Yyrkoon has all his grimoires, his favourite spells, his introductions to the demon worlds. We shall have to find a path of the ordinary kind if we wish to reach yonder monument, Warrior Priest of Phum.'

The Warrior Priest of Phum drew a red kerchief from within his tunic and blew his nose for some time. When he had finished he put down a hand, helped Elric to his feet, and began to walk along the rim of the marsh, keeping the black monument ever in sight.

It was some time later that they found a path at last and it was not a natural path but a slab of black marble extending out into the gloom of the mire, slippery to the feet and itself covered with a film of ooze.

'I would almost suspect this of being a false path – a lure to take us to our death,' said Rackhir as he and Elric stood and looked at the long slab, 'but what have we to lose now?'

'Come,' said Elric, setting foot on the slab and beginning to make his cautious way along it. In his hand he now held a torch of sorts, a bundle of sputtering reeds which gave off an unpleasant yellow light and a considerable amount of greenish smoke. It was better than nothing.

Rackhir, testing each footstep with his unstrung bowstaff, followed behind, whistling a small, complicated tune as he went along. Another of his race would have recognised the tune as the *Song of the Son of the Hero of the High Hell who is about to Sacrifice his Life*, a popular melody in Phum, particularly amongst the caste of the Warrior Priest.

Elric found the tune irritating and distracting, but he said nothing, for he concentrated every fragment of his attention on keeping his balance upon the slippery surface of the slab, which now appeared to rock slightly, as if it floated on the surface of the marsh.

And now they were halfway to the monument whose shape could be clearly distinguished: a great eagle with spread wings and a savage beak and claws extended for the kill. An eagle in the same black marble as the slab on which they tried to keep their balance. And Elric was reminded of a tomb. Had some ancient hero been buried here? Or had the tomb been built to house the black swords – imprison them so that they might never enter the world of men again and steal men's souls?

The slab rocked more violently. Elric tried to remain upright but swayed first on one foot and then the other, the brand waving crazily. Both feet slid from under him and he went flying into the marsh and was instantly buried up to his knees.

He began to sink.

Somehow he had managed to keep his grip on the brand and by its light he could see the red-clad archer peering forward.

'Elric?'

'I'm here, Rackhir.'

'You're sinking?'

'The marsh seems intent on swallowing me, aye.'

'Can you lie flat?'

'I can lie forward, but my legs are trapped.' Elric tried to move his body in the ooze which pressed against it. Something rushed past him in front of his face, giving voice to a kind of muted gibbering. Elric did his best to control the fear which welled up in him. 'I think you must give me up, friend Rackhir.'

'What? And lose my means of getting out of this world? You must think me more selfless than I am, Comrade Elric. Here...' Rackhir carefully lowered himself to the slab and reached out his arm towards Elric. Both men were now covered in clinging slime; both shivered with cold. Rackhir stretched and stretched and Elric leaned forward as far as he could and tried to reach the hand, but it was impossible. And every second dragged him deeper into the stinking filth of the marsh.

Then Rackhir took up his bowstaff and pushed that out.

'Grab the bow, Elric. Can you?'

Leaning forward and stretching every bone and muscle in his body, Elric just managed to get a grip on the bowstaff.

'Now, I must – Ah!' Rackhir, pulling at the bow, found his own feet slipping and the slab beginning to rock quite wildly. He flung out one arm to grab the far lip of the slab and with his other hand kept a grip on the bow. 'Hurry, Elric! Hurry!'

Elric began painfully to pull himself from the ooze. The slab still rocked crazily and Rackhir's hawklike face was almost as pale as Elric's own as he desperately strove to keep his hold on both slab and bow. And then Elric, all soaked in mire, managed to reach the slab and crawl onto it, the brand still sputtering in his hand, and lie there gasping.

Rackhir, too, was short of breath, but he laughed. 'What a fish I've caught!' he said. 'The biggest yet, I'd wager!'

'I am grateful to you, Rackhir the Red Archer. I am grateful, Warrior Priest of Phum. I owe you my life,' said Elric after a while. 'And I swear that whether I'm successful in my quest or not I'll use all my powers to see you through the Shade Gate and back into the world from which we have both come.'

Rackhir shrugged and grinned. 'Now I suggest we continue towards yonder monument on our knees. Undignified it might be, but safer it is also. And it is but a short way to crawl.'

Elric agreed.

Not much more time had passed in that timeless darkness before they had reached a little moss-grown island on which stood the Monument of the Eagle, huge and heavy and towering above them into the greater gloom which was either the sky or the roof of the cavern. And at the base of the plinth they saw a low doorway. And the doorway was open.

'A trap?' mused Rackhir.

'Or does Yyrkoon assume us perished in Ameeron?' said Elric, wiping himself free of slime as best he could. He sighed. 'Let's enter and be done with it.'

And so they entered.

They found themselves in a small room. Elric cast the faint light of the brand about the place and saw another doorway. The rest of the room was featureless – each wall made of the same faintly glistening black marble. The room was filled with silence.

Neither man spoke. Both walked unfalteringly towards the next doorway and, when they found steps, began to descend the steps, which wound down and down into total darkness.

For a long time they descended, still without speaking, until eventually they reached the bottom and saw before them the entrance to a narrow tunnel which was irregularly shaped so that it seemed more the work of nature than of some intelligence. Moisture dripped from the roof of the tunnel and fell with the regularity of heartbeats to the floor, seeming to echo a deeper sound, far away, emanating from somewhere in the tunnel itself.

'This is without doubt a tunnel,' said the Red Archer, 'and it, unquestionably, leads under the marsh.'

Elric felt that Rackhir shared his reluctance to enter the tunnel. He stood with the guttering brand held high, listening to the sound of the drops falling to the floor of the tunnel, trying to recognise that other sound which came so faintly from the depths.

And then he forced himself forward, almost running into the tunnel, his ears filled with a sudden roaring which might have come from within his head or from some other source in the tunnel. He heard Rackhir's footfalls behind him. He drew his sword, the sword of the dead hero Aubec, and he heard the hissing of his own breath echo from the walls of the tunnel which was now alive with sounds of every sort.

Elric shuddered, but he did not pause.

The tunnel was warm. The floor felt spongy beneath his feet, the smell of brine persisted. And now he could see that the walls of the tunnel were smoother, that they seemed to shiver with quick, regular movement. He heard Rackhir gasp behind him as the archer, too, noted the peculiar nature of the tunnel.

'It's like flesh,' murmured the Warrior Priest of Phum. 'Like flesh.'

Elric could not bring himself to reply. All his attention was required to force himself forward. He was consumed by terror. His whole body shook. He sweated and his legs threatened to buckle under him. His grip was so weak that he could barely keep his sword from falling to the floor. And there were hints of something in his memory, something which his brain refused to consider. Had he been here before? His trembling increased. His stomach turned. But he still stumbled on, the brand held before him.

And now the soft, steady thrumming sound grew louder and

he saw ahead a small, almost circular aperture at the very end of the tunnel. He stopped, swaying.

'The tunnel ends,' whispered Rackhir. 'There is no way through.'

The small aperture was pulsing with a swift, strong beat.

'The Pulsing Cavern,' Elric whispered. 'That is what we should find at the end of the Tunnel Under the Marsh. That must be the entrance, Rackhir.'

'It is too small for a man to enter, Elric,' said Rackhir reasonably.

'No...'

Elric stumbled forward until he stood close to the opening. He sheathed his sword. He handed the brand to Rackhir and then, before the Warrior Priest of Phum could stop him, he had flung himself head first through the gap, wriggling his body through – and the walls of the aperture parted for him and then closed behind him, leaving Rackhir on the other side.

Elric got slowly to his feet. A faint, pinkish light now came from the walls and ahead of him was another entrance, slightly larger than the one through which he had just come. The air was warm and thick and salty. It almost stifled him. His head throbbed and his body ached and he could barely act or think, save to force himself onward. On faltering legs he flung himself towards the next entrance as the great, muffled pulsing sounded louder and louder in his ears.

'Elric!'

Rackhir stood behind him, pale and sweating. He had abandoned the brand and followed Elric through.

Elric licked dry lips and tried to speak.

Rackhir came closer.

Elric said thickly: 'Rackhir. You should not be here.'

'I said I would help.'

'Aye, but...'

'Then help I shall.'

Elric had no strength for arguing, so he nodded and with his hands forced back the soft walls of the second aperture and saw that it led into a cavern whose round wall quivered to a steady pulsing. And in the centre of the cavern, hanging in the air without any support at all were two swords. Two identical swords, huge and fine and black.

And standing beneath the swords, his expression gloating and greedy, stood Prince Yyrkoon of Melniboné, reaching up for them, his lips moving but no words escaping from him. And Elric himself was able to voice but one word as he climbed through and stood upon that shuddering floor. 'No,' he said.

Yyrkoon heard the word. He turned with terror in his face. He snarled when he saw Elric and then he, too, voiced a word which was at once a scream of outrage.

'No!'

With an effort Elric dragged Aubec's blade from its scabbard. But it seemed too heavy to hold upright, it tugged his arm so that it rested on the floor, his arm hanging straight at his side. Elric drew deep breaths of heavy air into his lungs. His vision was dimming. Yyrkoon had become a shadow. Only the two black swords, standing still and cool in the very centre of the circular chamber, were in focus. Elric sensed Rackhir enter the chamber and stand beside him.

'Yyrkoon,' said Elric at last, 'those swords are mine.'

Yyrkoon smiled and reached up towards the blades. A peculiar moaning sound seemed to issue from them. A faint, black radiance seemed to emanate from them. Elric saw the runes carved into them and he was afraid.

Rackhir fitted an arrow to his bow. He drew the string back to his shoulder, sighting along the arrow at Prince Yyrkoon. 'If he must die, Elric, tell me.'

'Slay him,' said Elric.

And Rackhir released the string.

But the arrow moved very slowly through the air and then hung halfway between the archer and his intended target.

Yyrkoon turned, a ghastly grin on his face. 'Mortal weapons are useless here,' he said.

Elric said to Rackhir. 'He must be right. And your life is in danger, Rackhir. Go...'

Rackhir gave him a puzzled look. 'No, I must stay here and help you...'

Elric shook his head. 'You cannot help, you will only die if you stay. Go.'

Reluctantly the Red Archer unstrung his bow, glanced suspiciously up at the two black swords, then squeezed his way through the doorway and was gone.

'Now, Yyrkoon,' said Elric, letting Aubec's sword fall to the floor. 'We must settle this, you and I.'

# Chapter Four
## *Two Black Swords*

A ND THEN THE runeblades Stormbringer and Mournblade
were gone from where they had hung so long.

And Stormbringer had settled into Elric's right hand. And
Mournblade lay in Prince Yyrkoon's right hand.

And the two men stood on opposite sides of the Pulsing Cavern and regarded first each other and then the swords they held.

The swords were singing. Their voices were faint but could be
heard quite plainly. Elric lifted the huge blade easily and turned it
this way and that, admiring its alien beauty.

'Stormbringer,' he said.

And then he felt afraid.

It was suddenly as if he had been born again and that this
runesword was born with him. It was as if they had never been
separate.

'Stormbringer.'

And the sword moaned sweetly and settled even more smoothly
into his grasp.

'Stormbringer!' yelled Elric and he leapt at his cousin.

'Stormbringer!'

And he was full of fear – so full of fear. And the fear brought a
wild kind of delight – a demonic need to fight and kill his cousin,
to sink the blade deep into Yyrkoon's heart. To take vengeance.
To spill blood. To send a soul to hell.

And now Prince Yyrkoon's cry could be heard above the thrum
of the sword-voices, the drumming of the pulse of the cavern.

'Mournblade!'

And Mournblade came up to meet Stormbringer's blow and
turn that blow and thrust back at Elric who swayed aside and

brought Stormbringer round and down in a side-stroke which knocked Yyrkoon and Mournblade backward for an instant. But Stormbringer's next thrust was met again. And the next thrust was met. And the next. If the swordsmen were evenly matched, then so were the blades, which seemed possessed of their own wills.

And the clang of the metal upon metal turned into a wild, metallic song which the swords sang. A joyful song as if they were glad at last to be back to battling, though they battled each other.

And Elric barely saw his cousin, Prince Yyrkoon, at all, save for an occasional flash of his dark, wild face. Elric's attention was given entirely to the two black swords, for it seemed that the swords fought with the life of one of the swordsmen as a prize (or perhaps the lives of both, thought Elric) and that the rivalry between Elric and Yyrkoon was nothing compared with the brotherly rivalry between the swords who seemed full of pleasure at the chance to engage again after many millennia.

And this observation, as he fought – and fought for his soul as well as his life – gave Elric pause to consider his hatred of Yyrkoon.

Kill Yyrkoon he would, but not at the will of another power. Not to give sport to these alien swords.

Mournblade's point darted at his eyes and Stormbringer rose to deflect the thrust once more.

Elric no longer fought his cousin. He fought the will of the two black swords.

Stormbringer dashed for Yyrkoon's momentarily undefended throat. Elric clung to the sword and dragged it back, sparing his cousin's life. Stormbringer whined almost petulantly, like a dog stopped from biting an intruder.

And Elric spoke through clenched teeth. 'I'll not be your puppet, runeblade. If we must be united, let it be upon a proper understanding.'

The sword seemed to hesitate, to drop its guard, and Elric was hard put to defend himself against the whirling attack of Mournblade which, in turn, seemed to sense its advantage.

Elric felt fresh energy pour up his right arm and into his body. This was what the sword could do. With it, he needed no drugs, would never be weak again. In battle he would triumph. At peace, he could rule with pride. When he travelled, it could be alone and without fear. It was as if the sword reminded him of all these things, even as it returned Mournblade's attack.

And what must the sword have in return?

Elric knew. The sword told him, without words of any sort. Stormbringer needed to fight, for that was its reason for existence. Stormbringer needed to kill, for that was its source of energy, the lives and the souls of men, demons – even gods.

And Elric hesitated, even as his cousin gave a huge, cackling yell and dashed at him so that Mournblade glanced off his helm and he was flung backwards and down and saw Yyrkoon gripping his moaning black sword in both hands to plunge the runeblade into Elric's body.

And Elric knew he would do anything to resist that fate – for his soul to be drawn into Mournblade and his strength to feed Prince Yyrkoon's strength. And he rolled aside, very quickly, and got to one knee and turned and lifted Stormbringer with one gauntleted hand upon the blade and the other upon the hilt to take the great blow Prince Yyrkoon brought upon it. And the two black swords shrieked as if in pain, and they shivered, and black radiance poured from them as blood might pour from a man pierced by many arrows. And Elric was driven, still on his knees, away from the radiance, gasping and sighing and peering here and there for sight of Yyrkoon who had disappeared.

And Elric knew that Stormbringer spoke to him again. If Elric did not wish to die by Mournblade, then Elric must accept the bargain which the Black Sword offered.

'He must not die!' said Elric. 'I will not slay him to make sport for you!'

And through the black radiance ran Yyrkoon, snarling and snapping and whirling his runesword.

Again Stormbringer darted through an opening, and again Elric made the blade pull back and Yyrkoon was only grazed.

Stormbringer writhed in Elric's hands.

Elric said: 'You shall not be my master.'

And Stormbringer seemed to understand and become quieter, as if reconciled. And Elric laughed, thinking that he now controlled the runesword and that from now on the blade would do his bidding.

'We shall disarm Yyrkoon,' said Elric. 'We shall not kill him.'

Elric rose to his feet.

Stormbringer moved with all the speed of a needle-thin rapier. It feinted, it parried, it thrust. Yyrkoon, who had been grinning in triumph, snarled and staggered back, the grin dropping from his sullen features.

Stormbringer now worked for Elric. It made the moves that Elric wished to make. Both Yyrkoon and Mournblade seemed disconcerted by this turn of events. Mournblade shouted as if in astonishment at its brother's behaviour. Elric struck at Yyrkoon's sword-arm, pierced cloth – pierced flesh – pierced sinew – pierced bone. Blood came, soaking Yyrkoon's arm and dripping down onto the hilt of the sword. The blood was slippery. It weakened Yyrkoon's grip on his runesword. He took it in both hands, but he was unable to hold it firmly.

Elric, too, took Stormbringer in both hands. Unearthly strength surged through him. With a gigantic blow he dashed Stormbringer against Mournblade where blade met hilt. The runesword flew from Yyrkoon's grasp. It sped across the Pulsing Cavern.

Elric smiled. He had defeated his own sword's will and, in turn, had defeated the brother sword.

Mournblade fell against the wall of the Pulsing Cavern and for a moment was still.

A groan then seemed to escape the defeated runesword. A high-pitched shriek filled the Pulsing Cavern. Blackness flooded over the eery pink light and extinguished it.

When the light returned Elric saw that a scabbard lay at his feet. The scabbard was black and of the same alien craftsmanship as the runesword. Elric saw Yyrkoon. The prince was on his knees and he was sobbing, his eyes darting about the Pulsing Cavern seeking Mournblade, looking at Elric with fright as if he knew he must now be slain.

'Mournblade?' Yyrkoon said hopelessly. He knew he was to die. Mournblade had vanished from the Pulsing Cavern.

'Your sword is gone,' said Elric quietly.

Yyrkoon whimpered and tried to crawl towards the entrance of the cavern. But the entrance had shrunk to the size of a small coin. Yyrkoon wept.

Stormbringer trembled, as if thirsty for Yyrkoon's soul. Elric stooped.

Yyrkoon began to speak rapidly. 'Do not slay me, Elric – not with that runeblade. I will do anything you wish. I will die in any other way.'

Elric said: 'We are victims, cousin, of a conspiracy – a game played by gods, demons and sentient swords. They wish one of us dead. I suspect they wish you dead more than they wish me dead. And that is the reason why I shall not slay you here.' He picked up the scabbard. He forced Stormbringer into it and at once the sword was quiet. Elric took off his old scabbard and looked around for Aubec's sword, but that, too, was gone. He dropped the old scabbard and hooked the new one to his belt. He rested his left hand upon the pommel of Stormbringer and he looked not without sympathy upon the creature that was his cousin.

'You are a worm, Yyrkoon. But is that your fault?'

Yyrkoon gave him a puzzled glance.

'I wonder, if you had all you desire, would you cease to be a worm, cousin?'

Yyrkoon raised himself to his knees. A little hope began to show in his eyes.

Elric smiled and drew a deep breath. 'We shall see,' he said. 'You must agree to wake Cymoril from her sorcerous slumber.'

'You have humbled me, Elric,' said Yyrkoon in a small pitiful voice. 'I will wake her. Or would...'

'Can you not undo your spell?'

'We cannot escape from the Pulsing Cavern. It is past the time...'

'What's this?'

'I did not think you would follow me. And then I thought I

would easily finish you. And now it is past the time. One can keep the entrance open for only a little while. It will admit anyone who cares to enter the Pulsing Cavern, but it will let no-one out after the power of the spell dies. I gave much to know that spell.'

'You have given too much for everything,' said Elric. He went to the entrance and peered through. Rackhir waited on the other side. The Red Archer had an anxious expression. Elric said: 'Warrior Priest of Phum, it seems that my cousin and I are trapped in here. The entrance will not part for us.' Elric tested the warm, moist stuff of the wall. It would not open more than a tiny fraction. 'It seems that you can join us or else go back. If you do join us, you share our fate.'

'It is not much of a fate if I go back,' said Rackhir. 'What chances have you?'

'One,' said Elric. 'I can invoke my patron.'

'A Lord of Chaos?' Rackhir made a wry face.

'Exactly,' said Elric. 'I speak of Arioch.'

'Arioch, eh? Well, he does not care for renegades from Phum.' 'What do you choose to do?'

Rackhir stepped forward. Elric stepped back. Through the opening came Rackhir's head, followed by his shoulders, followed by the rest of him. The entrance closed again immediately. Rackhir stood up and untangled the string of his bow from the staff, smoothing it. 'I agreed to share your fate – to gamble all on escaping from this plane,' said the Red Archer. He looked surprised when he saw Yyrkoon. 'Your enemy is still alive?'

'Aye.'

'You are merciful indeed.'

'Perhaps. Or obstinate. I would not slay him merely because some supernatural agency used him as a pawn, to be killed if I should win. The Lords of the Higher Worlds do not as yet control me completely – nor will they if I have any power at all to resist them.'

Rackhir grinned. 'I share your view – though I'm not optimistic about its realism. I see you have one of those black swords at your belt. Will that not hack a way through the cavern?'

'No,' said Yyrkoon from his place against the wall. 'Nothing can harm the stuff of the Pulsing Cavern.'

'I'll believe you,' said Elric, 'for I do not intend to draw this new sword of mine often. I must learn how to control it first.'

'So Arioch must be summoned.' Rackhir sighed.

'If that is possible,' said Elric.

'He will doubtless destroy me,' said Rackhir, looking to Elric in the hope that the albino would deny this statement.

Elric looked grave. 'I might be able to strike a bargain with him. It will also test something.'

Elric turned his back on Rackhir and on Yyrkoon. He adjusted his mind. He sent it out through vast spaces and complicated mazes. And he cried:

'Arioch! Arioch! Aid me, Arioch!'

He had a sense of something listening to him.

'Arioch!'

Something shifted in the places where his mind went.

'Arioch...'

And Arioch heard him. He knew it was Arioch.

Rackhir gave a horrified yell. Yyrkoon screamed. Elric turned and saw that something disgusting had appeared near the far wall. It was black and it was foul and it slobbered and its shape was intolerably alien. Was this Arioch? How could it be? Arioch was beautiful. But perhaps, thought Elric, this was Arioch's true shape. Upon this plane, in this peculiar cavern, Arioch could not deceive those who looked upon him.

But then the shape had disappeared and a beautiful youth with ancient eyes stood looking at the three mortals.

'You have won the sword, Elric,' said Arioch, ignoring the others. 'I congratulate you. And you have spared your cousin's life. Why so?'

'More than one reason,' said Elric. 'But let us say he must remain alive in order to wake Cymoril.'

Arioch's face bore a little, secret smile for a moment and Elric realised that he had avoided a trap. If he had killed Yyrkoon, Cymoril would never have woken again.

'And what is this little traitor doing with you?' Arioch turned a cold eye on Rackhir who did his best to stare back at the Chaos Lord.

'He is my friend,' said Elric. 'I made a bargain with him. If he aided me to find the Black Sword, then I would take him back with me to our own plane.'

'That is impossible. Rackhir is an exile here. That is his punishment.'

'He comes back with me,' said Elric. And now he unhooked the scabbard holding Stormbringer from his belt and he held the sword out before him. 'Or I do not take the sword with me. Failing that, we all three remain here for eternity.'

'That is not sensible, Elric. Consider your responsibilities.'

'I have considered them. That is my decision.'

Arioch's smooth face had just a tinge of anger. 'You must take the sword. It is your destiny.'

'So you say. But I now know that the sword may only be borne by me. You cannot bear it, Arioch, or you would. Only I – or another mortal like me – can take it from the Pulsing Cavern. Is that not so?'

'You are clever, Elric of Melniboné.' Arioch spoke with sardonic admiration. 'And you are a fitting servant of Chaos. Very well – that traitor can go with you. But he would be best warned to tread warily. The Lords of Chaos have been known to bear malice...'

Rackhir said hoarsely: 'So I have heard, My Lord Arioch.'

Arioch ignored the archer. 'The man of Phum is not, after all, important. And if you wish to spare your cousin's life, so be it. It matters little. Destiny can contain a few extra threads in her design and still accomplish her original aims.'

'Very well then,' said Elric. 'Take us from this place.'

'Where to?'

'Why, to Melniboné, if you please.'

With a smile that was almost tender Arioch looked down on Elric and a silky hand stroked Elric's cheek. Arioch had grown to twice his original size. 'Oh, you are surely the sweetest of all my slaves,' said the Lord of Chaos.

And there was a whirling. There was a sound like the roar of the sea. There was a dreadful sense of nausea. And three weary men stood on the floor of the great throne room in Imrryr. The throne room was deserted, save that in one corner a black shape, like smoke, writhed for a moment and then was gone.

Rackhir crossed the floor and seated himself carefully upon the first step to the Ruby Throne. Yyrkoon and Elric remained where they were, staring into each other's eyes. Then Elric laughed and slapped his scabbarded sword. 'Now you must fulfil your promises to me, cousin. Then I have a proposition to put to you.'

'It is like a market place,' said Rackhir, leaning on one elbow and inspecting the feather in his scarlet hat. 'So many bargains!'

# Chapter Five
## *The Pale King's Mercy*

Yrkoon stepped back from his sister's bed. He was worn and his features were drawn and there was no spirit in him as he said: 'It is done.' He turned away and looked through the window at the towers of Imrryr, at the harbour where the returned golden battle-barges rode at anchor, together with the ship which had been King Straasha's gift to Elric. 'She will wake in a moment,' added Yyrkoon absently.

Dyvim Tvar and Rackhir the Red Archer looked enquiringly at Elric who kneeled by the bed, staring into the face of Cymoril. Her face grew peaceful as he watched and for one terrible moment he suspected Prince Yyrkoon of tricking him and of killing Cymoril. But then the eyelids moved and the eyes opened and she saw him and she smiled. 'Elric? The dreams... You are safe?'

'I am safe, Cymoril. As you are.'

'Yyrkoon...?'

'He woke you.'

'But you swore to slay him...'

'I was as much subject to sorcery as you. My mind was confused. It is still confused where some matters are concerned. But Yyrkoon is changed now. I defeated him. He does not doubt my power. He no longer lusts to usurp me.'

'You are merciful, Elric.' She brushed hair from her face.

Elric exchanged a glance with Rackhir.

'It might not be mercy which moves me,' said Elric. 'It might merely be a sense of fellowship with Yyrkoon.'

'Fellowship? Surely you cannot feel...'

'We are both mortal. We were both victims of a game played between the Lords of the Higher Worlds. My loyalty must, finally, be to my own kind – and that is why I ceased to hate Yyrkoon.'

'And that is mercy,' said Cymoril.

Yyrkoon walked towards the door. 'May I leave, my lord emperor?'

Elric thought he detected a strange light in his defeated cousin's eyes. But perhaps it was only humility or despair. He nodded. Yyrkoon went from the room, closing the door softly.

Dyvim Tvar said: 'Trust Yyrkoon not at all, Elric. He will betray you again.' The Lord of the Dragon Caves was troubled.

'No,' said Elric. 'If he does not fear me, he fears the sword I now carry.'

'And you should fear that sword,' said Dyvim Tvar.

'No,' said Elric. 'I am the master of the sword.'

Dyvim Tvar made to speak again but then shook his head almost sorrowfully, bowed and, together with Rackhir the Red Archer, left Elric and Cymoril alone.

Cymoril took Elric in her arms. They kissed. They wept.

There were celebrations in Melniboné for a week. Now almost all the ships and men and dragons were home. And Elric was home, having proved his right to rule so well that all his strange quirks of character (this 'mercy' of his was perhaps the strangest) were accepted by the populace.

In the throne room there was a ball and it was the most lavish ball any of the courtiers had ever known. Elric danced with Cymoril, taking a full part in the activities. Only Yyrkoon did not dance, preferring to remain in a quiet corner below the gallery of the music-slaves, ignored by the guests. Rackhir the Red Archer danced with several Melnibonéan ladies and made assignations with them all, for he was a hero now in Melniboné. Dyvim Tvar danced, too, though his eyes were often brooding when they fell upon Prince Yyrkoon.

And later, when people ate, Elric spoke to Cymoril as they sat together on the dais of the Ruby Throne.

'Would you be empress, Cymoril?'

'You know I will marry you, Elric. We have both known that for many a year, have we not?'

'So you would be my wife?'

'Aye.' She laughed for she thought he joked.

'And not be empress? For a year at least?'

'What mean you, my lord?'

'I must go away from Melniboné, Cymoril, for a year. What I have learned in recent months has made me want to travel the Young Kingdoms – see how other nations conduct their affairs. For I think Melniboné must change if she is to survive. She could become a great force for good in the world, for she still has much power.'

'For good?' Cymoril was surprised and there was a little alarm in her voice, too. 'Melniboné has never stood for good or for evil, but for herself and the satisfaction of her desires.'

'I would see that changed.'

'You intend to alter everything?'

'I intend to travel the world and then decide if there is any point to such a decision. The Lords of the Higher Worlds have ambitions in our world. Though they have given me aid, of late, I fear them. I should like to see if it is possible for men to rule their own affairs.'

'And you will go?' There were tears in her eyes. 'When?'

'Tomorrow – when Rackhir leaves. We will take King Straasha's ship and make for the Isle of the Purple Towns where Rackhir has friends. Will you come?'

'I cannot imagine – I cannot. Oh, Elric, why spoil this happiness we now have?'

'Because I feel that the happiness cannot last unless we know completely what we are.'

She frowned. 'Then you must discover that, if that is what you wish,' she said slowly. 'But it is for you to discover alone, Elric, for I have no such desire. You must go by yourself into those barbarian lands.'

'You will not accompany me?'

'It is not possible. I – I am Melnibonéan...' She sighed. 'I love you, Elric.'

'And I you, Cymoril.'

'Then we shall be married when you return. In a year.'

Elric was full of sorrow, but he knew that his decision was correct. If he did not leave, he would grow restless soon enough and if he grew restless he might come to regard Cymoril as an enemy, someone who had trapped him.

'Then you must rule as empress until I return,' he sad.

'No, Elric. I cannot take that responsibility.'

'Then, who...? Dyvim Tvar...'

'I know Dyvim Tvar. He will not take such power. Magum Colim, perhaps...'

'No.'

'Then you must stay, Elric.'

But Elric's gaze had travelled through the crowd in the throne room below. It stopped when it reached a lonely figure seated by itself under the gallery of the music-slaves. And Elric smiled ironically and said:

'Then it must be Yyrkoon.'

Cymoril was horrified. 'No, Elric. He will abuse any power...'

'Not now. And it is just. He is the only one who wanted to be emperor. Now he can rule as emperor for a year in my stead. If he rules well, I may consider abdicating in his favour. If he rules badly, it will prove, once and for all, that his ambitions were misguided.'

'Elric,' said Cymoril. 'I love you. But you are a fool – a criminal, if you trust Yyrkoon again.'

'No,' he said evenly. 'I am not a fool. All I am is Elric. I cannot help that, Cymoril.'

'It is Elric that I love!' she cried. 'But Elric is doomed. We are all doomed unless you remain here now.'

'I cannot. Because I love you, Cymoril, I cannot.'

She stood up. She was weeping. She was lost.

'And I am Cymoril,' she said. 'You will destroy us both.' Her voice softened and she stroked his hair. 'You will destroy us, Elric.'

'No,' he said. 'I will build something that will be better. I will discover things. When I return we shall marry and we shall live long and we shall be happy, Cymoril.'

And now, Elric had told three lies. The first concerned his cousin Yyrkoon. The second concerned the Black Sword. The third concerned Cymoril. And upon those three lies was Elric's destiny to be built, for it is only about things which concern us most profoundly that we lie clearly and with profound conviction.

# Epilogue

THERE WAS A port called Menii which was one of the humblest and friendliest of the Purple Towns. Like the others on the isle it was built mainly of the purple stone which gave the towns their name. And there were red roofs on the houses and there were bright-sailed boats of all kinds in the harbour as Elric and Rackhir the Red Archer came ashore in the early morning when just a few sailors were beginning to make their way down to their ships.

King Straasha's lovely ship lay some way out beyond the harbour wall. They had used a small boat to cross the water between it and the town. They turned and looked back at the ship. They had sailed it themselves, without crew, and the ship had sailed well.

'So, I must seek peace and mythic Tanelorn,' said Rackhir, with a certain amount of self-mockery. He stretched and yawned and the bow and the quiver danced on his back.

Elric was dressed in simple costume that might have marked any soldier-of-fortune of the Young Kingdoms. He looked fit and relaxed. He smiled into the sun. The only remarkable thing about his garb was the great, black runesword at his side. Since he had donned the sword, he had needed no drugs to sustain him at all.

'And I must seek knowledge in the lands I find marked upon my map,' said Elric. 'I must learn and I must carry what I learn back to Melniboné at the end of a year. I wish that Cymoril had accompanied me, but I understand her reluctance.'

'You will go back?' Rackhir said. 'When a year is over?'

'She will draw me back!' Elric laughed. 'My only fear is that I will weaken and return before my quest is finished.'

'I should like to come with you,' said Rackhir, 'for I have

travelled in most lands and would be as good a guide as I was in the netherworld. But I am sworn to find Tanelorn, for all I know it does not really exist.'

'I hope that you find it, Warrior Priest of Phum,' said Elric.

'I shall never be that again,' said Rackhir. Then his eyes widened a little. 'Why, look – your ship!'

And Elric looked and saw the ship that had once been called The Ship Which Sails Over Land and Sea, and he saw that slowly it was sinking. King Straasha was taking it back.

'The elementals are friends, at least,' he said. 'But I fear their power wanes as the power of Melniboné wanes. For all that we of the Dragon Isle are considered evil by the folk of the Young Kingdoms, we share much in common with the spirits of air, earth, fire and water.'

Rackhir said, as the masts of the ship disappeared beneath the waves: 'I envy you those friends, Elric. You may trust them.'

'Aye.'

Rackhir looked at the runesword hanging on Elric's hip. 'But you would be wise to trust nothing else.' he added.

Elric laughed. 'Fear not for me, Rackhir, for I am my own master – for a year at least. And I am master of this sword now!'

The sword seemed to stir at his side and he took firm hold of its grip and slapped Rackhir on the back and he laughed and shook his white hair so that it drifted in the air and he lifted his strange, red eyes to the sky and he said:

'I shall be a new man when I return to Melniboné.'

# Aspects of Fantasy

## (1963)

### 1. Introduction

WHAT *IS* 'FANTASY fiction'? It is, of course, a broad field but, on the other hand, fairly easy to define. It is fiction which deals in the fantastic, in what is outside of ordinary human experience.

It contains many sub-categories of which science fiction is one, it is written on many levels by writers of varying ability who use it for a great number of purposes. Today it ranges from the ill-written ghoul-operas published in poor-quality paperbacks to the well-written extravaganzas of Peake, Tolkien and others.

A more interesting question, and one which I hope partially to answer in these articles, is *why* is fantasy? Why is it written, why is it read, what is its appeal?

H. P. Lovecraft, that well-known describer of the indescribable, says in his book *Marginalia*:

> Modern Science has, in the end, proved an enemy to art and pleasure; for by revealing to us the whole sordid and prosaic basis of our thoughts, motives, and acts, it has stripped the world of glamour, wonder, and all those illusions of heroism, nobility, and sacrifice which used to sound so impressive when romantically treated. Indeed, it is not too much to say that psychological dis-covery, and chemical, physical, and psychological research have largely destroyed the element of emotion among informed and sophisticated people by resolving it into its component parts...

That I disagree with this judgement will be obvious, for I believe that dissection of the fantasy story into its component parts does

343

not detract from the story but rather adds a new dimension to it – a dimension which, to me, is far more interesting and rewarding. In an article published in the WOMAN JOURNALIST for Spring 1963, J.G. Ballard writes:

> I feel that the writer of fantasy has a marked tendency to select images and ideas which directly reflect the internal landscapes of his mind, and the reader of fantasy must interpret them on this level, distinguishing between the manifest content, which may seem obscure, meaningless or nightmarish, and the latent content, the private vocabulary of symbols drawn by the narrative from the writer's mind. The dream worlds, synthetic landscapes and plasticity of visual forms invented by the writer of fantasy are external equivalents of the inner world of the psyche...

Lovecraft was writing forty years ago, Ballard is writing now and I feel it is likely that the developments in physics and psychology which have taken place since 1922 would have caused Lovecraft to revise his views if he were living today, for Einstein and Jung between them have, by analysis, broadened rather than destroyed the scope of the artist.

The increasing interest in the fantasy form seems to show that intelligent people are, indeed, looking beyond its purely sensational and romantic aspects and finding it a rewarding literary field. Those critics who still decry it for its usual lack of deep characterisation do not see that it completely reverses the 'real' world of the social novel – placing its heroes in a landscape directly reflecting the inner landscape of the ordinary man. The hero ranges the lands of his own psyche, encountering the various aspects of himself. When we read a good fantasy we are being admitted into the subterranean worlds of our own souls.

Therefore the fascination of the fantasy story may well lie in its concern with direct subconscious symbols. The mingled attraction and revulsion felt by its readers may well express the combined wish to see into themselves and at the same time withdraw into 'normal' life when they begin to feel they are probing too deeply.

Generally speaking, fantasy stories can fall into two broad categories. There is the kind that permanently disturbs and the kind that comforts. Part of the purpose of the child's fairy story is to describe the horror and then, by means of an easily identifiable hero, destroy it, thus laying the ghost. The child is full of fears and fancies. Therefore one of the differences between fairy stories and the major proportion of adult fantasy stories is that an adult story rarely produces a comforting end. Whether the hero wins through or not, the reader is left with the suspicion or knowledge that all is not quiet on the supernatural front. For supernatural also read subconscious and you're still with me.

The typical UNKNOWN WORLDS story is a kind of rational ghost-laying substitute for the child's fairy story – it diminishes that which is described to the level of whimsey and makes it appear harmless – but it avoids the essential nature of the horror story / supernatural romance and is in many ways a corrupt and unproductive form. Most of the Gothic novels, incidentally, tried to tack 'rational' explanations of their horrors on to their last chapters, although here the rationality was so totally superficial that it did not, in most cases, convince – whereas the supernatural episodes *did*.

The fantasy which we read today is not really very much different from the fantasy of, say, 2000 BC. It is the oldest form of storytelling and, essentially, it has not changed much.

We are all familiar with the Greek legends, English folktales and the stories of King Arthur and his Round Table, even if we haven't read them since our schooldays. One thing is obvious in all of these, and that is the repetition of certain kinds of characters (archetypal characters) and situations (classical situations). They recur constantly and they recur in Chivalric and Gothic romances, in Goethe, Wagner and the Jacobean tragedists, the works of Poe, Hawthorne, Melville, Bierce, Dunsany, Blackwood, Machen etc. – through the first half of the twentieth century with

James Branch Cabell, E.F. Benson, Charles Williams, Lovecraft, Howard and the WEIRD TALES school, to Bloch, Leiber, Bradbury and others in the USA and Peake, Tolkien, Powys, etc., in this country. And, apart from complexities of plot, more sophisticated means of storytelling and the odd change of scenery, the basic form has not changed since Cervantes took the mickey out of it in *Don Quixote*. It is romantic, it is sensational and, at its best, illuminating.

There are writers who go directly to their source of inspiration and write within its context (Thomas Burnett Swann or Treece, for instance), others who remove the whole machinery to an imaginary setting (Merritt, Howard, Leiber, Tolkien) and yet others who specialise in a contemporary setting, contrasting the prosaic with the supernatural to produce their effects (this particular talent seems to have been all but lost since the days of the Edwardian school). There is the kind of story intended only to horrify (the typical WEIRD TALES story) and the kind which seeks to entertain the reader on a wider canvas (the typical Lost Land or Sword-and-Sorcery story). The difference between these is that the one *hints* at entities, worlds and events existing beyond ordinary human ken, whereas the other attempts to describe them in more concrete terms. Other writers go further – they make use of the symbols, archetypes and narrative machinery of the fantasy story – and attempt to weave them into a structure which, in its implications, causes the reader to sense more deeply the nature of his existence. Cabell's Poictesme mythos and, I suppose, Lewis's *Perelandra* trilogy are obvious examples of authors consciously exploiting the form in order to discuss their own ideas about the nature of Man.

This use of archetypes and classical situations is, of course, to be discovered in the entire body of literature, but only in fantasy, whether it is intended merely to entertain or to enlighten as well, is it at once apparent. This is one of the reasons why writers like Iris Murdoch, William Golding and John Cowper Powys find a sympathetic audience amongst adherents of fantasy fiction, for all three writers use only a thin disguise to clothe their central characters. Indeed, far from limiting the writer, direct use of mythic material increases the richness and range of the work, whether he's a Realist or a Romantic.

As Lovecraft shows, there is no need for the writer to be aware of his real sources, though, as Ballard's work illustrates, it can be greatly improved if he is.

Having sketched in these few initial ideas about the form, I shall now sketch in its development.

First, if we leave aside the basic mythologies and religions of the world, we come to a body of Western literature which, in the form we know it, emerged from the Dark Ages. This literature, though still disguised as hero legends, was created by men who made it their living to journey from place to place telling stories of mighty deeds and supernatural horrors, usually in verse. *Beowulf* is the best-known of these.

Later we begin to find examples of what are generally called Chivalric Romances, stories of brave knights, doomed hero-villain knights (such as Lancelot), fair maidens, dark sorceresses, mysterious magicians and foul monsters. The legends of King Arthur and his Table Round are probably the best-known in Britain and America, though there are two other important bodies of Chivalric Romance – Charlemagnian and Peninsula. The Charlemagnian cycle involves a set-up similar to the Court of King Arthur, with a king uniting his nation and vanquishing the pagan, helped by a group of paladins (usually twelve in number) who are his right-hand men. If Lancelot and Galahad are the best-known Arthurian knights, then Roland and Oliver are the best-known Charlemagnian knights.

The Peninsula Romances are not quite so complex. Many are based on the character of El Cid, the legendary champion of Spain who drove the Moslem invaders from his homeland. It is in the Peninsula Romances that we find the main body of what are termed by the experts 'decadent Romances' and it is in the decadent Romance that we find our first real examples of the fantasy story as opposed to the folk-legend for, from about the fourteenth century on, the romance-chronicler ceased hanging his stories on to already existing heroes and began to invent new ones.

Chief of these is *Amadis de Gaul*, probably created by the Portuguese Vasco Lobeira, comprising in the original four long books but, in sequels by a host of imitators, making up some fifty books in all. Whereas the original Chivalric Romances were a mixture of ancient pagan legend, later Christian revision, history and myth, the decadent Romances, though borrowing heavily from the original body, were of definite authorship. They were, in fact, the first novels. The fourteenth, fifteenth and sixteenth centuries produced a vast spate of these with titles like *Palmerin of England* (a four-volume Romance reprinted in 1807, translated by Southey), *Tirante the White*, *Felixmarte of Hyrcania*, *The Mirror of Chivalry* and hundreds more.

It was these Romances that Cervantes satirised in *Don Quixote* and, in rejecting the Romance form, laid the foundations for the modern novel in his pastoral and picaresque stories.

About fifty years after *Don Quixote* debunked the form, the last of its examples was published. It had given way to the novel of country life and the colourful novel of thieves and vagabonds, though, in drama and poetry we still find evidence of its appeal – *The Faerie Queene*, for instance, makes direct use of Romantic imagery, while the Jacobean Tragedy, with its emphasis on gratuitous horror, was later to influence the Gothic.

For over a hundred years, as the Age of Reason reigned, the prose romance was unpopular with intellectual and general public alike and it took an aesthetic and antiquarian politician, Sir Horace Walpole, to instigate the return of the romance in Britain with what is generally thought to be the first real Gothic novel – *The Castle of Otranto*. Though there were one or two hints in other works that it was coming, it was Walpole's short novel that launched the Romantic Revival in English literature. This was published in 1764. It deals with all kinds of sensational supernatural events in and about the grotesque Castle, makes no attempt to rationalise them, from the mysterious appearance one day of a gigantic helmet in the first chapter, to the 'awful spectre' who reminds one of the characters of his duty in the last chapter.

Since later articles will deal with examples in detail, I won't bother to describe the best of the Gothics here. These included the works of Mrs Ann Radcliffe (*Mysteries of Udolpho*), Matthew Gregory Lewis (*Ambrosio; or, The Monk*), Mary Shelley (*Franken-stein*), Charles Maturin (*Melmoth the Wanderer*) and many, many more. For fifty years, from 1770 to 1820, the Gothic novel was the most popular form in England and its influence remained with later writers such as Scott, the Brontës, even Austen, Le Fanu and, of course, Poe and the Victorian/Edwardian school of horror-story writers. In fact it never really died after *The Castle of Otranto*, but continued to develop to the present day (my own early 'Elric' stories are written, I feel, in the tradition of the Chivalric and Gothic Romance).

The fantasy story, with its overtones of romance and its under-tones of the 'inner world of the psyche', has never lost its appeal, though it often goes through periods where serious critics abhor it and a large section of the public disdains it. If we take into con-sideration folk-epics and religious works such as the Bible, the *Bhagavad Gita*, traditional tales such as *The Arabian Nights* and the Norse *Eddara*, we can see that its development has been continu-ous since primitive man first began to invent stories. For better or worse, this can hardly be said of any other form.

I should like to finish this introductory article to a series which will deal with specific works of fantasy with a quote from Jung (*Modern Man in Search of a Soul*, Routledge and Kegan Paul, pages 180–181):

It [the second part of Goethe's *Faust*] is a strange something that derives its existence from the hinterland of man's mind – that suggests the abyss of time separating us from pre-human ages, or evokes a super-human world of contrasting light and darkness. It is a primordial experience which surpasses man's

understanding and to which he is therefore in danger of suc-
cumbing. The value and the force of the experience are given
by its enormity. It arises from timeless depths; it is foreign and
cold, many-sided, demonic and grotesque. A grimly ridiculous
sample of the eternal chaos ... it bursts asunder our human
standards of value and of aesthetic form. The disturbing vision
of monstrous and meaningless happenings that in every way
exceed the grasp of human feelings and comprehension makes
quite other demands upon the powers of the artist than do the
experiences of the foreground of life. These never rend the curtain that veils the cosmos; they never transcend the bounds of
the humanly possible, and for this reason are readily shaped to
the demands of art, no matter how great a shock to the individual they may be. But the primordial experiences rend from the
top to bottom the curtain upon which is painted the picture of
an ordered world, and allow a glimpse into the unfathomed
abyss of what has not yet become. Is it a vision of other worlds,
or of the obscuration of the spirit, or of the beginning of things
before the age of man, or of the unborn generations of the
future? We cannot say that it is any or none of these ... In a
more restricted and specific way, the primordial experience fur-
nishes material for Rider Haggard in the fiction-cycle that turns
upon She...

It is in this more restricted and specific way that I intend to look at
some of the more important works of fantasy in subsequent
articles.

(Note: Most of this essay was originally written earlier for an
unpublished magazine.)

# Introduction

(to *Elric of Melniboné*,
graphic adaptation,
1986)

R IGHT FROM ELRIC's earliest appearances (in SCIENCE FAN-
TASY magazine, 1961) he has attracted the attention of some
of the best fantasy illustrators. Indeed, Jim Cawthorn (who depicted
him on the covers of SCIENCE FANTASY and the first edition of
*Stormbringer*) was more than a little responsible for my descrip-
tions, since Jim and I worked for years in very close liaison
(including a commissioned illustrated serial done for the ILLUS-
TRATED WEEKLY OF INDIA in the late '60s) and sometimes were
hard put to say who had invented an image first.

I have always placed a high emphasis on illustration, both in
my own books and in NEW WORLDS, the magazine I edited for a
number of years. I'm inclined to plan my books in terms of scenes
and images. The fantasies in particular are always very thoroughly
worked out in what I like to think of as a coherent pictorial
vocabulary. This is singularly important to someone who works,
when actually writing, at the kind of speed and intensity which
has enabled me to complete the majority of my fantasy books in
less than a week and frequently within three days. Everything
must be 'in tune' – there must be an internal logic of images, just
as there is in dreams. This much, I think, I learned from the surrealists. Like the surrealists, too, I found Freud and Jung of great
help in maintaining this coherence.

All of which is a roundabout way of reiterating just how much
I care about illustration.

Over the years, since Jim Cawthorn's first (and still in many
ways the finest) portraits of Elric, there have been a number
of interpretations of the albino. The first strip version to be

published was actually in French, by Philippe Druillet, in an obscure magazine called MOI AUSSI in the mid-'60s (reprinted as a portfolio, 1972; in English, 1973) which was given an altogether idiosyncratic cast, since Druillet spoke no English and the stories were *told* to him by a friend, whereupon he drew his interpretation! The second version was Jim Cawthorn's black-and-white, large-format *Stormbringer*, which was published with somewhat limited distribution by Savoy Books in the mid-'70s.

Thereafter, all the other versions have originated in America. One of the best of these was Robert Gould's original Elric tale (with Eric Kimball) published by Star*Reach, 1976. I have always been a huge admirer of Gould's work and am especially delighted that he is now illustrating virtually the entire Eternal Champion cycle on recent paperback editions (chiefly by Berkley). A very odd version of Elric came from the pen of that excellent Conan illustrator, Barry Windsor-Smith, in a Marvel CONAN comic. Jim Cawthorn and I were responsible for the scenario, Roy Thomas wrote the script, and Barry, having no clear idea of what Elric should look like, based his interpretation on the early US covers of *Stormbringer* and *The Stealer of Souls* by Jack Gaughan, not knowing that I had heartily disliked Gaughan's Elric! This was not Barry's fault, but it meant that the Conan meets Elric story, 'A Sword Called Stormbringer' (CONAN THE BARBARIAN Nos. 14 & 15, March & May 1972) always remained something of a disappointment, visually, for me.

In 1979 Frank Brunner produced a tremendously powerful twenty-page story in HEAVY METAL magazine (reprinted in *Star*Reach Greatest Hits*, together with the Gould story) – a rendition which almost got Elric into his first movie. I was approached by a film producer to do an Elric movie entirely on the strength of having seen Frank's story. Sadly, the project fell through for a number of reasons. Another Hollywood proposal came from Ralph Bakshi, but I wasn't prepared, in the end, to subject Elric to his kind of trivialisation and I pulled out very early. I am also disappointed that although Howard Chaykin and I have worked together on projects (notably *The Swords of Heaven, The Flowers of*

*Hell*) Howard's only Elric work remains the early portfolio he did in the mid-'70s.

It seemed for some time that Elric projects were doomed to founder after one or two enthusiastic attempts. Mike Friedrich, who was offered control of US comic rights to the Eternal Champion in 1976, had worked very hard to get a regular Elric series running in America and at last things began to come together in the 1980s when Roy Thomas and P. Craig Russell first teamed up to produce the Marvel Graphic Novel version of 'The Dreaming City' (1982) and then (in EPIC ILLUSTRATED No. 14) 'While the Gods Laugh'. With Friedrich as editor, Thomas as writer, Russell and Gilbert as illustrators, a winning team had finally been fielded.

In April 1983 the first regular Elric comic book began to appear, published by Pacific Comics. The fey, eery quality – especially experienced in the large set-piece pages – is like no other version of the Elric stories, and the strangely etiolated figures make the characters seem genuinely of another, more magical and alien world. Some of the work is extraordinary, both in detail and colour, in the originality of imagination which the artists have brought to their interpretation. I was greatly impressed and, in looking through the pages again, continue to be surprised and delighted by subtle touches which I had not taken in at first reading. I have never had the opportunity to congratulate the artists before, but am glad to do so now.

*Elric of Melniboné* is chronologically the first in the Elric series, although it was written as one of the last (in 1972). With the comic's first publication in paperback form I very much hope it will lead the way to the entire Elric saga being eventually available in illustrated versions. First Comics, who have already produced a further Elric series (*The Sailor on the Seas of Fate* by Thomas, Gilbert and Freeman) and who are, as I write, beginning an excellent interpretation of *The Jewel in the Skull* (featuring Dorian Hawkmoon) by a new team (Gerry Conway, Rafael Kayanan and Rico Rival), continue to prove themselves both reliable and conscientious in their treatment of writers and artists and this, in itself, is fairly unusual in the world of comics.

A long time ago I used to edit and write comics myself. I have lost track of the vast number of science fiction, Western and historical stories I produced in the '50s and '60s, chiefly for Amalgamated Press (later Fleetway Publications), but I well remember how I longed to be able to expand my imaginative range, how I tried to convince conservative editors and publishers to do something a bit different and how frustrated I used to feel when I was refused. Eventually I gave up my attempts to talk people into doing more interesting comics and looked elsewhere for a living. Now, through the new generation of comics publishers, writers and illustrators, I can at last feel encouraged that the old frustrations are ended and enjoy work which expands the medium and actually revels in the possibilities of the form.

My thanks, as ever, to Mike Friedrich, to Roy Thomas, to Messrs Russell, Gilbert and Freeman and, of course, to Rick Oliver and all at First Comics (who nobly took up Pacific's fallen banner) for these wonderful pages. They have succeeded in making a fairly old man pretty damned happy...

# El Cid and Elric:

## *Under the Influence!*

### (2007)

E LRIC AND EL Cid! The similarity between the two names is
not entirely coincidental, since the legends and romances of
El Cid were a huge influence on my juvenile imagination.

I was brought up, like most British boys – I suspect like most
boys of my generation everywhere – on stories of idealism, hero-
ism and self-sacrifice. Macaulay's *How Horatius Held the Bridge*,
Tennyson's *The Charge of the Light Brigade*, Newbolt's *Vitai Lam-
pada*, Chesterton's *Lepanto* and many, many more were the stirring
narrative poems we recited not to please teachers but for our own
delight. Much of our history was already mythologised – the cool
courage of Francis Drake and the brave death of Nelson were
mixed in our minds with the fictional death of Sidney Carton in *A
Tale of Two Cities* and a whole army of heroes who, in true Christian tradition, gave their lives for the benefit of others. Usually
these heroes were depicted, like Robin Hood, as underdogs, fighting against the rich, the powerful and the thoroughly unjust!

The movies were the same. The stories were often of brave
'ordinary' men who sacrificed themselves for the good of the
many. *High Noon* represented this theme in Westerns while *Quo
Vadis* and *Ben Hur* offered it in what were known as 'toga and san-
dal epics', Humphrey Bogart sacrificed his own desire in *Casablanca*
and in the urban thrillers which eventually were given the generic
name of 'noir' by French critics. These were the popular entertainment of my day, but I had another enthusiasm, not shared by
any of my peers. This was for all the books on myth and legend I
could find, as well as for the few adult stories which in those days
were still to be given the name of 'Fantasy', including Lord

Dunsany, Edgar Rice Burroughs and, when I came across them, the American pulp magazines with names like PLANET STORIES or STARTLING STORIES, specialising in a Burroughs-influenced 'sword-and-planet' fiction. Early on I came across a series which told the stories of Greece and Rome, Scandinavia and Britain, most familiar to English children, but also included a volume on Peninsula Romance and it was in that book I first came across the story of Rodrigo Díaz, El Cid Campeador, whose story especially thrilled me.

Perhaps I was impressed by the fact that Díaz was an historical figure living at one of the most colourful and romantic times in Spanish history, when Christians and Moslems were enjoying perhaps the highest level of civilisation either had ever known, when chivalric knights on both sides exemplified the highest ideals, irrespective of religion, while on the other hand there were villains amongst both communities, and El Cid fought with Moslem allies against corrupt Christians or with mixed armies of both religions to secure Valencia for himself. I was thrilled when Díaz was named El Campeador – 'The Champion', bearing his sword Tizona in man-to-man combat and I am sure all this went to inspire my own character Elric and the background of his world. When I wrote, at seventeen, the first draft of my story 'The Eternal Champion', there is no doubt that El Cid was influencing it. Like Elric, the Champion fights first for one side and then another, turning 'traitor' as he learns more about those he fights for and against. He is moved not by loyalty to a certain flag, but by loyalty to a certain ideal. And in the end he perishes as a result of the destiny he sets in motion. But, in perishing, he saves the world for others!

Noble self-sacrifice still brings me to tears to this day, irrespective of the loyalties of the man or woman who performs the deed. Their loyalty is to a higher ideal, to a noble ethic. To this day epic films, like Ridley Scott's recent *Kingdom of Heaven*, have shown the noblest hero to be the one who rises above simplistic loyalties to serve what is best in mankind and what is universal in mankind's religious or political systems. When, long after I first read of his exploits, I saw Charlton Heston as El Cid have the arrow pulled from his body and strap himself to his horse in order to rally his troops against the invader (even though I knew that in real life Díaz had died in his bed) I enjoyed the same sensations. All this went to inspire my own troubled characters who wonder, in the words of E.M. Forster, whether it is best to betray one's country or one's friend – or, indeed, oneself.

To me, no attempt to mirror the great epics of our ancestors can succeed, even marginally, without an understanding of death. My quarrel with many of the fantasy romances written in the past fifty years or so is precisely that they do not understand the issue of mortality. All they do is keep us wondering *whether* the protagonist will live or die. This is scarcely important to us or Malory would not have called his work 'Morte d'Arthur'. 'All death is certain' says the Hospitaler over his shoulder as he goes to certain doom against Saladin in Scott's film. It is the *meaning* that we give our deaths (and, of course, our lives) that is important. This idea is at the root of all our great chivalric epics. How the hero dies is as resonant as how he lives. This is the point I have tried to make in my own stories. El Cid's legendary end at the battle of Valencia reminds us that courage without sacrifice is an empty quality. Elric's death, to herald in a new and better era, must be equally meaningful if I am to do even modest justice to those great epics which meant so much to me when I was a child.

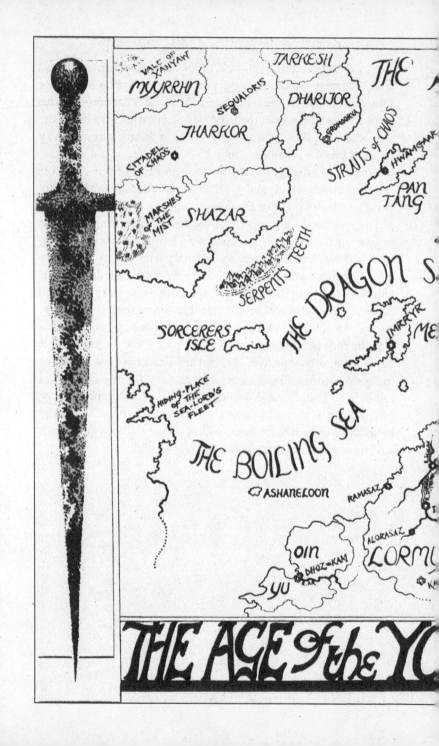

# Acknowledgements

'The Return of the Thin White Duke' first appeared in *Elric: The Stealer of Souls*, Del Rey, 2008.

'Putting a Tag on it' first appeared in AMRA Vol. 2 No. 15, edited by George Scithers, May 1961.

'Master of Chaos' first appeared in FANTASTIC STORIES OF IMAGINATION, edited by Cele Goldsmith, May 1964.

*Elric: The Making of a Sorcerer* was first serialised by DC Comics, 2004–2006, and was first collected as a single volume in 2007.

'And So the Great Emperor Received His Education…' first appeared as a spoken-word introduction to an audiobook edition of *Elric of Melniboné*, AudioRealms, 2003, and first appeared in print in *Elric: The Sleeping Sorceress*, Del Rey, 2008.

*Elric of Melniboné* was first published by Hutchinson, 1972.

'Aspects of Fantasy' (part one) first appeared in SCIENCE FANTASY No. 61, edited by John Carnell, October 1963.

The introduction to *Elric of Melniboné*'s graphic adaptation, First Comics, was first published in 1986.

'El Cid and Elric' first appeared in Argentina, in COMIQUEANDO No. 100, August/September 2007.

## All artwork by James Cawthorn:

'Elric in the Young Kingdoms' map, 1992 (based on the map by John Collier & Walter Romanski), first published in *Elric of Melniboné*, Millennium Books, 1993.

'Master of Chaos' interior artwork, 1979, from *Der Zauber des Weissen Wolfs*, (*The Weird of the White Wolf*), Heyne, Germany, 1980.

*Elric of Melniboné*, interior artwork, 1978, from *Elric von Melniboné* (*Elric of Melniboné*), Heyne, Germany, 1979.

'The Age of the Young Kingdoms' map first published in *Elric of Melniboné*, Hutchinson, 1972.